Pilorum

By C.S. Ramahon

Chapter 1

No one could predict or perceive the inexplicable events about to occur.

* * *

It is late April in Trenton, New Jersey. The skies are a deep azure blue and it is seventy-six degrees on this beautiful spring morning. Fifty-two-year-old college professor, Harold Simpson, sips his warm coffee from a porcelain cup bearing the slogan, "World's Best Dad" printed on it. Wearing a cotton robe and slippers, he leans back in an outdoor chaise lounge. He slowly opens his expressive gray eyes and squints upward at the rays of morning sunlight streaming through the tree branches above him. A gentle breeze brushes his mane of thick, gray hair.

Resting, he breathes deeply of the cool fresh air and then cocks his head slightly at the sounds of spring and the approaching summer. He listens to the chirping young birds in a nest their parents fashioned in the large magnolia tree ten feet away from his backyard cedar fence. He hears the gurgling sounds of clear water as it flows over the stones and flat boulders to then spill into his nearby, lavish swimming pool. He's glad he had the pool service remove the winter covering earlier this year, as he longs for temps to rise so he can start his mornings with a daily swim.

He blinks several times and rubs his unshaven face with an opened hand. A swiftly fluttering image darts past his eyes and he catches the glimpse of a bright, blue butterfly circling just above him. On a whim, he holds out one finger ... as if beckoning to the gentle creature. Astonished, his face displays his surprise when it does land on his outstretched digit. His eyes widen and his lips form a wry smile.

He softly whispers, "Good morning little friend. What wonders might this day hold for the two of us?"

* * *

In Paris, the President of France, Renee Armand, and his wife, Adeline, step forth from the curb onto the pavement. After partaking of a nice, filling dinner at his residence in the Palais de Elysée at number 55 rue du Faubourg-Saint-Honoré in the 8th arrondissement of Paris, a government agent opens the rear door of the limousine sent to transport them to the Paris Opera House for a relaxing evening out. They slide in and each seems enthused and looking forward to this night of relaxing entertainment away from the rigors of politics. The agent carefully closes the rear door, glances about, and enters the front passenger side of the vehicle.

In front of the limo is a black sedan car carrying government security agents responsible for the President's safety. Behind the limo is a second sedan, also carrying security agents. The agents inside the trio of vehicles begin communicating via radio, coordinating their planned route to the Opera House where the President and his wife will be let out to avoid reporters and the public.

Inside the limo's plush rear compartment, Renee kisses his wife on the cheek and holds her hand. She smiles at him and squeezes his hand lovingly.

He tells her, "I hope you enjoy the evening, darling. I know it's been hectic for the past few weeks, but if the Cabinet's proposal to Parliament passes, things won't be so chaotic. When that happens, we'll take a few weeks to vacation on the Riviera."

His cell phone rings, he lets go of her hand and answers the call from the Prime Minister.

As he converses next to her, she takes out her compact and powders her nose. There is a sudden bright flash of golden light. She winces and turns to ask him what caused it. Instead, she screams and begins to pound on the Plexiglas divider between the limo's front seat and the rear compartment.

The agent riding shotgun notices her agitation and slides open the clear divider door between them.

"She screams again, "Help! Stop the car!"

The agent, noticing the President is missing panics.

"Where's the President? My God, he didn't fall out, did he?" he asks excitedly.

As white as a ghost, she's mystified by what's happened.

"No!" She yells frantically. "He was on the phone ... and—"

"And what, ma'am?"

"Before I could blink ... he just vanished."

Hearing this, the limo driver's foot flails against the car's brakes and it comes to a skidding stop in the middle of the busy road.

The agent declares, "Vanished? That's impossible."

After the lead car and trailing car screech to a stop, agents from each vehicle exit with their pistols drawn and expressions of puzzlement and anxiety etched on their faces.

* * *

In Florida, a CBS mobile news team scrambles to set up a breaking news story. A male reporter holding a microphone faces the technician holding a field television camera. The cameraman's head appears momentarily from behind the camera lens.

He tells the reporter, "We're going live in twenty seconds."

"Very well, make certain you get a clear shot of the launch pad behind me, plus all the activity going on over there."

The cameraman lifts a hand and begins a silent countdown using his fingers.

Live on a local channel that is going Network-wide, the reporter clears his throat and begins his story.

"We're live here at the Cape where it appears there is going to be an unscheduled launch of the Space X rocket. We've been monitoring NASA channels and something is occurring on the International Space Station. Exactly what is unclear and NASA authorities are not commenting about it.

"We don't know if there's an emergency at the ISS, or if this is merely a routine flight re-scheduled. We do know that a Space X re-supply launch to the ISS is supposed to happen later next month, but there is every indication that the launch has been moved up and will occur tonight. This mission will feature two U.S. astronauts onboard the flight. From our vantage point miles away, we have been able to derive that they are indeed suited up and seem ready to go. We'll keep observing from here and let you know more as soon as we do. Bob Nash ... for CBS News."

* * *

On the Launch Complex 49-A at the Kennedy Space Center in Florida, the countdown begins at 2200 hours for a Space X Falcon Rocket. The Falcon consists of cargo and a ship known as the Crew Dragon 65 carrying two NASA astronauts. Captain, Rick Marshall, and the Engineer and Co-Pilot, David Carlson, are dressed in their new state-of-the-art spacesuits and helmets. They carefully monitor the controls and gauges inside their capsule, as the countdown continues toward launch.

When the launch sequence reaches zero, the powerful solid-fuel engines on this privately funded and built projectile roar and come to life, slowly lifting the sleek rocket and two astronauts into the dark firmament ... and toward the orbiting International Space Station two-hundred-fifty-three miles away.

About ten minutes into the flight, the Dragon reaches its preliminary orbit. This rocket, also filled with supplies and payloads, deploys its solar arrays. It then begins a carefully choreographed series of thruster firings to reach the ISS above Earth that is traveling at a speed of over seventeen-thousand miles per hour. This procedure is accomplished in less than an hour.

Inside the Rocket's capsule, Rick, the Captain of this hastily-planned flight monitors the telemetry of the approach to the Space Station. By his side, his Co-Pilot, David, verifies the information he's receiving from the instruments and flight control.

"The fuel burn is within the acceptable parameters and the trajectory appears to be spot-on."

Rick replies, "Excellent! That's the game plan."

He opens a switch on the Radio Communicator panel in front of him and then speaks into the microphone attached to his helmet. The craft's radio connects to NASA's Johnson Space Center in Houston.

"NASA Control, this is Captain Marshall. Air Pressure in our EMU Suits is holding and so far, all systems are functioning.

NASA responds, "Dragon 65, we're monitoring your rendezvous with the Crew Docking Port on the ISS. Expected capture is a "Go" within the next ninety seconds."

"Roger that, Houston," states Rick. "We comply. The docking port is coming into view now, and we concur with the trajectory of the capture. Any word yet from the six crew members?"

"Negative, Dragon 65. Have you tried hailing them on the emergency channel?"

"Affirmative, Houston, but we've received no response," declares David in a deliberate voice.

NASA responds, "We're still monitoring all available video transmissions, as that equipment seems to be functioning. Nonetheless, neither we nor the others of the joint venture's five agencies have received a confirmation of the crew's condition or presence within the ISS. Each bodily monitor reportedly ceased working at the hour of 2107, and per the video being broadcast to us here in Houston, in Russia, Japan, and to the Europeans ... the images and voices of the crew members ceased, and they disappeared from the video screen."

Rick inquires, "How is that feasible? Can there be a glitch in the transmission equipment?"

"That was our first reaction and consideration, but in testing it from NASA Control, we show no defect or anomaly in the equipment. The crew was running the Alpha Magnetic Spectrometer experiment when we lost contact with them. That's why you've been sent up there; to find out what's going on and to determine if the crew is there, alive, and well. Hopefully, this is some undetected malfunction of their equipment."

"Houston, we're now approaching the docking port and readying for capture," reports David.

He then switches radio frequencies and activates his mike, "Alpha Station, this is Dragon 65, do you copy?"

Getting no reply, he makes another attempt to connect, "Alpha Station, this is Dragon 65. We are preparing to dock with the ISS. Please respond."

There is no response.

NASA Control inquires, "Dragon 65, from your vantage point, do you see any structural damage to the transmitting antennae? Is there any evidence of a possible breech to the interior of the station?"

"Negative, Houston. From what we can tell, everything is as it should be."

"Dragon 65, Are there any Soyuz capsules missing?"

Rick shakes his head and states, "Negative, Houston. They are all intact to the ISS and none have been deployed for re-entry."

David questions, "Is the oxygen level readouts inside the ISS still reporting as normal?"

"Affirmative, Dragon 65, our data indicates ample air quality and pressure inside."

"Houston, docking maneuvers are in progress."

From mission control in Houston, commands are sent to the station's arm to rotate and install the rocket on the bottom of the station's Harmony Earth-facing port. Once this connects with the ISS, this process is completed. Rick sighs and glances at David. Rick readies himself to open the hatches and enter the Space Station.

"Dragon 65, we have you being a lock onto the ISS. Do you confirm?"

Rick queries, "Roger, Houston, we have docked and all systems are green. Are we a go for entry into the ISS?"

"Affirmative, Dragon 65. As per your directions, only one of you enters at a time. Remain suited and proceed carefully with the mission. Report directly what you ascertain inside."

"Roger, Houston. I'm preparing to open the outer hatch."

"Understood, Dragon 65. Good luck and do be careful."

Rick first opens the outer hatch. Now weightless, he slowly drifts inside the tunnel leading to the inner hatch of the ISS. He turns and closes the outer hatch behind him. The oxygen level and pressure quickly equalize. Slowly, he then spins the screw-like door lock of the inner hatch. Once he completes that, the latch disengages and the door opens. He sighs deeply and floats inside.

"Houston, I'm entering the ISS."

Slowly, he makes his way into the crew compartments and then proceeds to explore the station.

"Houston, it's a bit creepy, for there's no one in the crew compartments, in the Soyuz capsules, and as far as I can tell ... I am the only one onboard."

"Dragon 65, do you notice damage to any equipment or signs of radiation? Is there any evidence that the crew may have evacuated the station via their spacesuits?"

"According to the instrument readings, there is no indication of excessive radiation exposure. Stand by, I'll check the suits."

Rick cautiously makes his way to where the spacesuits are stored within the station. When seeing none are missing from their racks, he reports.

"Houston, all the EMU, and Russian Orlan suits are still on their racks. Not a one is missing."

"Very well, Dragon 65. Do the instruments verify the Co-2 levels and presence of adequate oxygen?"

"Affirmative, Houston. I confirm the oxygen levels are sufficient and there is no suggestion of any malfunction with the video or other equipment. I have no obvious explanation or indication of how six crew members could just vanish without a trace.

"He mumbles, "Where they are, God only knows."

The dejected NASA controller sighs and utters, "Understood Dragon 65."

"Houston, this rescue mission isn't one of replenishing supplies, for there is no one to resupply or to recover." His voice quivers, "We space sailors that ride Dragons like the one that brought us here at times expect to undergo a baptism by fire, but none of us anticipate having our bodies and souls ripped from existence by who knows what ... or how."

He pauses, and then asks, "So, we're here ... what are your orders as to what we do now?"

There is an awkward moment of silence from NASA Control, and then Rick hears, "Standby, Dragon 65."

After about two minutes, he receives word, "Russia is scrambling at Baikonur, Kazakhstan to get a Soyuz ready to launch. Even though we've made clear what you've found, as usual, they seem suspicious and plan to send three of their cosmonauts up to try to determine what happened. The two of you will enter the station and resume your investigative mission. Welcome the soon-to-be additional crew members when they arrive in a few days, but make certain the Russians do nothing to compromise the ISS or your ride home."

"Understood, Houston. My Co-Pilot and I ask ... How long will it be before that ride takes place? I can't pretend that either of us is comfortable in this ghost story environment where six brave colleagues evaporated without a trace."

Chapter 2

A day later in his office at the Apache Point Observatory in Sunspot, New Mexico, astronomer, Dr. John Lumpkin, regards with troubled eyes the data he carefully reads from the computer screen he's observing. He removes a mangled cigar from his mouth and crushes it, angrily into an ashtray. Appearing puzzled, he shakes his head and re-checks the readings. Finding the same results, he mumbles to himself, as if he's disgusted and somewhat worried. He sends the data on the computer screen to his printer and saves the documented data onto a jump drive. Picking up his cell phone, he dials a number. There are four rings before the party he's calling answers.

Dr. Albert Goodfellow responds, "Hello, John. So, do your calculations match my own?"

"Albert, I've experienced lots of unexpected strangeness in the vastness of our universe, and there is a lot of weird stuff, but this one ... Ken at Apache Point, and I are dumbfounded by what you've discovered."

Yes, we here at McDonald's Observatory are as well; also, are those from Mount Haleakala in Hawaii, and the Côte d' Azur Observatory in France. They and several more astronomers concur with our findings."

Albert's tone is tinged with anxiety.

He then states, "I assume you performed your analysis and that your data determined whether or not my findings and those of our other colleagues are correct."

"Regrettably, yes. The data does appear to be unquestionably accurate. The demonstrated truths of our math and logic, plus with the practical application of our instruments ... I would say that we're all in deep doo-doo if this continues."

"If the world hasn't had enough of a challenge from the Covid-19 pandemic. Putin's war against Ukraine, plus all the other life-threatening storms and viruses, we now have this with which to contend."

A concerned John asks, "How are the others dealing with this?"

"I've spoken to theoretical physicists at MIT, an astrophysicist at Aachen University in Germany, and a physicist in Stockholm, plus all our astronomer colleagues. Since we don't know the reason for it or how much more of a deviation will occur, I've asked them to quell any notification of this for now."

"I agree. If the public and media get wind of this before we are absolute about the degree of the dislocation, we'll have chronic, worldwide pandemonium. It's in the new phase of its elliptical apogee orbit now, so the casual observer will only notice the 'exposure effect' and not relate that to any impending threat. That is until it becomes obvious as to what's happening. Let's just hope this is an anomaly and that no further displacement occurs."

Albert moans and decries, "Yes, let's hope ... and pray that's it. In the meantime, continue to take your measurements, as shall I and all our colleagues. We can speak again in a couple of days. Goodnight, John,

And may God help us."

* * *

A day later on Friday, Princeton Physics Professor, Harold Simpson, downs his second cup of hot coffee. His bloodshot eyes note his lack of sleep from the night before. Shaking off a throbbing headache, he pours a third cup of coffee and removes the small patch of toilet paper covering the nick on his chin that he got while shaving. He'd stood under the shower for almost twenty minutes hoping to shrug off the night sweats and insomnia he's had of late.

Somehow, he manages to slip into the same pair of slacks he wore the day before, plus a clean shirt. He takes a sip of the coffee from his "World's Greatest Dad" cup, sneers, and spits out a small batch of grounds that lie upon the bottom of the cup. He's never been good at fixing any beverage ... even black coffee.

He shakes his head, whimpers, and thinks, "I feel as if I've been mugged. I need a direct transfusion of caffeine into my veins."

He yawns, stretches, and tries to get to his feet. He moans and bends to tie the shoelaces on his wingtip shoes. As he does, his effort only serves to have one of the laces fray and break into. Frustrated, he loosens the one he just tied and angrily kicks off both shoes, replacing them with a pair of black, slip-on loafers from his disheveled closet. From a hanger in the large walk-in closet, he removes and puts on a grey sport coat with suede leather elbow patches.

He glances into a mirror and ponders, "Elisa always liked me wearing this coat."

She told him it made him seem professorial and matched his distinguished-looking silver hair and ice-blue eyes. He then studies the array of ties available on the spinning, circular tie rack. His fifty-year-old left-hand reveals the wedding ring she gave him ... that he still wears, even though she passed away five years ago. He glances at the vast array of dresses, shoes, purses, and accessories that remain in the closet where she last left them. He's never had the heart to remove them.

He chooses the tie she always liked best to go with today's shirt and coat. More frustration sets in when he stands before the closet door mirror, and fumbles with the tie, but cannot seem to get the knot or the lengths done properly. He looks into the mirror and admonishes himself with a bout of self-deprecation.

"Knucklehead! You understand quasars, quarks, and photons, but after all these years still can't tie it right."

Elisa was always the one to help him get the knot and ends to come outright. Her nimble fingers always seemed magical when working on a tie, or doing almost any task around the house. After four attempts, he finally settles on the fact that it's the best he can do, so he leaves the fourth try as his best effort.

Off to the kitchen, he goes, throws open a cabinet door, and removes a box of cold cereal. He saunters to the kitchen sink, picks up a dirty bowl, runs it over cold water from the faucet, and then swishes a wet rag through the bowl, managing only to clean off most of the caked-on spaghetti sauce from his dinner the night before. A grimy plate, fork, and spoon are yet to be washed from that same meal. Not bothering to dry it, he slides the bowl onto the breakfast table and pours the cereal into the still-wet container.

As he stands and heads over toward the fridge, he hears his cell phone begin to chime out the tune from Star Wars. He sneers at the phone and is annoyed by this being the third call he's had since he shaved at 6:00 a.m. and downed his three cups of coffee. By the ring tone, he knows that the call is from his university Dean, so he does not answer this time either. One belligerent text message from his boss was enough. As a tenured professor, he did not have to take this exploitation of his goodwill. Besides, he is worn out and Saturdays are his clothes to the cleaners and sorting day. It is also the anniversary of Elisa's fatal car crash, so if the weather allows, he plans to visit her gravesite tomorrow, as he has each of the past five years. It was thinking of her that robbed him of his sleep last night.

He grumbles and looks at the phone. He imagines his conversation when he does have to confront the Dean after his classes today. In his mind, he envisions that in the ensuing ultimate, unavoidable confrontation he will be forceful and will mince no words.

He imagines, "Sorry, Dean Kelly, I'll be busy this weekend, so I cannot agree to take Professor Stewart's class. Get someone else to do it."

He nods his head, confident that he can avoid the bother and annoyance of such an assignment. At the fridge, he opens the door and peers inside. Grabbing the gallon jug of milk, he removes the cap and takes a quick sniff of the half-filled contents. His reaction time is measured in milliseconds, for he jerks his head away from the foul-smelling lactose and declares the two-week outdated white liquid to be null and void. Strolling to the sink, he holds his nose and disposes of the chunky sludge down the drain. He then glances at the bowl of dry cereal, snarls his upper lip, and then decides on an alternate solution to quell his hunger.

He states aloud his intent, "Elisa, it appears to be another sausage, egg, and biscuit morning from Mr. McDonald's house."

* * *

That afternoon, inside the room of his physics class at Princeton, Harold dims the lights and turns on a slide projector. As he lectures to this second semester of advanced students, he points at the slide projected onto the rolled-down screen behind him.

He tells them, "This first slide is of an Antarctic station. Pictured here, is the university's Ice Station facility, which is about ten miles from McMurdo station."

Clicking a button on the projector, changes to the next slide.

He adds, "Attached to a large helium-filled balloon and carried aloft by circumpolar winds, the SPIDER, as it is called has reached an altitude of around 120,000 feet, which is literally to the edge of space."

As his interested students all focus their attention on the screen, he clicks the button again, and another slide projects on thereon. It displays various cameras attached to the SPIDER.

"Attached to the balloon are sensitive instruments inside sun shields with six cameras that will search for gravitational waves left over from the Big Bang during the rapid expansion of our vast universe. That is ... if there was a Big Bang. Evidence from the James Webb telescope seems to question that possibility. Yet, despite that, in effect, we should be able to view as far back as to the beginning of time."

He stops the projector and switches on the classroom lights.

"This is a noble experiment made possible by a grant from NASA, and one that I eagerly await the results. Now, as our university's brightest physics students, what basics do we know about gravity?"

A young male student confidently raises his hand and Harold calls on him. Glancing down at his seating chart, he takes note of the young man's name.

"Yes, Mr. Hawkins, what is your response?"

"Professor, we know that all bodies experience the same gravitational force regardless of composition."

Harold smiles, nods his head, and replies, "Yes, Mr. Hawkins, and can someone tell me what else?"

A bright co-ed raises her hand and knowing her name he calls on her. "Yes, Ms. Jamison, what's your response?"

The lovely young woman sits up straight.

She replies, "That it's a fundamental consequence of the structure of space and time, as proved by Einstein."

"Correct, Ms. Jamison. Everything in the universe attracts everything else, and Einstein's Theory of Relativity defines the space-time curvature.

"So, for the remainder of this semester, we will be discussing various laws of physics, like dynes, differential measurements, testing equivalence, gauging the invariant, and more ... all in a way to better comprehend gravity and why here on our beloved home planet that we don't all float off into space from Earth. In general, we'll discuss why it is that stuff falls when you drop it."

* * *

That same day, at the interior operations room of Princeton's Antarctic Ice Station, it's been two days since the SPIDER balloon descended. It and the data from the months-long flight are retrieved, and now, Dr. Samuel Marshall, another leading physics professor from Princeton, focuses on his computer screen that displays the information and numbers that he attempts to decipher. A grad student colleague peers over his shoulder and notices a sudden blip in the stream of data.

"There, did you see that? There was a spike. As I mentioned before, that gravitational wave seems far too powerful to be coming from outside our solar system. From the strength of it, perhaps the anomaly is happening right here on Earth. Is that possible, Professor?"

The team leader pushes the mouse button and a graph begins to print out. Once it is printed, he nervously tears it away from the machine and closely examines the resulting data. His hand grasps his forehead, displaying his growing concern. He sighs deeply.

"Mark, I fear you may be right. SPIDER couldn't have been picking up this intense signature from deep space. The timestamp for the radio emission was six days ago."

He pauses and apprehensively shakes his head.

"If this data is true, we have a real problem to deal with here. We've only begun to examine the numbers, so keep at it, and let's see if this is a reoccurring event. We break camp tomorrow, but we best inform Professor Simpson of this situation right away."

* * *

A day later, inside her California home, a young housewife struggles to exit her bathtub. After she does and begins drying off, she glances at her figure in the vanity mirror. Patting the slight bulge of her stomach, she gathers and wraps a towel around her wet hair, and then steps onto her bathroom scale.

Seeing the numbers that proclaim her weight, she leaps off the scale, and then steps back on it, as if to confirm the poundage that it displays. Hearing her scream, her husband tumbles from the couch. He throws off his newspaper and rushes into the bathroom.

"For heaven's sake, Betty, what's wrong now?"

She frowns and points at the reading on the scale.

"This infernal machine asserts that I have gained fifteen pounds in two days."

He smirks and remarks, "Well, you have been eating a lot this past week."

"You do know I am pregnant? There is no way I could've gained that much weight so rapidly."

She steps off the scale and issues him instructions, "Get rid of this horrid thing and go buy me one that is accurate."

Chapter 3

As a fetal child pushes against its mother's cervix, Lilly, a birthing nurse at Harris Methodist Hospital in Fort Worth, Texas watches for the head of a struggling newborn to crown, as it attempts to leave the womb. The mother tries dealing with the pain and with great effort pushes to help the baby through the birth canal. As the infant's head crowns, Lilly smiles and holds one of the mother's hands, while the other is held by the wide-eyed nervous father standing beside the bed.

The doctor prolifically goes about grasping the child's head and assisting in its birth. Once the child is drawn from its mother's vagina, the umbilical cord is clamped and cut near the navel. This ends the baby's dependence on the placenta for oxygen and nutrition.

Lilly stimulates the baby to cry by massaging and stroking the skin to help bring the fluid up where it can be suctioned from the nose and mouth. As the baby takes its first breath, air moves into its lungs. The welcome sound of a crying baby fills the room. The proud father smiles and kisses his wife on the cheek. Lilly immediately shows the child to the happy couple and the relieved mother. Lilly gently places it upon the mother's bosom. She cuddles it and kisses its cheek.

"Congratulations, you have a beautiful baby girl," Lilly declares in a pleasing voice.

As the doctor turns his attention to the mother and begins removing the placenta, the father's knees weaken; he sneers, wilts, and looks away. Lilly quickly takes charge of the child. The newborn baby is wet from the amniotic fluid, so Lilly dries the baby and uses warm blankets and heat lamps to help prevent heat loss. She weighs the child, measures it, takes its temperature, checks its respiratory rate, measures the circumference of its head, and then places a knitted hat on its head.

After that and right away she begins a health assessment of the new baby. One of the first checks is the Apgar test, whereby Lilly evaluates the condition of the newborn at one minute and five minutes after birth. The child's health seems to be normal ... except for one odd birthmark on its right heel. There, Lilly discovers an alignment of three small red dots, each about the diameter of the plastic plunger that engages the ink stick of a ballpoint pen. She shrugs off the peculiarity and begins to sponge and clean the child, taking care to keep the umbilical cord stump clean. Before letting the recovering father hold his child, she captures its footprints, not using an old-fashioned ink stamp, but rather she employs a device that scans the infant's footprints into a database where the computerized document is saved into a medical record. Lilly doesn't say anything to the parents about the red dots.

Two hours later and before the end of her shift, she strolls into the maternity nursery to check on the child. One of her best friends is on duty.

Lilly asks the nurse, "Hi Betty, how'd it go today?"

Betty tells her, "We've had four births during my shift," she says. "This is the little darling with whom you worked." She touches the hospital crib where the child sleeps.

"Yes, she's a pretty little thing," replies Lilly. However, there was one oddity about her that I've never seen."

Betty takes Lilly's arm and shushes her. She quietly guides Lilly over to the other three cribs with sleeping babies. Gently, she lifts the blankets on each of the other three infants, revealing their wiggly toes and feet. As the babies react to the chilled air and squirm about, Lilly beholds that each of these three infants also has the same red dot markings on their heels.

"Strange birthmarks, huh?" Lily remarks with a question.

Betty nods in concurrence and then replaces the blankets. She guides a stunned Lilly into the glassed-in supply area behind the nursery.

"We can talk in here," she says in a quiet voice. "I took photos of all four of the infants' heels, for it seemed impossible to me that such a thing could occur on that many unrelated babies."

"I quite agree," states a puzzled Lilly. "It seems impossible, but I guess it's not."

"I posted the photos on the Facebook page of the 'Maternity Nurses Association' asking if anyone else has seen anything like this."

"Did you get any responses?"

"As of twenty minutes ago, about eighty-six posts from hospitals all over the nation ... all citing they have newborns with the identical anomaly ... three red dots on their right heel."

* * *

It is a mid-Saturday afternoon at Conny Land Amusement Park in Switzerland. The sixty-year-old President of the Swiss Federal Council is enjoying a fun weekend out with his grandkids. He enters a roller coaster ride, seating himself at the rear of the ride and alone in the car behind his two grandchildren.

His wife, two sons, and two daughters-in-law, plus a horde of media wait on the ground next to the ride. The coaster jerks, his grandkids joyously yell, and the coaster begins its backward ascent up the tall vertical track. Once at the top of the track, the underneath release engages and the coaster begins its rapid downward plunge along the track. The kids onboard all scream with delight. The coaster races past the boarding area from whence the riders loaded, and speeds along until it gets to yet another upward-sloping rail ... climbing to its top. The President smiles but seems a bit queasy from the rush of the gravitational pull.

Gravity again takes hold, and the coaster races backward down the rail and comes to a sudden stop moments later in the same spot from where it began. There is a sudden, bright flash of light, similar to a lightning strike. It's as if a strong sunbeam falls from the clear, blue sky. In the excitement, few pay it little heed. The kids are excited and laugh with glee. The wife and her grown children smile broadly at her grandkids' mirth. However, it takes but a few seconds before she, any one of them, or the media realizes ... that the President ... isn't in his seat. The wife panics and the kids scream.

Her alarmed voice yells out, "My, Lord! Where is Arnsberg?" Immediately, the kids hop out of the coaster and begin searching for their grandfather. The ride's operator, the park's staff, and the media all begin searching around the track area. It seems to be an impossibility that he might have somehow fallen out, for the operator points out that the over-the-shoulder restraint is still locked and in place. Several minutes of frantic searching turns up no President. He just seems to have vanished.

* * *

That same afternoon on the Krossbannen Aerial Gondola in Norway, Einar Gnudson, the Minister of Foreign Affairs sits inside the classic tramway gondola glancing down at the beautiful Rjukan and countryside below him. With him, are several other riders consisting of local and national dignitaries, plus the Ambassador of the United States.

The Minister stands as the gondola slowly makes its way toward the top of the tensioned cable three-thousand feet above sea level. There, at the foot of Hardangervidda, Norway's largest national park in the scenic view cafe, there is a planned dinner party for all.

The jovial Minister gently puts an arm around the U.S. Ambassador's shoulder, who is happily taking in the breathtaking views of the ride up the mountain.

He asks, "So, Thomas, as one of your country's most loyal allies, is your U.S. President still agreeable to a meeting before the NATO summit next month?

"Yes, of course, Einar. He's looking forward to it and to seeing you again.

In the crowded gondola, the two men are shuffled between other occupants. They are momentarily blocked from the view of the two Norway photographers assigned to cover the dinner for the media. When the primary photographer squeezes past a couple of dignitaries to where he last saw Einar and Thomas... he is surprised that he does not see them. Puzzled, he carefully looks around, politely moving people as a means of locating the two men that he's assigned to photograph. As the gondola gets close to the summit of its climb up the cable, a light fog rolls in and ascends around the tram. Suddenly, he and the others must shade their eyes from a bright, blinding flash of light.

The stunned photographer glances about, but the Minister and Ambassador are nowhere to be seen.

"One dignitary remarks, "Whoa! That's odd in this fog. It was as if someone reflected the sun in a mirror."

The anxious photographer's wide eyes search the forest and trees below. The tram is still moving ... but he cannot locate either man in the confined gondola. He checks the locked, secure doors, and seems convinced that they didn't jump or fall out.

Upon reaching the top, despite interviewing the other riders and having the crewmen, plus the authorities search... but the two men completely disappeared.

* * *

Back at the Apache Point Observatory, Dr. John Lumpkin squeezes into the seat at the controls of the observatory's Lunar Laser. Once the computerized instrument is lined up properly with the retro-reflector on the Moon, he pushes a green button. In two-hundredths of a second the laser beam, consisting of one hundred quad-trillion photons of light fires at the surface of the Moon. The beam, precisely directed at the reflector prism thereon instantly returns the beam along the same path from which it came ... therein, the laser's computer instruments become a recording source to measure an accurate distance between the Earth and the Moon.

John prints out the data and carefully studies its computations. All the hairs on his arms stand on end, as he gets goosebumps. Shaking his head and somewhat troubled, he removes a cigar from his coat pocket. He turns in the swivel seat and glances at his office. Slowly he stammers back there, where he stares at the bottle of Scotch whiskey he's had on a shelf for the past five years. Seemingly mortified, with the truth landing on top of him like a dropped piano, he blinks sweat from his eyes, smirks, and then grabs the Scotch off the shelf. He anxiously removes the top of the bottle and chugs down a huge slug of the strong liquor. His knees go limp as he chokes down the whiskey. He rolls the cigar in his fingers. He's been saving it for what he hoped would be a more cherished and cheerful occasion. Quite disturbed, he exhales deeply, lights the cigar, inhales, and plops down into a chair. His face seems frozen in a blank stare. Exhaling smoke rings, vague thoughts swim through his troubled mind, as he watches the smoke dissolve and float away.

His mind silently mumbles, "It was no use saving these for a more congenial or noted occurrence. If this keeps up we can pull the plug, for that which is terra firma will become Ragu sauce, and all of us here primordial soup."

John again calls his old friend and colleague, Albert, who quickly answers.

An anxious and nervous John asks, "What was your reading last night, Albert?"

"Exactly, 214, 674 miles and 127 feet and—"

A ghastly whiteness spreads over John's face and he finishes Albert's sentence, "And 7 inches."

Albert sighs into the phone, "Yes, I'm afraid that's it exactly. You and all of the observatory astronomers I've heard from on the Internet, plus those I've spoken to this morning confirm the same thing."

"We can't' keep quiet about this anymore, Albert. We must inform government officials of the world and let them know the severity of our findings. Our colleagues should do the same."

Albert declares, "You're the Nobel Prize winner among us. The others and I have been awaiting word from you to unerringly do that."

John's voice cracks and is emotional, "Very well, I deplore dealing with ivory tower, toe the line, fife, and drum-type politicians, but in this case, it must be done. I'll contact the State Department at the White House. They can pass it on to NASA and the U.N. plus get in touch with other nations and governments. Most likely they'll require several of us to come to New York to explain our findings and make a presentation to the U.N. General Assembly or maybe the Security Council. The sooner the better, I suppose."

Albert chides, "Yes, but to what avail? We're in a barrel going over Niagara Falls. There is nothing known that can stop this. Already on the news wire, they report U.S. cities and other coastal nations are experiencing imposing tidal bulges. I also heard from one source that an Antarctic station experiment by a group from Princeton recorded a variable spike and an increase in a gravitational wave. They think it might be coming from somewhere inside our solar system."

"We both know the source of that unimaginable abnormality," John states in a reserved manner.

Albert contemplates and asks, "I cannot fathom a reason for it, can you? According to all the experts, such a thing isn't supposed to occur for another two billion years or more."

"In the expanding universe, our Moon has been inching away from Earth at the rate of 1.6 inches per year. Now, within the past few days, somehow it has been drawn from its orbit and is thousands of miles closer ... by about 4%," declares John.

Albert's expression turns to one of abject terror, "And there's no sign that it is receding or slowing down."

John quickly turns and enters a complex program and equation into his computer. He waits for the printout to calculate the numbers. The printer whirs and begins to feed the paper through.

John clears his throat and peruses the figures before him.

His arms flail and he somberly states, "With the attraction and current rate of acceleration, according to my calculations ... the perturbation and variation of Earth's natural satellite and its twenty-nine-day elliptical orbit, it should distance itself from Earth to a point where the convergence reaches the Roche limit ... in exactly ... forty days.

A distraught Albert scribbles down some math problems of his own and then sneers.

His face reddens and flushes, "Which won't matter, because when it gets to within about 180,000 miles of Earth, tides will become absurd, and the coasts will be non-inhabitable because they shall be periodically submerged by the oceans. The effect will be such that the whole world will be completely flooded twice a day."

He cringes and rubs at the grey streaks in his short beard, "After that, it's Goodbye to New York City, London, Los Angeles, San Francisco, New Orleans, and Hong Kong ... to mention but a few."

With squinted eyes, John dismally adds, "I wager the politicians, military, and media will expect us to provide them with a solution to this problem, but there is none.

Albert states with conviction, "No, the consequences of it are dire indeed."

After the phone call ends, Albert slowly saunters to his office, plops down into a chair, and stares at the framed photos on his desk. One photo is of three people, two young adults, and one smiling, blonde-haired girl. His eyes moisten with tears, as he no doubts grieves for his son, daughter-in-law, and his six-year-old granddaughter.

Chapter 4

A remote news crew sets up near the NASA space center in Houston, Texas. A reporter with a cameraman is set to give an update to the NBC nightly news airing nationally. In the New York studio, the NBC anchor, Teri Louis, prepares to switch the feed to the reporter in Texas.

"As we reported a few days ago, there was a recent unscheduled launch of the Space X Falcon Rocket toward the orbiting International Space Station. Since then, NASA control in Houston has been vague as to the purpose and nature of that launch. NBC has attempted to question officials at NASA to explain what's going on in space, but our efforts to determine the intention of that flight have been kept secret. Our investigative reporter, Don Giles, is in Houston now with an update on the situation."

The live feed switches to Don Giles in Houston. "Thank you, Teri. After days of endeavoring to get at the factual basis for the unscheduled Space X launch and rendezvous with the ISS, it has been determined by our team that something is amiss within the ISS itself. Although all communications with the ISS by the Space X crew were and are being done via a NASA scrambled, confidential radio frequency, we were able to monitor a European channel that described concern for the six crewmen aboard the ISS. From what we heard, there doesn't appear to be any malfunction within the ISS itself, but rather that the crewmen are not responding to calls from Houston control, nor are they sending back any videos to confirm they are okay up there."

Teri asks, "Then is NASA concerned that something might have happened there to threaten the lives of the onboard crew?"

"It's speculation of course, but certainly seems like a viable concern. We do know that Russia is preparing to send a Soyuz Rocket with three new crewmen to rendezvous with the ISS."

The feed switches back to NBC in New York, where Teri continues with the news.

"Thank you for that update, Don. Let us know if you hear any more about what's going on up there.

"In other news, the media and officials in France refuse to comment on the confounding disappearance of President Armand. All that is known thus far is that his wife is being treated for hysteria, but the prime Minister's vague denial insists the President's absence from public view is not the result of a terrorist or military action."

Moving on to the next topic, a startling video plays onscreen showing a chaotic scene in New York and San Francisco.

"Also today, here in New York, Los Angeles, New Orleans, and San Francisco, extremely high tides are causing havoc with the loading and unloading at cargo container docks. Some machinery was flooded and several beaches along both coasts have been closed due to large waves, high tides, and dangerous winds. All the low-lying islands across the globe are beginning to experience flooding. As of yet, there's been no explanation as to what is causing this."

Another video displays geysers propelling nearly double their normal height and intensity into the air.

"Equally as alarming, the geysers in Yellowstone National Park have increased in their frequency and strength, causing some boardwalk lanes for visitors to be closed. Park officials are also concerned about the rising water temperatures in nearby lakes and measurable bulges in the landmasses around the park. Officials are considering closing the park to all visitors.

"In light of concern over all these strange occurrences, we've learned that the UN has called for a special emergency meeting."

* * *

Six hours behind Norway's time, on Saturday morning, a contrite Harold Simpson makes his way to a local graveyard in nearby Trenton, New Jersey. Carrying a bouquet of pink roses, he respectably strolls past several grave headstones until he comes to the one he seeks. Thereon, he bends and sweeps away the leaves gathered upon the base of the granite monument. He then replaces the withered flowers in the attached vase with fresh-cut roses. His eyes water, but he is more relieved than somber to be here to connect in spirit to his beloved wife, Elisa. Although she was a believer in life after death, he is more a practitioner of the laws of biology and physics, plus the reality of death being our final act. Still, in his waking confliction, he comes and speaks to her as if she is still alive and in his presence.

"Good morning, my love. I brought your favorite ... pink roses."

He stands and looks around him at the trees. Among the groupings of evergreens is the early evidence of springtime blooms peeking out on the limbs of Pink Dogwoods, Cherry Trees, and Elisa's favorite tree planted near her gravesite ... that of the Japanese Snowbell Tree.

Suddenly, a swift current of cold air wafts over him. The wafting, pleasurable scents tickle at his nostrils, making this place of death seem more like a rebirth of life itself. In the bright morning sunshine, his thoughts linger a bit upon that concept. A moment later, he returns his attention to Elisa's grave.

"You always loved spring, when from the long winter the Earth warms and renews life within the plants, trees, and animals. I know you never compromised your own beliefs, so ... I hope you are where it is always springtime."

The warming of the sun wraps around him like a comfortable blanket. He smiles down at the grave, although he hates the thought of being contained in a box for all of eternity. He much prefers the idea of cremation, but Elisa opted for burial.

He verbalizes his emotions, "The world is not near as beautiful without you in it Elisa. To me, you were the one that made it so glorious. It's hard to believe you've been gone now for only five years. It seems like an eternity."

The cell phone in his pocket rings, but he ignores it.

He continues, his voice calm and deliberate, "I'm okay, I guess. I try to stay busy and am thankful for my position at the university. If I didn't have that, I'd lock myself at home and wither away ... doing silly things like nailing my head to the floor. With all the complicated algorithms and computations I make every day, you were the one common denominator that kept me sane and gave my life purpose. Living is so miserable without you, Elisa."

Harold bends to one knee and places his right hand over Elisa's engraved name on the headstone. His mind reels in a past land of voice and memory, as he recalls her smile and warm embrace. Her voice whistles in his psyche like the wind through a keyhole. Yet, as quickly as her image comes to him, it then fades as if a vaporous fog in his remembrance. The world wavers as if he's in a dream. His heart sinks and his eyes moisten. The reality of her being dead crushes him like a great mirror in time shivering and breaking into a million pieces. In his somber reverie, from behind him, a human-shaped shadow breaks the sunlight upon the headstone.

He hears a soft, familiar voice, "Dad, are you alright?"

Harold quickly swipes an index finger across his cheek and under his eye in an attempt to erase and conceal the show of doleful emotion to his twenty-three-year-old daughter, Morgan. He shuffles around, stares up into the bright sunshine, and eases to his feet. In the glow, he notices her shiny blond hair and her sharp, angular features. He gasps and is momentarily silent as he stares at her. The sound of her sweet voice is as warm honey poured upon his brain.

Morgan's eyes narrow and she again voices her concern, "Dad, I'm here, are you okay?"

Harold inhales deeply and gathers his senses. The air returns to his lungs and blood to his wandering brain. Momentarily, when he first caught glimpse of Morgan in the glare of the bright sunshine, he'd thought it was Elisa he was seeing.

He rises and holds out his arms to her. She quickly rushes into them and warmly snuggles into his safe embrace.

"I'm fine, dear one," he tells her. "You cut your hair. For a moment there, I thought you were your mother."

He holds her at arm's length. "Thank you for coming."

Wearing a light green tunic with a knee-length skirt and sandals, she looks up into his face with her bright, cobalt-blue eyes and long, fluttering eyelashes.

"I came by the house, but when you weren't home, I reasoned that you'd probably be here."

They break the embrace and he glances down at the grave. "Yes, it's been five years since she passed. My coming here is like a leaf returning to the tree from which it fell."

"I know," she says. "Come on, Dad, let's go back to the house. We can talk there and I'll make some tea. You do have tea, right?"

He shrugs and the joyous sound of her soothing voice drives away some of his melancholy.

"Of course, I do, plus we can heat the three-day-old half-eaten package of sweet rolls in the pantry."

Morgan playfully snarls her lip and then takes his arm leading him toward his car parked along the street curb nearby. He leans and blows a kiss toward the grave. To him, Morgan has always been like a calming, flowing river that slows the current of creeping loneliness inside him. She helps him satiate a peace within him with her loving touch and presence. As they near his car, his cell phone again rings, and again he ignores it.

Morgan remarks, "Hadn't you better answer that, Dad? It might be important."

"Whoever it is can leave a voice mail."

"I spoke to Ted; he told me he would phone you today. Perhaps it's him that's calling."

Harold glances down at the cell phone and takes note of the area code and number of that which was called.

"No, it's from a different area code than where your brother lives. Besides, it's only 7:30 a.m. in California, so probably he hasn't even woken yet. Let's go."

Cheery and bright as a diamond in the sun, Morgan kisses her dad's cheek and watches as he enters his sedan. She closes the door behind him.

"I'll follow you in my car, Dad. Is there anything I can stop to get that you might need?"

He pats her on the hand and smiles, "No, my child. It is enough that you are here. I need nothing more."

***

When the two of them arrive and park at Harold's spacious and luxurious suburban home where Morgan and her brother, Ted, grew up in Trenton, he and his daughter adjourn to the gourmet kitchen. Morgan urges her dad to take a seat at the breakfast table.

"Rest, while I put on the tea."

At the sink, she sees the stack of dirty dishes and four to five pans still brandishing the remnants of previously cooked meals. She grunts and bends to pull out a drawer underneath the gas range top. In the drawer, she finds but one clean pot with which to boil water. She holds up the solitary pan, taps her shoe against the floor, and stares at her father,

"Thank goodness there's at least one clean pot in the house with which to boil water."

Morgan sneers, fills water into the pot, and then places it under the gas burner on the range top. She then rummages through the cabinets for two clean mugs. Finding but one, she runs water in the sink and washes off another located within the pile of dishes. She dries the mug and then opens the pantry door to find the tea bags.

Harold's face forms a sheepish grin and he remarks, "Yes, well, I wash dishes on Sunday and it's the maid's day off."

"Holy smoke! Do you mean you finally hired a maid? It's about time, and besides ... it's not like you can't afford one."

He snickers and waves off that assumption, "You know me better than that. I have a laundry cleaner down the street that washes and irons my linens, shirts, pants, and socks, plus dry-cleans my suits. I have a man that cuts the lawn and trims, plus I have a handyman on call if I need a house repair. So, no, I don't need a maid. I can handle any other chores."

"Too bad you don't have someone to dress you."

"Well, your mom always helped with that, but I've learned to manage it okay."

"Dad, you have on one red sock and one blue sock, plus your pullover shirt is inside out."

Surprised, he raises the legs of his pants and glances down at his dual-colored socks. He then reaches behind his neck and feels the inside-out label tag, realizing that she's right.

"Oh, I'm just making a fashion statement like that of my many young students."

She rolls her eyes and sarcastically remarks, "Yeah, sure, Dad!"

Shrugging off her mild scolding, he points at the boiling pot of water on the range top.

"Your water's ready."

She shakes her head and grins at him, seeming exasperated by his denial of needing help.

Taking the pot off the range, she then notices the bread shelf with stale bread ripe with green mold. The half-opened package of sweet rolls lies beside it. She picks up the rolls and sniffs them, apparently relieved that they too are not mold-infested. She then tosses a tea bag into each mug and fills the mug with boiling water.

Watching her, Harold mentions, "You know, in the south where I was raised, we drank iced tea. It wasn't till after I met your mom and moved up here to Yankee-Land that I learned to drink hot tea."

"Yes, I know Dad, but that's how Mom taught us and I know you like it that way too."

"I do. If you will ... put the usual two cubes of sugar in mine."

With their tea poured, the two settle down at the table, sip their warm drinks, and begin to converse. Both avoid the questionably stale sweet rolls.

"So, Morgan, how long will you be here this time?"

"Just a few days, Dad, and then I'll meet Steve at his parent's cabin in the Adirondacks. He likes going fishing this time of year before it gets too hot."

"Sounds like fun. I'm glad he's got you spending time in the wild again. You never seemed fond of that after you grew up."

"Yeah, I'm doing better with it, but last year when we went there, I was bombarded by bugs that bit me ... mosquitoes, chiggers, ants, plus I brought home a tick that settled on me in a place I'd rather not mention."

Harold laughs and states, "As a kid, I recall you used to like bugs. When we went to your grandmother's farm, you'd gather ladybugs, fireflies, and butterflies, and then help her gather honey from the beehives. Your favorite was playing with the doodlebugs on the barn's dirt floor."

She giggles and agrees, "Yes, I loved their little conical dirt holes. It looked like a Hersey Kiss turned upside down and pressed into the dirt."

Harold grins, "You were a bit of a tomboy back then, but when you got older you became a frilly and femme princess ... as radiant as the rose ... like your mom. Then your interest in the natural world waned."

She lifts the cup and drains the last few drops of her tea. "Well, Steve is determined to revive that interest. I must admit, I do like the solitude and the amount of rest I get up there. And yes, it is nice being out in nature again."

"Good! And how are things going with my son-in-law?"

"He's working toward getting his commercial brokerage license and hopes to open up his own company next year."

"Outstanding! How about you? Are you still working toward defending your dissertation in May?"

"Absolutely! I have developed some bio-chemistry philosophies that I will present in my dissertation."

"Excellent, I can't wait to read your papers and ponder your insights and discoveries. I'm very proud of you, Morgan. Getting a doctorate in chemistry is not an easy accomplishment. I'm so glad you are doing so in a scientific discipline. God help us, for your brother became a lawyer instead."

She playfully swats him on the shoulder, "Dad, don't pretend you're not proud of Ted. He's a prominent attorney in Las Angeles with one of the most prestigious law firms in the nation."

Harold snarls his lip and nods, "Yes, you're right. I'm very proud of both of you."

The cell phone begins to ring once more. Morgan insists he answers it this time. He takes the last sip of his tea and swipes his finger diagonally across the face of the cell phone to answer it. The voice on the line seems agitated and anxious.

"Hello, Harold! Thank goodness I finally got hold of you."

He recognizes the voice of his friend and colleague, Dr. Fred Nelson, from the University of Michigan Astronomy Department.

"Hi, Fred, and what tangible and inspiring results from your astronomy observatory have you today?"

Morgan nods at him and slips away towards the restroom, allowing him to speak with his colleague.

"Harold, have you been keeping up with the observable celestial events of late?"

"Not so much, I have been heavily involved in lectures at the university, plus reporting on the findings of the SPIDER project in Antarctica. If this crisp weather holds, I'm scheduled this coming week to meet at the Peyton Observatory for our monthly open house and observing session. Why? What's going on?"

"Use that Lunar Laser Range Finder Experiment that your Princeton student developed in 1969 and take advantage of today's precise and accurate measurement of the distance between us and the Moon."

"Yes, my doctoral student will do that before our meeting next week. Why is that so important?"

"Though our Moon has serenely and inexorably circled the Earth for millennia, it has now developed an alarming variation in its orbit. Harold, it's several thousand miles closer than it should be."

Harold almost drops the phone. He switches it to his right ear, "What? Are you telling me that instead of inching away from Earth, it's begun a perturbation toward it? That can only be due to some increased gravitational influence attracting it toward the Earth. Have you spoken to anyone at NASA?"

"No, but Steve at Ohio State's physics department did. So did Iva at Harvard. As reported, NASA is experiencing some sort of emergency on the ISS. Once they realized this lunar anomaly, they are as confused and concerned about it as we are. Harold, the Moon's on a trajectory that's causing the high tides coastal cities are experiencing, plus I hear there are already seismic and volcanic disturbances in the Earth's core and crust. My department measured the Earth's rotation these past few days, which resulted in learning that the days have grown shorter by about fifteen minutes per day."

Realizing the seriousness of this revelation, Harold is stunned. He feels his stomach twisting and turning in agony. As Morgan returns to the kitchen, he cannot bring himself to look her in the eyes, choosing his words carefully and hoping not to alarm her.

"Hold on, Fred, let me go into my office and I'll check on that."

Fred seems confused by Harold's words but then overhears him.

"I hope you don't mind, Morgan, but I have to get some information for my friend, Fred here. I'll just be a few moments."

Fred nods and whispers, "Yes, I understand what you're doing. I'll wait."

Morgan smiles at her dad and acknowledges that it's okay. Harold quickly adjourns to his home office. This private sanctuary has walls that are filled with framed certificates, diplomas, and notable merit awards he's received. He sits in the chair behind his elaborate wooden desk and ponderously glances at the calendar thereon and the noted display of the Moon's phases. Raising his eyebrows, he tilts his head to the left.

He speaks into his cell phone, "Okay, Fred, I'm back. I didn't want to discuss this in front of my daughter."

"I surmised as much," replies Fred.

"What you're telling me may also explain the gravitational anomaly we discovered with the SPIDER project. What are other observatories reporting?"

"I'm told, Harold, that the authorities have now been alerted to this phenomenon in Washington and across the globe. They're having a General Assembly meeting tomorrow at the U.N., and a Security Council meeting scheduled for Tuesday. They are putting together a committee of astrophysicists, astronomers, and scientists from all around the world to meet at the Security Council meeting in New York, plus a prequel meeting at the Pentagon Monday. Your name is on that list of attendees, as are others of our discipline from almost every continent and nation on the planet."

"I understand, Fred. However, unless by some miracle that trajectory alters and the Moon ceases to come closer, the astounding result is ... it will become an apocalyptic calamity."

Fred's voice cracks, "Yes, you're right, but as it's been said, 'Life is 10% of what happens to you and 90% of how we react to it.' So, perhaps by meeting, we may at least present some semblance of hope to the world."

"This is unbelievable, Fred. My daughter's visiting here from Albany, so I'd hoped to spend some time with her." He sighs, "Keep me posted on travel plans to D.C. and New York."

Fred replies, "So long, Harold, I'll be praying for all of us."

"Yeah, okay. For all the good it'll do, go ahead."

Harold returns to the kitchen where he forces his face into a weak smile that he flashes to Morgan. He winks at her as if to suggest the conversation was routine and no big deal. She reacts by nodding her head and going about the small task of washing the teacups and removing the garbage liner from the trash can.

Still, she senses he's uncomfortable and to her appears to be anxious about something.

"Dad, you seem edgy, is everything alright?"

Not realizing his body language and demeanor are transmitting his angst, he attempts to defray her concern.

"What? Oh, yes hon. I just had a moment when my mind slipped back to when your mom was with us."

She walks past him and pats him on the shoulder.

For him, the impact of the news Fred told him begins sinking into the tissues of his brain and saturating his soul with images and delusional visions of a world being torn apart by shifting in the Earth's crust, huge waves, and volcanic eruptions.

Morgan waves at him, noting that she's taking the trash into the garage to place in the city-supplied garbage container. He nods and then thanks her.

Harold glances toward the garage where his daughter is innocently going about her simple task. His expression is one as if he is in gut-wrenching pain ... like someone just stabbed him in the heart. Harold hears Morgan's high heels clicking against the concrete floor of the garage.

His mind recalls all the many prayers Morgan and Ted said for their mother and him. None of their pleas to God ... in whom he doesn't believe ... could save her. He envisions that out-of-control car that slammed head-on into the SUV she was driving. She never had a chance.

Morgan opens the back door leading into the kitchen. She again joins him at the breakfast table.

"Everything alright with your friend?" Morgan asks.

Avoiding what was discussed; Harold affirms that and shakes his head.

"Huh? Oh, yes. He just wanted to tell me about his physics department's experiment."

Morgan changes the topic, "Dad, I know that you still miss Mom. We all do, but it's been five years now since she passed. Ted and I worry about you being here in this big house alone all the time. You don't drink, so you don't go to any bars with friends. You don't go dancing anymore, to the theater, or concerts, and you only went to church because Mom made you."

Harold holds up a hand to deter her comments, "Hold on there, Princess. Yes, your mom is gone, and yes, I am alone here, but that's my choice. Besides, I have my students and work to keep me busy."

"I know, Dad, but have you considered that Mom wouldn't want you to be alone? You're only in your early fifties. You're handsome, affluently successful, and have a lot to offer any woman that might be searching for a good man. Isn't there some single lady that attracts your interest?"

Harold bristles, "Morgan, you're out of bounds with such questioning. Your mother was the only woman that ever stirred my heart. If some lady wants to be a part of my life, it will have to be her that makes the effort to do so. At this stage in life, I'd think twice before reserving another space in my heart for one that didn't make an effort to stay. As of yet, I've discovered no one like that."

"Perhaps that's because you've lessened the opportunity. Before you quit attending church, I know of several lovely widowed ladies there that might be candidates to seek your affections."

"Alright, just stop it. As you know, church, religion, and an eternal soul are something your mother believed in, but that I know to be nonsense."

"You know? Come on, Dad. You say that, but I refuse to believe that you have no faith in God."

"I am a scientist, Morgan. Given the immense scale of the observable universe, there is almost certainly life elsewhere in the cosmos, perhaps including intelligent civilizations. That said, my vision of the origin of humanity, this small planet, and its destiny does not include some grand plan designed by a single omnipotent Creator."

"You know, Mom, Ted, and I have always disagreed with you about that. Do you think that Mom's death only promised her oblivion? I refuse to believe that there is no life after death. The soul is eternal and is animated beyond the dependency upon the body. As the Bible states, the soul is a vital life force ... that Jesus proved by His death and resurrection."

"I know the arguments, and I do not mean to lessen your faith, but to me, the current scientific paradigm does not offer any proof or recognition of a spiritual dimension to life."

Frustrated, Morgan seems to realize the futility of attempting to change his mind on the subject. Tears fill her eyes and she takes her dad's hand.

"Dad, you're the smartest man I know, but you have a materialistic approach to reality. The paradigm you suggest leads only to insoluble enigmas that are ultimately irrational. I hope someday you'll realize that."

"One day, I hope to be convinced that I'm wrong about it, but as I see it, we're all just dust orbiting the sun. I've never seen a soul under a microscope, through a telescope, nor found one in a test tube."

"And you've never actually seen electricity, the wind, microwaves, or broadcast signals either, but they exist."

"Sadly, life is but the activity of atoms and particles, which spin around for a while and then dissipate into nothingness."

"At church, the pastor once quoted a brilliant man that said the hope of another life gives us the courage to meet our death, and to bear with the death of our loved ones; we are twice armed if we fight with faith in God. Surely, when you stand over Mom's grave and speak to her, you must feel that her soul is with God."

"Yes, I do speak to her, but it isn't as if I believe that your mother is present somewhere in a mysterious afterworld, or on some other plane of existence. It's just that when I think I hear her voice it is because she was so much a part of me that her being lives on inside my mind."

Harold's mind whirls as he recalls Elisa, and then the previous conversation he'd had with Fred. He knows the peril facing humankind and his family. His eyes water, as he stares into his beloved daughter's beautiful face. He wonders if this short visit may be the last time, he has to ever be with her again. Based on the information Fred gave him, that seems to be a real possibility. He sighs deeply.

"Okay, Princess, I am glad you have your faith and I value your input. In my case, knowledge has been at times a curse. I haven't any proof that there is no God or soul, any more than you do of proving there is one. In that regard, I suggest we move on to another topic."

"Dad, you know I love you, and God loves you even though you deny His existence."

"Great! I love you as well. Good grief, I'd rather we hadn't gotten off the discussion of my dating women than what we just wrangled over."

She sheepishly grins and shrugs, showing her obvious disappointment.

"Okay, but don't forget that it is said, 'Faint heart wins not the lady fair."

Still stunned by the News he got from Fred, Harold forces a laugh and a faint smile.

He remarks, "Are you certain you're not the one that graduated from law school?"

Chapter 5

It is a week before ... and two-thousand miles west of Chile in the southern Pacific Island known as Isla de Pascua, better known as Easter Island. The mysterious triangle-shaped island is famous for its Rapanui Indian heritage and the more than nine-hundred Moai statues scattered about the island. The southwestern part of the island is the largest of three volcanic craters. It's called, Rano Kau, which means in Rapanui language that water is stored there. Rainwater, which is one source of freshwater for the island's inhabitants, is indeed collected in the large lagoon below. With a lake depth of around thirty-two feet, Totora reeds are prevalent on the lagoon's surface.

Near the base of the lagoon's caldera's sloping north side and six-hundred-fifty-six feet below the circular walls are a team of geologists from the University of Chile in Santiago. Chunks of basaltic lava and some pyroclastic materials of obsidian are scattered about within the walls. The native Rapanui Indians once utilized those materials to create stone axes, spearheads, and to use for the Moai eye pupils.

The geologists came to the island on a field trip to learn more about the geologic composition of Isla de Pascua and the effect of land erosion caused by rising seawater and tides. Upon visiting the lagoon, they became troubled when they noticed dead bodies of the caldera's single species, Mosquitofish, floating to the top of the freshwater lake. Immediately, they gathered their equipment and now are busily sampling the temperature of the water. This unexpected discovery seems to greatly alarm them. In addition to the dead fish, there are moments when steam bubbles up from the bottom of the caldera. Realizing that this is not normal, one geologist looks over at another after taking the temperature. He ambles over to his colleague to compare readings.

Dr. Benecio Juarez asks, "This is most disturbing. What does your gauge read?"

Dr. Jose Ramirez expresses a grim and shuddering fascination.

"Two-hundred-degrees ... right near the boiling point."

Both geologists seem stunned and very much alarmed by this discovery.

Dr. Juarez's anxiety heightens and he sighs deeply.

"I must conclude that this caldera is reacting to an underground seismic rise in magma temperatures, which suggests that volcanic activity is reawakening. It seems that after one-hundred-eighty-thousand-years ... the crater and volcano are ceasing its dormancy."

Dr. Ramirez concurs, "Notwithstanding, I'd say this build-up of water temperatures indicate the summoning of seismic pressure ... leading to an all-out, formidable, and probably soon-to-be enormous eruption."

"Yes, and Rano Kau's phenomenal reactivation would also cause the activation of the other two dormant volcanoes ... essentially devastating the population of this island."

"Agreed! We must warn the populace of this impending disaster."

"Let's get out of here. An eruption could occur at any moment. The entire island must be evacuated as soon as possible

* * *

The geologists warn the authorities in the major island town of Hanga Roa. Already, there are the beginnings of rumblings within the Earth and tremors causing the populace of the island to panic. Several of the Moai in line on stone pedestals tumble over. Chaos reigns among the occupants of Easter Island. Distress calls are made to Santiago and Hawaii to send ocean liners and airplanes to assist in evacuating the island as soon as possible. The island's one airport, Matavari International, busily routes passenger jets to ferry people away as often as possible, but planes alone are not enough to evacuate almost 7800 people.

When one scheduled ocean liner finally does get to the island two days later, with no docks in which they can pull up to the island, ferries must be used to transfer the evacuees onto the ships. This proves not to be an easy task, for the high winds create choppy seas. Nonetheless, with the assistance of other cruise liners from three countries, in five days the island is void of its human occupants. By now, the Rano Kau crater has boiled away some of the lake water and is sending ash several miles into the skies above the island. It seems inevitable that a major eruption could occur at any time.

* * *

Again on this present Saturday ... aboard the Russian Presidential Aircraft, a Llyushin 11-96 Airjet, takes off from the Moscow airport. Inside the luxurious plane, Russia's head of state, Leonid Rosknova, settles in for the hour-long flight to Kazakhstan to check out the progress of the Soyuz rocket launch to the ISS. A few minutes into the flight, his aides and generals gather in the meeting area of the plane to discuss the reported progress.

The stern-looking Russian Prime Minister sits at a table before them reading over transcripts of conversations recorded from the ISS. After doing so, he animatedly shakes his head. By his slapping an open palm upon the table before him, he makes a strong indication to those present of his displeasure.

"This last transmission from the ISS depicts a normal telecommunication briefing between the onboard crew and those at NASA control and the Roscosmos main Mission Control Space Center in Korolvov. So, why did the broadcasts instantly cease, and why did the Americans so rapidly send up two other crewmen to investigate what occurred up there? Why weren't we ready with a Soyuz rocket to send up? I want answers."

The nervous, frustrated aides and generals can only speculate, for there seemed to be an infinity pool of illogical answers presented to them by Russian scientists and rocketry technicians, none of which seemed plausible to repeat to their 'fit to be tied' Prime Minister.

One brave aide spoke up, "Sir, even though 50% of our space program is dedicated to the ISS, no one could foresee anything like what's supposedly happened up there."

The squinting eyes of the Russian leader bore into the aide.

"What exactly has occurred up there?"

The aide swallows hard and glances around at the myriad of blank stares he receives from his colleagues, all of whom seem intent on playing dumb and not answering that question.

"Well, to be honest, Sir, according to our video feeds and those at NASA, all six of the crew just ... vanished."

"You're the third person to tell me that in the past three days. I don't deal with the impracticable. Six crewmen are not misplaced nor can they disappear from inside a contained spacecraft. They do not simply vanish. There must be another reason and I demand to know what that is."

Suddenly, the aircraft pitches to the left causing a strong jolt that tosses the Prime Minister to the floor of the plane. As his aides and generals gather themselves, two rush to help their leader to his feet. When they do, a bright golden flash occurs. They are astounded and quickly become befuddled. Shielding their eyes, they squint and rapidly scan the area behind the desk, as the others too attempt to see what it is that causes them alarm.

"One confused aide yells, "What happened to him? He's gone!"

Another grimacing aide, who is startled proclaims, "He has to be here! He was seated before us in that chair just a moment ago."

Frantically disbelieving, one general questions, "Where'd that flash come from?"

An aide casts him a wary glance, "We're flying at 30,000 feet, where could he possibly go?"

The pilot of the aircraft announces over the intercom system.

"Sorry for the lurch there. We hit a rough patch of air. I hope everyone is okay back there."

One aide covers a hand over his mouth as if to stifle a scream. Another plops down into his chair, looking as if he's just taken a quantum leap into the unknown.

The bravest among them that spoke up to their leader states, "The noble truth may be ... that we've entered another dimension, for I have no other explanation for what just happened."

His body shaking, another aide comments, "None of us has any clarity as to where he went, how he vanished, nor why he did. It's incomprehensible, but for certain he's not on this plane."

* * *

At the same time in London, their Prime Minister stands before the House of Commons and House of Lords making a speech about their new King, the state of the nation, and its recovering economy. Nearing the end of his diatribe, he suddenly seems distracted. He gets a catch in his throat, his hands travel to his head, and then he faints away onto the floor of the Parliament. Two of his Cabinet members quickly react, stand, and rush toward him to offer help.

To their complete surprise and all present, right before their disbelieving eyes ... a bright golden flash occurs, as the Prime Minister's body rapidly fades and disappears from view. This astounding occurrence leaves the entire governing body in stunned silence. They all rise and exchange shocked glances. Murmurs of astonishment vibrate through the assemblage. The two Cabinet members standing where their leader was but a few seconds before seem about to shout out. Their mouths are open, but their lips cannot speak any words to describe their bewilderment. They wildly wave their arms through the place where he sat only a moment before.

Finally, one man among them bellows, "We must all be dreaming, for what happened is impossible."

Another man remarks, "I'd agree with you, but then we'd both be wrong ... because it did happen ... or was what we saw just a hologram?"

* * *

Meanwhile in Washington D.C., in the Pressroom of the White House, President Nash Garrett, enters and stands at his podium before the packed assemblage of the press corps. The eager grouping of reporters waves their arms seeking the President's granting of them to ask him a question. He points at one reporter.

"Thank you, Mr. President. Is there any further word on the disappearance of France's President Armand?"

"No, only speculation and rumor. I'm sure they'll tell us more when they know more."

Another reporter asks, "Some sketchy reports have come in suggesting that there was an emergency that occurred on the International Space Station. NASA has refused to clarify what that emergency entails. I think most Americans and others around the world deserve to know what's going on up there. Can you enlighten us?"

President Garrett clears his throat and dodges the question as best he is able.

"I guess for you guys in the press you don't need to understand things to argue about them. The truth be known, your network should be put on mute and Google itself. Quit jumping to conclusions and complaining about my office or NASA not explaining something that is highly classified. If we wanted you to know, we'd tell you. Next question!"

Many more hands anxiously wave and the frenzied gathering yells out their requests to be heard. Reluctantly, the President calls on another reporter.

"Thank you, Mr. President. I understand the need for classified secrecy, but why all the mystery and avoidance of answering one simple question. Don't sugar coat it ... are the six crewmen aboard the ISS alive and well?"

The President snarls, "Well, unlike you, I didn't have a bowl of sunshine this morning sweetened with a thundercloud. I sure hope they're alive and well. That's all I'll comment on about the ISS. Any other questions?"

He recognizes a third reporter, "Yes, you, go ahead ... and don't ask me about the ISS."

"Thank you, Mr. President. We're told there will be an emergency meeting at the U.N. starting Tuesday. It's been reported from coastal cities all over the world that the tides have become so high that the bays and rivers near the cities are slowly being flooded. We know that downtown levees in New Orleans are close to overflowing and that commerce has been halted there along the docks and also in New York, Boston, Houston, and L.A. They are but a few that are having tidal surges. Is there any explanation as to what's causing these intrusive tides? Are the polar ice caps melting?" Also, we've heard rumors that Yellowstone is acting up. We all know what that means if it blows."

The President reaches and takes a sip of water from the bottle inside the podium. He coughs into his bent arm and seems to be searching his mind for the proper response.

He then states, "So far as I know the polar ice caps are not melting. Let's hope things at Yellowstone calm down. As for the exact cause of the higher tides, I'm told that it is symptomatic of a lunar event known as the 'Super-moon' phase of its orbit around the Earth. In other words, it's closer now to its elliptical orbit, and that causes higher tides and other phenomena. I'm told the reason is just consequential that they are larger now than normal."

The skeptical reporter comments, "Such flooding as this is unorthodox and has never been known to occur before. So, why now? Something else besides a Super-moon must be provoking the tides."

"If so, I am not privy to what else might cause it. Perhaps we'll learn more about it when the U.N. meets. Next question."

The President takes about a half-dozen more questions from the press, before he tires of their nagging inquiries about France's President, the tides, and the ISS. He finally puts a halt to the proceedings and turns to leave.

As he does, what happened in Britain instantly occurs within the press room. One moment President Garrett is standing and walking away toward a blue sliding door. The next, there is a bright flash of golden light ... and he disappears into thin air. A Secret Service agent only a few feet away from him grabs his arms toward the President, only to have them swipe out at nothingness. Cursing, he and other secret service men almost spastically yank their pistols from chest holsters and wield them at the ready. They wave and aim them, but can find no definable target at which to do so.

The room of reporters gasps and begins to chirp with incessant disbelief at what so quickly occurred. One female reporter faints. The News networks covering the press conference quickly re-wind their video footage, attempting to view what happened. At the exact moment he vanished, the video feed develops a static that scrambles his image for a second or two. None of the talking heads can explain nor comprehend what transpired, nor how it was even remotely possible.

One shaken, but sarcastic news reporter yells into his microphone.

He mockingly exclaims to his network, "Some unknown force did in an instant what the Democrats have been trying to do for the past three years ... make President Garrett ... disappear."

* * *

Sunday morning the event is posted in every newspaper. Bold headlines scream the news of the strange disappearances. On television, normal programming is interrupted. Internet feeds around the globe and all news outlets overflow with reports pouring in about the strange unexplainable vanishings of heads of state from nations around the world. Besides the French, Russian, British, and U.S. President, it includes the Chinese President, and the leaders of Pakistan, India, Israel, North Korea, and also South Africa, to mention but a few. All of the disappearances mysteriously occurred instantly after a bright golden flash, leaving no clues as to what could cause such a phenomenon. The one commonality between the ten nations is they all have nuclear capabilities, which makes their nervous nations all the more dangerous. Each one is filled with anxiety and suspicion. Around the globe, militaries are put on high alert. Some governments and scientists suggest that an unknown, undiscovered technology might be the only plausible explanation as to how such a thing could take place. All nations deny that capability or awareness of such a sci-fi-like technology. Various terror organizations and radical religious leaders make absurd claims about who is responsible for the disappearances.

A political superpower, Russia accuses China, and Chinese politicians seem certain that the U.S. is somehow responsible for creating a secret superweapon. However, almost all scientists claim that even if some nations did have such teleportation capabilities, they scoff at the idea of being able to teleport a human being from an air jet traveling at thirty-thousand feet and over four-hundred miles per hour. They also note the reported incident involving the Governor-General of Australia that disappeared while scuba diving in the ocean. A well-trained and experienced diver, he was down almost one-hundred-twenty feet deep and swimming alongside four other divers, when after a bright golden glow, he too vanished. The scientists claim that no teleportation device should be possible that deep under the sea.

The bottom line is no one truly has any comprehension as to how these things could happen, nor why so many heads of state were targeted. As one newspaper stated, it's almost as if in reality we are experiencing life inside the Matrix.

Chapter 6

That same Sunday morning, Harold wakes just before dawn and rolls out of bed. In boxer shorts and wearing a white undershirt, he stretches and wipes at his eyes. Glancing at the alarm clock near his bed, sleepily, he reaches to shut off the button disengaging the alarm. It is 6:08 a.m. and the brilliant glow of sunshine streams into his bedroom from the east-facing window. It takes him a few moments before his mind wraps around that fact. Then, he recalls what Fred had told him the day before about the days becoming shorter due to the gravitational pull of the Moon upon the Earth. He realizes that in late April the sun shouldn't be rising until around 6:45 a.m.

Harold sighs and strolls into the hallway. He quietly saunters to the bedroom down the hall, stops at the door, gently opens it, and peers into the room where he sees Morgan sleeping peacefully in the bed. He feels his emotions racing and his eyes well up with tears. How wonderful it is to have her here.

His memory recalls the myriad of times before while she was growing up that he cracked open this door to get a last peek at her before retiring for the night. Most times, Elisa joined him in their nightly routine of kissing their two children goodnight, tucking them in, and then returning to their bedroom after they'd fallen asleep. Peeking in to watch their children safe and sound in their beds always brought a smile to Harold's face and a warm glow to his heart. Even though Morgan and Ted are both grown and married now, the thrill it brings to him watching her ... once again back home, if only for a day or two is wonderful.

He lets her sleep and silently closes the door. His mind reels as he ambles back to his bedroom, with what he imagines will be a catastrophic event if the Moon does not cease its current trajectory. He saddens even more at the thought of that impending apocalypse ... of not ever having grandchildren, and both his life and the lives of his children terminated terribly. As he enters his bedroom, a sudden flash of anger overcomes him. His mind becomes engulfed by rage and he is gloomy and depressed. A shiver runs down his spine and he feels goosebumps trickle up his arms.

"Damn it all!" He shakes a clenched fist toward the ceiling and is boiling mad. His limbs feel as if they are chained to iron shackles and his stomach twists and turns.

He stumbles to the bathroom, but before he can make it to the toilet, he begins to heave up the salad, steak, and potatoes he wolfed down last night when he took Morgan to his favorite restaurant. He blinks sweat from his eyes and crawls on his knees to the bathroom sink. Pulling himself up, he turns on the water and with his hands splashes it onto his face. His watery eyes attempt to focus on his face in the mirror over the sink. His face is frozen in a glassy stare of fury.

He grumbles as if yelling at the world and wildly waves his arms frantically, "Where is your God now? If he loves us so much, how can he allow this to happen? I'll tell you why, because he doesn't exist ... that's why. He's just some imagined entity created by humankind to give them false hope and soften the fact that death is real and the grave is final."

As he finishes and slams more water upon his face, when he rises back up he notices Morgan's reflection in the mirror. Standing behind him in her gown, her head begins to shake and she too begins to cry. Harold wheels about realizing that his private outburst was overheard by her. This was the second time in two days that she'd surprised him with her presence. He cannot bring himself to meet her eyes and he cannot muster words to say to her.

She wipes away a tear and her voice cracks, "What's happening, Dad? Are you ill? You don't have cancer or something, do you?"

His face contorts and apologetically he tells her, "What? No, dear one, I am not ill."

"Then what's going on and why are you angry at God, yet claim not to believe in Him?"

Harold rushes to her side, grabs her in his arms, and kisses her on the forehead.

He withdraws but notices her odd expression. He reasons that the way she's looking at him suggests she's appraising him and is suspicious that he's hiding something from her. He shuffles his feet and stands a few feet from her intense gaze.

In his mind, he wonders what it is about a woman that makes her so perceptive and aware when a man is covering up something. Elisa was also that way with him. She always picked up apprehensive vibes when he was melancholy, or when he was trying to hide bad news from her. That sixth sense must have passed onto Morgan as well. But this is different. It is as inexplicable and real as existence itself.

"Come on, Dad. Something is going on that you're not telling me."

Harold can't bring himself to frighten her by divulging all of what he suspects will happen. Instead, he only mentions sketchy facts about the next few days.

"My friend and colleague, Fred, the man I spoke to yesterday on the phone texted me. There's a meeting he and I have to attend at the Pentagon Monday before the military's Joints Chiefs of Staff. It's just a Q & A session that I'm told needs the input of astronomers and astrophysicists. Others of my colleagues will also be there."

She turns her head and brushes a strand of hair from her eyes. He watches her reaction closely hoping that his explanation will quell her intuitive female mind.

"I see, and does this have anything to do with the secrets being kept from the public about the incidents happening on the ISS?"

Relieved to hear her pretense, he quickly agrees with her false assumption. He neglects to tell her that he's also got a meeting Tuesday at the U.N. in New York.

"Yes, most certainly that must be what it is. They probably need us to help explain the astrophysics of whatever is going on up there."

Not entirely convinced she poses a comeback, "Okay, but then why are you so upset if that is the happening you mentioned?"

Also quick-witted he replies, "Because it means I'll have to leave here Monday and miss being with you the next few days."

"I know that's disappointing to me as well, but you must go to that meeting." She ponders a moment and says, "Look, I'll meet with Steve Monday, but when our outdoor venture is done, I'll swing back here for a couple of days before going back home. That still gives us some time together tomorrow."

Harold's face lights up, "Terrific! That'll be wonderful, Morgan. By then, maybe Ted's trial litigation case will be over and he too can get away for a visit with us. It's been over three years since I've been with the two of you together."

"Okay, Dad. Now, let me help you pick out the right clothes for your meeting at the Pentagon."

* * *

After sharing some pancakes and sausage that Morgan fixed for breakfast, Harold pats his tummy and leans back in his chair. He sips his coffee and a broad smile crosses his lips.

"Wow! I haven't had pancakes like that since your Mom—"

She interrupts, "I know, Dad. That's why I made them for you. It's a good thing I fried up the sausage now, for its expiration date was two days ago."

Harold winces and his mind focuses on the words, 'expiration date' that she used. He struggles with the thought of it coming too soon.

"Well, it was wonderful, Morgan. Thank you!"

As Morgan cleans off the table and sets the dishes into the dishwasher, Harold stands and walks outside to the front yard to retrieve his morning newspaper. It is rolled up with a rubber band around it, so it isn't until he comes back inside and sits in his recliner in the den that he removes the band and opens the paper, revealing the huge headlines on the front page:

"U.S. PRESIDENT DISAPPEARS –
MILITARY PUT ON HIGHEST ALERT."

Harold begins reading and is stunned by what he learns of the myriad of high-profile disappearances and how each person basically vanished. It also reports that after this, NASA explained that the incident with the ISS was a similar disappearance, as all six of the crew mysteriously vanished while a video from the ISS was broadcasting back to Earth.

Morgan, in a good mood, joins him in the den. She wipes her hands with a dishtowel and saunters toward Harold whose face is sheltered from view by the newspaper.

She asks, "Any more news about the ISS, Dad?"

He drops his arms and lowers the paper. Her expression quickly changes as she notices the sudden color change in his startled face and frown.

After reading the articles explaining the dilemma, he reaches for the remote control and turns on the television.

"Yes, I'm afraid there is. You better sit down, Morgan, and let's see what's on the televised news."

On every network, the normal programs are pre-empted with breaking news about all the mysterious happenings. Again, and again, they show the video of President Garrett and the British Prime Minister disappearing. They also show videos of flooding coastlines, and dormant volcanoes around the globe waking and churning out steam and ash clouds. Network anchors are interviewing scientists that notice the shortening of days and the many unexplainable gravitational anomalies occurring that make things heavier.

Astronomers note this is supposed because the tug of Earth's gravity is lessening in strength as the Moon's pull becomes stronger as it comes closer. Astronomers across the world indicate their concerns about the deviance in the lunar orbit. They are not specific as to what causes it or what the repercussions might be. All around the world, people are beginning to panic.

A reporter standing away from one of the geysers in Yellowstone National Park explains how the government has warned everybody within three hundred miles to immediately evacuate as far as possible because an eruption seems imminent. He claims that the same is true for Kilauea in Hawaii and Mount Fuji in Japan. However, there is no reference to the building volcanic threat on Easter Island.

Global reporters assigned to Russia, China, Pakistan, Israel, and Korea provide videos of military build-ups and chaotic, panicky crowds in the streets. Some reports are going live to churches and mosques around the world to show how the faithful are praying and conducting somber prayer services.

Harold's thoughts are flooded with incomprehensible questions. He can't fathom how such disappearances are possible and despite his brilliance, he can come up with no rational explanation for how or why the Moon has begun to ascend toward the Earth.

A distraught, inquisitive Morgan turns and gazes at him with great curiosity and distress.

"Dad, how are people and things vanishing in plain sight even possible?"

"I have no answer that would make any sense, Morgan. As an experimental physicist, I attempt to prepare for every eventuality, but in this matter, I haven't got a clue."

Her shoulders slump and she asks, "And what's going on with the Moon's orbit?"

His eyes avert her questioning stare. Her query hits him like a right hook to the jaw.

Words stick on his lips and it's as though every neuron shuts off in his brain. He flails like a fish on the end of a hook, sighs, whimpers, and then small muffled sounds come out of his mouth.

"Baby girl, my brain is short-circuiting right now from overload. Please don't ask me any more questions."

"Dad, you don't call me, Baby Girl, unless there's something you're trying to hide from me, or when you don't want to scare me. I appreciate your intent, but not telling me only heightens my anxiety."

"I'm sorry, Morgan. If I were a drunkard, I'd look for the answer in the bottom of the glass of bourbon."

"You don't drink, Dad. So, what's a sobering answer to my question? Is our world in trouble?"

His reaction to this news hits her like the sting of a scorpion.

He reluctantly says, "I've always tried to keep you and your brother safe and out of harm's way, but in this case, not one of us can do anything except hope that the Moon's orbit stabilizes and comes no closer."

From other times when he's given her the bad news, she recognizes that his demeanor and indirectness means that this too is a dire situation.

"So, dad, are you saying that⏢?"

Before she can finish, he interjects, "Don't say it!" He grabs her and holds her to him.

"My Lord!" she exclaims and her hands fly to cover her face.

"Baby Girl, this is one time I wish I had your faith."

"Is there any hope that the Moon won't come any closer?"

"I suppose there is always hope, but if our world was for sale ... we'd be in no position to bargain or dictate terms."

Morgan sighs deeply and wilts into a chair beside him. Her eyes well up with tears and he too becomes emotional. They break their embrace and his weary body plops down in a padded armchair. Shaking, she quickly rushes over to him and sits down on his lap, wrapping her arms around him.

"Let's pray that God will help us." She then inquires, "How much time do we have?"

Not wishing to add to her anguish he tells her, "I expect there are a few weeks before things escalate to the critical point. As for avoiding the outcome ... I'm not sure. Yes, do pray that your God will intervene. For yours and your brother's sake, if he's real ... I hope He will."

The remainder of the day they spend glued to the constantly breaking news coverage of the global events and impending diversion of the Moon towards Earth. Panic and riots flare up everywhere, as the news spreads to terrified people around the globe. In California, Ted ironically notes that the TV networks are still playing commercials as if nothing is more important than commerce and profit.

After watching the news, Ted calls his dad at 7:00 p.m. He informs Harold that a continuance of the trial he's prosecuting was granted and that he and his wife, Rita, will catch a flight on Tuesday to Trenton. Harold and Morgan are both relieved to hear the good news. Ted realizes the severity of the things happening with the Moon. Harold also learns that all classes at Princeton and most universities have been suspended until further notice.

* * *

At 8:00 p.m. that evening, the networks break in for an important message from the former Vice-President, Dave Battle, newly sworn in as President.

He begins somberly, "America, I come to you tonight with a heavy heart, praying that you and each of your families are safe. As you've been hearing and watching on the newscasts, today at a press conference, for some reason as yet unknown, President Garrett somehow inexplicably vanished without a trace while turning to leave the press room. This tragic and unexplained incident would be bad enough, but as you've probably heard, heads of state from over twenty-eight nations have also disappeared instantly and without explanation or warning. As unbelievable as this whole scenario seems, no one has any comprehension as to how or why these things are happening."

President Battle pauses to take a drink of water from a plastic bottle under the podium. He clears his throat, coughs into his elbow, and then sighs deeply.

"If our battles with Covid-19 weren't enough, we now face these uncertainties. I know that you all must have dozens of questions about this and the other anomalies happening in our world and universe. I too want to know what's going on.

He looks down and pauses a moment for effect.

"Is the President and all those others still alive? If so, where are they and will they return? Where did they go, why were they taken ... and by whom? What is your government doing about it? If our military is on such a high alert, are we going to war? If so, with whom? What's going on with the rising tides, sudden volcanic activity around the globe ... and for God's sake, what's going on with our Moon?"

Although attempting to keep his calm and composure, President Battle's somber voice cracks, and then he stops for a moment to catch his breath and wipe the sweat from his brow with a handkerchief.

"I wish I had answers to all the questions you must have, but I don't. At this time, I can only tell you that our great nation has no plans to go to war, but we shall remain on max alert until we are certain from where this threat is coming, be it from another country or a terrorist organization.

"As for President Garrett, we can only hope and pray that he and all the others are indeed alive. Besides being the leader of our Great Society and our nation's Commander-in-Chief, he's a close friend of mine and a beacon of democracy.

"Until his return, I shall do my best to carry on with his policies. All of us here in Washington, our military, and all of you, my fellow Americans must perpetuate and preserve our world, our nation, and our way of life. I know you must be worried, but please, do not panic or allow pandemonium to prevail. Stay tuned to your televisions for news updates, your radios, and the Internet.

"We will provide you with any further information about these events. In the meantime, a meeting will take place with the Joint Chiefs of Staff at the

Pentagon, and then on Tuesday the U.N. Security Council shall meet with a panel of astrophysicists, astronomers, and scientists from all across the globe to hear from them and hopefully learn more about all the mysterious events that are occurring in our world." President Garrett bows his head solemnly, raises his eyes, and gazes into the television camera.

"Have faith and please pray for our world and all humankind. God bless America."

* * *

Monday morning, getting little to no sleep and having had an emotional goodbye with Morgan, Harold boards a plane to Washington D.C. He arrives there later that morning. Upon checking in at his hotel, and then going up to his room, there's a knock on the door. Opening it, the bellboy carries in his luggage, which Harold has placed on the bed.

He fumbles through his pants pocket for tip money, which the bellhop thankfully accepts.

The bellhop remarks, "I hope your accommodations are suitable, Sir."

"Yes, it is a very nice suite, thank you."

"I'm told a van will be outside the lobby at 2:30 p.m. to carry you and the other gentlemen to your meeting at the Pentagon."

Harold isn't exactly thrilled at the prospect of facing a grouping of military generals but knows he must.

"Very well, I'll be there."

The bellboy turns to go, but then stops and turns, offering a note to Harold.

"One other thing, Sir. A gentleman asks that when you are settled in, he would like you to meet him in the hotel restaurant for lunch at noon."

Harold reads the note from a man named, Nicolai Stalin. He's puzzled, for the man is unknown to him.

He frowns at the bellboy and says, "Who is this man and why does he wish to meet me?"

"I'm told that he's a Russian General. That's all I know, Sir."

Harold's annoyed by this Russian's request and is suspicious of why he'd want to meet. Still, he is also curious and thanks the bellboy, who smiles and politely dismisses himself.

* * *

After texting Morgan to report that he's arrived safely just before noon, Harold dresses in his best suit and strolls off to meet with the Russian stranger that invited him to lunch. Downstairs in the elaborate setting of the plush hotel's restaurant, a maître'd greets him with a broad smile.

"Good morning, Sir. Will you be dining alone?"

"No, I am supposed to meet a man named, Nicolai Stalin. Is he here?"

The courteous host checks his seating chart and nods and grabs a menu.

He nods his head, "But of course, Sir. Please follow me to his table."

As Harold trails through the busy establishment of diners, he is led to a table by a window overlooking the Potomac River ... and with a distant view of the Pentagon. The barrel-chested, blonde-haired man with a full mustache sips on a vodka cocktail. To Harold he's the stereotypical image of a communist Ruskie that's just gotten off the set of a cold-war movie set. He's dressed in a brown, Russian uniform with gold epaulets and a gold star depicting his rank of General. Over his left pocket are a string of bronze, silver, and gold medals, plus various ribbons denoting his 'been there – done that' service in global deployments and service to mother Russia.

The husky, six-foot-tall general quickly stands and offers a friendly hand toward Harold in a gesture of friendship. Still, puzzled and uneasy by this mystery man wanting to meet, Harold's eyes attempt to assess the man's sincerity ... but firmly shakes the General's hand.

"Professor, Simpson, it is such an honor to meet you."

"Call me, Harold. I presume that you are Nikolai."

Yes, Harold, I am. Please, take a seat and relax," as he points to a chair at the table.

As Harold does so, his eyes catch sight of the Pentagon across the river.

"Thank you for coming, Professor. Would you care for a cocktail before lunch?"

"No, thank you, I don't care for the drink."

Although he speaks English, Nikolai does so with a strong Russian accent.

"General, please tell me, how it is that you know me and why did you ask to meet?"

Nikolai raises his glass to toast, "Nostrovia!"

Harold acknowledges the toast, but his glaring stare signals to the General a growing impatience.

Raising his water glass, Harold states, "Salud!"

Then Harold quips sarcastically, "You say your last name is, Stalin? As in ... Joseph Stalin, I suppose."

Unhesitatingly Nikolai replies, "Yes, he was my father. Do I not favor him?"

Nikolai watches Harold's reaction closely, who chokes back a laugh and seems squeamish and suspicious. Nikolai then bursts forth in hardy laughter.

"I'm joking, of course. I have no family connection to him, which is good, for he was a cruel man. My true last name is, Belinski ... General Nikolai Belinski."

Hearing this, Harold's lips form a wry grin, but his expression remains stern. The two men make eye contact and smile, though neither blink.

"That's a relief, for a moment there, I was afraid I was going to have to shoot you."

"Yes," the Russian says robustly in a sarcastic manner, "I hope you don't regret omitting that opportunity. Forgive me, Harold, my wife tells me I do not take life seriously enough. Me? I say, enjoy it while you can, which may not be as long as we'd like."

Harold nods his agreement. Nikolai then bends and takes a manila folder out of a briefcase near his feet. He lays the folder down on the table. Harold orders a cup of hot tea from the waiter and turns to glance down at the folder. Nikolai's intense, emerald eyes look attentively over hooded eyelids. He carefully scans Harold's face for a reaction.

"Harold facetiously asks, "What's that, some secret formula for making Russian dressing?"

Nikolai smirks and replies, "Oh No, that concoction is top-secret information. This is merely a detailed dossier ... on you, comrade Harold.

Harold's pleasant expression instantly becomes a sobering, suspicious one.

"Go ahead, take it. Read it. Everything my country's intelligence people could come up with about you is in there."

Harold's jovial mood quickly fades and he angers. He grabs the folder, opens it, and begins to hastily peruse the contents.

Nicolai adds, "You will note, Comrade, the info tells me that you are fifty-two years old, were born in Alabama, and are five years a widower after your wife died in an auto crash. My condolences for your loss."

Harold nods his head acknowledging the sentiment, but his normal modest and unassuming personality nears the breaking point.

Nikolai continues, "You have two grown children, advanced degrees in astrophysics, nuclear physics, and quantum theory, plus you have been a department leader and tenured physics professor at Princeton University for more than fifteen years."

Harold's eyebrows raise, his eyes narrow, and he squints and continues to read. Seconds later he finishes and irritably slaps the folder down onto the table.

Harold scoffs, "That's not all it tells you, Comrade Nikolai. Go on!"

Nikolai holds his hands up in mock surrender and resumes, "No! As you read, it also states that you're a covert agent of the CIA and are involved with and are currently contributing to the Groom Lake, Area 51 development of a secret U.S. program called AURORA. You've also worked with aerospace engineers at the NASA Eagleworks Advanced Propulsion Labs in developing and experimenting with a new non-fuel propellant system known as an EM Drive that uses a high-powered magnetron to convert electricity into microwaves ... that then exerts a force against the walls of a chamber, whereby the stored energy is propelled out the rear resembling the effect of a propellant-less rocket engine."

He continues, "You were selected to research and work at the Supercollider in Cern, but decided to keep your professorship at Princeton instead. You were offered the position as Dean, but turned that down as well."

Harold's face turns red and his distrust and annoyance at this man increase.

Unfazed, Nikolai maintains, "This dossier also tells me that you are a key component to designing what our spies discovered to be a TR-3B, high altitude, stealth, reconnaissance platform with an indefinite loiter time. In effect, you helped build and design a working model UFO."

Harold dismisses the comment, "That's insane, for such a technology is not yet possible."

"Harold, I understand these things because being an ex-KGB agent before it disbanded, I was commissioned into the military. I also hold advanced degrees in astrophysics and I am also a nuclear physicist for my country."

Harold snarls and glares at Nikolai, "I see! I'm not surprised that your government tapped into that EM program and other covert-mentioned programs, but your spies need to update my dossier. I resigned from those projects and the CIA fifteen months ago. You should also be aware that my government knows you guys have your own type Area 51 ... and developed something similar to the EM drive, plus hypersonic rockets and a similar above-the-atmosphere craft about ready to fly."

Nikolai chuckles, "Yes, we know that you know, yet as you are also aware, neither of our programs yield mercury and plasma propulsion or EM drive crafts that can as yet traverse safely through the vacuum and other unfriendly elements of outer space."

"Hah! Are you certain of that? I wouldn't advise it."

Nikolai laughs again. He picks up the dossier and retrieves a cigar lighter from his pants pocket. As he fires up the cigar, his meat-hook-sized hands tear the dossier into shreds. He tosses the pieces into the folder and hands them to Harold.

He sternly comments, "I was given that information before leaving Russia to come here and meet with you and your colleagues at the U.N. meeting tomorrow. I want you to know, Comrade, I did not request it, nor will I use what info is in it in any way to cause your country or you embarrassment or harm. I also vow to never reveal your clandestine status with the CIA or the AURORA Project."

"Then, what is it you wish, Nikolai? And why is your country so interested in me? I'm just an ordinary old physics professor."

"Comrade, physics professor yes ... ordinary and old ... no! I consider it an honor to meet you. I believe you to be a brilliant man of great character, and one that shall consider all points of view when dealing with solving our planet's difficult problems. As you know, all of humanity is facing a huge dilemma threatening our very existence as a species. We must coordinate our efforts and understanding. In this matter, we can neither be Russian or American, but only citizens of this world."

Harold quickly reformulates his opinion of this man and his intent.

"That's true, Nikolai. You should come with me to repeat that speech tomorrow at the U.N. It's to our mutual benefit that all nations collaborate in our efforts to avoid mayhem and attempt to come up with a solution to this enormous challenge ... if there is a solution at all."

Nikolai states, "I deplore the political correctness method of dealing with others whose fate it was to simply be born into a different nation than my own. We're all passengers on the same spaceship. We all live under diverse means of governing with varying ethnic cultures where idealism and religious beliefs collide. Still, we are all just humans with our own needs, flaws, and frailties. Unfortunately, what some call tolerance toward others, I see as more indifference."

Harold smiles, "I agree with everything you've said, but you still haven't answered my question."

"For one, I hear that you've been designated as spokesman for the team of astronomers and physicists to meet tomorrow in New York ... of which I too am a member."

"Spokesman? Me? Are you sure?"

"Yes, I'm certain. Your background in astrophysics makes you the perfect choice. As a professor, you're used to making presentations and teaching others. Plus, you have been a former member of the CIA, so you are no doubt adept at briefing military chiefs about their options in a crisis."

"Well, as a general, you are no doubt adept at doing the same, taking command, making battlefield decisions, and plans, plus giving orders. You'd be as equally good a choice for that task."

"I'm guessing that's why they named me as the co-chairman of the team. That is my motivation for asking you to lunch ... to introduce myself before the U.N. meeting tomorrow."

Harold nods his head and quickly develops higher regard for this man.

"Then I shall be counting on your expert contributions and assistance. I was told a team of astronomers and astrophysicists would be present tomorrow. I was not aware that I'd be called upon to be the lead presenter. I would have thought that Harvard's head of astronomy would have been better suited for that honor. Nonetheless, your thoughtful gesture of inviting me here is evidence of your consideration and integrity."

Harold raises his water glass again in a salute, "No matter how improbable it may seem, here's to an alliance of goodwill aimed toward the commonality of facing a difficult predicament. I applaud you, Nikolai."

The two raise their glasses and share the toast.

Nikolai nods and replies, "God be with us all."

Harold's head nods, but his brain revolts at the idea of God blessing anyone. Although this incident would normally rankle him, causing a certain estrangement between him and a Russian general, he's taken an instant liking to this man and believes him to be honest and sincere.

About this time, the waiter brings Harold's tea and sets it down on the table.

Looking at Nikolai, the waiter informs him, "Your order will be out in a few moments. Would you care for another drink, Sir?"

"No, but I would like coffee."

"Right away, Sir. "

Nikolai glances at Harold and says, "I took the privilege of ordering lunch for both of us. I hope you like linguini, salad, and breadsticks."

Harold nods and agrees, "Yes, that sounds good. Thank you!"

* * *

In a hastily called secret meeting at the Pentagon in Arlington County, Virginia, a United States counsel of the Joint Chiefs of Staff sit around a conference table. Also attending are the Secretary of State, the Secretary of Defense, and the Secretary of Homeland Security. At the head of the table is the Army Chief of Staff, General Howard Franks.

The General stands and speaks, "Gentlemen, as you know, the U.N. has called a special emergency meeting for tomorrow. Along with our Commander-in-Chief missing, plus dozens of other foreign national leaders, there are more concerning issues to which we must contend for our nation and the world. As we learned from our experiences with the Covid-19 pandemic, we must have international scientific collaboration among all nations across the globe.

"The upcoming U.N. meeting will be one dedicated to achieving that. Our newly sworn-in President and the U.N. Security Council have asked us to bring in experts in the field of astrophysics and astronomy to help explain what's occurring and to try and answer your concerns and questions.

"Let me first introduce you to the team leader in astrophysics: Professor Harold Simpson is from Princeton University. His team will address the issues confronting us in this emergency."

He motions with his hand, "Dr. Simpson, please introduce us to your team."

The Chiefs and the others shift their attention to Harold.

"Thank you, General. The two gentlemen to my right are astrological experts assigned to observatories here in the U.S. The first is, Dr. John Lumpkin, from Apache Point Observatory in New Mexico. Dr. Lumpkin is a former Nobel Prize winner in the field of astrology. Next to him is, Dr. Albert Goodfellow, from the McDonald Observatory in Texas. Beside them is, Dr. Giles Edwards, from Mount Haleakala in Hawaii." Harold continues and introduces the other three physicists on his team.

"I suppose it's best if we first attempt to answer what questions you may have. Let me start by saying that of the strange anomalies reported and occurring recently, neither I nor any of my colleagues, have any actual knowledge as to how or why there have been all the mysterious vanishings. We conclude that because it's happened to such high-profile world leaders, it is an intentional targeting and not some random sequence of events. Although the method of such remarkable teleportation is unknown, it is our belief that is some unknown mechanism that is capable of instantly opening a portal into another dimension and transferring that person there."

The Navy Chief chides Harold, "Professor, have you any knowledge of the so-called 'Philadelphia Experiment' supposedly conducted on the destroyer escort, the USS Eldridge, by the U.S. Navy in October 1943?"

Harold nods his head, confirming that he has heard of that incident.

He remarks, "Yes, and as I recall in 1953, I believe it was then, that a writer sent to an astronomer presumed information about what he claimed was the destroyer being rendered invisible. There was a claim that it and the crew were teleported through time to another dimension ... where they were encountered by aliens. He reported that several sailors died in the process, some of whom were infused into the ship's hull."

The Navy Chief asks, "And do you believe such a thing happened?"

"It was a consensus that it was all a hoax, proclaiming that it defies the laws of known physics. Based on Einstein's idiom that he called, unified field theory, they supposedly used electrical generators to bend light around an object via refraction ... thus causing the object to become invisible. You'd probably know if this is true or not, Admiral, for it was said the Navy regarded this as a valued experiment to the military, so they sponsored it."

The Admiral comments, "I have no proof or documentation from archival information to verify that, but in the seventy-seven years since then, might someone or some covert government in today's computerized world have discovered the theory and refined it to include teleportation ... to work as it has in the reported vanishings?"

"Apparently so, Admiral, for what seemed an impossible abstraction and a defiance of physics has in effect become a reality."

The Chiefs and Secretaries murmur among themselves and several mention possible culprit nations that might have developed such a clandestine project.

One Chief remarks, "I'm telling you; communism is cancer upon our world."

The Secretary of State replies, "Yes, but what can they possibly gain by using such a weaponized device to make others and especially ... their leaders to also disappear?"

The Navy Chief responds, "For the same reasons many of you politicians from the party affiliation opposite that of our President wouldn't mind if he too vanished."

Seeing that the meeting is getting rowdy, Harold makes a plea to the gathering. He clears his throat and holds out his arms waving them about as if to display that he wants to continue.

"We will now attempt to answer questions you have based on the astronomical events taking place."

The Army Chief remarks, "Thank you, Professor. From time to time over the past few days, our field weapons have been performing well below normal ranges. Fifty caliber bullets should have a range of around seven-thousand-four-hundred yards, yet now seem to travel only seven-thousand yards. Our tanks can only effectively fire from a range of sixteen miles, down from the normal nineteen miles. Explosives scatter their destructive patterns a quarter less than they should."

The Navy Chief adds, "Yes, and all our jet fighters struggle to launch off our carriers, and land-based aircraft require full power to take off. There are many other examples of this odd phenomenon, so what may we ask is causing this? Is it all because the Moon's affecting the world's gravitational field and altering it to make things heavier?"

The military group listens intently, but mumbles amongst themselves.

Seeking to regain their attention, Harold raises his hand to ward off other questions.

"In a manner of speaking, no. Something I often do in the classroom is to have my students envision what it would be like if things in our vast universe differed from what they are. One such exercise we did was imagining that the Moon was closer to the Earth. What would the repercussions be of such an anomaly? The Earth has about eighty times the mass of the Moon. From its normal distance from our planet, we scarcely notice the gravitational pull of the Moon upon us here on Earth. Here, a man weighing one-hundred-fifty pounds would only weigh twenty-five pounds on the Moon. With the current deviation in its orbit, the Moon's center of gravity is moving much closer to us, and thus we, and all mass for that matter are affected in a manner that makes us more susceptible to the Moon's gravity, which therefore renders us heavier and weighing more. As for the Moon's gravitational pull on the Earth, in theory, we attribute it to an abbreviated, unstable progression in the force of gravity upon us and all other things on Earth."

The Secretary of Defense remarks, "I understand, Professor. I'm told you have some indication that the anomaly, as you call it, is also causing the rotation of the Earth to speed up and that days are growing shorter."

"That's correct, Mr. Secretary. The rising tides and volcanic activity are also the results of the Moon's orbital variation."

The Marine Chief asks, "I've been told that until now, the Moon's been slowly inching away from Earth, not toward it. What's caused it to all of the sudden deviate from that and come toward us?"

"My physics colleagues and I concur on the data that has been collected and reported from national and international observatories and their lead astronomers. The Moon's perturbation has it within 214,000 miles from Earth at its perigee, rather than the previous normal range of about 221,500 miles. Even the Chinese and Russians comply now with what's been discovered. As to why it's happening, none of us knows."

The Attorney General asks, "Is there anything we on Earth can do to stop it from getting any closer?"

Harold blinks and pauses a moment to exhale, as the Chiefs seem openly disturbed and their emotions in flux and conflict with their usual stoic behavior.

"If you don't mind, I'd prefer Dr. John Lumpkin address that question."

John acknowledges Harold's request and stands to reply.

"Besides what you've all noticed with weaponry, planes, and other equipment there will be shorter days to come as the Earth's rotation increases and its axis will likely wobble more. Anything I'd tell you about how or why this lunar deviation is happening would be mere speculation. We have calculated that by the time the Moon comes to within about 179,000 miles of Earth ... in its present trajectory, our entire planet will be covered by water and all landmass will cease to exist. Volcanic activity will be prevalent and it may even cause the oceans to boil."

The Marine Chief angrily states, "I'll wager it has something to do with all that hocus pocus crap going on over in Switzerland with that Large Hadron Collider. I heard they are making small black holes and something called quirks and strangles. They claim it isn't dangerous, but I don't buy it. Could that have affected the Moon's orbit?"

As a physicist, Harold comments, "That's quarks and strangelets but no, the collider experiments are not the cause. Could what they're doing there be dangerous? Perhaps, but I doubt their work caused any of our current problems."

The Secretary of State asks, "So, are we doomed then? Is the apocalypse upon us?"

John somberly states, "Think of our planet as a spaceship, self-contained and self-sustaining, yet vulnerable and not finite. Our world and universe face a constant threat, be it from solar flares or asteroid impacts. We've prepared some protections from those before they eventually hit us, but in this case ... the Moon, although much smaller than Earth, is still too massive to attempt to divert its trajectory with rockets or nuclear devices."

Harold glances around the room, noting the stunned faces of the men in the room.

He reads from a report, "Cosmologists using the European Space Agency's Planck satellite and the U.S. South Pole Telescope confirm the Earth has about another sixteen days until ... the Moon's current trajectory causes living on our home planet to become impossible,".

No doubt reflecting on what they just heard, the room abruptly becomes quiet. The Secretary of the Navy contemplates the depressing news and bows his head as if in a moment of silent prayer.

Harold notices the gloomy expressions on everyone's faces. He swallows hard and sips on some water to moisten his dry mouth.

He tells them, "I truly wish there was a manner in which to resolve our problem. It was with a great deal of reluctance that I have come here before you and confirmed the bad news. As my distinguished colleague from Harvard once pointed out:

"The universe consists mainly of hydrogen, helium, and heavy elements like carbon and oxygen that enable the chemistry of life. We are in essence formed from the nuclear burning of 'ashes' in the hot cores of stars. Our fleeting existence as a species has lasted for less than ten one-billionths of cosmic history on this tiny rock we call Earth. We are surrounded by vast, lifeless space."

Before he continues, he notices the blank, solemn expressions on these military men and politicians. goes on to write,

"We should be thankful for the fortuitous circumstances that allow us to even exist Now, unfortunately, the vulnerability of our Earth and the circumstance of the universe will soon take away that allowance."

The Air Force Chief asks, "Then, will the Earth be destroyed?"

Harold and John seem too emotional to answer that.

Albert stands and comments, "Almost all life will be extinguished before the Moon reaches the Roche limit at about 11,470 miles. That's the point at which the gravity holding the Moon together is weaker than the tidal forces trying to pull it apart. So, the moon will shatter into thousands of pieces and not make it to Earth, which will then have the appearance of Saturn and its rings."

The Marine Chief asks, "So, with all the military weaponry and technology at our disposal, plus that of the other nations of the world, we can do nothing to stop this from happening?"

Harold shakes his head denoting the answer to be, "Sorry, I know of nothing that can stop this."

The Secretary of Homeland Security says, "There's already speculation, panic, looting, and worry among the populous. I can't imagine the chaos, destruction, and terror to ensue once the certainty of the fate of the human race is revealed to all people."

Harold winces and remarks, "Neither can I imagine it. I have two grown children and should have liked having grandkids, but that dream seems to have vanished too. Gentlemen, if I were you, I'd go home to be with those you love. Any troops deployed abroad should be recalled and allowed to do the same."

The solemn meeting concludes. They dismiss and the Secretaries and Chiefs depart. After a cell phone call to his son, Ted, Harold asks him when his flight to Trenton will be. Harold cannot connect with Morgan, since she's gone up to the remote mountain cabin to get Steve.

Chapter 7

Harold has a silent, pondering taxi ride to the airport, where there is a state of mass confusion. Dealing with long lines and rowdy crowds, he manages to board his flight to New York with the others of his team for tomorrow's U.N. meeting. He imagines that the meeting will have a similar somber ending as the one at the Pentagon.

As he sits silently in the plane's first-class area casting his eyes out the small window, those flying in the coach section come on board and pass by him and those of the other physics team members going to the meeting at the U.N.

Hearing a boisterous laugh and a loud voice approaching the doorway to the jet, Harold instantly recognizes it to be Nikolai, who enthusiastically greets the attractive young flight attendants. His boisterous entrance on the aircraft and this flight is something Harold expected. Nikolai's jolly demeanor continues, as he makes his way toward Harold's seat, stuffs his bag into the overhead compartment, and then addresses his new comrade.

"Excuse me, Comrade, but I am seated there by the window. Yours is the aisle seat."

Nodding reluctantly, Harold politely gets up and scoots out of the way while Nikolai settles into the wide seat next to the plane's window and an exit.

"Since this is one of the last flights to New York today, I figured you might be joining us," states Harold. "But tell me, how'd you get seated next to me?"

Nikolai grins and says, "We Russians have many ways of getting what we want."

"I see that," remarks Harold. "After take-off when the seatbelt sign is turned off, I'll introduce you to the rest of the team. Do you have dossiers on them as well?"

Nikolai grunts out a hardy laugh and slaps Harold on the shoulder in a friendly way.

"No, Comrade, there are a few physicists, but most are astronomers and mere analysis trackers whom I consider to be the universe's, Peeping Toms.

I'm sitting next to the most fascinating, clandestine astrophysicist and genius among them." He then comments, "Yet, even without dossiers, I'll be happy to meet the team."

Harold casts Nikolai a scathing glance, thinking this mouthy man would make a very good used car salesman.

As the jet taxis down the runway, Nikolai taps Harold on the arm and stares him in the eye.

"So, tell me, Harold, how did your Pentagon meeting go? Did you offer those distinguished gentlemen any encouragement, or did you speak the truth and present the worst-case- scenarios ... to then strategically withdraw afterward?"

"I told them the facts as I and the others of the team know them to be. That truth, as you call it, left them diminished with every indication that they realize our situation is dismal."

"Yes, yet ... no doubt you were not selling what they wanted. Military men, like me, want direct answers that leave no gray areas."

"And I attempted to do just that, presenting our findings in a simple manner that was packaged right off the scientific shelf."

"Yes, but the problem no doubt was that they wanted answers that required no guessing as to who the good guys are ... and who are the bad. None of us can identify that with any certainty."

Harold leans back in his seat and casts his eyes upon the ceiling. He nods and acknowledges Nikolai's statement.

After take-off, Nikolai glances out the window and waves goodbye to D.C.

He remarks in a cynical tone, "So long to Washington, the hot seat of eternal dissidence, on the front lines of your government's two-party congressional system, partisanship, bias, and prejudice prevail ... and seldom is heard an encouraging word."

Harold grins and quips, "Yes, and mother Russia has set all sorts of sad new trends by engaging in war upon a sovereign state, and with scam elections that allow into office power-hungry men that reign over the homeland ... for what seems like forever. At least in our system, the people have the opportunity to vote the power mongers out of office every two, four, and six years."

Nikolai starts to raise his hand in protest, but instead, both men nod their heads and break out in mocking laughter.

"Let's face it, Comrade Harold, in both our nations; they're all a bunch of selfish boneheads that get their checks on time, but have little to no idea of reality or what their less affluent and non-privileged constituents go through in life."

A few minutes into the short flight, the fasten seat belt sign turns off. Harold then escorts Nikolai around the first-class cabin to meet the others on the team. All except Harold partake of an adult beverage. Nikolai imbibes his choice of a glass filled with vodka. Harold previously informed the others of Nikolai's dry sense of humor, describing him as a backslapper. He even pulls a few antics on his new comrades as well, yet they seem to accept him and find him intelligent and amusing.

Returning to their seats, Nikolai removes a recent copy of the U.S.A. Today newspaper and hands it to Harold.

In a voice barely above a whisper, he tells Harold, "With all the other startling headlines and news events occurring, there is another most intriguing and amazing report that somehow only merited coverage on the back of page one. I suggest you read it, as I believe it is quite significant."

Curious, Harold does as Nikolai suggests and reads the story with the headline:

MYSTERIOUS MARKINGS ON RECENT NEWBORNS PUZZLE
EXPERTS

After carefully reading the article, Harold stares at the colored photo of an infant's right heel and the three small red dots that appear thereon. His mind flutters with what the article states, and then he looks up at Nikolai who is holding a hand to his chin and has the most serious expression Harold has yet to see on this Russian's face.

"This is astounding," says Harold. "They claim here that in all known births for the past three days, the infants have these red dots on their heels. That is truly bizarre and although humans vanishing is also incredible; I am bewildered how something like this is even remotely possible. I mean, there is no adequate way of explaining how such a biological oddity can be identically introduced into the inheritable DNA of infants of all races and sexes. I'm flabbergasted by this."

"Hold onto your flabber and your gasted," declares a smirking Nikolai. "Take a gander at what else I found remarkable this afternoon following my reading this story."

He shows Harold an enlarged version of the photo with the red dots.

"Does that dot pattern suggest anything familiar to you?" he asks thoughtfully.

Harold stares at the infant's heel and the dots but does not quite follow what Nikolai's implying.

Nikolai asks again, "They are three small dots in a row. Does it remind you of anything ... say, celestial?"

Nikolai then hands Harold a transparent piece of plastic with three shiny dots on it.

He tells him, "Place the transparent image with the three dots over the infant's three red dots."

When Harold does so, it's as if a light bulb goes off in his brain.

"My word! I see what you're inferring. This transparent image matches that of the three sisters in Orion's belt, the three bright, blue supergiant stars in the constellation Orion: Mintaka[1] (Delta Orionis), Alnilam[2] (Epsilon Orionis), and Alnitak[3] (Zeta Orionis). That's it, isn't it? The Orion dots are an exact match and mirror the marks on the red dots on the infants."

Nikolai leans back, grins, and scratches the top of his head. He shrugs and confirms Harold's realization.

"That's the way I see it, Comrade. When I saw the photo, I knew it seemed familiar. After a few moments of pondering, it dawned on me why it was familiar. I had my office in Moscow fax me an enlarged photo of the dots and one matching the size of Orion's belt. I then got a clear plastic notebook sheet and copied and marked the position of each Orion star. When I placed it over the photo, it lined up perfectly. Like you, I am fascinated, and ... my flabber is also gasted."

"This is incredible. Have you shown this to anyone?"

"Only you, but tomorrow we best inform the U.N. members about this phenomenon."

---

1. https://www.star-facts.com/mintaka/

2. https://www.star-facts.com/alnilam/

3. https://www.star-facts.com/alnitak/

"Most certainly. We can add it to the increasing list of perplexing mysteries and inexplicable events. As much or more of knowing 'how' these things are happening, is why and for what purpose are they taking place? I cannot connect them to any rational reason."

"Nevertheless, Comrade, those in attendance tomorrow will be looking for us to provide them with answers to what you describe as a mostly imponderable mystery."

Harold moans, "Yes, and what our team will be telling them will no doubt be a redundancy of what we explained to the military officers at the Pentagon."

* * *

Harold, Nikolai, and the other members of his scientific team arrive that afternoon at the plush hotel where they'll temporarily reside in New York City. The hotel manager notifies them of a called meeting in the conference room after dinner that evening to discuss their plans for addressing the U.N. Security Council meeting tomorrow.

Later, at that meeting are dozens of the world's brightest astrophysicists, astronomers, and physicists from over twenty nations. Harold is humbled that they chose him to be their leader in presenting their findings to the Security Council.

With interpreters present to explain to all members, Harold and Nikolai call the meeting to order and begin the discussion about the ominous lunar situation. This august gathering of twenty-eight men and two women is guided by their best and highest principles with an all-absorbing desire to transmit the stark realities of this ominous situation to their nation's ambassadors and politicians. Like Harold and Nikolai, the others are mesmerized by the news of the heel dots on newborns. That, plus the vanishings of all the heads of state is being presented in a short, candid video put together by the State Department in D.C. displaying the Moon's convergence and what it means to humanity.

When the meeting adjourns, Nikolai and Harold join several others of the team for a private dinner at the 'Tavern on the Green' restaurant in

Central Park. Working his way through a choice cut of steak with a salad and a loaded baked potato, Nikolai also savors the taste of his chocolate pudding dessert, even ordering a second dessert of a hot fudge sundae.

Topping that off with a hardy belch and his usual glass of vodka, he raises his glass in a toast to the three others that joined him and Harold. He urges them to fill their glasses, which they do with liquor, while Harold abstains again by preferring to drink water. They all stand up and raise their glasses.

Nikolai's brows crease with reflection, "Here's to good food, good comrades, to tomorrow ... and God willing many more to come. Nostrovia!"

Harold and the others acknowledge his toast and after downing their drinks they again sit. By now, he can't help but like Nikolai, who seems like an old friend and acquaintance. Still, there is much that Harold doesn't know about this remarkable man.

Harrold then chides Nikolai, "Two desserts? Be careful, General, you'll get fat from all that sugar and alcohol."

Nikolai smirks and pats his full stomach.

"I quit worrying about that years ago. At my age, cremation is the only way I'll ever get a smoking hot body ... which may occur sooner than I ever imagined."

Harold nods and understands Nikolai's inference. His heart aches from thinking about those that will die when the moon's distance to Earth reaches the point where life cannot survive. The prospects and the reality of it make him feel ill. He needs fresh air, so he excuses himself from Nikolai and the others. He wants only to get back to the hotel to call Ted and hopefully get ahold of Morgan tomorrow. He's had enough conversation for tonight and there isn't much about all this doomsday talk that has been left unsaid.

Nikolai gives him a big bear hug and a mock salute.

"Get some rest, professor, you'll need all your strength and wits tomorrow. Let's meet around 7:00 a.m. for breakfast in the hotel before going to the meeting," he says to Harold.

Harold agrees and exits the restaurant. He inhales the sweet aromas of nature and strolls through the green grass area of the park, across a busy street, and then hails a taxi back to the hotel. After undressing, he takes a long, hot shower, dries off, then gets into his jockeys and an undershirt. He plops down on his bed and fluffs the pillow under his weary head. Exhausted, he picks up the phone receiver and dials the front desk asking for a 6:00 a.m. wake-up call.

He then tries to call Ted on his cell phone, but there is a recorded message that the connection cannot be made due to technical difficulties. Annoyed by that, he attempts the call via the hotel phone but gets the same response.

Unable to get through, he yanks back the bed covers and kicks out the tightly tucked blanket at his feet. He lays back and reaches for the remote to turn on the television to get an update on the news. What he sees and hears from that electronic medium does nothing to alleviate his angst.

The first images he sees are those from Saint Peter's Square at the Vatican, where thousands of faithful Catholics gather to hear the Pope present prayers and a message of hope. More images appear of church sanctuaries, synagogues, temples, shrines, and mosques around the world filled beyond capacity with believers holding candlelight services and pastoral leaders praying to God:

"Please, Lord ... Remove this cup." Then they state, "Thy will be done."

Across the globe, people of faith are petitioning their deity and the divine to intervene and spare the world from disaster. According to the reports, some Christians see this as being the apocalyptic time of the second coming of Christ. The world seems to be coming apart and the news from that electronic medium doesn't alleviate Harold's anguish.

Harold's own opinion of their reaction is indifference, for he's certain nothing divine exists. His stern thoughts and deadpan expression towards all these people are they're like frightened children in the dark, pulling the covers over their heads and hoping for an eternal, omniscient, supreme being to save them. To Harold, humanity subsists on this small planet in the universe where we are all just tenants whose existence can be terminated at any moment without warning.

There are also reports of numerous GPS satellites being disabled and many other types experiencing decreasing orbital speed and direction, before finally vanishing ... in a similar manner as had all those heads of state that disappeared. Amazingly, no communication satellites are disabled and none of those that are have come crashing back through the Earth's air to be destroyed by atmospheric friction.

Harold realizes all this is the probable reason that the cell phone and communication systems have been interrupted, but does not comprehend how that would affect the landlines. Like so many of the other quandaries, what he fails to understand is how or why it's happening.

There is also a quirky report coming from Las Vegas of an inexplicable black-out there and that the entire city and surrounding electrical grid has gone out, stranding thousands of Vegas gamblers, performers, and revelers in the dark. They claim even flashlights, vehicle headlamps, and all electronics have ceased working. Hoover Dam is reporting that despite all hydroelectric generators turning and seemingly operable, they have mysteriously ceased to output any electrical power. Thousands of people throughout the states of Nevada, California, and Arizona suffer from a complete blackout causing chaos and panic. Harold suspects that some powerful type of EMP attack was aimed at Vegas, yet he has no clue as to how hydroelectric generators can become dysfunctional. The bigger question again is why and how was that achieved.

Harold's thoughts buzz through his mind like a swarm of wild bumblebees. He isn't sure how much more of this unheralded, untamed, and unknown mysteriousness he can take. People vanish like vapors before the sun, and then our ancient celestial friend the Moon advances like a great fire-breathing dragon that's become an unknown enemy. The world wavers within a circle of uncertainty like a bad dream. His fatigued brain flutters as if he's a blind, bewildered moth under a blazing streetlight. This watcher of the skies realizes that the years of hope and promise that once stretched before him ... now wilt like a dying flower and a falling leaf from a tree. To him, the world is now bitter as a tear.

The former quiet benevolence of a Father watching his children at play now fractures into shards and pieces of a past that is soon to become like the withering of a rose. His weary eyes fill with tears as bitter as blood and his mind implodes with anger and annoyance.

He switches off the television and the lamp next to his bed. He slams a fist into the pillows, grabs one, slips under the covers, licks his lips, and then fidgets a moment as he tries to relax. Like one of those frightened ones he thought of, he too pulls the covers over his head and moans.

Despite his efforts to do so, his brain is too engaged in the blinding, unyielding fear and frustration that he can do nothing to stop all this madness. He has a faint feeling of being encased by some invisible force. A dreadful chill engulfs him as the arrector **pilorum** muscles on his arms cause the hairs on his arms to develop goosebumps. The hairs on the nape of his neck stand up.

He slowly levers himself into a more comfortable position, but his mind reels with thoughts of what the members of that Security Council might ask him tomorrow. What can he tell them? He's no clairvoyant, but surely they all know by now that our only hope is that somehow something dispels the moon from any further approach to Earth. Something inside him triggers an inner response to flee.

Despite his weariness, he hops out of bed with an overwhelming, all-absorbing desire to rent a car and drive the sixty or so miles to Trenton as quickly as possible tomorrow morning.

He somberly talks to himself in the dark, "I should just skip that stupid meeting. There's nothing I can add to it. Besides, the credentials of the others are just as valid as mine ... so why do they need me? There are tidbits of information that will be adequately explained via the video that will be presented. Then it will become quite clear that there is no rational explanation for any of this."

Adrenalin being the main thing keeping him upright, he shuffles toward the thick, floor-length closed curtain that blocks out the bright night-time lights of New York City. He needs to fill his lungs with fresh air, so he yanks on the cord that draws back the curtain revealing the sliding glass door leading to the hotel suite's veranda. From his room on the eighteenth floor, the view is quite impressive. Once outside, the marvel of lighted buildings, flashing signs, and hurrying cars below make him feel like a caged creature being freed into the wild.

At that instant, he wishes he had wings so he could just fly away back home to where he belongs. This day ... today ... will never come again, and all tomorrows will become fewer and fewer.

He glances up into the night sky to see the enlarged appearance of the Moon he has studied for much of his adult life. The chilled air embraces his senses and lungs somewhat renewing his vigor. Though still angry, he allows himself to exude a piercing cry of frustration like a seabird into the wind. Just as he finishes his screeching shout, he's stunned when he sees the lights of New York City rapidly beginning to shut off, in a manner as if someone has shoved over a stack of dominoes that trail along with their stood-up-route falling over in a sequence and switching off the lights as they fall. In but a few moments, the city is blacked out, with the only light coming from the Moonglow.

At least, that's what Harold thinks, until he turns and notices that although there is no reception, the television in his room is still on and the lamps beside his bed still burn brightly.

From the balcony, he notices below that in a similar reaction to that described in Vegas, not even the headlamps from cars are visible. There are no secondary, generator-powered emergency lights either. He glances toward the skies and can see approaching jet planes with their running and landing lights still working.

Despite the lateness of the hour, in this city that never sleeps, he imagines the primeval chaos that must be occurring among those who stir in the nocturnal masses below. It takes very little time before he hears the shrill sounds of sirens whining and darkened rooms being dimly lit by candles gleaming through the windows of buildings that adjoin this hotel.

An undefined, brooding reaction befalls him, for he ponders how this hotel can retain its electrical power, while all other backup sources in the city fail. Five minutes later, he walks to the room's door that leads into the open hallway. Upon opening it, he's surprised to be greeted by several other guests waiting there in the abject darkness. Several of them have cigarette lighters that provide dim illumination. He cautiously acknowledges them and strolls two doors down from his room to the hotel elevator. There's no lighted button to retrieve the lift.

One of the other men in the hall states, "There's no use pushing the button, mister. The elevator's not working either. It seems the power's out all over the hotel and throughout the city."

As people gather in the halls conversing about the outage, Harold quietly makes his way back to his room and shuts the door so that no light filters into the hall. He has no explanation for how he could be the only room with lights and power. He shakes his head vigorously as if to attempt waking from a bad dream.

Once back inside, he shuts off the television with the remote, sits on the edge of the bed, and glances at the illumination coming from the two bedside lamps. With an unsteady hand, he fumbles for a lamp's switch, flicking it to the off position, but to his surprise, the bulb does not turn off. He pauses a moment and then flips the switch back to the on position. The light remains bright as ever. He checks the room's main lights, the ones in the bathroom and the one on the veranda. They all work and shine brilliantly. It's as if the doorway to an unseen world is ajar, for he can make no sense of this matter.

His grim face flashes a look resembling shock. He sits down on his bed, stares at the phone, picks it up, and then dials the number to Nikolai's room. A note of despair races through him when there is only silence and it does not connect or ring.

Suddenly, a strong breeze whistles in through the open glass door to the veranda much like it's a leviathan plowing through the sea. It rustles his bed covers and tumbles over one of the bedside lamps, knocking out the bulb when the lamp crashes to the floor. A sudden blast of lightning cleaves across the night sky as if shot from the quiver of some infallible, mysterious bow. A moment later torrents of rain begin to gust sideways through the open door. Harold struggles against the stiff winds and rain, yet manages to close the glass door and pull the curtain shut. As a lightning bolt strikes nearby, intense bursts of light from the flash streak around the edges of the drape and slither across the ceiling like swift serpents. He shudders at the loud bellows of deafening thunder that follow. He staggers to the room's door. Slowly opening it and peering down the hallway, he sees even more people gathering there. All seem puzzled and frustrated. Several yield flashlights that do not work and a few more hold their lit cigarette lighters that manage to cast some minimal amount of illumination upon the hallway. For a moment, he considers trying to make his way to Nikolai's room five floors above him. However, when he attempts to open the stairway door, it too is shut and won't budge.

A man noticing Harold's failed attempt comments, "There's no use, mister. Somehow, that doorway seems welded shut. We've tried, but it won't open and there is no noticeable locking mechanism that we can tell that's causing the door to lock. I'm afraid we're all stranded here for the night. We might just as well sack in and try to get some sleep because we're not going anywhere."

After returning to his room, for almost an hour, he tries to turn the one still-lit lamp off, but it stays lit and seems to be even brighter. The television also came back on and now won't shut off ... despite both it and the lamp being unplugged from their electrical sockets. In the bathroom, he turns on his electric razor and a hairdryer. Both of them are unplugged and yet still work and seem to be getting ample power from some mysterious force.

His senses swim as if he's in a dizzying cloud of fantasy. He mentally compares this irrational event to water running uphill. These impossibilities peal through his scientist's brain like a muffled bell, staggering and defying all sensibilities and the laws of physics to which he so proudly attests. Unless he's lost his mind, it is futile to deny what's happening, other than it being some odd enchantment of which he has no understanding. When he wraps a cloth handkerchief around his hand and uses it to unscrew a lamp's bulb ... it continues to shine brightly. Angry and startled, he flings it across the room into a wall. It crashes and breaks into shards, finally extinguishing its eerie glow. He shudders and wipes his brow in wonderment. What sort of wizardry is causing this impossibility?

Hours later, lying in bed, he tosses and turns. Though he resists sleep, sheer exhaustion forces his hyperactive mind to surrender and run its natural course ... and finally give in to a restive slumber.

Chapter 8

However, sleep brings him very little respite, for his mind drifts into an iridescent dream world whereby he's standing in an open field of bright green clover. A shallow brook of babbling water runs next to him, cascading happily over stones as it flows downstream. Above him are snowy white clouds and a brightly lit sun. Huge butterflies flutter in the wind. Trees with flowery blooms burst forth with a sweet-smelling fragrance that teases and soothes his nostrils. A great, red moon twice the size of the sun lingers near the western horizon. Tall grasses around him dance in the gentle breezes like a wave upon the ocean.

Suddenly, the trees darken as if bending together to present whispering secrets. The sunset is rapid, giving way to cold darkness as deep as a fathomless sea. A profound well of sorrow invades his thoughts and despondency clings to him like a cast-off cloak. A shadow looms above him, lit dimly by the huge, red moon. The unrecognizable vision grows larger and closer, until it covers the entire sky, bringing about an eerie dimness.

With feet that cannot move and eyes that cannot close, he beholds the faint image of a large, odd-looking creature in an upright position emerging from within what appears to be some sort of enormous craft. Silvery, glowing dust-like specs begin falling like dew from beneath the craft. They sift upon his body and cause his skin to tingle like that from opening a deep freeze. Odd sensations shimmer through his being and his fears slowly subside giving way to an inner peace that chases away the gloom that somehow breathes into him ... anticipation. It is as if a sudden burst of sunshine chases away the storm clouds in his life.

In his fairy dream state, the shadow of his melancholy lifts, and he hears the sweet, caroling voice of the extraordinary, vague creature standing before him. Any sense of fright vanishes and his attention is drawn to this amazing, tall entity before him.

The voice transmits, "Be not afraid. You have been chosen to receive the word."

To Harold, this indefinable creature's smooth voice is like a golden-caged nightingale whose symphonic words drift over him as comforting as a soft pillow. All that's beautiful drifts across the neurons of his mind.

Again, it speaks to his mind, "This world stretches before Him that made it like the open palm of a hand. Though blessed with an immortal spirit that dwells within you, that which is the frail flesh of your species must be humbled and taught to live in peace. Obey Him that created all. Do so, and your world and all in it shall survive. Failure to comply with His commands ... and all shall be lost. The choice is yours, as shall be explained at your meeting. Go now, for morning approaches."

* * *

Harold wakes the next morning and stares at the digital clock next to him on the nightstand next to his bed. His weary brain struggles to recall memories of the odd craft and the amazing creature that spoke to him in his dream. He attempts to focus on what that entity looked like, but despite his efforts to do so, he cannot categorize or accurately describe its appearance. That frustrates him and he wonders if the dream was a mere fantasy brought on by his state of exhaustion.

So, was the incident real or imagined? Whatever the case, he cannot deny the unfathomable oddities he experienced last night with the blackout, light bulbs, T.V., razor, and hairdryer. For the first time since all this began, he considers that some unknown, foreign power ... perhaps not of this world ... is responsible for all the amazing, inexplicable events that have been occurring.

It is 6:30 a.m. and the sun has risen. The air outside on the veranda is fresh and clean, the rain has washed away a lot of the carbon dioxide aromas emitted from the exhausts of vehicles upon the avenues of this huge city.

After showering, shaving and dressing in his best suit, Harold exits his room. He's relieved to learn the hallway lights are back on and that the elevator is working again. Once in the lobby, he strolls into the Hotel's restaurant where he sees Nikolai, John, and Albert sitting at a table. He approaches them and they invite him to join them for breakfast.

Nikolai's usual jolly manner has him commenting first in Russian, "Syadyem Na Dorozhku! Priyatnogo Appetita!

He uses a Russian phrase that friends say when someone is getting ready to eat. Harold realizes the gnawing discomfort in his stomach is because he's hungry.

He smiles and surprises Nikolai, "Yes, we should eat before hitting the road. Bon appétit!" He then adds, "Da! Dobroye utro, Nikolai!"

Nikolai laughs heartily and tips a hand to his forehead, "And good morning to you as well, Comrade Harold." His brows raise and he displays amusement, "Like I was taught English, I see that you were also taught Russian."

"Yes, I do speak it, but still cannot read it, as your kooky writing makes me dizzy."

John yawns and remarks, "I've no idea what you each said, but I'm worn to a frazzle after all the excitement last night with that blackout and the fierce storm."

Albert rubs a hand across his temple, "Thank goodness the lights came back on about 4:00 a.m. They say on the news there's no indication of how it occurred. At least the tempest blew away soon after that,"

Harold scoffs, "The storm may have passed, yet I'm convinced the tempest remains."

Nikolai stretches and remarks, "Very true! I must have been asleep when the thunder and lightning came, for neither it nor the blackout woke me. How about you, Comrade Harold, did you sleep well?"

His face is gray with fatigue, as Harold replies, "Nyet! I did finally give in to exhaustion, but my dreams were ... unusual and disturbing."

Albert asks, "Did you hear on the news where some satellites have been disappearing and many others have been disabled? Nations are scrambling all over the world in hopes that televised signals that bounce off satellites aren't affected."

"Yes, I saw that on the news before the blackout here, in Las Vegas, and elsewhere occurred," says Harold.

John adds, "I cannot endeavor to explain such strange incidents. I can only conclude that they can't be random. Some astonishing source has to be in control of it all."

Yes, but who and how?" Harold asks. "The bigger question is ... why and what can we add at the meeting that they won't already know?"

Albert states, "For certain, the prevailing winds suggest the elephant in the room will be that which is happening to the Moon's orbit. As for all the other oddities, who can say?"

Harold somberly states, "To paraphrase the author, Margaret Atwood, "I'm like nothing more than a man of sand left by a careless child too near the water's edge ... and now it washes over me ... over all of us."

Nikolai detects the haunting quality in Harold's voice and tells him, "At any rate, Comrade, I can tell you that those stiff-necked ambassadors and politicians you are soon to address aren't enjoying themselves either. Most of them have lived lives of privilege thinking they are invulnerable and that nothing can happen to them. Consider them all as bees that listen and report back to their queen or king of the colony ... always attempting to bring back enough sweet pollen for the hive to make their honey. You just go in there, play their game, move the pawns a few spaces, and let them figure out their next moves."

"Some there will no doubt have been military men ... like you," states Harold. "I can't believe they'll react favorably to an American scientist like me?"

Nikolai scoffs, "You know the ropes, Comrade, so I suggest you just toe the line, allow the video to do the educating, and remember that you're as tough as they are. As for them being military men, I wager the only time most of them has seen blood is when they nicked their chin while shaving."

The foursome order and eat a hasty breakfast. Afterward, as they await the arrival of the limo to take them to the U.N., Nikolai lights up one of his Cuban cigars. He offers one to both Harold and Albert, who decline, but John takes him up on the gesture. Both men seem pleased with their stogies and exhale enough smoke to set off fire alarms if they'd been inside the lobby.

Soon the limo arrives. Snuffing out their cigars first, Nikolai and John join Harold and Albert inside the limo as they all pile into the rear passenger compartment. Ever the one to be prepared, Albert brings his umbrella. As with such vehicles, there is a clear petition between them and the driver up front. As the long sedan pulls away from the hotel, Harold is surprised to hear his cell phone ringing. When he checks to see who's calling, his spirits are quickly lifted.

Relieved to know the cell phones are working again, he smiles and tells the others, "Thank goodness, it's my daughter."

Nikolai winks and makes small talk with the others while Harold swishes his finger across the front of the phone to answer the call.

"Morgan, how are you, Sweetheart?"

"I'm fine, Dad. I've been trying to call you since yesterday, but the phones were out."

"Yes, I know. We're in a limo heading toward the meeting with the U.N. Security Council. I've tried calling you too for the past two days."

"Steve and I drove back to Trenton last night, but all the phones were offline then too. Many places still don't have any cell coverage. When do you expect to be coming home, Dad? We're picking Ted and Rita up at the airport when they arrive here later today."

"That's wonderful, Morgan. As soon as we're done with the meeting here, I plan to scoot to the airport to rent a car and drive back later this afternoon."

Alright, Dad. I love you and good luck with your meeting. It's being televised everywhere, so we'll be watching. Is there any good news you can share ... or does the outlook remain the same?"

Harold avoids answering her direct question, "I love you too, Sweetheart. Give my love to Ted and Rita. We'll talk more when I get home."

"Goodbye, Dad. Safe travels and God be with you!"

Hearing from her is the medicine he needs to help him through the stress and tension he feels from being designated as the lead speaker at the meeting.

Nikolai pats him on the shoulder and grins, "I too have a daughter back in Russia. I love her and she's a dear girl, but she's mud ugly like her mother. If I'm to ever have grandchildren, she'll have to marry a not too particular peasant in the army that I can convince and command to wed her."

With that, he bursts forth in laughter and shakes his head.

Then he corrects himself, "I'm lying, of course. My wife is amazing and as lovely as a spring flower. Even the angels envy my daughter, for she is the most beautiful creature in Russia."

Harold grins and not to be out-bragged comments, "Then we are both fortunate, for my daughter, Morgan, makes Helen of Troy look like a handmaiden."

Chapter 9

As they both boast, the limo turns a corner and heads down the street that houses the U.N. building. The street is blockaded and there is a line of police officers that cordon off the area in front of where the limo will stop to let them out. Seeing the throng of bewildered people along the sidewalks and in the streets before them makes Harold rest his head against the cool window glass. Something keeps nagging at the back of his mind, namely the words from the peculiar creature in his dream.

The limo pulls up in front of the tall glass and steel U.N. building. A horde of news reporters and media from around the globe are already gathered. Things are rapidly coming to a boil in New York and across the nation and the world. Besides reporters, an anxious, panicking crowd is in front of the building. A madhouse of screaming humanity waves signs warning of the end of the world and urging people to repent. The weary, worried faces of men and women from all age groups and ethnic backgrounds seem unsure of what they or the government can do to ward off the impending lunar disaster.

They strive to get past the lines of police to protest and display their intentions. Some protest the governments that are there for the meeting, declaring their abuse of war crimes, violation of human rights, and promoting slavery and human trafficking. There are signs protesting government cover-ups and demanding to be told the real reason why the Moon is coming closer. All in all, it is an unruly, chaotic scene and one that has all the earmarks of erupting into a genuine, violent riot.

The limo stops and a guard then opens its rear door. Nikolai gestures to Harold to be the first to exit.

He comments, "After you, Comrade. It's time we entered the chamber pot where you have the catbird seat."

Harold answers Nikolai's sarcasm, "Thanks a lot, Comrade. You have a remarkable way of making me even more nervous than I already am."

As Harold scrambles out of the seat and stands in the open, a chorus of boos and hisses pour forth from the rowdy crowds gathered in the streets around the U.N. The reporters surge like a swarm of hornets attempting to get close to him.

One sticks a microphone in his face and asks, "Professor Simpson, what do you make of the GPS satellites being disabled or destroyed?"

Another chides, "Do you think the Russians or Chinese have anything to do with all this chaos?"

One more query, "What do you think happened to the President and the others that disappeared, and is there any way to stop the Moon's path toward Earth?"

"You see!" chortles Nikolai, "They know who you are and they all think you should know the answers ... while others rebuke you and us with their taunts."

He and the other two men exit the limo and receive a similar snide reception. With police and security guards warding off the protestors, Harold ignores the questions and the four men are escorted into the building and down the hallways to the chamber where the Security Council meeting will take place in less than a half-hour.

The chamber is known informally as the Norway Room and gleams with new trimmings and beige carpet. The high-ceiling room captures the essence of what the U.N. strives to create: An atmosphere that is fair, judicial, and stylish. Twenty-six seats are reserved for Harold's team and over one hundred seats in the amphitheater-style layout are for the international press. Due to the nature of this meeting, the remaining three-hundred-seventy-five or so seats are not available to the general public. Besides the press and the U.N. television network, invitees of the nations that are not members of the Security Council are also to be present today. Given the tight security measures in place at the U.N. today, things are very tense.

There is a large, C-shaped table, from which the Security Council ambassadors and members preside. The chamber's original Zen qualities of peace and calm prevail, while the huge picture windows overlooking the East River capture long views of Brooklyn and Queens. Although they are bordered with heavy drapes, the sunlight glows through to remind members that their work here affects the world far beyond their priestly quarters. An oil canvas mural, painted by a student of Matisse, covers most of the east wall.

Its purpose is to emphasize a phoenix rising theme that depicts the U.N.'s birth from the cinders of World War II.

As Harold glances around the stately room, he recalls why the U.N. was created in the first place. It consists of one-hundred-ninety-three countries formed in 1945. The Security Council consists of fifteen members among which are five permanent members ... China, France, Russia, the United Kingdom, and the United States ... who are responsible for responding to world crises and maintaining peace through cease-fire orders, collective military action, sanctions, and peacekeeping operations. It is the only U.N. body with the authority to take legal action. The remaining ten seats on the Council are temporary and non-permanent members that are elected by the UN General Assembly for two-year terms.

Harold notices the myriad of media present and is aware that the television cameras in the chamber will focus upon the enormous C-shaped table and the colored wall painting behind it beaming into the people of the world a collective image of the proceedings through television screens everywhere via the UN Web TV Channel Live with on-demand videos of the meeting.

He's been told that although Norway does not have a permanent seat in the United Nations Security Council Chamber, since their head of state was one of the first to vanish, the foreign minister of Norway will be the opening speaker today. The Norwegians have always influenced the direction of the United Nations either subtly or directly, starting with the world body's first Secretary-General hailing from Norway.

Harold and Nikolai will then be introduced along with the others on his team. Other than he and Nikolai, the others will be seated with the media in the gallery.

Not familiar with how the proceedings for a video are to be shown, Harold asks, "How will the prepared video be presented in the chamber?"

An aide to the Secretary-General explains, "A screen in the chamber will drop down from the ceiling to display the video, plus each person in attendance will have in front of them a television monitor upon which to view the video that has been loaded into the master video player in the control room."

Satisfied that all preparations have been made, Harold goes over the notes he made to present to the Council and press. As the members of the Council begin filing in, like them, he and Nikolai take their assigned seats next to the Secretary-General.

Nikolai remarks, "If you have an urge to answer a call of nature, now would be a good time to do it."

Harold nods and the two men jointly stand and ask the aide where the facilities are located. They excuse themselves and stroll off to the restrooms. Moments later, returning to their seats, the chamber has almost filled with members around the tables, plus there was an overflow of people in the gallery.

Flashbulbs going off are like streaks of lightning and newsmen scramble to get a chair with a monitor. With but a few moments left of clarity before the storm begins, Harold stretches at his necktie. Although it is cool in the chamber, sweat rolls down his forehead.

Nikolai Notices Harold's edginess and angst.

In a calm and stoic voice, he whispers, "Easy now, Comrade, pretend you're addressing a freshman class of physics students. They're all ignorant and waiting to hear from their professor."

Soon after saying that, the huge drapes pull shut, and the overhead lights dim. A metal podium is set up outside the C-shaped table for the speaker from Norway, and the Secretary-General stands to gavel in the opening session of the meeting. He introduces Harold, Nikolai, and the others from the international physics and astronomical team. The members around the table all watch their monitors and listen to their interpreters through their earphones.

Once the speaker from Norway is finished with his introduction concerning the vanishing of the heads of state, Harold is invited to speak. His nervousness somewhat fades as he begins by speaking into a microphone in front of him. He summarizes the obvious threat of the Moon's trajectory toward Earth. He then urges the control room to start the prepared video.

He tells them, "For those present, please watch the video screen and your monitors. Afterward, General Belinski and I will attempt to answer whatever questions you might have for us or our team."

As the video plays on the drop-down screen and the monitors, Harold sadly observes that pointing out the inexorable facts seems to close in on those present like a prison warden handcuffing a convict. There are mournful murmurs about the darkness of the predicted fate of the world. It sweeps over them as a black maelstrom that ends with the Earth becoming a heap of crumbling ashes. Like a scroll unfurled, the video and its computer animation display the end of humanity due to massive flooding by oceans, rivers, and lakes boiling ... while massive volcanoes spew their thousands of degrees of heated lava upon the Earth.

When the video finishes, the dropped-down screen ascends to the ceiling and the lights are turned back up. All those there seems shocked. Harold's presented with moments of deathly silence. Although the news media presented the world with a similar fate, none of what was shown to the public was as stark or as vivid as what those in the chamber just viewed. Harold is relieved that the ten-minute video was blocked from being televised to the public.

Finally, as one member from France manages to speak, his question and meeting are abruptly interrupted—

The large mural in the chamber unexpectedly transforms into a video screen to display the words from Isaiah 2:4 engraved on the walls of the Ralph Bunche Park across from the U.N. building. In the earphones comes an amplified male voice communicating via an unknown method and source to all those present in the chamber. The astounded members and international press listen intently as the voice transmits in words that are received in their various languages.

The voice then recites verbatim:

"They shall beat their swords into plowshares and their spears into pruning hooks; nation shall not lift up sword against nation; neither shall they learn war anymore."

Harold's jaw slacks open, for he quickly recognizes the familiar voice as being that of the peculiar creature in his dream last night. He recollects the voice and its distinctive and soothing but never changing timbre.

Suddenly, the image on the wall evolves into one displaying the Moon, Earth, and the Sun. To everyone's shock and surprise the theme music from "2001 A Space Odyssey" is heard. The symphonic arrangement by Richard

Strauss in 1896 is entitled, "Also Sprach Zarathustra." It starts low and slow, but then after a few moments has loud drums and instruments that produce pulse-pounding music. In synch with the triple view of the three celestial objects, the music soars to its highest crescendo.

At that point, the voice again transmits, "Be not afraid! This world stretches before Him that made it with the open palm of His hand. Though blessed with an immortal spirit that dwells within you, that which is the frail flesh of your species must be humbled and taught to live in peace. Obey Him that created the universe. Do so, and your world and all in it shall survive. Failure to comply with His commands … and all shall be lost."

Harold slumps in the chair and his breath catches in his throat. He realizes those are the exact words he heard the voice say in his dream. Nikolai also seems stunned and has a very bemused expression. Everyone in the room seems mesmerized by whomever or whatever is speaking to them.

The music pauses momentarily to display on the wall the scene from the "Space Odyssey" where the ape-like creatures surround and touch the mysterious, dark, rectangular monolith. This event supposedly has them drawing wisdom from it. Then the music restarts from the beginning as one ape strikes the ground using a large bone, presumably to use it later as a weapon.

The voice conveys more, "Mankind was made in the image of the Creator and did not evolve from apes such as these. For you who claim humans came about that way, I would question then … who made the apes? Although we've been observing and coming to your world for thousands of your Earth years, there has not been any known ancient visitor to your planet that has left a monolith to increase your wisdom. Instead, you have been gifted by living flesh, human monoliths … such as Abraham, Moses, Isaac, Isaiah, and even the Creator's own Son, whom your kind crucified."

In the control room, one of the astonished technicians in a muffled voice murmurs to a camera operator and sound man, "Please tell me you're both getting all this recorded." They nod slowly affirming that they are and shake their heads in puzzlement.

The voice states emphatically, "As you've suspected, there are many worlds that teem with living beings in the vastness of space. Life takes on numerous shapes and sizes, though the substance varies. We too are flesh and blood, also created in the Maker's image, yet formed from a different mold. Our technology, as you will soon see, is far beyond anything your scientists have developed or conceived.

"We are capable of interstellar travel and have been to the edges of the universe. The Creator has sent us to your planet to present ourselves as messengers and harbingers to caution you to obey His new commandment. He has given you a sign as to where we are from that's depicted on the heels of newborns in your world. The two men of science that you chose to speak to you this day have the answer to that, and it is through them that we shall hereafter communicate."

All eyes quickly turn towards Harold and Nikolai, who in slack-jawed awe seem in a dream-like trance as they listen to the voice.

Next on the wall, there is the image of an in-session meeting inside the General Assembly Room from the morning of July 7, 2017. Amidst a standing ovation, loud cheers, and joyous tears, one-hundred-twenty-two national states voted to adopt the Treaty on the Prohibition of nuclear weapons.

The voice continues, "This was an encouraging moment in your planet's history as your assembly voted to delegitimize nuclear weapon possession by emphasizing the devastating humanitarian consequences of their use. Though a noble effort, your species remains far too tribal and warring against others that have differing philosophies about governing that might inhabit more fertile land and natural resources.

"From your stone age until now, you humans have been locked into bloody wars fought with swords, knives, spears, guns, and explosives. Since the discovery of and development of nuclear weapons, the nations of your world have stockpiled warheads onto missiles, rocketed them into space for covert deployments, made nuclear torpedoes, and other methods of delivery. If ever used in an all-out thermonuclear war, the degree of destructive power released into the atmosphere would no doubt destroy all life upon this planet."

At this point, the wall begins to display an image of the Red Planet, Mars. However, instead of being a barren, bone-dry world, the image displays a vibrant society with beings scurrying about in airborne vehicles and massive, highly technical appearing cities surrounded by huge lakes and brilliant foliage.

"The images you see here are of your neighboring planet, the one you call, Mars," the voice declares. "The images are not fictional. At one point in the history of that world, it was an active and blessed civilization with a populous like your own. They too were given free will and all that they needed to self-sustain life in their world. A plasma physicist and scientist here on Earth recently discovered via information from your planet's Mars rover, Curiosity, that there is evidence of relatively high concentrations of radioactive xenon isotopes found emanating on the surface of Mars.

"As you see, that planet also once teemed with life ... until nuclear warfare wiped out all evidence of it. Your physicist found evidence of a nuclear winter wiping out all ancient Martian existence. Life on Mars was cut short by the power of the atom and the deliberate use of nuclear weapons by a foreign force. The researcher further warns that humanity stands on the brink of a similar cataclysm unless such devastating weaponry is destroyed. Based upon your species' violent history, it is plausible that whether deliberate or by accident, the employment of nuclear weapons upon the populace of your planet seems inevitable.

"Such an action constitutes a violation of cosmic laws put forth by the Interstellar Planetary Justice System set up by all member planets in our galaxy. Such action also disrupts the plans of the Creator. Thus, your species presents Him with a great deal of ire and disappointment. Therefore, He will simply not allow such a thing to occur to your Earth.

"With all your egotistical ambitions, world tensions, distrusting self-interests, crimes against humanity, and the warring state of mind among your world's competing nations and leaders, the Creator's patience is near to being exhausted. This world that He so loves and the decent, faithful souls within it will be spared spiritual oblivion, yet all mortal life is in danger of being destroyed by the approach of the natural satellite that you call the Moon."

The image on the wall shows the Moon's ascending trajectory toward Earth and all the carnage that will occur when it comes within a lethal distance of the planet.

The voice then issues a warning and offers a gesture of hope.

"As beings that are also given free will, the Creator herein presents humanity with a choice. Although my species has the capabilities of neutering all your nuclear weapons and neutron bombs, plus disposing of all chemical and biological weapons, the Creator has chosen to offer to cease the oncoming trajectory of your Moon toward Earth and to place it again in its previous orbit at the same distance it was from your planet ... if ... all nations possessing these weapons agree to denuclearize, destroy and cease making any future nuclear weapons, plus destroy all biological and chemical weaponry.

"Do this and your Moon will cease its current trajectory. As a gesture of hope, your Moon will be put in a holding pattern beginning at 4:00 p.m. Eastern Time here in the United States. After that, you shall be given fourteen days to complete a universal agreement to be presented back at this chamber two Earth weeks from now."

The room buzzes with anxiety and there is a churning of voices whispering and mumbling about this cautionary warning and command.

The voice cautions, "The actual disarmament shall be performed by our technology, but we must warn you that all nations must agree to this offer. Otherwise, this opportunity to avoid destruction will be voided and the outcome obvious if there is a refusal by any nation to dispose of its nuclear arsenal. As a means for displaying to you the Creator's power, though there have already been numerous examples of it, others shall be forthcoming and exhibited to you until the agreement is reached."

While those present focus on the wall, the voice issues another stern statement, "What is about to happen here in this chamber shall not seriously harm you. Rather it will demonstrate and convey to you how insane and immoral it would be to ignore this warning. Watch the wall."

All eyes turn toward the wall on which the 3-D images of a B-2 bomber are seen flying from a distance away and toward them. They are all amazed because the three-dimensional image appears to be coming from the skies outside the building. In but a few moments, the scaled-down bomber's image exits the wall and flies over the C-shaped tables. Its bomb doors open and in slow motion down from the tall height of the ceiling ... a projectile tumbles toward the floor. Before it hits the floor, the room is rocked by a blast of bright light followed by heat from a shock wave that thrusts the tables, monitors, and all those sitting and watching backward and onto the floor.

Several members received minor cuts and bruises. Harold and Nikolai are each bowled over in their chairs and onto the floor. Everyone scrambles to avoid what follows as a mushroom cloud begins to form within the center of the C-shaped setting ... its roaring, rumbling fury tumbling across the ceiling and raining down ash upon all in the room.

Horrified, everyone in the room begins to crawl toward the exits, but all of them are locked and cannot be opened. They cough, choke and try not to breathe in the dust cloud's air. To their added horror, as they crawl around on the floor, the very ground beneath them becomes glass-like and transparent. Horrified, they view smoldering, molten beds of red-hot lava churning below the clear surface of what they lie and stand upon.

This unbelievably frightening scenario soon fades and the room returns to the way it was. The members all stand again upon a solid concrete floor and the mushroom cloud disappears. They dust themselves off and replace their chairs, as do Harold and Nikolai. The whole of those present seems filled with blind and unyielding fear caused by this unexpected event.

The voice returns, "What you experienced was not a real nuclear detonation, but if it had been, all of you would be dead now. What occurred beneath you is what your planet's crust would and will be like should you fail to follow the Creator's commandment. Tend to your nicks and bruises, and do not falter in achieving that which has been demanded of you. Save yourselves and save your world." The voice pauses and bluntly states, "The choice is yours."

With that, the images on the wall fade and the voice ceases to be heard. All those attending sit in dumbfounded silence. Harold and Nikolai look at each other in momentarily stupefied amazement. The Secretary-General gavels the meeting to a close and quickly the international press races through now unlocked doors from the room to call their networks, thus making certain this story gets out to the entire world. Several members scurry to exit the room as well. Numerous representatives from foreign nations flock toward Harold and begin peppering him and Nikolai with questions. There's a sense of urgency in their voices and all are curious about what the voice's reference to the newborns meant.

Harold explains to them about the three red dots and their lining up to be an exact representation of the three sister stars in Orion's Belt. Reporters swamp the two men with other questions about the vanishings and how it is possible that an alien presence could do what they just experienced. Many want to know if they believe the aliens have an ulterior motive and simply seek to have the world's most powerful defenses neutralized so that the aliens can take over and enslave humanity by forcing us to submit.

Harold is disheveled and exasperated.

He tells them, "I've no idea how such things that occurred here today are possible, nor have I any clue as to how the vanishings were made to happen. I can only hope that all the nations of the world take this warning seriously and their government's leadership will quickly act to come to a disarmament agreement. Look, people, before this mysterious voice entered the equation offering us a choice, we had no hope of saving our planet. So, if indeed this powerful demonstration doesn't convince all of humanity to humble itself and give up the suicidal weapons of mass destruction and chemical and biological weapons ... then it shall be our undoing and stubbornness that leads to our end."

As Harold answers questions, inside the chamber, technicians closely begin to check the wall and all outlets for what might be a powerful projector that may have cast those images upon the painted wall. Finding no source for what occurred; they check the sound system to try and find out how the voice overcame all the secure frequencies developed for this chamber's member nations. Again, they can find no source to explain how the voice took over and communicated in all those differing languages. When asked by a ranking official if everything that happened was recorded, those in charge of the video equipment confirm it has been. However, when trying to re-run the digital recordings from four cameras strategically located in the chamber, all of them only display static and scrambled images.

The remaining members argue and chortle among themselves, some denying that this could be real and that a rogue technology must have been used to dupe them into thinking this was a legitimate extraterrestrial encounter.

Those who received minor cuts and bruises obtain treatment and the other members of Harold's team are also bombarded with questions and asked their opinions. Nikolai's government representatives pull him away and intensely interview him, casting suspicious glances at those from the U.S.

The whole scenario becomes like a bad soap opera and Harold's only desire is to leave it all behind him. He's fed up with being in the spotlight and only wants to return home to be with Morgan, Steve, Ted, and Rita. Working his way toward the exits, he waves at Nikolai, who is trapped by his counsel and cannot get away from their prying inquiries. John and Albert both manage to slink off and exit to the outside where the limo they came in awaits to carry the foursome back to their hotel.

Harold makes an end-run and attempts to squeeze in among the Russian representatives. He grabs Nikolai by the arm and drags him back. He begs the others to excuse him and tells them he needs to speak with Nikolai in private. Nikolai acknowledges Harold's request and the two quickly back away and stealthily exit out of the doorways.

"Thanks, Comrade. They were grilling me and asking things that I could not answer."

"I know, plus they seemed as if you were cavorting with Satan by speaking to me. Let's get out of here and back to the Hotel. I have to check out and pick up a rental car in a couple of hours. We can discuss what happened here on the way back."

Nikolai nods, agrees, and then asks, "You wouldn't happen to have a Geiger counter in your briefcase, would you?"

Harold remarks, "No, but my body feels as if it's made of lead. I'm so tired I just want to go dig a hole and crawl into it."

Chapter 10

Once inside the limo again, the astonishment of what occurred in the chamber is still evident.

John breaks the ice by asking, "What in God's name did we just experience? Was that voice truly alien, or were we somehow tricked by some clever use of a technology we don't understand?"

Nikolai turns his palms upward toward the ceiling and shrugs his shoulders.

He comments, "Maybe rain, maybe snow ... maybe yes, maybe no. Still, I think it's safe to say that what we saw and heard was not staged by any known entity. As to the origin of that being, there's nobody I'm aware of that's capable of doing what we encountered. I'm certain it's not from this world. At least not from the world we know."

Harold adds, "Yeah, and I didn't mention it to you guys, but last evening after the blackout, for some odd reason the lights in my room still worked. When I attempted to shut off a lamp, the bulb continued to burn. Even my hairdryer and electric shaver worked ... even though they weren't plugged into a socket."

"Huh? How is that possible?" Albert asks.

Harold grimaces, "I've no idea, but that's not all. When I did finally drift off to sleep, in the dream I had I saw a huge craft that I could not identify. Then I saw and heard a voice from a creature I still cannot describe. The words it told me were the same as first expressed by the voice in the chamber today. It was the identical voice I heard last night in my dream."

The three men look at Harold with amazement. Nikolai scowls, puts his hands behind his head, and then leans back in the seat.

Harold states, "The voice did point out that you and I would be the ones contacted and chosen to communicate with him, them, or whatever it is."

Harold feels the gurgle of his blood pounding through his veins. He exchanges a glance with Nikolai and coughs into a fist, as his head spins and thoughts keep running through his mind about what the voice said. The part where it mentioned a Creator and that our species possessed an eternal spirit, which Harold assumes is a reference to the soul and God. That statement truly causes him to struggle with a viewpoint he has always privately denied. His mind battles against his lack of belief that an immortal soul might exist after all. If indeed a godly presence can save the world, then he must certainly admit he's been wrong about his philosophies and rejections of divinity and accept what great gift humanity is being given by possessing something that lives on even after physical death.

"Yes, Nikolai, the voice did say that, so I am assuming that you and I will have further contact with it and hopefully come to a better understanding of what and who it is."

Nikolai nods his head in agreement, "If that's the case, then this is just the intermission and the rest of the show is yet to come."

Harold pauses a few moments, and then answers, "I'm afraid so, and I have serious doubts that the world's governments, even faced with oblivion, will be able to agree upon nuclear disarmament and do so in a mere fourteen days what they haven't been able to achieve in the past seventy-seven years," remarks Harold.

Albert cites anxiously, "The voice mentioned more demonstrations of the Creator's power. Hopefully, that will be of even more amazement to provide enough incentive so that all nations will comply with the disbanding of nuclear weapons, plus the chemical and biological ones as well."

John glances at his watch, with it being 11:45 a.m., "The voice said the Moon's trajectory would pause and cease coming closer at 4:00 p.m. eastern time today. I'll call my observatory and have my assistants confirm if that indeed occurs. If it does, then we can be certain this mysterious voice is what it claims to be."

The tension among the four men eases a bit, but they still seem weary and profoundly on edge. Harold silently wonders if the 'Creator' the voice mentioned is a singular masculine deity and if perhaps the religion of his daughter and son is indeed one based upon truth ... for the voice did also mention the Creator's Son was sent to Earth and crucified. This voice caused Harold's psyche to take an unfamiliar route to a destination that he has not known. Always guided by logic and the laws of physics, he is now bedazzled by what's happened. He's become a bit more optimistic about the outcome for humanity and what might await all humanity after we face physical death.

In this new state of mind, he finds himself for the first time ... saying a silent prayer.

* * *

At the airport's rental car counter, Harold and Nikolai must part to take separate transports home that afternoon. Harold reaches to shake hands with his Russian friend. Instead, Nikolai grabs Harold and again gives him a huge bear hug.

"So long, for now, Comrade Harold. Our separation may not be for long, for I suspect that voice will be in contact with us soon. I cower to think what will be demanded of us then."

"Yes, I've come to the same conclusion. Therefore, I want to be able to spend a few days with my kids before that demand becomes evident."

"Do svidaniya, my new good friend. Yes, I'm confident that shall come as sure as two times two is four. But if we take hold of the burden together, maybe it won't seem as heavy."

"Do svidaniya, Comrade Nikolai. For whatever reason, I suppose our job will be to cry cockle-doodle-do and then let others of the world determine if the new dawn comes or not."

The two men part and Nikolai heads toward where he will board a jet back to Saint Petersburg. Harold continues his rental car checkout but is soon interrupted and met by three mysterious men in black suits that forcefully ferry him away from the terminal and toward a separate, private room usually arranged to interrogate those suspected of trying to smuggle in drugs or contraband. To Harold's surprise, Nikolai is also being led into the room.

They both protest vehemently, yet their mild resistance is met with defiance, as the larger of the men opens his coat to reveal a holstered pistol. Nikolai complains, claiming he has diplomatic immunity, yet the men ignore that fact.

Inside the room, the men flash badges and documents depicting them as members of the NSA.

One speaks, "Professor Simpson, our apologies for keeping you and the General from your trips home, but we have been sanctioned by our superiors to request your and the General's presence elsewhere. We have your luggage and contacted your daughter and son to let them know of your delay, and General, through your embassy we had them contact your wife and daughter."

He stands and again opens his jacket to reveal a pistol. He then directs Harold and Nikolai to follow him.

"Your co-operation in this matter is not open for discussion, so please do not resist and follow us to the car waiting outside. We will escort you both to a private airstrip where an Air Force jet is ready to depart."

In not too polite a method, Harold and Nikolai are quickly shuffled out the door. When out of the terminal, one of the men scans them with a radiation detector. Having no conversation, they're urged into the rear seat of the black vehicle waiting outside. Nikolai has a bemused expression on his face. The doors slam shut and the sedan races off towards the private airstrip and an awaiting aircraft.

Harold sarcastically remarks, "I'm sorry, Nikolai. I have no idea why our shadowy tormentors here are ushering us away."

Nikolai snarls and states, "No matter, we've been taken by iron fists in velvet gloves; whom I suspect have velvet paws that hide sharp claws."

When they arrive on the tarmac of the airstrip, they are shown their way onto and inside the Air Force jet. Both are then seated in the plane and secured into their seatbelts. After take-off inside the militaristic simple interior of the jet with bench seats and but three porthole-type windows, each is given a choice of what they'd like to drink. Of course, Nikolai chooses vodka straight up with a cube of ice, while Harold asks if they have hot tea. Told they have no tea; he settles for a Coca Cola. To his contentment, Nikolai's given a half-filled bottle of Gray Goose vodka, which he gladly accepts and begins to gulp down.

Harold sneers at Nikolai, and then queries one of the men, "Where is it we're going ... and why?"

The most menacing-looking of the men replies, "Relax, we'll be in the air for several hours. There are snacks in the canvas bag there on the floor next to you. You'll be fed dinner after we arrive at our destination."

Harold asks, "If you have a method of phoning from this plane I should like to call my son and daughter in New Jersey. I'm sure they're worried about me."

"No, as we told you both, your families have already been notified of your delay home. There can be no outside contact from the plane. Don't be concerned, we explained to your son and daughter that you were not in any danger."

"Then why are we being kidnapped like this?" asks Nikolai.

"Everything will be explained after we land."

Harold's and Nikolai's curiosity grows with each passing hour of the trip. After being in the air for over two hours, both men become uncomfortable and fidgety in the hard bench seats. Though mostly silent, each man casts questioning glances at the other. Finally, Harold feels invaded and festering anger boils within him. He's done his duty and now he should be allowed to go home to live whatever remains of his life.

A silent Nikolai seems lost in his thoughts. As usual, he lights up a cigar and anxiously tosses it about from side to side in his mouth. He glances at Harold and points toward the front of the plane, where the three men have gone to sit in seats behind the pilot.

He comments, "I see Larry, Curly, and Moe have settled in upfront. Have you noticed the air in this aluminum box car is getting more and more chilled?"

Harold shivers a bit and wraps his arms around his body.

"Yes, that could be because of the altitude, or else we're flying north and it's getting colder outside."

"My gut instinct is you're right about us going north."

Harold bemoans, "Apparently we're invited to this party, but don't know who's conducting it."

Nikolai nods in agreement. "I'm not so sure even our three stooges up front know that, but if they are truly with your NSA, then the superiors they mentioned must be some chiefs high up in your Defense Department."

"Yes, maybe, but if that's who they are, why were you also made to come along? You've no connection to our Defense Department."

A few moments later, two of the men come back carrying several items in their arms.

One of them says, "In about forty minutes we'll be landing at an airbase about seven hundred miles north of the Arctic Circle. Since it's late April, the sun does not set here until late August. It's sort of a cold desert, and we'll be in the northernmost part of the world with current balmy temps of around 25 degrees. The ground and permafrost are so solid that the building's foundations are raised off the ground."

The other man tosses thick, hooded parkas and gloves with fur linings to Harold and Nikolai. He also hands them each a pair of polarized sunglasses.

The second man continues, "After we land and before you leave the plane, put on the parkas, gloves, and sunglasses. With the sun glistening off the snow it's difficult to see without sunglasses. You'll first be driven to a base hospital to be checked out, and then on to the dining hall before you're assigned to an NCO dormitory for the night."

"Why are we going to a hospital, we aren't sick?" Harold questions.

"Professor, I'm just informing you as to what's been told to us. You're not prisoners, or else we'd handcuffed you both and put you in leg irons. You know as much as we do about why you're being sent up here."

* * *

A half-hour later and somewhat bored, Harold stares at Nikolai in a moment of reflection. Brushing away cigar smoke that Nikolai exhales toward him, Harold studies this man he's been coupled with these past few days.

After a quiet moment or two, he states, "You know, in the CIA, because of my proficiency at judging human behavior, I was sometimes asked to profile members of your KGB and governing communist leaders. I have no dossier on you, Comrade, but I have determined a few things about you."

Nikolai playfully and intentionally exhales smoke rings at Harold, who again swipes them away with his hand. Downing another slug of chilled vodka, Nikolai grins and nods his head.

"Very well then, Comrade, fire away and tell me what you've learned."

Harold returns Nikolai's cynical grin with one of his own.

"To start with, in the restaurant this morning, sans your uniform when you wore only a shirt and slacks, I noticed your beefy arms stressed the seams of that pullover to the max. You have a barrel chest as well, so I imagine that although you've gotten older and ate two desserts ... I'd say you're about fifty-five years –"

"Nikolai corrects him, "Nope, fifty-eight."

"Really? Okay, fifty-eight years. I wager that you work out regularly. As a leader of military men, you do so for you do not want any of your superiors or underlings in the army to think you're not fit."

"Nikolai smiles and confirms, "Yes, I do one sit-up and push-up each morning for every year of life that God has provided me. Thus, I did fifty-eight each in my room this morning before breakfast." He then scoffs, "Come now, Comrade, my fitness is obvious and requires only observation and no real skill on your part to determine it."

Harold raises a hand to indicate there is more. His vivid gray eyes twinkle and he maintains his ongoing critique.

"I noticed the way you sliced your steak last night at dinner, and how you place your cigar in your mouth using the predominate left hand."

Nikolai laughs and holds up his left hand, "Most certainly, I am left-handed. That too is easy to determine to be simple observation. You're mountain climbing over molehills, Comrade."

"Okay, how's this?" Harold grins and states, "You present a tough front to others, especially the men you lead, but underneath it all, you're a loving, and sentimental man."

Nikolai scowls and shakes his head at Harold, "Hold on now, I am no such thing and there's no indication that I've presented to suggest that."

"On the contrary, before breakfast, I watched you in the hotel gift shop picking out a card to send to your wife and daughter. Through the glass window, I saw you pause, smile, and then write some loving sentiment on it to them. You then exited and asked the hotel concierge to mail it for you, giving him a handsome tip to do so."

Nikola sighs and confesses, "Okay, I admit I love my family, but who doesn't?"

In a sarcastic, but facetious way, Harold quips, "I haven't met yours yet, so how can I love ... them?"

Nikolai good-naturedly growls. "Come on, Comrade, you know what I meant."

"Indeed, my friend. So, continuing with my scrutiny, you have a very distinctive, deep bass voice and I suspect you are an excellent singer. I've noticed that you hum a lot, so I imagine there are all sorts of melodies floating through that thick noggin of yours."

"You are astute to notice that. Truly, I do love music. My father was a classical pianist. I was his prodigy and became proficient at playing the piano even before the age of ten. Later, I also learned the organ, performing several times as an adult at the Great Hall of the Moscow Conservatory. I also love to sing when I'm off duty. As recently as a month ago, there was a Music Festival held in The Moscow Kremlin Museum at the Armory Chamber. I joined famous musicians from Great Britain and Russia to perform notable Russian and English compositions, presenting their visions of the musical traditions of both countries."

"That is indeed impressive, Nikolai. You are a gifted man. I wager you no doubt used that talent and your vocal connections, bringing them to the U.S. as a means to scout and report to the KGB any tidbits of information that might benefit your Russian comrades."

"Nikolai's face forms a sheepish expression, "Had I gotten hold of any stolen American secrets, such info would've just made us technically three more years behind your country. I ask you, Comrade Harold, would I do an underhanded thing like that?"

Harold teases, "Where there's smoke, there's fire."

"Nyet! That's just the scent from my cigar, for there's no news in ashes," sites Nikolai in a teasing manner.

"In truth, I think that you'd like to become an American citizen. What would it take to make that happen and have you switch camps?"

Nikolai chortles and mockingly responds, "Chloroform." He laughs and adds, "If we were to invite you into the communist party, what would it take for you to become a citizen of Mother Russia?"

Harold's wit clicks into gear and he removes a quarter from his pocket. He flips it up in the air, catching it in his palm.

"I'll tell you what. I'll flip this coin and let it fall to the floor of the plane. If it lands on heads ... I'll shut up and we can relax and get some sleep. If it lands on tails, I'll stay an American. If it lands on its edge ... then I'll defect and become a Russian."

Nikolai grins, looks out a porthole-like window of the plane, and remarks. "I think we just missed our exit." He then winks at Harold and teases, "Now I know what you took up in college ... space."

Harold flashes a sarcastic grin, "Well, that is appropriate for one who becomes an astrophysicist." He counters. "Still, to go on, because of your rank, I believe you're a grand leader of men that they admire and respect. Heck, I've only known you a few days and even I respect you."

Nikolai feigns modesty, "Please, don't make a fuss over me. Just treat me as you would any other great man."

Harold chuckles, "It's a mystery how your head got so big without any nourishment."

"And here I thought I had a good friend on the jury," quips a jovial Nikolai.

Harold mocks, "To continue, I don't think you were coerced by your government and instead studied English voluntarily to expand your worthiness to your superiors."

Nikolai's expression becomes solemn, "Actually, as I stated, my father was an American citizen and classical musician that toured Russia before settling in Saint Petersburg where he met my mother. He was a concert pianist. It was him that taught me English. He was also a skilled pilot and flew himself to his concerts often held in other nations of Europe and Asia. When I was six years old, he chartered a plane to attend a concert in Poland. Somewhere over Lithuania, his plane went down in a snowstorm and neither the plane nor his body was ever recovered."

Harold winces and remarks, "That is tragic. So, did your mother raise you after that?"

"Yes, she never remarried but saw to it that I received a quality education and more musical training to prepare me for the future. I won't go into how or why I was later recruited into the KGB, for that in itself is a remarkably long story."

"We have something in common," states Harold. "My mother was from Poland and my father was from Lithuania. When my mom became pregnant, they came to America as immigrants to the U.S. Thus, I was born a naturalized U.S. citizen."

"Wow! Yes, that connection is most unusual," proclaims Nikolai.

Somewhat astonished by that coincidence, Harold attests, "My mother spoke Russian and Polish and my father spoke fluent Russian. I never really got the gist of Polish, but it was my father that taught me Russian when I was a young boy. Tragedies followed me too, for both my parents and my wife were killed in vehicle crashes. That's my curse I suppose and one of the reasons I've been so bitter at the God that doesn't exist."

Harold's voice cracks as he tells Nikolai the story.

"I was thirteen when my parents sent me off to a summer camp for two weeks. They were coming to pick me up after the camp term ended. They topped a hill on the narrow two-lane highway when a semi-driver in a gasoline tanker dozed off and wandered over into their lane. The collision was so violent that the truck exploded and poured fuel all over my parent's car. The tanker driver was badly burned but lived. The authorities told me my parents were probably killed instantly. By the time help could arrive to douse the intense blaze, there was nothing left of their bodies inside the vehicle ... only ashes."

"My word!" exclaims Nikolai. "So, who raised you after that?

"I had no living relatives, so I was placed in a state home where I remained until I graduated high school. I received an academic scholarship to the University of Alabama and you know the rest."

"I truly am sorry for those loved ones you've lost," confirms a contrite Nikolai.

Harold nods appreciatively and quickly reverts to his assessment, "I don't know why, but despite your jolly, backslapping, huggable ways, I surmise that you present a visible effort to use humor as a means of controlling your temper. And for some reason ... I feel you too are hiding some other sadness."

Nikolai's square jaw stiffens and he tightly clamps his lips.

Harold then remarks, "I know losing your father was a dreadful thing, and I'm sure you love your wife and daughter. Are you perhaps also sad because you wish you had a son to pass on your legacy?"

Nikolai's expression again turns sour. He sighs deeply, stands inside the plane, and turns on his heels. His emerald green eyes and his mind seem to lock upon a vision from his past.

He wipes a finger across the bridge of his nose.

He then unhappily states, "I had an eighteen-year-old son, a brave young man that was killed in 2003 at Chechnya during combat with insurgents of the second Russian-Chechen war."

Harold grimaces and apologizes, "Nikolai, I did not mean to—"

Nikolai grabs Harold's arm, "It's alright, Comrade. You didn't know. It was a rough time for his mother, sister, and me. He was a wonderful son whom God loaned to us for eighteen years. I loved him and was very proud of him and every man under my command and those that died that day."

Harold states somberly, "You lost your beloved son ... I lost my beloved wife, and we each lost a beloved parent ... or two. Such shared sorrow as this pierces one's heart like a knife. Still, the stab of that dagger cannot carve away the precious memories that we have of them."

Nikolai's eyes blink sternly as he pounds a fist into his chest and sits down.

Harold comments, "With you being Russian and me an American, I should cherish the initial misconceptions I had about you. Instead, we have a commonality between us and I believe the beginnings of a true bond."

His eyes meet Nikolai's and both men settle back in their seats, allowing this solemn, but a heartfelt moment to savor between them. Soon, they'll be landing and the purpose of this forced trip becomes evident.

Chapter 11

Back in Texas at the McDonald's Observatory, Albert Goodfellow celebrates the fact that at exactly 4:00 p.m. eastern time, just as the voice at the U.N. predicted, the Moon ceases its forward course towards the Earth and holds in a stationary path. He and other observatories check at fifteen-minute intervals and each determines that the moon is, for now at least, stopped its path toward destruction.

Near dusk, from Mount Locke near Fort Davis, Texas, Albert's again at the controls of the computerized L.E.D. readouts from the reflecting mirror lens telescope. He awaits data taken from Orion's Belt and the Horsehead Nebula. Soon, another image comes through on his console, one that stuns and alarms him. He checks, attempting to find out which observatory is posting this data and the ensuing image. To his frustration, there is no identifiable source of what he's witnessing. Once the image is completed, he records it and sits in stunned silence.

When his cell phone rings, he springs to attention and almost leaps out of his skin. Startled, his trembling hands answer the call from his colleague, John Lumpkin in New Mexico.

"Albert, for God's sake, are you getting the image that's just been posted?"

Albert's voice cracks and he swallows hard, "Yes, but who's sending it? This must be some hacker or a hoax. It can't possibly be real … can it?"

"That was my reaction as well, but then I turned on my television. There are live images of it. The radio is saying this thing is being broadcast worldwide on every televised network to every nation."

With that news, Albert scrambles to locate the remote for the forty-inch television he has in the office. He quickly leaves the console room, enters his office, and switches on the set. In this remote region of Texas, he has satellite T.V. service. Holding the phone to his ear, he stares at the screen, which begins to show the same image on each of the channels he scrolls through.

"My Lord, John, this is inconceivable."

"Well, as amazed as we were at the U.N., and then by the Moon's ceasing its divergence, this certainly leaves no doubt that the voice we heard was that of a being from another world."

"Yes, but with technology like that which I'm witnessing, we'd best hope the words he spoke at the U.N. are true and that they mean us no harm."

The image Albert and John view appear to be that of an enormous spacecraft exiting from behind the Moon.

"For sure! Based upon the scale of the image, I'd estimate the craft to be over one hundred miles long and about twenty miles wide. It's amazing that something so large can travel through the cosmos."

Both men note the craft's bell shape and the array of colorful lights rotating around what appears to be a revolving metal belt around the thicker edge of it.

"I wonder who's taking these images. They almost appear to be coming from near the Earth."

"Apparently, they are, for just after the images began, on the NASA feed they announced that the cameras outside the ISS that were aimed at the Earth, somehow digressed and now are aimed at the Moon. NASA lost all control over those cameras."

Like the rest of the world, both astronomers are amazed ... all except for an inexplicable blackout of the coverage to those at Thule Airbase in Greenland, all watch in awe as this massive craft pulls away from behind the Moon and begins to advance toward the Earth. As it progresses steadily, Albert's reminded of something from a movie.

He chides Stephen Spielberg's vision of a mothercraft, "I'm glad that the voice from the U.N. speaks our language. I'm not sure I could take another episode with the diatonic sounds from 'Close Encounters.' Those eight notes and seven intervals of quavers, semitones, and whole tones would drive me crazy."

John points out, "Given its enormous size, notice the apparent rapid acceleration. The first Apollo Moon mission traveled at seven miles per second, roughly 24,700 miles per hour. It took three days to travel the expanse between the Earth and Moon. At the speed this craft is advancing, it might be upon us in less than a couple of hours."

* * *

On the ISS, the two USA crewmen are concluding with the three Russian cosmonauts an experiment with anthropomorphic Zucchini done in microgravity in the environment of space. They are all notified by NASA and the Russian government that because of what occurred at the U.N., they are all to exit the ISS within the next thirty minutes and return to Earth.

All of the sudden, the Paycom-1 controller at the Payload Operations Center in Huntsville, Alabama interrupts.

"Alpha Station, this is Paycom-1. Please cease your experiment and check the switches for the outside cameras. We have lost all control of them, for they are now pointing toward the Moon."

"Roger, Paycom-1, we're also getting that view on our monitors."

Awestruck, Rick Marshall, the new U.S. commander of the ISS orbital laboratory watches their station's monitors as the huge spacecraft ascends rapidly from behind the Moon toward the Earth. His co-pilot, David Carlson, on the Dragon 65, plus the other three Russian crewmen all become alarmed by what they're watching.

"Paycom-1, is what we're seeing real?"

"Roger, Alpha Station. It appears to be some sort of colossal, alien spacecraft, probably connected to the situation that occurred at the U.N. Security meeting yesterday."

Rick glances at the other four crewmen, all of whom seem very anxious.

"Paycom-1, as I view the monitors, I am struck by the fact that we are the only humans orbiting in space ... and from the looks of it, that mammoth craft is heading directly toward us."

"Roger that, Alpha Station, we concur. Both Russia and NASA control urge you all to as rapidly as possible make ready to evacuate the ISS. All systems on the station seem operable, so we'll direct its functions from the ground."

"Roger that, Paycom-1. We're all ready for the ride home to be with our families during the next two weeks. We'll get in our spacesuits immediately. Any word on how the discussions on nuclear disarmament are going?"

"Alpha Station, the prevailing wind has it that there's been some high-stakes maneuvering and posturing going on, but it's only been a few hours. We imagine the ball game is only in the first inning."

"Roger, Paycom-1. Let's hope that the political and military leaders of all nations understand the urgency of working toward the same goal ... and saving our planet. From up here, one can easily see it being a beautiful Garden of Eden amongst the cold, deep, darkness of outer space."

"Roger that, Alpha Station. Indeed, it is. Godspeed and good luck with your rides home. The Russians are standing by to retrieve their Soyuz capsule. NASA will be tracking your Dragon 65 capsule for retrieval."

* * *

In space, the palpable presence of the vast phantom craft steadily powers its way toward the blue planet that all humans call home. Upon the Earth, ocean tides swell this night to again flood coastal city shores and threaten many islands that aren't far above sea levels. Krakatau in Indonesia and Nishinoshima in Japan seem less threatening. A rise in the land around Yellowstone warns of increased activity beneath the magma caldrons below. Several other dormant volcanoes along the 'ring of fire' that before were rumbling are now mellow somewhat, but still, appear dangerously close to erupting.

Throughout the world, billions of people stop to watch with sheer amazement and trepidation the images on the screens of their televisions. High-ranking political figures and military officers from every nation around the globe assess the threat and move quickly to prepare some manner of defense plan should the beings from space directing this massive craft be hostile. If that's the case, then the entire world will become ground zero. The President calls for a meeting at the White House to discuss options.

Many hysterical populations around the world take to the streets in panic and adamant protests demand a quick response to the alien's demands. People insist certain government, military, and scientific officials come forward and make the agreement to ban nukes, plus all chemical and biological weapons. The crowds swell and become vicious and violent, with masses of usually stoic and reasonably civilized, law-abiding citizens screaming, panicking, and insisting their leaders resolve this matter swiftly and completely.

After meeting with the President, the Joint Chiefs gather at the Pentagon. One general grumbles and makes his point.

"Look, we all know that those rogue nations that practice gunboat diplomacies are going to be flies in the ointment when it comes to negotiating and disbanding nukes ... no matter the cost."

"True, but ... take another look at that incredible, enormous machine that's speeding its way toward us. Nobody has ever been faced with such an opponent. Any government or terrorist group would have mad cow disease if they think they can fend off those in that huge craft with rocket launchers, tanks, planes, missiles, or even stolen or purchased suitcase nukes," adds a Marine general.

A Navy admiral remarks, "I agree, as odd as it seems, the low-lying fruit among nations are those that have the most warheads and missiles. That being: the U.S., Russia, China, France, Pakistan, India, and Britain. I see all of those being realistic and understanding the circumstances necessary to avoid an Apocalypse by complying with what God and that alien commands. It's the other less logical and maniacal loner nations like North Korea that fear regional threats that worry me. We know they will likely resist reason despite the consequences."

The Marine general states, "Then, they are like the stubborn Emperor and military leaders of Japan that during World War II allowed their nation to be bombarded by an atomic bomb ... not once, but twice before they submitted and agreed to cease warring and surrender. In this case, the world cannot brood and try holding the fort, for we are surely walking through the valley of death. We, as a species, cannot refuse to abide by the directive and warning placed before us. Ignore it, and we will suffer annihilation, and in effect be committing global suicide."

As their discussion and plans proceed, in space the crewmen on the ISS enter their return capsules, detach and set their small lifeboats on trajectories that will bring them back to Earth. On television, the world watches as various satellites and space debris crash into the enormous alien craft, yet some sort of shielding prevents these objects from damaging or reaching the outer shell of the craft itself.

When the spacecraft descends to within a few hundred miles of the ISS, what happens next stuns and amazes everyone. From the underside of the spacecraft, colossal-sized bay doors open like a mammoth giant opening its jaws. Then, steadily as a panther clinging to its prey, the craft lowers toward the ISS, swallowing the two-hundred-forty-foot long by three-hundred-fifty-six foot wide, two-hundred-ton behemoth station into the bowels of the enormous, alien craft. All the TDRS tracking and data relay satellites quickly lose their ability to send information about the former geosynchronous orbit of the ISS.

Inside the meeting room at the Pentagon, the Joint Chiefs stare at their television monitors in disbelief. The jaws of the alien craft close slowly, capturing the single most peaceful example of international scientific cooperation. NASA control and Roscosmos focus on the retrieval of their crewmen, and in the meantime lose all contact with the ISS itself.

Breaking the silence, an admiral states, "Gentlemen and ladies, what other examples of the power before us must we witness before we comply? Consider the astonishing act we just witnessed, the vanishing of astronauts, plus the disappearance of our commander-in-chief, our Moon's divergence, and now the presence and incredible act of this astounding craft. How much more proof does our world need for us to convince our governments to do as we've been directed?"

Chapter 12

After the five-and-a-half-hour flight, the jet carrying Harold and Nikolai begins to descend into the darkness and onto a snowy runway. As the plane taxis toward a large outbuilding, Harold sees a sign on the building that reads:

THULE AIR BASE — HOME OF THE 821st AIR BASE GROUP
BASE MOTTO: "PROUD TO BE"

Nikolai leans back and nods his head. He remarks, "We're in Greenland, Comrade Harold. Your nation's airbase here houses the new Space Wing and Space Force. There's a reported network of sophisticated sensors providing for early missile warnings and space surveillance ... should my country or some other threatening nation decide to start a suicidal nuclear war and fire missiles over the northern polar ice cap."

Harold puzzles over why they are here. He asks, "I suppose it's your job to know all that, Nikolai, but can you explain why they'd be bringing us here?"

Nikolai casts a glaring look of disdain at one of the men in black. One of the men glares back at him with a smug scowl.

Nikolai quietly whispers, "I'm sure we'll learn that soon enough."

As the plane slowly turns and they can see out their windows, they observe a line of warmly clothed airmen lined up and waiting in the cold breeze outside. Harold and Nikolai put on their sunglasses, gloves, and heavy parkas before deplaning.

When the jet's engines stop and the front exit door is opened, Harold and Nikolai are escorted out and down the steps. The female Base Commander ushers them and the three men in black into a waiting Air Force sedan. Even though it's close to the start of an Arctic spring, the chilled air causes each man to shiver and their cheeks quickly turn red.

Harold and Nikolai notice the gathering of airmen bearing weapons. They seem like guards of some sort. Both men also take note that there are Asian soldiers, plus ones wearing Russian uniforms.

The sedan makes its way down an icy, dirt roadway to the base hospital, where both men are told to exit. Even though they've been checked a couple of times already, one airman steps forward and scans them for radiation.

Convinced they are okay, he nods to another airman that escorts Harold and Nikolai into the hospital.

Inside, they are taken to a room where there is X-ray equipment. A couple of technicians have them remove their parkas and sunglasses, then one at a time step up to an X-ray machine. Then they are each stationed in a position to take cranial X-rays of each man's skull. This inexplicable action causes Harold to get an overpowering urge to scream out in protest but seeing he has no choice; he clamps his lips shut and ignores the instinct.

Once the X-rays are complete, the two technicians study the results, whispering amongst themselves. Harold reasons something is amiss, for whatever they noted on the X-ray seems to intrigue them. They murmur to the guards and men in black, who then tell Harold and Nikolai to retrieve their sunglasses and parkas and follow them back to the sedan.

They are then driven to what's called a dining hall, where they exit and are escorted inside. They remove their sunglasses, gloves, and heavy coats, hanging them on a rack near the door. To their surprise, there is a cafeteria-like line where prepared food is being served. There's a wide choice of several types of entrees, vegetables, desserts, bread, and drinks. Since both men are hungry, they each get in line and load up their plates and trays with an array of quite tasty-looking food. They are then led to a crowded, nearby long dining table where several Air Force officers also partake of their evening meal. Harold sets his tray down and wraps his hands around a mug of hot coffee.

He overhears one NCO officer's remarks, "Yeah, control is all out of synch and we've somehow lost surveillance capabilities on the ISS and several other satellites. The radar is also on the fritz. Though they're working to find out what's causing it, they seem to have no idea why surveillance, communication systems, and satellite television reception isn't working."

Another NCO officer replies, "That's a major equipment glitch for a base whose mission is to protect and forewarn the Pentagon against missile launches."

They quiet down after Harold and Nikolai sit down. The two men begin conversing with several of the airmen, and Harold asks for an explanation of what he just heard, but the NCO airmen clam up and realize they shouldn't discuss the matter further in front of Harold ... especially not with a Russian.

In truth, they seem to marvel at even being in the company of a Russian general.

One sergeant makes a snide remark, "I never thought I'd be sharing a dinner table with a Russian general here on a top-secret U.S. airbase. These are indeed strange times."

Nikolai's wide smile reveals his set of white teeth. With an amused expression, he confirms the truth in the officer's comment.

"Let me assure you, Comrade, I am as astounded as you. The two of us each had other dinner plans that didn't include being hijacked and brought here to this top-of-the-world airbase. It's been a very long day and to say I feel like a fish out of water is an understatement."

The Air Force Seargent chuckles and nods his head, "Understandably so, General."

Harold takes a bite of his mashed potatoes and slices off a piece of chopped steak, eagerly attempting to quell his hunger.

After swallowing, he then replies, "Do any of you men have an idea about why we've been brought here?"

The sergeants shake their heads indicating they do not.

Nikolai nibbles at his food and asks Harold, "Why do you think they X-rayed our skulls?"

He answers, "I've no idea, but I imagine we'll soon find out."

The two men make small talk with several of the NCO officers and finish eating their meals. Once they're done and their hunger's satiated, the three NSA musclemen escort them back into the sedan. From there, they are taken to an NCO dormitory where they are told they'll be quartered for the night. Each is given a single bed in a room. They will share the facilities with other NCO airmen in the barracks-like building.

Although Harold has never actually been in the military, he did on occasion while a CIA agent spend time in group military sleeping quarters when training at Virginia's one-thousand-acre Camp Peary on "The Farm," as it is called. It was there that he and others received covert CIA training with the Defense Clandestine Service.

The NSA men tell them, "The showers and latrine are located down the hall to your right. You'll be waked at 0600 for breakfast, and then afterward by 0730, you'll be escorted to a field office where you'll await the arrival of those with whom you will be meeting. Lights are out in forty-five minutes, so get some rest, you're going to need it."

Harold does not care for the NSA men's condescending attitudes.

He says to them, "There is no cell phone coverage up here. How are we supposed to contact our families to let them know we're safe and when we'll be home?"

One of the men in black tells him, "Cell phones do not work here and the Tetra communication system in place is for classified use only. Do not worry about your families; they were notified that you're okay and will be away for a few days."

"Harold then protests, "You claim we're in no danger. Then why are we here and why were those cranial X-rays taken?"

"We've no idea, Professor. We just do what we're told." The mystery man then adds an unexpected touch of wittiness, "Our thanks to both of you for cooperating with us. We'd have hated to have to shoot you."

Nikolai mocks, "We appreciate your restraint and followed your path of least assistance."

The tall, muscular man snarls, forces a grin, salutes, and then turns to exit.

After they leave, Nikolai and Harold remove their parkas, store their gloves and sunglasses by their bedsides, and are happy to learn their luggage has been brought inside. Nikolai stretches and plops back onto his bed. He then removes his shoes and opens one of his suitcases. Inside he finds and removes a nearly full bottle of vodka. He laughs, removes the bottle's top, and chugs down a slug of the strong liquor.

He declares, "I like it cold. Thankfully, it got that way by being stored with the luggage in an unheated compartment on the plane."

"Harold winces and remarks, "Gad! How can you drink that stuff? As I said, I have a severe dislike for the taste of it."

Nikolai wipes his mouth with the back of his hand and takes another slug. He smacks his lips and issues a hardy belch afterward.

"Aw, that's better. I can face just about anything if I've got this magic brew of liquid courage."

"It's a good thing you weren't operating any machinery today. Your blood-alcohol level must be three times the legal limit for gauging drunkenness."

"Most certainly, Comrade Harold, I have enough anti-freeze in me so as not to congeal if I go outside."

Harold laughs, "Yeah, you no doubt have enough to keep your blood flowing at temps as low as -50 degrees."

"True, but to a Russian vodka is like air. We need it to breathe and feel alive. Besides, I was weaned on it. Never has it negatively impaired my mental abilities."

"Well, I hope your invulnerability holds. I have a feeling tomorrow's meeting will be quite demanding. A hangover will not make your day any easier."

"I shall have spring in my step and be prepared for anything that comes our way."

Harold looks at his watch and ponders, "It's after 10:00 p.m. on the east coast, I wonder if after 4:00 p.m. the moon did as the voice predicted and stopped its trajectory toward Earth?"

"I've got a strong hunch it did exactly that. Now we must convince all governments to avoid a firestorm and agree to disband nuclear weapons. Simple, eh?"

Nikolai smirks and swallows another slug of vodka.

Harold concludes, "Oh, sure! It'll be like trying to rope and tame a housefly."

With that, Nikolai begins to strip off his tunic. He removes his pants and shirt, getting down to his boxer shorts and undershirt. Harold notices the tattoos on each of Nikolai's forearms but pays no heed to one resembling a fish on his upper arm near the shoulder.

"Are those tats on the forearms of your two kids?" Harold asks curiously.

Nikolai sighs and has the expression of a creature in pain.

"Yes, the one on my left arm is that of my lovely daughter, Anya." He holds out his other arm to Harold and in a brooding voice says, "And this one is my son, Viktor, who was once my strong right arm."

Harold nods and watches as Nikolai removes his undershirt and shorts, prancing about nude in front of Harold displaying his muscular body. He grabs a towel from off a nearby rack, waltzes towards the door, and then toward the showers down the hall. Harold's amazed to see that Nikolai has another large tattoo, this one being on his back about eight inches down from his neck and shoulders.

Harold loudly comments, "Wow! That's an amazing image on your back."

Nikolai turns and glances over his shoulder, "Yes, that's an icon of the Virgin Mother, Mary, The Birth-Giver of God." He then looks back at Harold, "Not all of us are faithless hounds or slaves of Russian communism, Comrade. Some of us love the God that created us and sent us His son to die for our sins."

After saying that, Nikolai's bowels churn. His face turns red, and then he loudly farts, slapping himself on the butt as he expels gas. Afterward, he smiles broadly and winks at Harold.

Harold sneers and holds his nose, then remarks, "Good Lord, that smells as foul as all of Arabia."

He then begins to undress and watches as Nikolai disappears into the area where other soldiers are showering. He hears the back slaps, that hardy bass voice, and thunderous laughter as Nikolai begins to joke and converse with the NCO airmen there.

Harold strips down to his underwear but decides to skip the showers and just crawl into bed. The very long day has sapped him of all energy, and despite being thousands of miles away from home, this military bed feels awfully good.

Chapter 13

At 0400 of the following morning, as Harold and Nikolai sleep, they are startled awake by the shrill sounds of base siren alarms going off. They hear rousing, excited voices and the scampering of feet, as airmen career down the hallways in varying stages of dress; some in partial uniforms, but wearing parkas to investigate what the outside commotion is all about. The loud calamity stirs Harold and Nikolai from their bunks.

Harold rubs the sleep from his eyes and staggers from his bed. Aware that something is awry, he and Nikolai rapidly scramble, grasping for socks, shoes, boots, and clothing to race outside to find out what's happening to cause such a chaotic awakening of the troops.

Once they have enough clothing, each man dons their parka, gloves, and sunglasses, and then streaks out of the building into the outdoors where the troops are assembling. What they and other stunned airmen and officers on the base see is beyond belief.

There, in an open snowfield about two hundred yards from the base camp, hovering about ten feet off the ground is the entire International Space Station. It remarkably bobs up and down like a tethered balloon filled with helium. Apparently, some unknown, ominous force is holding it there, preventing it from crashing to the ground where it would crumble under its bulk and extreme weight.

None of those present can conceive of such a thing being possible. Everyone marvels at the sight of this amazing image before them. Harold is in awe of the power that's responsible for this astonishing achievement. Nikolai too seems aghast at what he's seeing.

Guys with guns cautiously make their way across the tundra toward the suspended ISS. As they near it, they hear a muffled sound like that of air being let out of a car tire. When a couple of the men stretch and attempt to reach up to touch it with their rifles, they quickly experience an electrical shock. They jerk away as if being stung by wasps. Everyone steps back from the hovering ISS. Those who were stunned soon recover and experience no serious wounds. Whatever force holds the ISS has a defensive response to anyone attempting to touch or move the station.

The Base Commander directs those in charge of communicating with NASA and other government agencies to quickly repair whatever equipment isn't allowing the base's outward communiqués to be sent. She issues additional orders to others that surprise Harold and Nikolai.

"If there is no communication between the tower and Air Force One, then get out there to the runways and use flares, flashlights, fires, or any means necessary to be certain it and the other dignitary's jets are going to be able to land safely."

Harold's eyebrows raise, "Air Force One?" he mumbles. "That can only mean that President Battle will soon be arriving here."

He and Nikolai are then directed back toward the NCO dorm and told to wait until someone comes for them. Before entering, they take one more gawking look at the floating ISS. Neither man can seem to fathom how it got here or what's holding it up. Harold's fascination far exceeds his apprehension, and his mind attempts to summon how many laws of physics this scenario shatters.

About a half-hour later, Harold and Nikolai hear the thundering sounds of large jet engines soaring above the base and landing nearby. In all, Harold counts four such jets arriving, hopefully carrying what he suspects and hopes are those dignitaries who will be explaining why he and Nikolai were brought here.

Each man rests in their bunk and is brought breakfast items, including hot coffee, eggs, bacon, toast, and orange juice. After eating, Harold and Nikolai both shave, and then dress in their best attire, thus displaying readiness and anticipation for whoever comes for them.

* * *

Back in Trenton, New Jersey, Morgan, Ted, Steve, and Rita are all sitting at a breakfast table where the ladies prepared a meal. The forty-inch television mounted to a kitchen wall is turned on and they all watch and listen to a special news program where scientists, astrobiologists, and commentators discuss the events of the day and those at the U. N.

One male host asks an astrobiologist, "Thus far, all we know of the alien is that it transmits in Earth languages, but we haven't yet actually seen what they look like. Any ideas on how they might appear?"

The astrobiologist tells him, "There are folks touting theories that our ancient ancestors were visited by advanced, intelligent alien forms from other worlds. Supposedly, those aliens are responsible for helping to build amazing structures like the Pyramids of Giza and those of the Mayans, perhaps ones in India or even Stonehenge. Besides these archeological wonders, the aliens allegedly helped mankind develop and advance our civilization. Some were even said to be worshipped as gods. Some believers view these beings as imagined, strange, and powerful 'sky' creatures that were everything from being birdlike to small gray humanoids, reptilian, and some even believed they were similar to us and not much different looking than ourselves."

The host then states and asks, "Okay, so we've seen in movies and on television many representations of what aliens might look like. Mostly they resemble humanity's form, supposedly because human actors portray them. What then is your scientific opinion of what their actual appearance might be?"

"Trying to pinpoint or predict what extraterrestrials might be like and look like is dependent on so many factors that it's impossible to sort them into only one category. Since Professor Simpson at Princeton pointed out that the dots on the heels of newborns is a replica of the three sisters of Orion, one might start with an assumption that merits Orion as being the star system from where the extraterrestrials originate. In recent new images of the Orion Nebula, there's been an indication of it possessing an unexpected wealth of planet mass objects possibly being Earth-like. They are, however not in orbit around stars, but trail through the galaxy like stars. If the aliens come from within that Nebula, then it would be most unlikely that they are not anything like us physically."

"Do you mean, they'll be monstrous-looking, or something like those mysterious-looking creatures from the sci-fi movie, Arrival?"

"Possibly, but that too is all speculation. Since one of those Orion stars is a gaseous giant, perhaps where the aliens come from, instead of breathing oxygen, they may breathe hydrogen or even methane ... if they breathe at all.

The only true model of life we have comes from our planet. On Earth all life is carbon-based. However, the biochemical foundation of life forms from another world might be silicon, iron-based, or who knows what else. Maybe aliens wouldn't even live on land. If they do it might be so cold that humans wouldn't be able to survive there. On Jupiter's moon, Titan, liquid methane lakes may just as easily as water develop life. On extremely arid worlds, life might take on an entirely different chemical element. The chemist turned author, Hal Clement, created many such worlds in his books."

Yet another scientist comments, "It's true that anything is possible. They may have symmetrical bodies; however, it is doubtful they'd be bipedal like us with two arms and two legs. They may only have but one gender, or perhaps several. Unlike us, they might be cold-blooded and possess any number of legs and arms, or perhaps have none at all. Our planet has many diverse biotypes, so there's no reason to believe other worlds wouldn't also. I expect this baffling alien, when he, it, or whatever it is does reveal itself, it will be nothing like anything we've been able to imagine or comprehend."

The astrobiologist confidently declares, "All these amazing possibilities are why we are so excited and anxious to have the alien whose voice we all heard, disclose his true form to us; unmask itself and allow us in science to converse with it."

The host then replies, "I'm certain the entity would face a barrage of questions by the media and by you in astrobiology, especially since we know it speaks our language."

"We don't know for sure that it does speak ... at all. Although the voice was projected to all the nations represented in their language, we believe that perhaps it was not a verbal voice as we know it, but rather a telepathic one."

The host seems confused, "Telepathic? he asks. "Then how is it that we who watched on television heard its voice speaking to us?"

"I hope that it does speak verbally. As to how it could accomplish what I just mentioned, projecting itself telepathically via television is merely conjecture, but a definite possibility."

"If it does speak verbally, it would most certainly be advantageous to you in the media, but probably not to the extraterrestrial. I'm guessing that's why it designated Professor Simpson of Princeton and the Russian General,

Nikolai Belinski, as its contacts, and through them will it make most of its communications to the world," adds the other scientist.

Hearing this commentary, a worried Ted rises from his chair and anxiously refills his cup with hot coffee.

"As he does, he remarks, "If that's the case, I sure hope that alien can find Thule Airbase in Greenland because before those men told us of it yesterday, I'd never heard of it."

Observing this dialog, Morgan declares out loud, "I know! And why in God's name was Dad taken way up there? I wish he would call. I pray he's alright and will be home soon."

Chapter 14

On Fox News, there's a special report being shown about the ISS. An anxious news anchor clears his throat and a video plays on screen.

"As we all watched in sheer wonder and awe, the enormous spacecraft, estimated to be about a hundred miles long swallowed up the International Space Station as easily as if it were an entrée item on a dinner menu. We've learned that the six-man crew, two Americans and three Russians, have all evacuated the ISS and made successful returns to Earth. After the capture of the ISS, the feed seen here shuts off, and apparently, NASA doesn't possess the ability to follow where the huge alien spacecraft traveled into space from there

* * *

The airmen assigned to Air Force One wait for the deplaning of President Battle and to greet him with the customary salute. After the President descends, an Air Force sedan waits to take him and his entourage of advisors, the Secretary of Defense, and the director of the CIA, to the building where an important meeting is scheduled to take place. Russian soldiers and Asian soldiers escort their nation's leaders via their vehicles to the same building. A Japanese representative and one from Great Britain were also on board Air Force One. All are taken to the meeting place.

Oppressed by the thoughts racing through his mind, Harold despises the indefiniteness of this state of affairs. He's desperately impatient and wants the bell to ring that will dismiss this class. The toil of the long day and plane flight, plus the rude awakening by sirens so early that morning drains him of energy. He recalls the horde of newsmen that greeted him and the others yesterday at the U.N. In his head, he can still see the bright snap of flashbulbs ... seeming like the popping champagne corks one after another. What a joy it will be if he ever gets to again look at the pureness of the naked, star-filled heavens and not have to worry about the sky falling or it being clouded by unknown voices of beings that bring warnings to all mankind. He feels imprisoned like a bee in a transparent, glass hive.

Nikolai rolls an unlit cigar around in his mouth and under his tongue as if it is a sweet-tasting piece of candy. He leans back in a chair and seems as anxious as a thoroughbred horse for the race to begin. Like a snake struggling to free itself from a vulture, he leaps up and paces about the room.

He yells out to anyone listening, "Come on, people! I'm tired of being herded around this frozen palace like a sheep. Fish or cut bait, just get on with whatever it is that you want from us."

Joining Nikolai's frustration, Harold also issues a cry of unassisted woe; his pent-up frustration begins to boil over.

He expresses his sentiments to Nikolai, "I agree! These past few days have been like a great express train, roaring, flashing, and dashing headlong into a dark unknown tunnel. The future is but a mirage, vaguely lit and mysterious. I just want this over and for us to go home and be with those we love."

* * *

At 0930, the three NSA goons, as Nikolai starts calling them, arrive at the NCO dormitory and escort him and Harold outside and again into a sedan.

Annoyed, Harold quips, "I assume we're going to a meeting now, which you said last night would be at 0730. That was two hours ago."

The NSA man riding shotgun in the front seat says, "That was before we had the unexpected visitation by the International Space Station, now drifting around like a helium-filled dirigible over the tundra. As you might imagine, it sort of juggled the plans and schedules a bit."

"So, where are we headed now?" Nikolai asks.

"To a hanger just off the runway in a room set up to have a meeting."

Noticeably present on the short drive, Harold and Nikolai behold the jet, Air Force One, plus the planes of both Russia's and China's equivalent to it. Nikolai scratches his firm chin and seems a bit conflicted. He sighs and looks at Harold, whose nerves cause his throat to fill with bile. He feels an oncoming headache.

Moments later the sedan stops and six other men in suits and parkas, seemingly secret service agent types, come racing out to meet the vehicle. They open the car doors for Harold and Nikolai.

One of the NCA men comments, "We're done here. They're all yours."

With that matter-of-fact send-off, the NCA agents drive away and the new men in black escort Harold and Nikolai into the large, modern hanger, where they are then taken into separate rooms. Harold's room is about the size of a two-car garage and there is a long folding table with ten folding chairs around it. The lighting is sparse and upon the table are note tablets and pens. He also notices a recording device is set up on the table and there are video cameras near the ceiling in all four corners of the room. Two pitchers filled with water, plus ten glasses sit on a small table near one of the two doors to the room.

All of a sudden, Harold feels like an amoeba in a Petri Dish. He squirms about in the uncomfortable chair. After about fifteen minutes of sitting there alone and staring at a digital wall clock, he angers.

In an outburst of irritation and cynicism, he cannot conceal his displeasure, "Earth to whoever it is that abducted the general and me. Exercise some sense of decency and come tell me why we are here and what's this is all about."

Another three minutes pass, and then at last one door opens and a group of men, two being generals like those he met at the Pentagon, plus the Secretary of Defense, the CIA director, and others he doesn't recognize. They all stand next to the chairs supposedly assigned to them, leaving but the one vacant chair at the head of the table. The one to sit there became quickly evident. President Battle of the United States comes in, followed by several agents that are his bodyguards. Instinctively, Harold nervously rises to his feet out of respect.

The men present wait until the President is seated and then they too take their seats. A base NCO technician switches on the recording device. President Battle lays his hand on the table and turns toward Harold.

"Professor Simpson, I'm certain you're curious and anxious about why you were brought here. My apologies for the secrecy and for hauling you up here to this shivering, remote airbase. I assure you, it wasn't our idea."

Harold puzzles over that answer but doesn't question it.

The President continues, "We've come here to discuss the dangerous situations occurring in the past few days. Meeting here does somewhat compromise some of our nation's military secrets, but at this juncture, we felt compelled to overlook that because of the threat we all face. After the U.N. escapade, like all of us, you too must be stunned for having witnessed the base's new arrival of a two-hundred-ton air balloon from space."

"Yes, Sir! Stunned is an appropriate word for it. Are the members of the crew still aboard?"

"No, they were able to evacuate the station before it was captured by the huge spacecraft."

Harold reacts in a relieved manner, "Thank goodness they're safe, but what's that about a huge spacecraft capturing the ISS?"

"Yes, I forgot. I'm told all on the base here were not able to receive television transmission of the event. A spacecraft longer than Rhode Island approached and captured the ISS in its enormous bowels. The next thing we know, as you have seen the ISS was brought here, we assume by them. There was neither radar detection of it, nor any sign of another craft transporting it here ... it just appeared here in an instant."

Harold nods and acknowledges seeing the ISS, "Yes, Mr. President, I am stunned how something as large as the ISS can be made to defy gravity and be suspended out there the way it is. As a physicist, that's beyond all reason as we know it. I suppose down is up and up is down."

The President nods in agreement, "Equally alarming is the fact that all satellite surveillance was shut down, as was the ability to track missile launches. There was a glitch in the radar, and all communications from the tower were blocked. That occurred here at a base with equipment designed to avoid all that. Fortunately, it's all been restored and is working again, but it is most unsettling."

He then wriggles in his folding chair, attempting to get more comfortable. His face is gray with fatigue like a man with the weight of the world on his shoulders.

"He continues, "Now, Professor, as to why you're here. You and General Belinski were privately invited to be here."

"Huh? Invited by you ... or whom?"

"By the same voice that spoke, or however it communicated, at the U.N. After that meeting, I called one for my Cabinet and the Joint Chiefs at the White House. As it had at the U.N., a ball of bright light appeared wherein the voice plainly stated it wanted you two to come here to meet with it. It claimed it would show up here at 1100 hours today, telling us that we should come also."

The President waves his arms as if acknowledging the group.

"The Russians, Chinese, Japanese, and British all heard the same message by the same voice, and a contingent of each nation is here this morning. The voice said all would be explained ... by it communicating to you and the General."

Harold's reaction is to check his watch for the time and make a stammering reply.

"It is 1030 hours now. We each suspected it might again contact us, exactly why I don't know."

"We're guessing that since you two are nuclear physicists and the lead speakers at the U.N. meeting, it's the reason you've been chosen."

The Secretary of Defense adds, "The voice also informed us that you two should not be alarmed, but that it placed an implant into yours and the General's brain ... to be able to speak ... privately to each of you. The X-ray technicians here tell us that indeed you each have a small one-inch metal disk implant in the parietal region of your brain."

Harold gingerly rubs his head and thinks about the X-rays they did of his skull.

He pauses, ponders a moment, and then says, "Yes, it makes sense now. In a dream I had before the U.N. meeting, I saw a strange craft and a large, mysterious being that spoke to me. It was in the same voice as that at the U.N. meeting. I believe it must have somehow entered my hotel room that night, and while I slept it contacted me and somehow implanted this device in my head. I imagine that's when it did so to General Belinski as well."

The CIA director looks at Harold and states, "Professor, as a retired member of the CIA, we have no problem trusting you to represent your nation in a respectful, truthful, and honorable manner. However, the General is a Russian and a former KGB agent whose trust we cannot count upon to uphold our best interests."

Harold counters, "Having spent the majority of the past few days with him, I think I can say that he is an honorable man and one I trust. Where have you taken him?"

The President remarks, "The General is being briefed by the new Russian President. The other dignitaries are waiting till after your upcoming encounter with the voice to have more discussions about the disbanding of nuclear weapons. The General will be brought here momentarily, where you're both to confer with the entity, voice, or whatever it is."

An NCO airman speaks, "Mr. President, it is 1048, so we'd best vacate the room. The President thanks him and stands. So too do all the others, except for Harold.

"Please have the General brought in. Gentlemen, let's all reconvene in the outer area where the others are waiting. Good luck, Professor," adds the President.

Chapter 15

The door opens once more and Nikolai is ushered inside. He takes a chair next to Harold. The two men gaze at each other, and then at the rows of staring eyes that turn to leave the room. Each of them takes note that the recording device on the table is still on and they also are aware of the red blinking lights on the wall cameras, probably indicating they too are focused on recording.

Harold glances at his watch, as both men sit silently. Nikolai, sans his cigar, taps nervously with his fingers upon the table.

"What time is it?" Nikolai asks. "I'd rather be in a foxhole dodging bullets than be here right now."

"It is 1055 hours, and I'm wagering you too had a dream before that U.N. meeting, and that when we were both asleep that thing implanted a disk in our brains."

"That seems like the most logical explanation, for yes ... like you, I had a similar dream and heard the same words as you when the voice spoke at the U.N."

Harold annoyingly states, "You might have told me that before. Instead, I felt like I was the only one caught in some mental mousetrap."

Nikolai smiles and says, "Well, here we are, about to host our dream voice as we suspected, but not where we suspected. It's almost cock-a-doodle-doo time, Comrade."

Harold nervously looks at his watch again. It is 1059 hours and approaching the time the voice claims it'll arrive. He silently wonders if the voice will reveal itself and display its true appearance. He wonders, will it be grotesque, misshapen, and perhaps even frightening?

As he struggles to remain calm and his breath comes in gulps, Harold once more rubs the side of his head, hoping that he won't become like some of the so-called victims of close encounters of the third kind. He doesn't care for the idea of being probed or examined by space aliens. He doesn't like that somehow this mysterious disk was implanted in his skull. As if chilled, he suddenly feels goosebumps race down his arms.

He's then shocked as the room begins to glow with a bright light lingering a few feet above the floor. Nikolai sits up straight and grits his teeth in anticipation. Harold's imagination runs amok and he's impulsively overwhelmed with a moment of fear. He imagines a great scimitar appearing from within the light like that of a reaper's sickle ... rapidly swishing it toward his neck and slicing away his head and the implanted disk as if he's a turkey at Thanksgiving.

Moments after the initial shock, reality kicks in and Harold watches as within the light there appears a large intimidating image. Estimating the ceiling height of the room they're in to be about ten feet, the creature, alien, and extraterrestrial being ... stands before them only a few inches short of being as tall as the ceiling.

Nikolai's eyes also focus upon the gradually clearing image, as each man is awe-struck when they behold the apparition that begins to slowly materialize before them. Besides its height of almost ten feet, its copper-colored body shimmers with an alien flesh that ripples up and down it like ocean waves. Its massive chest ripples with what resembles a curvy umpire's chest protector, except it is fleshy, and not an appliance. It appears to be wearing some sort of protective helmet.

To their complete astonishment, the shape of it resembles that of a block, with shoulders topped by multiple spike-looking appendages and a long body with flexible arms similar to the trunks of elephants, yet without the constraints of bone, elbows, or ligaments. Instead of hands, it has four long, nimble finger-like protrusions for feeling and grasping. Instead of legs, it moves quickly about the room with eight each, approximately three-foot-long, thick, muscular protrusions like octopus tentacles that grasp the floor. The constricting muscles and suction cups on the legs provide the alien with rapid mobility.

On apparently what Harold presumes is a rectangle space helmet with a clear visor there appears to be a large, bony head with an uncanny resemblance to that of the Moai statues on Easter Island. It has a long, broad brow, forehead, nose, wide nostrils, and a narrow slit mouth with thin lips. Inside the helmet, there's a pair of unblinking, large oval white eyes with cobalt blue pupils. What's most peculiar is there appears to be a clear liquid inside the helmet and a backpack-looking device that Harold believes to be some sort of containment for life support.

Harold and Nikolai notice a rhythmic exhalation of what looks like gray smoke evacuating the helmet every few seconds. Harold immediately relates that as being a gas expelling during its breathing process. Only, instead of it breathing the Earth's oxygen and nitrogen combination, he suspects this liquid it breathes might perhaps be something similar to hydrogen or some other gas.

The alien displays no emotions. Still, as big as it is, neither man seems to find it particularly threatening.

As the two men continue to observe their visitor, each begins to hear in their minds the voice that has become familiar to them these past few days.

"Professor Simpson and General Belinski, I know you can hear me, but none of the others shall, so we may communicate silently together. In your language, Professor, I am called, Rehtorb. My species comes from the planet we call, Nongam in the star system you call Orion. Ours is a far colder planet than yours, and our lakes and seas consist of what you named, methane. We travel upon the land but can live either there or within the seas. Although we have no lungs, our systems respire methane through a photo genetic type method, which is what fills my helmet so that I may survive here upon your world."

Realizing what they hear is by way of thought transference; Harold attempts to answer the alien by projecting thoughts via his mind. To his surprise, it works.

"Welcome, Rehtorb! Though I'm not certain why you've chosen us, the General and I are honored to be your Earthly contacts. I hope you understand that national leaders of our planet are concerned that your coming here might be an incursion and to use advanced technology to enslave or else destroy us."

Surprising Harold, Nikolai joins in the mental discussion, "Yes, that is an apprehension of my government as well. They wonder if perhaps your demands to destroy all nuclear weapons will leave the Earth vulnerable and unprotected."

Rehtorb mentally responds, "I understand those suspicions, but as I explained at the U.N., we are here at the bequest of the Creator, the Supreme

Being. We serve as His messengers. It is with His blessing that we and all life in the universe exist. Beyond your degree of scientific knowledge, our advanced technology is such that we could destroy your small planet in just a few moments, but that is not our intent or our purpose. Besides, we are not a warring species like you Earthlings. The Creator considers your planet to be a favorite among those present in His universe, but still, he mourns at your violent tendencies."

Harold queries, "Why may I ask, have you used your spacecraft and technology to capture the space station ... and what caused the vanishing of so many of our world's leaders?"

"No, it was not us that caused the vanishings, just the capturing and relocation of the space station as an example of our technical capabilities. It will be returned to its original orbit once this encounter between us is over. The Creator has made those other things happen. For what exact reason, we do not know."

Nikolai mentally asks, "We know it must be Him that caused the Moon to leave its orbit and traverse toward Earth, for only the divine could possess such power. Was it Him that also caused the newborns of our planet to have the marks of three dots on their heels?"

"Yes, that too was done by the Creator," responds Rehtorb.

Harold curiously questions, "By calling Him the Creator, do you mean, God ... as in the Bible's Old Testament God?"

"Yes, He is the same, having referred to Himself as, 'I am' in your Bible. I sense, Professor, that you are not a believer."

"Not entirely, I'm not ... or rather I wasn't, but with what's happening it's hard not to believe in the validity that something almighty is causing it." He then asks, "Although Orion is the closest star-forming region to Earth, it is still over 1300 light-years away."

He pauses and then inquires, "How long did it take you to get here, and what sort of propulsion is capable of vaulting your craft through space to navigate that vast expanse in your lifetime?"

Rehtorb replies vaguely, "That's a question we'd expect an intelligent scientist like you to ask. It was your Einstein who theorized the bending of light and the existence of what you refer to as 'wormholes.'

"Indeed, there are portals that exist in the universe whereby the vast distances between galaxies and inter-dimensional multi-verses can be spanned or eliminated, providing a means to reduce travel from what you call light-years down to only a few of your minutes or hours. As for our propulsion methods, we shall not reveal that to your kind."

Although his body is quite flexible, Rehtorb doesn't appear to have what might be called a waist. Harold notices a bronze-looking band around the lower half of his body that seems to vibrate and give off a wave looking like a desert mirage on the horizon.

He questions, "What is that metallic object around your body?"

Rehtorb provides a practical answer, "Since the Earth's gravity is about ten times that of our planet, we devised this band that helps equalize the pull on our bodies and allows us to defy gravity and travel amongst you. Its power source in such a small device, however, is only effective for around a few hours of your Earth time. After that, we'd fold in two and be squashed like one of you stepping on a small bug."

"Then be sure to monitor your time here and not allow that to happen," declares Harold.

"You see, Professor," he explains. "Our bodies are what you refer to as cold-blooded. We are no more immortal than your flesh and blood, yet our lifetimes are many times that of your species."

Harold then asks, "Just how long is your normal lifespan?"

"If I were to compare my lifespan to your Earth years, I would be approximately 423 years old. Unlike you, we require no supplemental food source. Space is a vacuum, but not empty or devoid of everything. Our bodies receive energy from absorbing the life-giving tiny particles called cosmic dust and elements like hydrogen and helium distributed throughout space. This applies to interstellar space also and all the previously mentioned particles making up what's known as the interstellar medium."

His thoughts pause a moment and he points at Harold with his long, fleshy phalanges.

"However, like you, the Creator also infused in us an immortal soul, which by what you refer to as faith and a life lived righteously... can and will be given an afterlife. When judged by Him to be worthy, we too will share in His eternal Kingdom."

That a being from outer space and another world presents this to Harold causes him to seriously consider the concept's legitimacy.

Rehtorb continues, "We have monitored your species since the comet collision caused the extinction of the dinosaurs. We observed your slow human progress from the stone age to your present civilization and ever-growing understanding of science and technology. At this stage in your development, because of your violent nature and the divisiveness of differing ideologies and religions, the Creator has experienced great unrest. There's a consensus throughout the cosmos by more advanced worlds, like my own, that have come to consider your planet's weaponry a menace to the universe."

"I agree that we have our problems, but the idea of destroying our world and killing off billions of our people is the very definition of barbaric," declares an annoyed Harold.

Rehtorb deflects that premise and states, "Accepting your premise of physical death being but a reality of life, the Creator prefers to think of it as a freeing of the soul; to dispense with those that are evil and reward those that are good."

Harold scowls and mentally transmits, "Perhaps freeing souls sounds merciful, but to kill off all those we know and love seems contradictory and savage for a divine being. Besides, you said He loves this world, so why would he stubbornly destroy it and everyone in it?"

Rehtorb responds, "We too understand love and cherish our offspring and families. Although many of your predecessors survived savage, cataclysmic wars and territorial disputes, your present-day development of nuclear weapons and nanotechnologies, plus the advancing use of space exploration as a weapon threatens to jeopardize and destroy your world by your own making.

"You've continually been in defiance of peace and it is only a word without meaning on your planet. Therefore, you've been given a simple choice by the Creator. Agree to allow us to disarm those weapons I mentioned, or prepare for your end."

"Nikolai transmits, "Must all nations agree to rid themselves of the weapons you described? Why not give those that do agree to disarm some sort of a pass for the effort?"

Rehtorb answers bluntly, "Once before, long ago, when the people of Earth became so foul and sinful, your Bible proclaims He allowed one family to survive a devastating flood that swept over this planet. Afterward, a covenant was made with humanity not to obliterate humanity again via a flood. If it happens again, there will be a deluge of fire from the heavens via lunar asteroids. That within the Earth's bowels will erupt also causing your demise. I cannot guarantee that the Creator would spare even one nation or individual if all do not agree to disarm."

Nikolai somberly tells him, "World peace on Earth has never been a reality and I suspect its mere folly to imagine that any unanimous agreement to disarm all nukes will be forthcoming. Besides, there are other practical, high-quality uses of nuclear power that benefit mankind."

"That type of usage," explains Rehtorb, "The creator does not challenge ... only the weaponry. I urge you to try convincing the world leaders to put down their stones, cast aside this weaponry designed to destroy life, and avoid the consequences that will follow should they not comply with the directive."

Harold sighs, "I sincerely hope ... yes ... and pray for our children's sake and all of humanity that it shall come about, but like the General, I have sincere doubts that it will."

Rehtorb forewarns them, "To make the urgency more evident, as well as presenting the Creator's unmistakable, awesome supremacy over the universe, there shall be over the next twelve days more displays of His might and capabilities.

"If after that, an agreement is not rendered and forthcoming, then by His hand shall you suffer the calamity of which you've been warned. The outcome is solely up to you. And let you not forget that chemical and biological weapons are to be included in that decree to dismantle those types of weapons as well."

He then issues yet another warning, "One more caveat, the Creator has informed us that a malevolent entity has entered the arena."

With that, the light brightens again and Rehtorb vanishes like a wisp of smoke. Harold and Nikolai again sit anxiously fidgeting in their chairs and exchanging blank looks, no doubt as their minds try to assess all that they have just witnessed and try to mentally absorb.

"Wait!" Harold cerebrally pleads, "There are many more questions I want to ask. Come back, please."

A few moments pass and he realizes Rehtorb isn't coming back. He rises and goes to pour himself a drink of cool water. Nikolai joins him and the two doleful figures stand quietly pondering all that transpired. All of a sudden, the opening of the door startles them to a more conscious state, as the national leaders come storming in with their accompanying subordinates. They all seem somewhat annoyed and confused.

One angry Army general declares, "So, the mysterious voice didn't show up after all. Are we supposed to find this amusing ... to draw us up here and waste our time to provide a diversion while his spacecraft and technologies have the opportunity to invade and destroy our nukes?"

Harold corrects him, "Wait! What are you saying? Didn't you all see him? He came as he said he would and we spoke with him ... mentally I mean. His name is Rehtorb and he's from a planet near the Orion Nebula."

Nikolai confirms it, "He's right! The alien was here and we communicated with him as Harold says. He told us that there will be other displays of God's power. If after them there is no unanimous agreement from all nuclear nations to dispose of their nukes and the other types of weapons, the Moon will continue its plunge toward Earth and destroy us all."

President Battle also seems skeptical, "Professor, we've been watching on the monitors from another room. We saw only the two of you nodding your heads and acting a bit glib in moments of intense concentration. No words were spoken and for certain, we saw no alien being."

In reading the cynical faces of those present, plus being frustrated and seeing that no one believes them, Harold and Nikolai manage to resist the urge to argue.

"So, what now, Mr. President? Have you and the other leaders here discussed nuclear disarmament? Even if you don't believe he was here and communicated with us, the risks of ignoring the warning he gave us at the U.N. will result in our world being destroyed."

President Battle hears the grumbling among the military men present. The Russian President commands Nikolai to come with him back to Russia. The leader of the Chinese contingent seems to want no more of being among the capitalists. He sneers and dismisses himself and his communist associates.

Nikolai mentally communicates to Harold that their leaders are incapable of understanding the truth. Harold agrees with him as he shakes hands with Nikolai, who then is quickly steered away.

Before leaving the room, through his interpreter the Russian leader expresses a warning to the British, Japanese, and Americans.

"My nation has much invested in the Space Station somehow stranded out there over your base. I suggest that you do nothing to compromise any of our assets thereon and allow us time to study a way to retrieve them without causing damage."

President Battle bristles, but keeps his head, "My government had nothing to do with the space station being brought here. Most certainly, we too and all those present have major investments in it. I shall issue orders that it not be disturbed and no attempts made to disassemble it ... by anyone."

Harold states, "If I may, Mr. President, Rehtorb said the ISS will be returned to its original orbit. I assume that providing an agreement on the nukes is forthcoming."

Nikolai stops near the doorway and confirms it, "Yes, sir! That is what it told us."

"Let's hope that's true and that this pattern of distrust and argument will decrease and all nations can work together to solve this dilemma," says a stoic, President Battle.

One of the Russian soldiers already went to the NCO dorm and retrieved Nikolai's clothing and luggage. Nikolai's given his parka and sunglasses.

President Battle addresses Nikolai, "General Belinski, please allow me to offer our apologies to you as well for the way you two were brought here. It had to be done discreetly, as this clandestine meeting was top secret."

"Thank you, Mr. President. I hope there comes from this expedition some real fishing and not just a case of drowning some worms."

The President smiles and shakes Nikolai's hand. The others exit the hangar and all those from Russia are herded out and toward their nation's jet to prepare for take-off. Nikolai lights up a cigar and looks back over his shoulder at Harold. He stops before entering the plane and waves with his free right hand. Inside the jet, he takes a seat and watches out the window. Harold's garbed in his parka and also waves back at Nikolai.

To his complete surprise, Harold hears words transmitted to his mind. "I'm sorry, Comrade, Russia's new leader is as smart as he can be ... unfortunately. He's like the whale, who when spouting off is in the most danger of being harpooned."

Nikolai's equally astonished when he gets a mental reply.

"Oh, how I long for the days when the only voice I heard in my mind was my conscience."

Harold then again has words run through his brain.

"Comrade Harold, I'm not your Jimmy Cricket, but either we are somehow still linked together mentally, or else I'm going nuts."

"Oh crap, I can hardly wait to hear what I'm going to be saying to myself next, and it's Jiminy Cricket, not Jimmy Cricket."

Harold smiles as he imagines himself cerebrally transmitting that silly message.

"Nikolai laughs and thinks, "Nope, it's me, Comrade, not Jiminy. Testing ... one, two, three. Okay, try this: If everyone in America rode a horse, you'd have a more stabilized nation."

"Nikolai? Am I dreaming? Is that you? Are we now able to communicate mentally as we did with Rehtorb?"

As the Russian jet revs its engines and bolts down the runway, Nikolai sends one more mental message to Harold.

"Apparently so, Comrade. Hi Ho Silver ... away! Be careful what you think from now on, for I might be listening."

He laughs, confusing the soldier sitting beside him that isn't aware of the joke.

Harold's amazed, "This must be some lingering effect from the disk implanted in our heads. So long, Comrade. I hope your President doesn't get us all harpooned. A man without reason or wisdom is as a sword in the hand of a fool."

Harold then turns to ask President Battle, "If you have nothing else for me, Mr. President, I should like to get my gear and have a return flight home to be with my children."

Having finished giving the Base Commander instructions for guarding the ISS, the President asks his staff if Air Force One is prepared to leave for Washington.

Assured that it is, he says to Harold, "Your gear's already onboard. We're leaving, Professor, and I'd like you to be my guest and come on board with us. After the crude way you were brought here, you deserve a more comfortable ride home. We'll land at Trenton so you can indeed spend time with your family."

"Thank you, Mr. President, I appreciate it."

Chapter 16

Once underway, Harold muses and admires the luxurious interior of this magnificent plane. He's escorted to a comforting lounge near the center of the plane, where he is served a cup of coffee and given a choice of entrees to eat from the lunch to be served. Though Harold does not favor his company, the CIA director comes to sit next to him.

The Director says, "So, how do you like being part of the inner circle, Professor?"

"I wasn't aware that I am."

"Come now, Harold, we both know that little charade you and the General pulled off back there was just an ill-conceived maneuver to keep yourself visible to the President and governing body of the party."

This accusation angers Harold and he sneers.

"Director, your pattern of ridiculing and disrespect of subordinates is the primary reason I left your covert agency. Of course, you weren't there then, but you've inherited that same arrogance and suspicion. Your kind erects walls around our nation instead of building bridges to allow for the options of peace. I no longer sail on that ship, but mister ... like it or not, we're now all in the same boat. So, for the record, what the General and I said back there is gospel and not a fabrication, and I don't give a tinker's damn if you believe me or not."

With that, Harold stands and strides away in a frenzy to find another seat away from the Director.

* * *

On the Fox News Network, there's a special program viewing with four expert panelists and a moderator discussing nuclear weapons.

The moderator speaks, "Gentlemen, thanks for joining us on this program. As we all know, there has been a directive given by a mysterious voice that is presumed to be from an alien being that a global nuclear disarmament agreement must be reached within the next thirteen days.

Being that you're all experts on this type of weaponry, please help us understand more about the strength of such bombs and what effects a nuclear explosion has on human beings."

Dr. Ralph Zukor explains, "Those unlucky enough to be in the immediate blast range would receive flash burns and radiation heat from the shock possibly causing them to incinerate and vaporize. Farther away, there would be serious burns and mechanical injuries from the destructive blast wave. Others farther away that might be in the radiation fallout zone would likely develop radiation sickness leading to cell damage, cancer, or death."

Dr. Carl Hughes says, "There are different types of nuclear weapons and devices. For instance, atomic bombs like the ones dropped on Japan in World War II were fission devices. The far more powerful hydrogen bombs use fission to power a fusion reaction. Therefore, an atomic bomb is used to activate a hydrogen bomb."

Dr. Zukor declares, "Then there are the many other devices such as the neutron bomb designed to kill living organisms, the salted bomb that acts as a doomsday weapon designed to produce a large amount of radioactive fallout, which could extend outward and spread globally.

"Then there's the nuclear device that's known to produce EMP, an electronic magnetic pulse. A nuclear explosion high in the atmosphere over the U.S. would disrupt all electronic equipment, cause massive blackouts of the electric grid, and instantly disable any vehicle with an electronic ignition system ...which is almost every automobile on the roads today. It would disrupt all cell phones, computers, and television reception, interrupt all commerce, and essentially throw us back into the horse and buggy days.

"The bottom lines being ... that all nuclear weapons are far too dangerous to even consider using, which is why I pray that every nation that has them in their arsenal will heed the warnings given by that alien voice."

* * *

Harold waits till things settle down a bit inside Air Force One before finally getting hold of an attractive young, female Presidential aide.

"Pardon me, Miss, but if I may ask, is there a way I can communicate with my son and daughter in New Jersey? By now, they must be really worried about me, so if possible, I'd like to call them."

"Yes, Sir! There is a line we can let you use, but I must get the President's okay before allowing it. If you'll wait here, I'll go ask him."

Harold nods politely and takes a seat nearby, "Most certainly, and thank you so much."

A few minutes later, the aide returns and motions for Harold, "Sir, if you'll follow me, I'll take you to the communication area of the plane. They'll place a call for you from there."

Harold smiles and follows the woman into a private area of the plane overflowing with all sorts of high-tech equipment, video monitors, several computers, and no doubt other clandestine-like machines that he assumes contain, and disperse top-secret information. The woman taps one of the men assigned to work this area and he turns and looks at Harold. He hands Harold a headset with a microphone. Harold slips the device over his head and adjusts the microphone in front of his mouth.

"What's the number you wish to call, Sir?"

Harold states the number, which the man dials from his console. Harold then anxiously anticipates hearing Morgan's or Ted's voice. Morgan is the one that answers.

Looking for, but seeing no listing of who's calling, she answers briefly, "Hello!"

"Hello, Morgan! It's me, Dad. How are things in Trenton?"

A relieved Morgan falls back into an armchair, "We're fine, Dad. We've been worried sick about you. Is everything okay? Where are you, and when are you coming home?"

"I'm alright, sweetheart. We're on the way home now, but it'll be a few hours yet."

"I hear a loud humming noise. From where are you calling?"

"You wouldn't believe me if I told you. This is the first real chance I've had to call since the U.N. meeting was dismissed. I'm calling because I knew you'd all be worried about me."

His voice cracks, "Listen, I have to go now. Get some rest and we can catch up when I get home. I'll call when we land."

"Alright, Dad. We love you and will see you soon."

"Goodbye, Morgan. I love all of you as well."

Harold's line disconnects and he hands the head-phone back to the man at the console. He thanks the man, and the aide, and then satisfied that Morgan and Ted know he's alright, returns to the seat he left when following the young woman.

* * *

A couple of hours into the flight, Harold is summoned by the same female aide.

"Pardon me, Professor, but the President would like to speak to you in his onboard office."

Mildly surprised, Harold states, "Very well, you lead and I'll follow."

Harold wonders why the President wants to speak with him, and though not nervous, he is curious.

The aide leads him toward the section of the large plane where the President has a private office area equipped with direct access to communicate with his staff and even other nation's leaders. There, he's able to conduct business and make known his decisions while in this flying White House.

As Harold follows her, he passes a young naval officer seated alone in a chair a few feet away from the President's office. Harold notices the metal briefcase in the officer's lap and that it is handcuffed to the officer. It's then that Harold realizes what the man is holding. Although he's heard of it, this is the first time Harold's seen the briefcase called the 'Nuclear Football' that holds all the codes that the President can unlock to order the use of the nation's nuclear weapons. A sudden feeling of great discomfort overcomes him as he contemplates the power held within that small briefcase.

As Harold is led into the office, the President stands from behind his desk and greets his guest.

The President tells the aide, "Thank you, Margaret."

He points to a chair across from his desk.

"Please have a seat, Professor."

Harold forces a smile, sits, and notices the folder the President lays down on the desk.

The President sits and shuffles some of the papers in front of him.

He states, "I hope this flight has been comfortable for you."

"Yes, Sir! This is a remarkably lavish plane offering many more conveniences. I thank you, Mr. President, for allowing me to phone my family. As I thought, they were worried about me and relieved to know that I'm okay and coming home."

"That's great! The President replies. "My wife and family are also glad I'm returning to Washington."

He pauses and then taps his hand on top of the papers he's been reading.

"I've just been reading more about you, Professor. You are a very interesting man indeed."

Harold raises an eyebrow and asks, "Is that a dossier on me, Sir?"

"It's the vetting report done before and during the time you were assigned to the CIA."

"I see," states Harold. "I wonder if it's as complete as the one the Russians did on me before General Belinski met with me in D.C.?"

"They did that?" he chuckles. "I'm not surprised. At any rate, you've had a remarkable life and career."

He continues, "Your parents were immigrants from Poland. They moved to Alabama in 1964 and you became a naturalized citizen. As a high school salutatorian, you received a full scholarship to the University of Alabama, where you graduated magnum cum laude with a degree in physics. From there, you attended Princeton and received a doctoral degree in advanced nuclear physics and astrophysics."

Harold listens politely but is curious about where all this is going.

The President continues, "Although you wanted to teach, in 1989 at the age of twenty-nine you were recruited into the agency. Though not a field agent, you were a liaison to many agents that were; whom you worked with on numerous top-secret projects over the next sixteen years. You received numerous accolades for your distinguished service and meritorious awards. Our nation thanks you for your devoted service."

"It was an honor to serve my country in such a manner, Mr. President."

"In 2005, you retired from the agency and followed your dream to become a college professor at Princeton. You have had numerous accomplishments in the field of astrophysics and have assisted our nation when dealing with proliferation agreements with other nations that have nuclear weaponry."

He lays down the papers, sighs, and then stares at Harold.

"In short, Professor, you're a lot smarter man than I am ... and I'd like to get your expert opinion on how we can best approach others to resolve the dilemma of coming to a unanimous agreement to ban nuclear weapons."

Harold breathes deeply and chooses his words carefully.

"I indeed assisted others with the wording and methods of disarming nukes, but I'm no politician, Mr. President. Besides our own country, I've no connection to any of those other seven nations that have had detonations of nuclear weapons. Of course, Israel might as well be listed as one of them too, plus who knows how many nukes might be in the hands of terrorists as well as those known to be lost at sea or otherwise unaccounted for by terrorists or other of our enemies. However, it's common knowledge that between them, the U.S. and Russia possess over 90% of all nuclear weaponry."

"Yes, all that's true, but I want your input on how we can go about solving this problem in the next twelve days."

Harold is straightforward, "As I told you before, either those other leaders come together as a whole to agree on banning nukes, or as Rehtorb told Nikolai and me ... the Moon will again ascend toward Earth and all will perish. If they or anyone refuses to comply, they'll be committing suicide and take all of us with them."

"Do, you still contend that the alien was there at the airbase ... and that he appeared before you, and then spoke to you and the General telepathically?"

"You have my word of honor on it, Sir. He did indeed and these disks in our brains allowed that. Unlike any of you or even that video camera, we were able to speak to him and see him."

The President exhales deeply and crosses his arms. He leans back in his chair, glances out the plane's windows and seems momentarily lost in thought. He slowly exhales a long breath, and then he turns toward Harold and leans forward.

He tells Harold, "I believe you, Professor. In your communication, did it ... rather did he mention what happened to my friend, President Garrett, and the other leaders? What did he do with them?"

"We did ask about that, Sir, but he claims the Creator did that and not them. He also said he has no idea where they were taken or if they're alive."

The President grimaces, and then remarks, "I'm reminded of a quote by a famous leader that once said, politicians are the same all over. They promise to build a bridge even when there is no river."

Harold smiles and answers, "Yes, Sir! I remember when Nikita Khrushchev said that. He was a blustering bully, but also smart enough to know when to back away from a nuclear confrontation."

"Indeed, he was. I hope his new predecessor will be also."

He then places both hands on the desk and looks Harold sternly in the eye.

"What all did you learn about your Russian friend, the General? Did you know that he was on the plane when the Russian President disappeared?"

"No, Sir ... I didn't."

"He was later questioned about the incident by the Central Committee and Politburo. When they asked him if he knew what caused the disappearance, he told them he had no idea. When one committee member asked him what he'd done about it, he simply replied, "I yelled, 'Man Overboard."

Harold chuckles and remarks, "Yes that sounds like something he'd say."

The President smiles and asks, "You like that big Russian, don't you?"

"Yes, Sir, I do. He's an honorable, intellectual, and talented man ... one with a sense of humor and a lot of common sense."

"Then I hope the two of you working together will help to swiftly bring all nations to the table to reach an agreement. I'll see to it that the General and you have whatever assets and assistance you'll need from our two governments."

"I'll do my best, Mr. President, but I do first need some rest and to be with my family for a few days."

"Yes, of course. I understand that need. Take a couple of days, and then I'll send for you."

He then tightens his lips and raises his eyebrows.

He solemnly states, "As a child, I believed in Santa Claus. When I was ten, I no longer believed in Santa. Now that I'm an older adult, I became Santa to my grandchildren. In a way, I am also the reluctant Santa to the over three hundred million of our nation's citizens that expect me to bring home in my magical sack a joyful surprise for them to place under the tree of life and hope. I'm sad, Professor, for my sack of toys, is empty and I've no gift for them."

Harold clears his throat and says, "I believe in you, Sir."

"Thank you, Professor. I just feel so frustrated. The other two nuclear powers at that summit meeting were akin to turtles laying in the middle of the road, subject to being run down and squashed by both lanes of traffic."

"Yes, Sir! The turtles better move out of harm's way, or we'll all be squashed."

"Although several of the Pentagon Chiefs urge me not to, I'm calling for the nine nations known to have nuclear weapons to have another U.N. summit in three days, petitioning that all nine agree to the terms of the alien."

Harold's pleased to hear that and he thanks the President.

He then adds, "One other thing, Sir. As we told you before, Rehtorb stated that the Creator will be displaying more proof of His almighty power in the next thirteen days. Although I've been a skeptic and never truly accepted the idea of an almighty, omnipresent deity, the deviated lunar events and other inexplicable actions in the past few days have caused me to seriously reconsider that possibility. Therefore, Rehtorb's revelation makes me cringe when I think of what other disruptive episodes might be forthcoming."

The President replies, "Ordinarily, I wouldn't be too concerned over some prediction of a future event, as I don't put much stock in fortune-telling, but that was before witnessing the power of God and His unbelievable supremacy, plus the advanced, incredible technology of the aliens."

"Yes, Sir! It is amazing. I am encouraged by the fact that his species is attempting to help us rather than rule over us."

"Speaking of this Rey—"

"It's pronounced, Rehtorb, Sir."

"Yes, since you two were able to see him, what is he like? Is he humanoid or of some other form?"

As Harold specifically describes Rehtorb's species and features, the President listens and seems astonished by the revelation.

"Well, he certainly seems to be an amazing specimen of God's handiwork. I find it fascinating and encouraging that he detailed the fact that despite our variable physical differences, his race also has an eternal soul and that God is the Creator of both our species."

Chapter 17

A few hours later, Air Force One begins an ascent into the Trenton-Mercer Airport. As it approaches a landing, Harold's relieved to know that his cell phone works again. He immediately dials Morgan to let her know he's arrived.

She anxiously answers the phone, "Hello, Dad! Are you getting close to coming home soon?"

"Yes, sweetheart, we're soon landing at the Trenton airport."

"Wonderful! We'll leave right away and come pick you up."

"Great! I'll see you then. I might still be on the plane when you arrive, so be patient and I'll come out as soon as possible."

As Air Force One pilots steer the huge jet to a stop on the six-thousand-foot runway, Harold unbuckles his seat belt and stands peering out of the windows. The plane sits on the tarmac for almost twenty minutes before taxiing toward a nearby gate.

An anxious Harold notices though that it does not pull up to the gate. The engines are idle, but not shut down. Instead, a ramp is rolled out to the plane and the front exit door is opened. As Harold prepares to deplane, he is first met in the aisle by the Secret Service Agents, followed closely by several others, and then the President.

"Professor, I have just received news from NASA that the ISS has been returned to its previous orbit and that all systems on it seem to be working," states the President.

Harold nods and says, "It's good to know that Rehtorb kept his word about that."

"Yes, it is. I feel confident that what he told you and the General will also be truthful and happen. Let's hope this all comes to a peaceful end instead of the end of everything."

Harold nods in agreement with him and again bends to look out the windows. Four Secret Service Agents deplane down the ramp and stand vigilantly, as the President walks Harold to the door. The two men vigorously shake hands.

The President glances out the door and asks, "I'm told that you were able to call your family. Are they coming to pick you up?"

Harold glances out the doorway into the terminal. There, he sees Ted guiding his sister and the other two toward the large window overlooking the airport's gating area. He sees Morgan's hand fly up to her mouth and a huge smile breaks out on Ted's face. Turning to the President he thanks him and starts down the ramp.

He hears the President's final remark, "I'll have my aides send for you in two days. Enjoy your time with your family."

Once Harold reaches the asphalt, he races across the distance between him and the door to the terminal. One of the agents stops him just before he opens the door and hands him the suitcase he'd forgotten. He grabs it, smiles, thanks the agent, and then rushes in to be met by the loving embraces of his kids and their spouses.

Morgan's eyes fill with happy tears, while Ted's jaw drops as he notices the smiling President waving at them from the doorway of Air Force One. Harold hugs Morgan, Ted, and his in-laws. The agents return to the plane, enter it and the ramp is removed by airport personnel. In but a minute or two, the big jet taxis to the runway for take-off. Morgan, Steve, Ted, and Rita all watch in awe as the jet revs its powerful engines and rises into a glorious, all-rosy, and salmon-pink oncoming sunset.

Morgan comments, "Wow, Dad! Air Force One. What other surprises have you got for us?"

Ted grins and comments. "Yeah, that's super cool. Where have you been and why were you brought home on the President's plane?" He then takes Harold's suitcase, "Here, Dad, I'll carry that for you."

Harold's face glows with joy and he gathers the four of them into his arms and kisses each one on the cheek.

"I'll explain all about it later, but for now let's just go home."

"Have you eaten, Dad? Rita and I prepared a nice dinner for us," declares Morgan.

"I had a light lunch on the plane, but my appetite's always ready for one of your home-cooked meals," remarks Harold.

As the sun sets, the few thin strips of clouds on the horizon turn a shimmering gold. As the foursome turn to leave, they do not notice that two snooping newsmen took videos and were snapping photos of them through the large window when Air Force One pulled up toward, but not into the terminal. They recorded as President Battles shook hands and waved goodbye to Harold and his family.

* * *

In the car on the way home, Harold's head is still spinning with images from the U.N. meeting, the suspended ISS, and mostly of meeting Rehtorb as well as the President. Morgan and Ted have a myriad of questions they toss at him, but mainly he shuns being too specific about all that happened, especially avoiding any mention of meeting with the alien. Though he understands their curiosity, he prefers to offer them hope instead of causing them more worry by stating the imposed deadlines for nuclear agreements.

Once at home, Harold joins the four of them in a relaxing few moments before Morgan and Rita excuse themselves to set the dining room table for the meal they prepared. Harold silently wonders if Nikolai is experiencing the same joyous feeling of being reunited with his family. He attempts to communicate mentally with him but to no avail. He rationalizes that it's probably the distance between them that prevents it. He can't keep his mind off the fact that in a couple of days he'll be summoned to D.C. by the President.

Despite being mindful of that bittersweet reality, he endeavors to make this short visit with his kids a true celebration and a grateful time together with them. These four are living blessings and sunshine that warm his heart and bring harmony to his life. He cherishes the close connection he has with Ted and Morgan, whose presence helps him draw blissful memories of times they all shared with his beloved Elisa. Among them, he rediscovers and preserves precious treasured moments.

As Morgan calls them all to the table for dinner, they all gather, find their places, and sit. With the top sirloin entrées, side dishes of veggies and salads, plus wine glasses filled with a fine merlot, Morgan taps his glass with a spoon and directs their attention at Harold. Knowing that Elisa always insisted that the protocol before family meals required a bowing of heads and saying grace, asking God to bless the meal. Knowing this, Harold bows his head and they all join hands.

"Dad, it's wonderful that we can all be together during these trying times. If you would, please say a blessing before we partake of this meal."

Harold's startled by this and his head jerks upward as he stares at Morgan. All through the years that she and Ted were being raised, either Elisa or Morgan always said grace before meals. His lips tighten and he swallows hard, as his brain tries to recall some of the words and praises that both of them were so gifted at presenting. He stares at Morgan's pleading eyes, knowing she is anxious to hear him pray, something she's never seen him do at home or in church.

Harold gathers his thoughts, "God ... I want to thank you for this meal ... I love all those seated at this table. We appreciate that we are together as a family in these troubling times. See us through these trials and help us face the music, even if we don't like the tune."

He then pauses and they all notice tears beginning to trickle down his cheeks,

"For most of my life, I thought that Christianity and faith in a Creator was a falsehood and crutch, but now ... I realize I was wrong and express my gratitude to you for these my children ... and their belief."

He stutters, but finishes his first prayer, "And ... for helping me realize it was me that was the spiritual cripple, and not them. In my lifetime of denying your existence, it took but a miraculous moment of clarity for the conversion of my soul, and for that, I am humbled and thankful. Help us, Lord, for our future depends on what we do now in our present. Amen!"

There is a deafening silence at the table and all eyes are on Harold as he raises his head. Ted breaks the ice and reaches for his wine glass. Smiling, he lifts it toward the others.

"I propose a toast ... to my father, who once told us about a little girl that when asked where home is, she replied, 'Where Mother is.' That's true, but I would add to that now by declaring it's also 'Where Father is.' Here's to our, Dad, whom we love with all our hearts."

With misty eyes all around, they clink their glasses in a toast and partake of the wine. Harold's face delights in this loving and tender moment..

"Thank you, all. Let's hope He heard the prayer and that there is a good outcome to our predicament."

He adds some brevity to the occasion by saying, "Okay, in this glorious gathering let us linger no more, for suddenly I'm as hungry as a horse."

They all laugh, begin passing platters of food around and then partake of a fabulous family meal. Afterward, although Harold seeks to help with the dishes, he is urged into the den where he, Ted, and Steve all locate comfortable seating and chat. Steve describes Morgan's day on the lake.

"She caught a fish and got so excited that I had to help her reel it in. That darn thing almost weighed eight pounds. Even I haven't caught one that large. I wanted to keep it and have it mounted for her, but of course, she insisted on releasing it back into the lake. So, I did."

Harold grins and declares, "Yes, when she was a kid, I had to do that with the small sand bass that she'd catch when I took her river fishing with me. Her mom was the same way."

* * *

After playing an extended game of Monopoly with the four of them, Harold congratulates Ted on dominating the others by him placing hotels on Board Walk and Park Place, thus bankrupting all those that landed on those valuable properties. Enjoying the diversion helps calm Harold's nerves. Afterward, he and the others sit and watch the local news coming on the television.

To their surprise, the lead story of the news report from the airport shows the videos and photos the reporter and a colleague took of Air Force One landing there. The reporter introduces the video and explains to the News Anchor and viewers what's happening.

"Yes, Bill, we were at the airport to interview the mayor after his scheduled arrival at Trenton-Meyer. We'll show you that interview later, but before his flight landed, we were amazed to see this huge Boeing 747 land and taxi toward Gate 5. It didn't take us long to realize it was Air Force One. When it stopped on the tarmac and several men departed, we presumed they were with the Secret Service and that President Battle must be onboard.

The video then zooms in on the open doorway, where he describes who is inside the doorway.

"There in the doorway, you can see President Battle shaking hands with a man that then turns and walks down the ramp toward the terminal. After an agent gives him his luggage, he's seen inside meeting what we assume is his family. The video notices the President waving, and then the men rejoin the plane. The ramp is taken away and Air Force One takes off for what we believe is a return flight to Washington D.C."

Bill, the News Anchor asks the camera crew, "If you will, please put up the photo of the man shaking hands with the President. I understand, Phil, that you have identified him."

Phil replies, "Yes, Bill, he's Professor Harold Simpson, an astrophysicist that teaches at Princeton. He was the leader of the physics team that presented the video at the U.N. Security meeting the other day. We can only assume by his being on Air Force One that he's been working with the President in solving the issues mentioned there about disarmament of nuclear weaponry and other biological and chemical weapons. In checking with sources at the Pentagon, we were informed that there was a contingent of foreign leaders and ambassadors from several nations that were having a top-secret, hastily scheduled meeting at an undisclosed remote location to discuss the possibilities of nuclear disbandment."

I see! And it's good that he's one of our own, so let's pray that he's able to make headway in achieving that task."

"Yes, we were going to approach him and ask him about any progress on that front, but it was obvious that this wasn't a good time to do that. He looked tired and was sharing time with his family, so we allowed him that."

"That's understandable. Perhaps he'll consent to an interview when it's more convenient for him to do so."

Harold raises an eyebrow and notices the others staring at him as if awaiting his response.

"Is that true, Dad?" Ted asks, "Is that where you've been since Tuesday?"

"Yes," says Harold. "A Russian general and I were asked to come there, where we were questioned about the alien and the consequences of ignoring the directives, he gave to those with nuclear weaponry."

A nervous Rita asks, "And was there progress in the nations complying with that demand?"

Harold confesses, "That situation is pending, but the alien came and spoke there too, warning that the Creator, as he calls Him, will cause more displays of His power and command that all nukes be destroyed."

"What type of displays, Dad?" Morgan asks.

Harold is hesitant to tell them everything he knows for fear of sending them into a panic.

"We don't know, but after what I've seen at the airbase and with the Moon, I expect whatever it is to be quite astonishing ... and hopefully convincing"

A pent-up flood of emotions bursts forth from Morgan and Rita as the two of them slump in their chairs with worry etched upon their faces. Ted and Steve seem more agitated than worried.

Ted proclaims, "If the lunatics in charge of our world can't see the choice is obvious ... and agree to disband their nukes we should all revolt and make certain it's the decision that's made. In court, we would describe this as a slam dunk, open and shut case with but one obvious and rational verdict."

A few hours later as the girls are ready for bed, Harold decides to get some fresh air. Ted joins him. They stroll outside onto the veranda in his backyard. It's a cloudless night and the stars are brightly shining. Each takes a seat in one of the plush cushioned, outdoor patio chairs. Harold then glances up at the nearly full moon gleaming down from high above. Silently, he wonders where Rehtorb is at this moment and what he's doing. Although he attempts to connect with him, his efforts to do so fail.

Harold leans back and remarks to Ted, "You mentioned the lunatics involved with resisting the decisions to disband nukes. Indeed, there is apparent lunacy about it all. In Europe during the Middle Ages, there was the so-called, 'Transylvania lunar effect,' of the full moon when it supposedly transformed reasonable men into werewolves. I know that's only mythical folklore, but lunatic behavior is presently causing insane, violent, aggressive, indecision based on suspicion, distrust, and seeking to sustain an offensive and defensive posture ... even when faced with impending disaster. I fear that we can argue the matter till we're blue in the face ... and as we used to say in

Alabama ... till the cows come home, but I feel we're just be whistling into the wind."

Ted smirks, "Yes, I recall that slang term you taught Mom that she sometimes used on us when she got mad. She'd then assert, "Arguing with you kids is like hollering down a rain barrel."

Chapter 18

The next morning, a weary-eyed Harold rolls out of bed. He glances at the alarm clock on the nightstand that declares it's after 9:00 a.m. However, Harold notes that it is still dark outside, so the clock must be wrong. He yawns, stretches, stands, and goes into the bathroom to relieve his bladder. As he does, he hears the sounds of conversation coming from downstairs and wonders why the others would be up before sunrise.

Gathering his robe and slippers, he toddles down the stairs and into the kitchen where he's surprised to see all four of them sitting at the breakfast table and watching the news on the wall-mounted television set.

He again yawns, and notices that they're all fully dressed.

He inquires, "What's going on kids? Why are you all up so early and why have you dressed already?"

He notices the somber expressions on each of their faces. Morgan points at the kitchen wall clock. He turns his head and looks at the clock, which like his alarm has the time at 9:33 a.m. He sneers and looks back at Morgan who shakes her head and sighs.

"Dad, it's not early. It's after 9:00 a.m. and it's still dark as night outside."

Ted adds, "They say on T.V. that it's dark all around the world and that there is no sign of the sun. Temperatures across the globe are already falling well below normal."

Stunned by this news, Harold backs up to a chair. He then drops down into it. He tries to wrap his foggy mind around the possibilities. He cannot fathom that the world has stopped revolving and most certainly how is it possible for the sun to disappear? Such a thing isn't feasible by any alien technology ... is it? No, of course not. The only answer is it was caused by the Creator ... the Almighty Himself. Is this then the first of the events predicted by Rehtorb?

Morgan interrupts Harold's musings, "Dad, the news says that there is widespread panic across the globe. Wall Street closed due to the sharp tumbling of stocks and people are rioting, looting, and burning buildings and other property. They're demanding their leaders comply with the alien's commands. Religious fanatics are carrying signs declaring it's the end of the world, and churches are holding candlelight and prayer vigil services. That's where we're going now, to Saint Thomas' cathedral. Will you come with us?"

Harold's mind is racing and he becomes agitated.

"No, I must get in touch with my colleagues at the observatories and the President. We shouldn't wait on getting the leaders together to agree. This powerful display of God's has to awaken the sensibilities in them that we must comply as directed."

Morgan stares intently at her father for a few seconds and then nods her head in agreement.

"Alright, Dad. There's bacon, eggs, and toast that I made for you in the microwave. We'll go pray for our world and light a candle for Mom. I fear all these dangerous happenings may be the tribulation warned about in the Bible."

Not exactly sure what his daughter is referring to; Harold shrugs and embraces them all. Despite his shortcomings when it comes to religion, he's always known that Morgan and Ted's faith was bred into their psyches by their mother. Elisa made sure they lived by the precepts and principles she taught them as children, and thereafter they and she were always as one when it came to their belief in God and Jesus. He always felt a tinge of remorse, for he was the one unreliable factor that brought doubt into their otherwise orderly lives rather than reinforcing the concepts of faith.

When they break the embrace, Ted opens his coat to reveal a concealed holster and pistol.

He whispers to his dad, "Just in case we run into any violence and anarchy."

Harold nods and whispers back, "Be careful, Son. These are crazy times."

* * *

In Saint Petersburg, Russia, Nikolai, his wife, Katya, and his daughter, Anya, all are startled by the sounds of warning sirens going off in the city. It's 40 degrees outside and a chill wind is blowing. Nikolai glances at his watch. It is 4:00 p.m. and pitch-black outside. He stumbles to the window and pulls back the curtains. Below in the street, he sees the presence of military vehicles racing by and notices the myriad of people gathering outside with signs and placards of protest.

There are shouts of anguish and some are being arrested and restrained by armed soldiers. Others on the block are rushing to their windows to see what's causing all the sirens. Except for the street lamps and the headlights of the vehicles, plus an occasional flash bomb, there is complete darkness. Rioters are seen chunking bricks and rocks at the soldiers who have bloody wounds. There are also the sounds of gunfire. Nikolai cringes when he hears that.

Nikolai refuses to answer his phone, knowing that his superiors are attempting to contact him with orders to come in and direct the troops. He seems only interested in spending this time with his family during this crisis. His wife and daughter both seem terrified and they're watching television news that only heightens their anxiety.

His wife inquires, "What's going on, dear? The darkness, warning sirens, and gunfire indicate something awful is happening."

Nikolai backs away from the window and closes the curtains. His face is somber.

Dressed in his full uniform he tells her, "I expect at any moment they'll be knocking on our door and I'll be forced to report for duty. I'd rather stay here, but since that probably won't be an option, I want you both to know that I love you and that I'll see to it those rioting below will not get up here to bother you. Keep the faith and pray for our world."

His wife stands and embraces Nikolai, who wraps his arms around her and his daughter. They all join in the embrace. He kisses them each on the cheek.

His daughter asks, "How long do you think this darkness will last?"

"I wish I knew, but hopefully its effect will be to force our leaders to negotiate an agreement to ban nuclear weapons. Having heard what I did from the alien, I know that God wants to save our world, but the choice to do so is ours."

* * *

Harold attempts to contact John and Albert, but all the cell tower lines are busy and he can't get through to them. He has no better luck using the landline either. Now in his den, he switches on the television to get updates on the situation. The news he hears describes Earth's darkened situation, one that he already knows is critical and yet apparently is still not near as bad as it should be. According to the news, this darkness began in the far eastern areas of Russia when the sun did not rise there. That was more than nine hours ago.

Harold realizes that if the Sun disappears, the Moon, planets, asteroids, comets, and whatever else orbited the Sun ... retain their forward motion and fly off in a straight line into space. If that occurs, it would be thousands of years before Earth comes into the gravitational vicinity of another solar system ... if at all.

The worst of it would be that in the darkness, the world would become frigid with constant temperature drops. In just a few days, the world would be hundreds of degrees below freezing, which would freeze the atmosphere itself. That effect would fall to the ground and expose us all to the severe radiation of outer space. Harold knows that such a disaster is not what Rehtorb said would happen, so he prays this event, though incredibly dramatic, will not cause the world's end.

Like Nikolai, Harold expects the government and the President will be contacting him at any moment to find out if Rehtorb has been in contact with him or Nikolai. Harold silently wonders where the alien is and when he will again contact them.

* * *

Harold did not have to wait long, as an hour later and before Morgan, Ted, and the others return home from church, in a bright flash of light Rehtorb suddenly appears inside Harold's fifteen-foot-tall den. Still fascinated by the alien's odd appearance, Harold facetiously recalls an old slogan his dad used to tell him about a large neighbor of theirs in Alabama.

Harold's Dad would say, "That man's big enough to go bear hunting with a stick!"

To Harold, this ten-foot-tall alien surely suits that description. Harold waves vaguely at the alien and feels his mind being probed. Rehtorb's body seems aglow like a thousand fireflies are flitting about him as sparks are flinging off his body. Harold no longer takes for granted the normalcy of the world he knew, and instead now accepts this strange sensation of mental communication with this being from another world.

Rehtorb turns his attention toward Harold, who studies the alien with a serious and curious expression. No longer does Harold perceive Rehtorb as being an 'It,' but as incomprehensible as it seems, the alien is an intelligent, sentient being. With his lips valiantly compressed, Harold manages to focus his mind on what he wishes to express.

"Good evening, Rehtorb," he states mentally, "Welcome to my home ... although I've no idea how it is you manage to just materialize here or when you did at the airbase before."

Harold pauses, at least his mind does, but then his thoughts go on and he wonders about Nikolai and wishes he were here. It was odd how much he misses that husky, bushy eye-browed Russian and the smell of vodka and smoke from his Cuban cigars. He then realizes that Rehtorb has picked up on those thoughts that he let slip out. Harold licks his lips and prepares to ask a diminutive, mental question.

"I suppose this darkness issue we're dealing with is one of the four events you mentioned?"

"Yes," declares Rehtorb, "It is spectacular and exhibits the Creator's awesome power. Perhaps it's enough to convince your nations to comply."

Harold soberly answers, "I certainly hope so. I also hope that our sun reappears soon before all of us humans on Earth become frozen popsicles."

"This display I'm told will last another two days," pronounces Rehtorb. "At that time your Sun shall reappear. The Creator isn't going to allow the Earth to freeze."

"Thank you, I was hoping and praying that would be the case," replies a relieved Harold.

Rehtorb cautions, "Still, Harold, you must convince the others of your species that the Creator has eminent domain over this and all planets and stars in His universe.

"One other thing, Rehtorb," says a concerned Harold. "If darkness lasts for three days, plant life, crops, and other essential food sources will suffer from lack of light."

"Like the halting of your Moon toward Earth, while there is darkness the Creator has placed all plant life in stasis to prevent them from damage."

"Thank goodness for that," comments Harold.

Rehtorb comes closer and Harold winces a bit but remains still as the hulking alien stands over him. He reaches and with his long, limber finger-like appendages takes Harold's hand. Harold blinks as his mind begins to whirl and his vision of reality shifts.

"Close your eyes, Harold, and come with me. I've something to show both you and Nikolai."

Harold's mind drifts and he begins to doubt his own senses. He once again has a detached feeling of overpowering unreality. He blinks again and feels as if he's flying along, holding Rehtorb's hand as Wendy does with Peter Pan on their way to Never-Never Land.

Powerless, Harold's obliged to follow where he's being taken. Entranced by the surroundings whizzing past his mental vision, and then with wondering curiosity he peers into an approaching image of some strange swirling portal. He mentally hesitates, but Rehtorb's presence draws him into the gateway expressly opened to admit him through it into some unknown world. He's immediately aware of strange, exotic aromas that fill his nostrils and a sun-bright radiance that causes him to squint. Although seemingly traveling through the air like a bird, as he strains to see and make sense of all this, he avoids panicking, maintains his composure, and trusts Rehtorb to guide him safely in this unfamiliar new realm.

A feeling of great calmness and curiosity comes over him. His mind propels through this maze of the unknown. His eyes behold blurred visions and he has intervals of awareness that come and goes. He begins to recognize optical ports whereby myriads of star clusters seem to whiz past. Is it possible, he wonders, that he is inside some type of spacecraft? Is Rehtorb turning this dazzling mind trip into an actuality whereby this advanced propulsion turns science fiction into a reality?

Scanning carefully with half-closed eyes, he supposes they must be traveling at speeds well beyond that of light. His numb mind suddenly comprehends one other broken law of physics, for inside this enormous craft, if indeed his slowly increasing perception is correct, he is not weightless. There is no physical strain upon his limbs from whatever produces the gravity effectively now lowering him and Rehtorb to the floor of the craft. This delirium causes him no pain, but it's mentally discomforting. He has no comprehension of how much time is passing.

Still clinging onto Rehtorb's appendages, Harold begins to have lucid thoughts and a sense the craft is slowing down. The stars passing by the portals become less blurry. In his mind, he begins to hear the mental conversations of others coming from within the walls of this ship, if indeed that's what it is. The language he hears is incomprehensible to him, but Rehtorb knows what is said, for he responds to whatever voices transmit through their mind links. Harold experiences his body feeling very light and almost fluid, but his heart beats fast despite his apparent calmness.

He then has a moment of clarity and wonder, "Wait a second! Am I actually here in both mind and body, or is this some manifestation of projected mental images?"

Rehtorb answers for him, "You are physically present, Harold, within the bowels of the vessel my species uses to traverse the regions and firmaments of the universe. The quarters you are in are designated and designed to provide you with the proper amount of oxygen and nitrogen your body and lungs require for you to exist herein."

A doorway suddenly opens and almost a dozen helmeted aliens similar looking to Rehtorb all slither inside and surround Harold. Behind them, Harold is happily surprised to see a dozen more beings simultaneously escorting Nikolai into the chamber.

Harold telepathically greets his friend, "It's good to see you again, Nikolai. Are you alright?"

He replies verbally, "For someone that's been plucked from my Russian field office like an apple from a tree, I'm okay ... but I'm pretty sure we can't ring room service from here."

Harold adds, "For sure, we aren't in Kansas anymore!"

Rehtorb reminds them, "You need not converse orally while here, for your thoughts are sensed and known to us."

Harold's mind complies, "For a moment I forgot that. Hey, I thought you said you didn't cause all those vanishings of international leaders when it's obvious you do have the power of teleportation."

Rehtorb comments, "I didn't say we couldn't do it, I just said that we didn't."

Harold nods, "Come to think of it, you're right. Anyway, why have we been brought here, Rehtorb ... and where exactly is ... here? I'd ask how it is we came, but I expect I wouldn't understand it anyway."

Nikolai remarks, "In peering out the portals of this craft, I'm thinking we're in deep interstellar space and not on some virtual reality thrill ride at a Disney Park."

Rehtorb confirms, "We are approximately 7500 of what you call light-years from your planet on the backside of what your scientists deem to be the Carina Nebula."

"Hold on!" replies a startled Harold, "Are you saying we're 7500 light-years away from Earth?"

Nikolai groans, "Whoa! That's going to be one expensive taxi ride back home."

The other aliens look on but remain silent.

"We brought you this far to demonstrate our technology and to avoid any interception of our meeting by that malevolent entity I mentioned to you before."

"Yes, what is it that evil entity is attempting to do?" inquires Harold.

"We have no clear indication of its plans, but do know of the chaos and destruction it has caused elsewhere in the universe. We seek to keep private our transmissions to you. Our purpose herein is in keeping with the wishes of the Creator and revealing unto you some astonishing history of your planet and your efforts to help obtain an anti-nuclear weapon universe."

Nikolai asks, "That comment causes me to ask, are there other planets in the universe that also have nuclear weaponry capabilities?"

Rehtorb pauses before sending his mental answer to that.

"There were, but sadly two of those planets did not comply with the Creator's commands, so He destroyed them. Such is the reason both He and all of us want your planet to avoid the same fate and type of destruction."

Harold sighs and shakes his head, "He actually did that?"

"Yes, He most certainly did," affirms Rehtorb. "In another eon, your Bible states as I before mentioned to you, He became so displeased with humanity that he sent the huge floodwaters to destroy all but one family. He also sent fire and brimstone down upon the depravity and violent nature of those at Sodom and Gomorrah. He is a tolerant and forgiving Creator, but his patience with your world is growing thin."

Rehtorb has no chairs in the chamber, for his kind does not sit, but he offers a chair-like energy force to support them and urges them to become more comfortable. He also has one of the others fetch two glasses of water, brought from Earth, for quenching Harold and Nikolai's thirst. Once both men are in sitting positions and more relaxed, Rehtorb begins a soliloquy.

"You asked me before why did we choose the two of you. We did not. That was done by the Creator. In a way, you two have become like the two in your Bible named Moses and Abram, whom the 'Great I Am' renamed, Abraham. Moses saw a bush that did not burn and followed it up a holy mountain to speak with Him that created all. He told Moses, 'Take off your shoes, for you are on Hallowed Ground.' As was told to Moses by the Creator ... He considers the whole of your world to be Hallowed Ground."

Harold listens intently and his brow twitches with nervousness. His eyes swim across the amazing glory and strangeness of this incredible being. He assumes that Rehtorb has some special status and authority within his species.

Sensing Harold's thought, Rehtorb momentarily ceases his diatribe. He remarks, "Yes, Harold, I am what you might refer to as the magistrate of this mission and captain of this vessel."

Nikolai raises his water glass to Rehtorb, "Nostrovia!"

"And to you, Nikolai," replies Rehtorb. "As I was pointing out, you two are the chosen ones to receive the following disclosure. Being scientists, you will comprehend what it is I am revealing to you. Let me start by declaring that the book of Genesis in your Bible is divine dictation with the Creator explaining the beginning of Earth to Moses. You may speculate that He does so in an allegory and symbolism. I take it the way the "Maker" described it.

Nikolai then queries, "Wait, are you saying that there was an Adam and Eve and a Garden of Eden?"

Rehtorb states, "Of course, none of those among my species now were alive back then, but according to our archives and data, yes ... there was an initial seeding by the Creator of a pair of humans ... a male and female. As to the Garden of Eden, it is stated that the Earth they inhabited was wealthy with sustenance and flowed with purity and grace. Thus, the birthplace of humanity came about from the seeding of the 'Garden', which in reality may have been the entire Earth itself. "Accordingly, at some point, the Creator became disappointed at the two humans for disobeying Him and thus, sin came into your world.

Harold comments, "So, did there come upon our planet human beings from other galaxies and worlds much like your own?"

Rehtorb answers, "No, they were not from worlds like mine and not from other galaxies, just from the one you call the 'Milky Way.' The Creator will not allow inter-galaxy transport among the billions of other galaxies in the universe. The memories of those that were chosen to seed your world had memories of their past world and existence erased and they began a new life on Earth."

Harold says, "Evolution is a hoax, so God seeded the Earth with humans like us that came from other worlds that He created?"

"Essentially, yes, but He created and breathed life and a soul into them too," says Rehtorb. "In our galaxy, as many as a hundred million Earth-sized planets are orbiting in the habitable zones of sun-like stars. You may have heard of the Mediocrity principle that argues planets like Earth should be common in the Universe, and so they are. Those types of planets have liquid water and oceans, plus land surface and sub-surface, sunlight, oxygen, and nitrogen atmospheres, and multi-cell organisms with geothermal heat and earth-like conditions. The Creator harvested humans from those numerous planets.

"Those with fair skin and blue eyes were seeded among the lands where the Sun is not as intense. There came others, such as those with slanted eyes and darker skin to rein upon the land given to them known as Asia and the far northern lands of ice and snow. Your region known as Africa was seeded with a physically superior race with dark skin known to you as, Blacks. Arabia was sewn with brown skin humans that can survive desert climates. Other parts of the world were dispersed with what you call Hispanics. The one commonality among all these beings was that they were instilled with an eternal soul to be harvested upon their physical demise and judgment passed upon each one before entering the hereafter.

"Although over time some hybrids came into being and migrations ensued amongst some tribes, to each of these lands there came pioneers, sent into a new world to make of it their own. The Creator told them, 'Be fruitful and multiply.' Each of the domesticates brought with them their own languages and traditions from their worlds. They worshiped the God of the Sun and stars and have dominion over all other creatures here in your world. After the zoo-like large reptilian creatures known as dinosaurs were destroyed and their bodies covered up by the soils over millions of years where centuries later humans explored and extracted fossil fuels to use as an energy source. Thus, the Creator brought forth humankind."

Nikolai laughs and says, "That makes perfect sense. Did the diversity of plant life, animals, birds, fish, snakes, and insects arrive similarly?"

"Yes, each a creation of the Creator's infinite imagination and in the same manner, for the planets from where they came had similar climates and terra firma. Yours is mainly a water world, so a tremendous amount of abundant underwater life was transported to Earth. Even our cousin, the octopus was among those that were brought here and learned to survive in the seas.

"It is no accident that all the variety of plants necessary to sustain life is upon your world; trees to create shade, provide fruits, pulp and wood for housing, safe habitats for birds and various other animals, sap to make syrups and rubber, and beans to make chocolate and coffee. Even the rocks and soils contain elements and metals for making tools, dwellings of stone, and adobe. Some animals provided transportation, such as horses, camels, and even elephants. There are all manner of fowl to eat, plus cloven hoof animals, which became a main source of protein, like the cow, deer, elk, goat, sheep, antelope, and others. The seas and lakes teem with fish *to* eat, oysters, lobsters, shrimp, and crab. Colorful songbirds and majestic eagles, hawks, owls, and osprey fill the skies and forests. Fowl like the hen, quail, duck, goose, dove, and others are fruitful and provide humans ample food sources. There are winged creatures known as butterflies that like colorful flowers brightly decorate your natural world.

"Edible plants exist like the many varieties of garden vegetables, berry bushes, plus melon and grapevines. Even the rocks and ground itself are a treasure trove of gold, iron, silver, stone, copper, diamonds, gypsum, and other geometric elements placed here by the Creator.

"There are gases like helium, hydrogen, nitrogen, and other periodic elements that benefit mankind. All these and many more, such as the thousands of varieties of insects, microbes, bacteria, etc., plus the energy source from your Sun, fossil fuels, nuclear generators, wind turbines, solar energy, and hydro energy; all greatly boost Earth technology within the past two centuries.

"Yet, it also brought us to this moment in time when rendering to the Creator all nuclear weaponry and the horrid chemical and biological weapons must be done."

Harold inquires, "Am I being presumptuous in assuming that your species was responsible for collecting and transporting many, or even most of the foreign humans, plants, and animals to Earth?"

"We did transport several new species of plants and animals, but mostly the Creator himself brought all life here. Due to our nature of being resistant to radiation, our lengthened life spans, and the fact that we draw our sustenance from the energy of space itself, we and two other worlds with beings similar to our own were selected as cargo transporters, very much like the one you are inside of at this time," explains Rehtorb.

Nikolai, wearing his full uniform rustles through his pants pocket and retrieves a cigar case. He looks at Rehtorb, whose eyes reflect no emotion, and brings out a lighter from the other pocket.

Rehtorb holds up an arm and declares, "I suggest you not set that leaf on fire in here, General. This is a highly oxygenized cabin and it will cause an incendiary reaction."

Nikolai quickly puts his cigar away and apologizes, "Oops, sorry. It's a force of habit, but of course, you're right."

Rehtorb continues, "One other explanation is in order. We're told by the Creator that those recent newborns of your species have been marked with the dots so that if He must destroy your planet, those infants, plus their parents will be re-seeded onto other worlds, not unlike Earth, and they'll begin the seeding cycle once again. The Creator so loves your Earth that He sent His only Son to die as a ransom for your sins. Therefore, it is His and Jesus' wish that all be saved, now physically ... and later spiritually."

Nikolai, in deep thought, finds himself rubbing with his fingers at an old scar he sustained from a long-ago war injury. His index finger trails over a slight indention just under his brow line. He'd been grazed by a bullet and was fortunate that day that it ricocheted off his skull and didn't penetrate his hard noggin.

Rehtorb, sensing the two men are anxious to know when they'll be taken back home, turns to one of the other aliens nearby and gives him instructions in their language.

"We are almost done here. Set a return course for Earth. I wish to now escort our guests through parts of our vessel before transporting them back."

He then instructs another of his kind to bring forth a couple of backpacks and helmets. Once that is done, Rehtorb turns back to Harold and Nikolai.

He explains, "I'm sure you're curious about our vessel, so please allow my assistants to apply to your backs the oxygen life pack. After you've placed the helmet on your head, he will connect a line and open the valve so that you might breathe normally in the other areas of our vessel that I'm going to show you. Other gases you may encounter herein will not harm you, as long as you wear the helmet and life pack."

Harold and Nikolai do as they are told and soon each prepares for their tour. As large sliding doors open slowly, each man feels a chill, but soon gets used to the cooler air. The stone-faced aliens all follow Rehtorb's instructions and walk behind the two Earthlings. Once a second door opens, the view before them becomes extraordinary. Harold's cheeks tighten and his eyes open wide. The sweet, oxygen-rich air from the backpack enters through his nose and he's amazed at what he sees.

He's already imagining that some unknown element propels this massive craft, but he does not expect or envision the extremely long hallways with transparent panes that display the lake-sized aquariums filled with hundreds of aquatic species ... some unknown to him, and others like those found on Earth. A dozen or more kinds of sharks, beluga whales, sperm whales, killer whales, blue whales, stingrays, marlins, giant squid, turtles, eels, dolphins, and porpoises, plus too many species of smaller fish to name, crustaceans, mollusks, shrimp, and many other unknown species swim inside these huge aquarium tanks.

As they continue, they see sectioned-off into parcels many acres long all manner of small land animals, reptiles, birds, snakes, and larger predatorily land animals. Rehtorb explains that these terrariums and aquariums house a myriad variety of animals from several different worlds. Nikolai too is fascinated by the enormity of these "Ark" type exhibits. Rehtorb tells them the ship has four sections, the first being the one they are on now. The second section is one resembling arid Earth climates, plus other areas with lush valleys and fertile soils that grow fruit trees, grasses, and crops to feed the animals. The third section is halved into two parts. The first is a lush garden-like setting with thousands of plants, flowers, butterflies, ants, bees, wasps, numerous other bugs, majestic trees, freshwater streams, waterfalls, vines, and exotic animals like Harold and Nikolai have never before seen.

Rehtorb explains that the fourth section consists of the craft's piloting area, propulsion and gravity section, teleportation section, the crew's compartment, plus the navigation and engineering sections. He explains that it is only in that section that his kind can maneuver without helmets and life packs. It is mostly a fluid section filled with life-sustaining liquid methane.

All totaled, the guided tour takes over two hours. Harold is exhausted. Nikolai has more stamina and seems unaffected by physical exertion. The two are then led into the second part of section three on the third level where a mountain with snow on top has a cable-car-type lift operating at the bottom of it. Rehtorb motions for each to get in one of the transports, which they do. He gets into a transport behind them and begins to rise. The lift steadily climbs upward by cable toward the top of the tall mountain. Though expecting the air to greatly chill and become thin, making it hard to breathe, it remains a comfortable temperature and the height does not affect their breathing. At the summit, the lift stops, and all three shuffle off onto a platform.

The view from the summit reminds Harold of the Colorado Rockies and the expanse provides a view of what he imagines to be over twenty miles of scenic mountain tops. For a moment, he forgets they're inside a craft sailing through interstellar space. The most amazing aspect of it is that when Harold and Nikolai look upward, they see no Sun, but a bright, blue sky, just as if they were on Earth. Rehtorb motions for them to follow him, which they do into a resort-type building with an oval dome-shaped top. Inside, the bright blue sky disappears and the nighttime skies are lit up with stars ... as the craft has a transparent lens cockpit-type skylight about a hundred feet wide and long that amplifies and makes the stars visible. The interior is plush with sweet-smelling plants and herbs, some of which are very exotic and indefinable.

When Rehtorb waves at a lighted switch it clicks and a massive metal door opens where they can see inside. There in this vast cavern-like opening are hundreds of dwellings, streets, and familiar-looking neighborhoods similar to those on Earth. Some are more elaborate and futuristic than Harold and Nikolai have ever seen.

"This," Rehtorb explains, "Is where humans are housed while they are transported to their new worlds. They are clothed, fed, and have all the facilities needed to help them make the voyages that the Creator plans for them. No weapons are given to them and their degree of advancement is crude, so they must fend for themselves and build their new societies and civilizations from the natural resources available to them. For some, it takes many generations and thousands of years. For others, they learn much quicker and advance more rapidly."

Harold bristles a bit at this information, as he sucks air into his helmet and blinks his eyes.

He remarks, "So, those that are chosen to seed the other new planets, regardless of their status, affluence, or their world's technological advances ... on their new planet they must become primitives who have to grovel for food, shelter, and clothing to survive their new environs. That seems sort of like being abandoned on a deserted island."

"That analogy is not exactly as it is, for they are given enough sustenance to last for years, during which time they must learn to partake of the nourishment available to them in their new world. They learn the value of family and of toiling together to help carve out a new life devoid of wars and weaponry. In effect, they are somewhat like the indigenous tribes in your Amazon and other rainforests and jungles. The Creator chooses brave, faithful humans that are allowed to recall their religions and worship of an omnipotent deity that has for them a place when their physical struggles end."

Harold quips, "If God .is God, why does he need your help in removing and reestablishing these humans from other planets? He created them, why can't He do the same and just produce the new planet's races with His powers?"

"He could do that, yes ... but His will is His will and we simply carry out His instructions," replies Rehtorb.

Nikolai yawns and stretches. Rehtorb knows the two are tiring. He sends a mental message to the piloting area asking when they will arrive near the Earth.

"You may rest on the voyage back to your world. Two days will have passed since you left, so we shall return you both to Harold's home. Nikolai, we had your wife and daughter transported there also before leaving. They were notified of you being with us and are fine with knowing we'll keep you safe. Harold, your family is also aware that you two have been our guests. There is a U.N. meeting planned for tomorrow morning, at which time your Sun shall return. You will be expected to be in D.C. before noon, so we arranged for your early flights. All there at the U.N. will know of this time we have been together."

Rehtorb pauses and then announces the second of the Creator's coming displays of power.

"Among the Creator's major seeding of humanity on Earth upon a remote island in the south Pacific Ocean he placed a primitive tribe. From the air, one can discern that it is a delta-wing-shaped island where the current inhabitants have been evacuated. In three days, you should plan to visit that island, for the entire world will never have seen anything like what is about to occur there and to dozens of your famous world landmarks."

Harold ponders, "A delta-wing-shaped island in the Pacific?"

Nikolai asks a question, "Have any other kinds of advanced aliens sought to come to our planet ... who unlike you have plans to dominate or possibly conquer and take over our world?"

Rehtorb bluntly remarks, "In the past, thousands of years ago before your planet's population explosion there were other suitors whose motive it was to eradicate humanity from Earth and re-populate it with their species. The

Creator did not allow it, so the results of their efforts to do so were in vain and were forcefully ceased by my ancestors and those of a planetary alliance. Others who had interest and peaceful desires to co-exist with your species found the Earth too crowded, archaic, and too violent for their liking. There are, as I noted before, thousands of other more suitable and optional choices for integrating with humans on an exoplanet similar to your own."

"I see," projects Nikolai. "Well, crowded and archaic as it might be, to us it's still home. I was hoping you might swing us by your planet and give us a glimpse into what your society is like."

Rehtorb answers, "This was not an interplanetary trip and although we told you from which Nebula we derive, we prefer not to expose our world to anyone else. Remaining mysterious is one of the attributes of the Creator and we subscribe to the same philosophy."

Chapter 19

In what seems to be the passing of an hour or two, Harold and Nikolai find themselves transported back into Harold's guest bedroom downstairs. Harold's mind whirls and the same odd sensations he had before linger as his vision slowly begins to return.

Nikolai too has a similar reaction, sort of like a heavy sleeper being wakened and told to get up. They are alone and Rehtorb is gone, just as if he was a ghost and all that they saw and experienced was but a shadow of reality.

It is about then that each man realizes they still have on the helmets and oxygen packs they'd been given to use. Harold swoons but manages to stand and strain to remove the helmet and backpack. It tumbles over his head onto the king-size bed. Nikolai follows suit and does the same. Both men breathe heavily and their eyes lock onto the two items that seem much heavier now than when they were in the spacecraft.

Harold finally speaks, but realizes it isn't vocal but still a mental effort that he projects.

"Whew! For a few minutes there I wasn't sure if what we went through was real. Since you're here ... and these helmets and oxygen packs are too, I suppose it all did happen."

Nikolai starts to reply mentally, but instead clears his throat and says, "Yes, I suppose it was. May I pinch you to see if I'm dreaming? So, are we in your house, and if so, where are my wife and daughter?"

"They must be in the kitchen or den," remarks Harold vocally. "Give me a moment to gather my wits and we'll go find them."

"I know what you mean, Comrade. I feel like I've been in an accident where I had the right of way, but the other guy had the big truck."

After allowing their bodies to recover from the stress of space travel, they each plod down a hallway together where they find their families relaxing on the sofas and conversing in the den. The families are pleasantly surprised when they see Harold and Nikolai come casually strolling into the room. All but Ted is either sipping on coffee or hot tea. He's drinking a cold glass of milk.

Nikolai comments, "Milk! I've always wondered how a brown cow can gobble up green grass and still produce white milk."

Harold and the others laugh. He appreciates how Nikolai manages to make everyone feel more comfortable by injecting humor. The two excited families exchange hugs and greet one another. Harold introduces his daughter and son-in-law, plus his son and daughter-in-law to Nikolai; who in turn, performs the same honors and introduces his wife, Katya, and daughter, Anya, to Harold.

Morgan then tells Harold, "That alien brought Katya and Anya here from Russia—"

Nikolai interrupts, "About that ... exactly how did he transport you both here, Katya?"

"I wish I knew," exclaims Katya in English. "One minute we're sitting in our living quarters and the next thing we knew ... we're here in this house with these nice folks and a hulking alien gaping at us."

Anna adds, "I feel as if we've been removed and detached from reality."

Morgan continues, "Yes, for after we all got acquainted with his strange appearance and the fact that he just materialized here with Katya and Anya, we listened as he informed us that you both were going on a voyage with him into space. We were stunned by that news, by Katya and Anya's arrival, and by his weird form and the method by which we understood him.

"Still, he seemed friendly and sincere about keeping all of us and you safe. After he disappeared, we realized he hadn't been speaking to us, but amazingly somehow communicated with our minds."

Ted asks, "Were you transported back here in the same way as Katya and Anya? Where and how did you get on board an alien spaceship?"

"Well, as Nikolai said to me, it was one heck of a taxi ride. As I tell my students, be always eager to learn, even if you aren't certain of what's being taught. That's the case here, for we experienced things you wouldn't believe if I told you ... neither could you comprehend where we were or what we saw," declares Harold.

Nikolai's daughter has an intriguing Russian accent where she uniquely rolls her vowels.

She asks in English, "So, why were we brought here, Father?"

Harold's relieved but not surprised to know that Anya and Katya both speak English.

Before Nikolai can answer, Katya tells him, "As you know, things were getting very bad in Moscow and Saint Petersburg. The poor are still revolting against the establishment and the party leaders are not taking their protests well.

"Many of those that rebelled have been shot and either killed or arrested. In general, chaos reigns there now. Still, as Morgan and the others of us have been discussing, we may be no safer here, for the citizens of this country, as well as dozens of other nations, are experiencing turmoil, rioting, burning down buildings, looting, and marching on their capitols, revolting and demanding that nuclear weapons be destroyed."

Nikolai and Harold each find and sit in padded chairs near the two sofas. Nikolai withdraws a cigar from his pocket. He looks at Harold and waves the cigar in his left hand.

He says to Katya, "I'm sure the aliens brought the two of you here for a good reason … me too for that matter. I no longer try to guess their motives, only to accept that they are trying to help us." He sighs and asks Harold, "Do you mind if I smoke in your home, Comrade?"

Before Harold can answer, Nikolai's already removed his lighter and lit up, exhaling smoke rings throughout the den.

"No, I suppose not, Comrade," chuckles Harold.

Katya sneers and tells Harold, "My apologies, Professor Harold. He smokes so many of those dreadful cigars that when he kisses me … I suffer from nicotine poisoning."

Nikolai grins and replies, "I have to smoke, or else intelligent thought vanishes from my head as if it is in solitary confinement."

Katya facetiously scolds him, "And you lack only a few more obnoxious habits before that confinement may indeed become solitary."

Nikolai grabs her, they laugh, and then he hugs and kisses her on the cheek. Harold grins and then takes notice of the grandfather clock in his den striking the hour. He listens as the bong strikes ten times.

"My goodness, is it 10:00 p.m.?"

"Yes, Dad, it's almost bedtime."

He explains, "In space, we lost all sense of time, for it did not pass as we thought and days passed like hours. Nikolai and I had best retire for the night, as we're told that we must attend a U.N. meeting tomorrow in New York. Oh, and Rehtorb claims the Sun will rise again in the morning."

Steve remarks, "That's a relief, for people all over the world have been freaking out with all this darkness ... me included."

Harold adds, "Yes, and we hope light shall be cast upon that crucial vote tomorrow that will be taken ... and all nations will come to agree upon disbanding nukes."

Morgan tells Nikolai, "Anya can sleep in one of the downstairs bedrooms and use the hall bath. General, we have fresh linens for you and Katya in the upstairs guest bedroom. There's an on-suite bath and clean towels if you'd care to take a shower. Katya explained that suitcases with clean clothing were also transported here, but if you'd like us to clean and dry the clothes you're wearing, place them in the hallway."

Then she asks her dad, "What time should I wake you two tomorrow morning?"

Harold tells her, "Around 7:00 a.m. We'll need to get to the airport for our tickets, which Rehtorb told us is an early flight already reserved for us."

"Going to New York might be dangerous, Dad," states Ted. "What we've seen on T.V. from there is complete mayhem and chaos by gangs of desperate, frightened, faithless people that are revolting like a rampaging army. Most of them believe the end is near. Civil law and order are being tested and even the military has had a tough time preventing the unruly crowds from destroying property, outright slaughter, and threats to diplomats and other representatives that are at the U.N."

"Must you go, Dad? If so, how will you get from the airport to the U.N.?" Morgan asks.

"I imagine we'll either go by taxi or rent a car."

"On the news, they claim that taxi drivers have abandoned their cabs due to the violence," proclaims a worried Morgan. "Many taxis have been turned over and burned in the city. I'm not sure if you can even rent a car, since the rioters stormed into airports there as well. Marshall Law was declared and only when Army soldiers were sent in and stationed in the terminals was the airport re-opened."

Nikolai suggests, "I think she's right, Comrade, we should call ahead and ask that your President sends us some safe transportation to get from the airport to the U.N."

Harold says, "Rehtorb did tell us that our presence there is expected and that all there know of our trip with him into outer space. That idea does seem like the thing to do, but I'm not sure how best to get hold of Him."

Rita comments, "Try calling the FBI, Dad. Tell them who you are and what you need, then have them relay the message to the President."

"Yes, that makes sense. I'll try that right now," says Harold.

* * *

In the upstairs guest bedroom, while Nikolai undresses in the bathroom and steps into the hot shower, Katya opens the luggage that somehow mysteriously got transported with her and Anya from Russia. She starts with the one that is Anya's. Inside it are extra lingerie, nightgowns, two pair of comfortable-looking shoes, and several dresses. She seems both amused and pleased.

As she hears Nikolai happily tuning up his voice in the shower, she then opens her suitcase. Although there are similar types of garments in hers, she is puzzled by two items she finds there on top of her clothing. With her hands, she removes the two brass-framed portrait photos of Nikolai and his father that in their Russian home was prominently displayed on their bedroom wall. The photos were professionally taken about three weeks before his father's plane crash and disappearance.

Holding the two portrait photos, she mumbles, "Now why would that alien put these in with our clothing in the luggage? For that matter, how did he know what to put in them at all? This is most puzzling."

She carefully replaces the photos and closes the suitcase.

Chapter 20

Meanwhile, in a remote underground facility in Arizona, a clandestine meeting is taking place with a group of wealthy "One-Percenters." They are sitting around a large conference table, where the richest amongst them is explaining what they are about to see on the sixteen-foot wall screen at the end of the darkened room.

The tall, well-dressed multi-billionaire with a remote control in his hand pushes a button and a projector flashes the images onto the screen of three large, cargo-type rocket ships sitting on a launching platform in an undisclosed location.

"What you are seeing in this video is not science fiction. As you know, I have been planning to build a rocket that can be launched toward Mars to begin efforts to colonize the planet and make what is now inhabitable into a base that can support human life. In doing so, it offers an alternative to the Earth as our only choice of a habitable world."

One of the affluent men comments, "Yes, but I see three rockets, and isn't such a thing several years away from becoming a reasonable alternative."

"You see three rockets because they are not just concepts or computer animations. They are real and are prepared to send those of us in this room, along with our families on a voyage that although risky, might just save our lives if Earth is destroyed by the Moon's further ascension toward this planet."

A Japanese man speaks up, "So, are you saying these rockets are now able to carry us to Mars? I'm 63 years old and no astronaut. If by chance I survived the trip, what good would I be in trying to build or put together a colony on another planet?"

"Then you can choose to stay and die if you like, or chance the encounter. I have already assembled a team of strong, young men and women that will travel in one of the rockets, while the other two will hold fifty of those like you, your families, and more of the team that will work to put together the new stations and colony."

An Arab man asks, "What will we drink and eat when we get there and how long will supplies last? And what if the Earth survives and doesn't become inhabitable; will we be able to return once we leave?"

"The trip one-hundred forty-million-mile trip there will house almost five hundred pounds of cargo, which are ample supplies for those on the trip and when on Mars. As for returning, that is made possible by the fact the engines on the rockets can use methane as a propellant. That's because, on Mars, methane can be made using carbon dioxide for the Mars atmosphere, or using subsurface water. Thus, refueling is done and a return trip becomes possible."

The Japanese man again inquires, "So, how do we obtain oxygen, for a human cannot breathe on Mars? The gravity on Mars is a third of what it is on Earth, so what happens to our bones in a long-term stay in such gravity?"

Another man of color asks, "How does the launch window to Mars coincide with the timing of the Moon's colliding with Earth? And doesn't it take around six months to even get to Mars?"

The affluent tall man's becoming frustrated by their skepticism.

"Look, I know this scenario seems far-fetched to some of you, but what are the alternatives? I think most of us here believe there's no way most nations that have nukes will agree to destroy them in the next eleven days. We've witnessed the extreme panic and chaos that extended darkness caused, plus from the other incredible demonstrations of alien technology, we know the threat is real and will be carried out as stated. Admittedly, you'll be taking a chance by going on this voyage, but it is likely your only chance at survival.

"To answer the question about oxygen; by using large terrariums and hydroponics, plants can be grown as food sources, whereby we can use a filtration process to pull from the gardens to produce oxygen and water. That can be done before the stored food and water are depleted. As for the long-term effects of low gravity on the human body, there will be some loss of muscle mass and bone density. The greatest of these effects would occur on the voyage and not so much on Mars. There is indeed one-third less gravity there, but it is still not a weightless environment like space. Once your body gets used to less gravity, physical exercise regimens can help you maintain a healthy body."

A cynical Englishman quips, "Yeah, but are you going to smuggle a few cows, chickens, and hogs along on the trip and set up a ranch on Mars for us meat-eaters?"

"Let me first answer the question about the launch window and the time the voyage will take. Our cutting-edge technology has my engineers estimating that with our improved engine performance the voyage will be lessened from six months to less than three. As for the trajectory, once in orbit around the Earth, other rockets will be launched afterward to bring up the required amount of refueling for the Mars trip. This is not Noah's Ark, but there will be opposite-sex animals consisting of two live cows, two pigs, a dozen fish, and four chickens on the trip. There will also be animal embryos that can later be fertilized and cloned to make more if fertilization fails. There will be meat stored in the cargo and some left when you arrive, but after that is used up, you'll learn to become vegetarians until the animals reproduce and can be harvested."

The Englishman declares, "Well, I hope you grow crops that when fermented will taste as good as Scotch and Bourbon."

"Imbibing alcohol will not be permitted until the colony is established. After that, we'll have to see what plants might grow to be able to create such liquor. Any other questions or statements?"

A Hispanic woman asks, "What precautions have you made to fend off radiation and solar flares on the way to Mars ... and how about those that occur while we're there?"

"I don't see that it will be a major concern on the trip, as the ships are well protected from radiation. We have identified and intend to land close to several of the dormant vent tubes from ancient volcanoes. Thereby, we shall establish a habitable 'storm shelter' to lower the population into in the event of a severe surge of radiation from solar flares."

Tiring of answering their questions, the tall man concludes the discussion.

"Any other questions you may have should be presented to me via text, email, or by asking a member of my staff. The date of the launch will be two days before the deadline given to us by the alien. If you're wavering about your decision to go or not go, know that the preparations are underway and I shall not delay the launch. If you are ready to commit to the trip, then sign the ledger, and give me your contact information, plus the names and number of people you wish to take with you.

You will need to undergo some training to acclimate yourself to the environment you'll be in while in space. That instruction will begin in three days, so any commitments made after that will be voided. Keep in mind that on this innovative journey there is only room for two hundred seventy riders at this time; one hundred of those being my own family and the members of my assembly and service team. That leaves one hundred and seventy openings, which I suspect will quickly fill. Procrastinate at your own risk.

Those who sign now will be receiving an electronic confirmation and be directed when and where to arrive before the decided launch date. The communication will list the items you should bring along and items you will not be permitted to bring. This includes restrictions for things you may not bring, for all persons whatever the age, need to be healthy people that do not need a regimen of medications, such as diabetics, or dental issues. There will be medical doctors on the trip, but there will not be enough available drugs to sustain lengthy, adverse health conditions requiring long-term care. "

The meeting adjourns and this gathering of sixty very prominent, rich, and powerful individuals from around the globe dismisses. Several people with families sign the ledger right away. Others that are still unsure walk around mingling and mumbling amongst themselves. They seem anxious, but reluctant to sign up until more of their questions are answered. This revolutionary idea frightens and concerns them almost as much as the thought of the Earth being destroyed.

Chapter 21

The next morning, all in the house celebrate the rising and reappearance of the Sun. In a hurry to dress and get ready to catch their plane, Harold has no time to give Nikolai a tour of his home. In the kitchen, after a hardy breakfast, there's a tearful farewell and pleas for Harold and Nikolai to be careful in New York.

"Dad, please ...both of you be very careful and stay out of the subways. There's complete mayhem going on there," exclaims Morgan.

"Anya adds, "It's no exaggeration to say that New York is a chaotic mess, Papa, so don't go acting like a stormtrooper and just do what you each have to do and come back safe."

Having gotten an early morning phone call from the President, both men know that an armored vehicle will be waiting for them at the airport when they arrive, and then they'll go to the U.N. where the President and his team will meet them.

Ted and Steve drive them to the airport. Along the way, they encounter delays and are re-routed due to protestors and angry mobs.

Nikolai states, "These worried, angry people should be heard, for when one's hand is on a hot stove there is a scalding pain that warns us to remove the hand. Their angry pain exists because world leaders are spouting contemptible rhetoric and delaying a decision that must be made to save our planet."

* * *

Once in the airport, Harold ducks into a restroom while Nikolai browses through the gift shop. Soon after that, they board their plane. On the aircraft, they're guided to their side-by-side first-class seats. When Harold crosses his legs and arms, Nikolai notices that one shoe of Harold's is black and another is brown. He also has one black sock and one brown one.

Before going to bed the previous night, Katya washed Nikolai's uniform, and then pressed it before breakfast this morning. Anya shined her dad's boots and each one helped him dress. Harold refused any help and did his usual haphazard job of dressing. A worried Morgan distracted by her dad going to a dangerous city did not notice his shoes or his choice of socks.

As the plane accelerates for takeoff, Harold peers out the window at Trenton and the world that has been turned upside down and shaken in ways he'd never dreamed possible. The dominant political, social, and economic structure on which civilization is so dependent has become an intrusive frontier of chaos and turmoil.

He'd sat hunched over in his seat during breakfast and didn't have much to say. He now slouches and squirms in his seat, causing Nikolai to poke him gently in the ribs.

"Are you alright, Comrade?" Nikolai asks verbally. "You're very quiet. Are you in a somber mood?"

Harold's eyes blink and he comes out of his momentary daze. He turns his face to Nikolai, and forces a small grin, but remains silent. Soon afterward, the plane reaches its cruising altitude. Harold's so quiet that all Nikolai can hear is the pilot engaging the wing flaps of the jet. Deep in thought, Harold's weary brain begins to receive mental communication from Nikolai's mind.

"I know you're worried, Comrade, about your family and mine, and you realize this is but the calm before the storm. Everything that seems like fiction has become a stark reality, but I suggest you temper your paranoia and cling to hope, for like it or not, it's become our certainty to try and create a new reality without nukes and other WMD's. Maybe this U.N. security meeting will go well and the outcome of it all need not be sad, improbable, or unlikely."

Harold nods and remarks mentally, "Yes, hope is what the world needs right now, but all this bedlam seems to indicate for many that hope has vanished."

"Nyet! It's inconceivable to me that the leaders of all or any nation could ignore the power and commands of Him that made for these past days of darkness. Any country with nuclear weapons that denies making a unanimous accord to ban them will have a contrary argument from all of humanity for those that are not willing to do so."

"Harold replies, "Perhaps nothing's as bleak as it seems, but it's just all so disconcerting. How I long again for peace and serenity."

"Keep the faith. If today isn't the finality of all this, Rehtorb said there'll be another two chapters leading toward the story's climax."

Harold somberly replies, "Yes, that's what worries me."

Nikolai then muses, "I do wonder what he meant by telling us to make plans to go to a remote Pacific Island. I'm assuming he meant Easter Island, but as I recall the population there was evacuated due to geologic activity suggesting volcanic eruptions are evident."

Harold adds, "Yes, Easter Island was the one to which he was likely referring. He also stated that there would be some issues with world landmarks. I wonder what he meant by that?"

"I've no idea, but let's just focus on the upcoming meeting and hopefully stave off any further need for demonstrations and displays for not obeying the Creator."

* * *

When their plane flies over Manhattan on the way to the airport, the two men glance out of the windows at the city below. On this cloudy day, they see lots of dark gray smoke rising and many fires burning below. In the Hudson River, floating fireboats are spraying water onto burning buildings onshore. Masses of protesting humanity are on the streets that far exceed the number of police and motorized vehicles.

After landing, their plane does not taxi to a terminal but rather stops short of one and the captain addresses the passengers.

"Ladies and gentlemen, please remain in your seats. There will be a temporary delay while some baggage is removed and two honored guests deplane. When that's completed, we will continue to the gate whereby you may exit. Thank you for flying with us and please be careful and stay safe out there."

Harold and Nikolai are escorted to the front of the plane where they walk down a ramp and are met by several army soldiers that take their baggage and shuffle them into an armored Humvee. Once inside the vehicle, the plane's ramp is removed and the Humvee drives away down the tarmac to a designated safe area where private aircraft are kept. An army Major in the front seat of the Humvee turns and looks at his two passengers.

"Hello, Professor Simpson, General Belinski. I am Staff Sergeant, David Long. The President welcomes you to New York, such as it is. Our job is to see that you get safely to the U.N. and your meeting. It's a bit crazy in the city right now with a lot of people not playing by the rules. Therefore, rather than risk driving you there, you will be flown via a military helicopter to a landing pad atop the U.N. building. From there, you will be escorted on an elevator down and into the hall leading to the U.N. Security chambers."

As the Humvee pulls onto a secluded runway, Harold and Nikolai see the waiting helicopter. Harold notices that the aircraft is similar to one that ferries the President to and from the D.C. airport where Air Force One is kept. They hear the loud, chopping sounds of the helicopter, whose pilot is communicating with the Sergeant via radio.

"Delta Sierra One, are your packages ready for delivery?"

The Sergeant answers, "Roger, Whiskey Papa. Is Babe Ruth in the dugout?"

"Affirmative, Delta Sierra One. He's warming up and asks that we send in the other two players."

The Humvee pulls up as close as possible to the helicopter and the Sergeant gives his two passengers the thumbs up. Two soldiers from the helicopter meet at the Humvee and open the vehicle's back doors. They greet the Sergeant and then assist Harold and Nikolai out of the Humvee. They quickly lead them toward the aircraft, where Harold and Nikolai scurry up an attached ramp and onto the helicopter. The two soldiers scamper inside, shut and secure the door ramp, and then turn again to their two passengers. They seat their two guests and help buckle their seat belts. Harold and Nikolai cannot help but be impressed by the plush interior of this aircraft that smells brand new.

In a few minutes, the aircraft lifts off the tarmac and begins its journey toward the U.N. building. One of the civilian aides on board sits across from the two men.

The aide informs them of what to expect, "The area around the U.N. has been blocked off and secured for three hundred yards in every direction.

Only authorized personnel and vehicles are permitted within the perimeter. You'll be flown to a heliport atop the U.N., and then escorted down to the Security Council chambers. The President was flown there about a half-hour ago and he's expecting you."

As their flying entourage zooms over major city streets toward the U.N., Harold and Nikolai get their first close-up glimpse of the street chaos happening below within the city. Crowds with thousands of people of all races and ages swarm through the roads blocking traffic. There are burning cars, barricades, Molotov cocktails, and threatening firearms in the chaos below.

There is no sense of order, and from their lofty altitude, Harold thinks: They look like lost souls with no real idea of where to go or what to do other than causing vandalism and havoc. The fire trucks attempting to douse the fires are spraying fire retardant onto several of the tall, blazing high-rise buildings and apartments. The white foam they use is stacked high and resembles a small snowstorm.

Below, herds of people milling around seem alert but confused by all the mayhem. As the helicopter flies over Central Park, more demonstrators and arsonists are busy lighting trees on fire and setting off fireworks of all types. A disconcerted Harold watches out the large windows of the aircraft as they pass mile after mile of concrete and steel buildings, ones made with mirrored glass, and brick and mortar icons like the Empire State Building. Even it is not immune to arson, as small fires flare up from its ground floor offices and shops. Disgusted, Harold can see the immense array of spray-painted graffiti on its brick façade.

Nikolai witnesses more burnt-out buildings and rioters holding signs, some of which he's able to read as the aircraft passes by them. The maddening signs demand action ... against nukes, bioweapons, and chemical ones. Some of the signs state: "REMEMBER COVID-19 – ELIMINATE NERVE GAS AND VIRAL WEAPONS – ANNIHILATE NUKES–A-BOMBS B-GONE–BAN THE BOMB."

All of a sudden, the air below fills with bright flashes from the ground quickly followed by the sounds of lead popping onto metal. Harold and Nikolai realize the clunking thud is that of rifle caliber rounds as they hit hard steel. The pings from bullets ricochet off the bottom fuselage of the helicopter causing the pilot to evade them by swerving and altering his course. He flies away from the gunfire and over toward a different street with fewer anarchists.

Nikolai comments, "The safest and shortest distance between two points this day is under repair."

One of the soldiers informs them, "Don't worry, this new Sikorsky Marine One helicopter is armored and impervious to gunfire. Still, I'd rather not chance it."

Nikolai and Harold are each astonished by his revelation. Not just that the gunfire won't cause damage to aircraft, but also that the soldier called it, "Marine One," the President's private aircraft for ferrying him from the White House lawn to the airport where Air Force One is kept.

Harold curiously asks, "Did you say Marine One? I've seen that helicopter many times and this one doesn't look like it."

The soldier grins and remarks, "Yes, this is the updated and improved Marine One, VH-92 model that recently replaced the iconic VH-3D, Sea King."

Nikolai's face lights up and he laughs, "This just gets more and more interesting. I was flown to Greenland in a U.S. Air Force cargo plane, escorted around a highly restricted U.S. Air Base, and now I'm in a Presidential machine designed and built by the company my fellow countryman, Igor Sikorsky[1] began. If this keeps up, by Christmas I'll have enough democratic air miles built up to fly free to Australia ... where I'll probably have to hide out when my superiors hear about this."

Harold suddenly feels like someone has slung a bunch of heavyweights over his shoulders. He supposes it's a residual after-effect from having been in the much lighter gravity while on Rehtorb's craft. He's felt sluggish ever since they returned home to Trenton. Nikolai picks up on Harold's uneasiness and noticed it through his silence while on the plane trip.

He once more senses Harold's thoughts and concerns about what to do and say at the meeting.

Once again, they connect mentally and he sends a message to his mind-linked companion.

---

1.   https://en.wikipedia.org/wiki/Igor_Sikorsky

"Quit worrying, Comrade. You'll be fine. Whatever you say I'm sure will be convincing. They aren't expecting a sales brochure. All there is most certainly aware of what needs to be accomplished," Nikolai states emphatically.

Harold projects, "I know, but I just hope all those ambassadors and leaders needing to be there will be. All of them must by now be aware of the threat to our planet and will hopefully do what is necessary to avoid disaster.

"Yet, while many sovereign nations will seek peace and denuclearization, I worry that others might hold up progress using the world as a hostage and at the mercy of some unpredictable, rogue nation that refuses to accept banning nukes and claiming those weapons are their only deterrent and defense from their enemies."

Nikolai believes, "All we can do is our best and hope the outcome isn't pre-determined by those who might not be smart enough to exhibit common sense and know a revolt against God's demand is sheer lunacy."

Harold reflects, "People have been living on this planet for thousands of years. In the past seventy-seven years, despite the threats of an all-out nuclear confrontation we have managed somehow to avoid an Armageddon-type war. I hope that trend continues and common sense prevails."

Chapter 22

Nikolai muses out loud, "When we were up there ... out there, or in there with Rehtorb, I kept wondering what would happen if there was a hull breach in their craft, or perhaps had some radiation-shield failure. I asked myself, what it would be like to die in outer space 7500 light-years from my loved ones and home.

"Instead, all we experienced was a comfortable atmosphere inside a huge space cargo cruiser in a place where we were treated royally to a grand tour by one of God's most amazing creatures."

Harold responds verbally, "Yes, we saw and heard amazing things which no other human on our planet has been privileged to witness. The images and every detail of that adventure are ingrained in my mind forever, as I'm certain they are in you as well ... for as long as forever lasts"

"Indeed! So, Comrade, how will you approach speaking before those who have not seen or heard what we have? Your words and mine should be reflective of the feeling of amazement we encountered from that breathlessly remarkable journey."

Noting the two pilots seem to be listening, Harold goes silent and projects his answer, "I plan to temper that somewhat and won't reveal to them what Rehtorb told us when explaining about the seeding of Earth with humans from other planets. I doubt many would believe it anyway and it might offend some religious sects.

"Still, I do want them all to understand that humanity is but one family of God and that we are not some primordial ooze that evolved from a winning spin on life's 'Wheel of Fortune.' As Rehtorb stated, we are blessed with a divine, eternal soul and all of us are God's children. For most of my life, I didn't believe that, but now I do. Ours is a special place within the universe worthy of avoiding wrath. To do so, we must learn to live and let live, forgive and love one another. The start of a new world will happen if all agree to dispose of those destructive weapons that threaten to annihilate us ... and follow up on that agreement."

In less than fifteen minutes the big helicopter sets down on the U.N. building's heliport.

Nikolai sighs and states, "Whew! I feel as if we just flew through an asteroid belt."

Both men unbuckle their seat belts and are led down the ramp and to a roof-top elevator. The two soldiers escort them and moments later they are in the lobby area and on their way toward the Security Council chambers. Secret Service agents outside the doors wave metal detector wands over their bodies and then open the doors and point inside.

"Professor, you and the General follow our agent and he'll take you to the President and to where you'll be sitting."

Nikolai chides, "I hope this is a consensual meeting whereby I won't be forced to sit with my nation's contingent. I prefer to stay paired with you, Comrade ... to offer my support."

"I sense suspicious eyes already tracking us," replies Harold. "I also hear the sound of voices chattering in Russian. I imagine it's insufferable to think they'll enjoy allowing you to sit with a body of Americans while wearing the uniform of their nation."

"Yes, but I recall Rehtorb declaring that all here knows of our adventure with him and that I was brought here with you for a reason."

Harold sighs and remarks, "This is a new frontier ... for sure."

He glances around the C-shaped grouping of tables in the room, cranes his head around, and notices the icy stares he's getting from several communist representatives sitting across from where he's being led. The President notices the two men approaching him and waves for them to come over. As he shakes hands with Nikolai and Harold, he gazes out of the corner of his eye and notices the four members of the Russian contingent a few tables away staring back at them. The President invites Harold and Nikolai to sit next to him and they do. Nikolai looks uncomfortable but begins to sip on the glass of water before him.

He snarls and swallows, "Water! I'd best be careful ... I've heard this stuff just might be habit-forming."

The President laughs and winks at Nikolai for softening the awkward moment. Harold glances at the four Russians who appear to be incensed. He wonders if perhaps they're planning to harass Nikolai afterward.

Nikolai picks up on their cynical attitudes and declares mentally to Harold, "Comrade, don't let them spook you. That's just their angle of approach ... to appear angry, intimidating, and with ruffled feathers. It's just a ruse. Still, Siberia is very cold this time of year, and the prospects of my receiving a pension are greatly reduced. You will be generous with that chloroform when you adopt me and my family, won't you?"

Noting Nikolai's discomfort, the President states, "Just so you know, that alien Rheeabsorb, or whatever his name is—"

Harold assists the President, "His name is Rehtorb, Sir."

"Yes, well anyway, I wish he'd appear to us in person, yet his bright, golden orb and voice again came to us last evening. He told us he did so to the Russians as well, insisting via a mental connection that the General sits here with you Professor, at our side during the meeting. Your countrymen weren't thrilled by that, General, but when Rhea-whatever explained that you two were whisked away into space inside their super-large spacecraft, they agreed to allow it. So, relax General, you aren't in the dog house."

"Thank you, Mr. President, but you see, to my Russian colleagues, I'm wearing their dog tags and they have ready a collar with a very short leash."

As the chamber fills and each nation's ambassadors and representatives are seated, the Secretary-General stands at his table and gavels the meeting to order. Those present put on their earphones and watch the monitors before them.

The Secretary-General speaks, "Ladies and gentlemen, Ambassadors, Heads of State, Ministers of Foreign Affairs, Special Envoys, and Advisors, by your attendance today in this open meeting, whether or not your country is a member of this U.N. Security council, your nation has been recognized as one that has either nuclear weapons, biologic weapons, chemical weapons, or all of those mentioned.

"Therefore, after a few words from, Professor Harold Simpson, and Russian General, Nikolai Belinski, you will be voting on the issue confronting all our nations and our world. I ask for your courage and a decisive commitment that will result in all nations making an unconditional, universal accord for the banning of these types of weapons ... removing them ... forevermore.

"For the sake of our world, your nations, and our families, I pray you vote for disarmament. Our thoughts and prayers go out to the families of those national leaders and astronauts on the ISS whose presence somehow vanished from the face of the Earth. May God be with their souls."

He then welcomes Harold to the dais and invites him to speak.

Harold pauses a moment, looks at the notes he's made, and then speaks from his heart.

"For all of us, the past days and weeks have presented humankind with the astounding truth and revelation that we are not alone in the universe, that God almighty exists, and that He has eminent domain over this Earth on which we live. He's sent us an amazing messenger that presents us with a simple choice ... to either continue living upon this planet we call home, or else have it destroyed by refusing to obey our Creator's command.

"In our gathering here, the problem is not to come up with an answer to avoid God's wrath. The problem is to face the answer and realize our continued existence depends on something so uncomplicated as to agree to disband the scourges of our technology ... nuclear weapons, chemical weapons, and biological weapons.

"As a nuclear physicist, my colleagues and I know all too well, as do all of you, the threats that these types of weapons pose for humanity and our world. There are so many and some so powerful that if ever used in a war would lead to the annihilation of all human and animal life on Earth.

"I dare say that all of us in this room have lived our entire lives with the threat of nuclear war hanging over our heads and those of our children and grandchildren. It's insane to think that these awesome powers of death and destruction can be forever contained. Sooner or later, either by accident or by design, missiles will be fired whereby atomic and hydrogen bombs will be exploded over foreign soils, leading to mutually assured destruction. That's a recipe for disaster and a matter of when not if, it will occur. Afterward, mass extinction is inevitable."

Harold's voice cracks and his pleading eyes redden and moisten. Picking up on the turmoil building within Harold, Nikolai stands and walks to the dais, comforting his Comrade with a pat on the shoulders.

Nikolai continues the thought as Harold's knees weaken and he slumps down in his chair.

He speaks in his native Russian language, "Eventually, a more powerful pandemic than Covid-19 will be loosed and become uncontrollable; more people will die because of chemical weapons used upon those people or governments that are seen as a threat to some monarch or tyrants' power over their citizens.

"Gathered here, are those of you from various ethnic groups and nations, many differing in how you govern and what your leaders believe is the best way to protect and preserve your nation's safety and way of life. I get that, but what we should all remember is that we are one family of God ... and to God. All of us have red blood in our veins and breathe the same air. We live on the same planet ... which is in serious jeopardy of being destroyed ... unless you here and all those that possess the weapons mentioned decide not to unanimously agree to disband them.

"We've been given the message and have seen the display of God's power and supremacy through the days of darkness, by the re-positioning of our Moon, and the disappearance of national leaders. Our Creator has been patient with us, but His restraint is not inexhaustible. If we do not or cannot come to terms today ... then we will have but a few tomorrows left before an Apocalypse occurs. Please, I implore you ... vote your conscience and for the welfare of our species and our world, agree to God's demands."

The room is mostly silent and somber as Nikolai joins Harold and returns to his seat. Harold shakes his hand and nods his head, confirming mentally his appreciation for the relief and the words spoken.

The Secretary-General then stands and calls for a vote. He then makes a bold statement.

"As you can see, there is a large contingent of the international press in attendance. Therefore, I ask that all representatives forgo the usual theatrics and do not attempt to defend their positions or attack an adversary by playing to the cameras and the audience at home. I merely ask for your vote to disband nukes aa all WMD weapons."

There are mumblings and some dissent, but as the clerk begins the roll call of nations in alphabetical order, each is asked to privately register their vote into the computerized console at their table. As all nations register their votes, Harold and Nikolai hold a private cerebral conversation between them.

Harold projects at Nikolai, "I do worry about some of these nations that have always exhibited no susceptibility or motivation to achieving peace.

They sometimes remind me of omnivorous beasts of prey, eager to swallow up any living thing that differs from them."

Nikolai mentally states, "Yes, and some seem to have in mind the chief occupation of exterminating those that differ from their beliefs, and whose rhetoric and extremism infest their populations with hate and a suicidal boldness."

"Let's just hope this meeting doesn't become a farewell party for the world. I know some of these cabbage heads have delayed or prevented the progress for world peace, but maybe today they'll practice common sense and decency," Harold adds somberly.

Nikolai quips, "Yes, trying to be clever now would be dumb, yet the difference between genius and stupidity is they say, genius has its limits."

After the last vote is taken, the clerk begins to tabulate them. He then hands the results to the Secretary-General, who stands and faces the council, the press, and the television cameras before him. His unchanging expression does not present any indication of the results, but Harold does note the presence of a huge smile forming on the face of the clerk.

The Secretary-General speaks, "According to the votes tabulated, the vote to disband nuclear weapons, chemical weapons, and biologic weapons ... has passed ... unanimously!"

The room breaks out into a raucous and joyous response. Men slap each other on the back, women weep, and cries of relief exude from everyone present.

Nikolai immediately grabs Harold and embraces him with a huge Russian bear hug, which causes Harold to groan and momentarily lose his breath. Afterward, Harold grins and thanks his Comrade. Nikolai then reaches into his vest and removes a flat slab of bubble gum. He breaks it into two pieces and gives half of it to Harold. As the two men happily chew on the dried gum, Nikolai removes two photo cards the same size as the flat gum. Harold quickly realizes they are baseball cards of two pro players.

Harold questions, "This gum is from a pack of baseball cards. Where'd you get them?"

"I bought them in the gift shop at the Trenton airport. Who are the two men in the photos?"

Chewing vigorously on his gum, Harold laughs and says, "Alex Rodriquez and Derek Jeter. They are two of the best pro baseball players that ever played the game."

"They were?" inquires Nikolai.

"Yes, they're both retired now and played right here in New York City for the Yankees."

"Oh!" he says, "I saw that their cards mentioned the Yankees, but I thought that was referencing what all of you Americans are called."

"Yes, I suppose to Russians we are all Yankees." As Harold chews his gum, he asks, "Why bubble gum? Why not light up one of your cigars?"

"Nyet, doing that now would be too much like your American sci-fi movie, 'Independence Day.' Besides, I only have two Cubans left and I might need them again before this is over."

The reporters in the press celebrate and even old enemies among the nations present begin to hug and congratulate each other. In the billions of homes around the world, people leap from their couches, yelling and exclaiming their joy to their families and television sets.

Outside in the streets of New York, church bells can be heard ringing and car horns blaring. The city that was in turmoil and boiling with anger and fear is quickly extinguishing the fuse of protest that exploded so vigorously before. Those in the streets and in Times Square begin to celebrate the news and hope seems restored to humanity.

President Battle shakes Harold and Nikolai's hand and a broad grin forms on his face. In Trenton, Harold's and Nikolai's families celebrate their elation by popping bottles of champagne and raising a toast. All around the world, this is the news they hoped would be forthcoming. One can almost sense the entire human race resounding with a huge sigh of relief. Humanity has given its Creator what was asked for and saved Earth from destruction ... or ... has it?

Chapter 23

As those in the chamber continue to celebrate, President Battle informs Harold and Nikolai, "Congratulations, gentlemen, you both gave powerful and impassionate speeches that no doubt helped those present decide on this remarkable outcome. I have to confer with our ambassador, so let's meet at the roof helipad ... in say, twenty minutes. You'll fly back with me to JFK airport. I'll deplane onto Air Force One and then have my Marine One fly you back to Trenton."

Harold and Nikolai nod in agreement, but before they know it they are swarmed by news reporters. It's like being surrounded by a pack of wolves as the curious members of the press begin to fire off question after question at the two men.

One asks, "Professor, we understand you and the General here got taken aboard that huge alien spacecraft that captured the ISS. What was that like and what does the alien look like?"

Harold's uncomfortable with all this clamoring and attention but realizes they all are curious and expects answers.

"Yes, General Belinski and I were privileged to have been escorted onboard to the craft you mentioned. What we experienced there is indescribable and defiant of all known laws of physics. As you might imagine, their technology is far more advanced than our own. The alien voice that communicates via telepathic means was our guide."

Another reporter anxiously queries, "Tell us, Professor, what did it look like, and was it friendly?"

"I'll let the General here explain that," replies Harold. Nikolai groans and answers in English.

"Yes ... well, first off, he's not an 'IT," but is rather a remarkable presence difficult to describe."

Before he can finish, another asks, "Try anyway. Was he humanoid and bipedal?"

"Nikolai sneers and comments, "Although not bipedal or humanoid, his form is functional and quite amazing. His species requires no intake of food as we know it and their lifespan far exceeds that of our own. As for being friendly, they must be or else they could have easily destroyed our planet with their superior technology."

More reporters scramble to ask questions, "Did you meet others of their kind and where did they come from in the universe? Did they traverse through space via some black hole to get here?"

Harold attempts to answer without revealing too much about Rehtorb, "A Black Hole? No, those aren't used for interstellar travel or anything except the disposal of matter. Even we know that if one enters a black hole, they will be compressed down to the size of a gnat. He did, however, mention the use of wormholes as a means to navigate through vast distances of space.

"Yes, there were others of their kind on the spacecraft, but we did not converse with them. As for where they come from, all we know, and all he would admit to is that their planet is somewhere in the Orion Nebula."

"Do they have water on their planet and breathe oxygen like we do to survive?"

Harold again motions toward Nikolai to answer, "No, they do not breathe oxygen and their planet's surface is mostly covered in liquefied methane. Also, their planet's gravity is about one-tenth that of Earth."

Questions continue, "If they aren't bipedal, do they have legs, wings, skin, feathers, heads, hands, or what?"

Getting annoyed, Harold quips, "No feathers! They have multiple limbs that allow them to move about and long arms with appendages similar to fingers. Of course, they have a head, two eyes, what appears to be a long, thick snout-like nose, and thin lips. They wear helmets with life-support backpacks containing their required methane inhalant to exist in our atmosphere."

Another reporter then asks, "So, why is it that out of all humans on Earth, you two were selected by the alien to be the ones to meet with him and become the envoys for delivering news of the Creator's demands?"

Nikolai states emphatically, "The alien explained that he did not choose us, but that we were selected by God to bring word of his demands to the world. As to why the Almighty chose us ... only He knows."

Harold raises his arm and hand telling them, "We know you're all curious about the alien and his species, but out of respect for them we prefer not to divulge any more. Besides, we have to go. Like all of you, we wish to return to our families and celebrate the decision made here today."

"One last question, Professor," asks an aggressive reporter. "Do you think this decision to disband the weapons mentioned will prevent wars and truly save our planet and humanity?"

Harold sneers his nose and pauses a moment before answering.

"Neither I, nor any of you has a crystal ball to predict the future, but disbanding these weapons is only one step in reducing the dangers to our planet and humanity. We still have to deal with environmental issues, like the pollution of rivers, lakes, seas, and oceans. Carbon dioxide from millions of auto emissions and other pollutants traps heat causing global warming and the melting of polar ice packs.

"The world's remaining rainforests are being depleted by deforestation that reduces the oxygen produced by the trees and fauna. This threatens many species of plants and wildlife. Even with the depletion of nuclear weapons, there will still be nuclear power plants that produce nuclear waste that will require being disposed of in better, safer methods. Then too, although it is rarely mentioned, the world is becoming over-populated, and producing enough food, shelter, employment, and basic economic and health services for everyone is becoming more difficult to accomplish. Human trafficking and even slavery still exist. The poor and the homeless among us seem to be increasing ... so my answer, as you can see is that ... no, although eliminating these weapons is a major step toward restoring hope to our world, there is much more work to be done before humankind solves all its threats and dangers. Besides, conventional weapons are still lethal and futile wars will likely still occur between opposing nations."

With that, Harold dismisses himself and Nikolai also refuses to answer any further questions. Though the reporters follow, the President nods towards his bodyguards and bids them stop to the onslaught, which they do. Still, on their way toward the exit doors and the elevator to the roof, Nikolai is confronted by the ambassador to Russia. As they await the elevator, the tall distinguished-looking Russian takes Nikolai by the arm and faces him.

He speaks, "Congratulations General, your speech was quite convincing and powerful."

He pats Nikolai on the shoulders and seems friendly.

He remarks, "By your being in uniform, I assume you are still loyal to mother Russia and embrace plus uphold the principles which our nation values. You are still accountable for your actions and command decisions, are you not?"

Nikolai chooses his words carefully, "My principles and bond of trust with the Russian Army, Navy, and those others I lead has not faltered nor lessened. Please understand, neither I nor my family is responsible for having been brought to Professor Simpson's home. That was accomplished via transference from Russia by the alien's technology. As you were told by the alien, so too was my presence here with the Professor. I maintain my command discipline is intact and that I strive to accomplish my assigned missions as best I am able."

The ambassador smiles and shakes Nikolai's hand.

"Good, then my report to your superiors will be to accept your word, expect that you will maintain your decorum, and not divulge any information that would be detrimental to our nation. I'll ask for tolerance of your situation here in the U.S.

"The President has asked that you report to him within three days for duty and return to your troops as soon as possible. Transportation back to Russia is being made and you will be contacted. He glances at Nikolai's head, pauses, and then adds, "I notice you are not wearing your service hat. It would've been nice to have you display it with its Russian military heraldic crest."

Nikolai rubs a hand through his thick hair and remarks, "Yes, Sir! It would've been nice, but the last I saw of it before I was swiftly transported to America by the aliens, was it lying on my desk in Russia where I put it."

The soldier in Nikolai is silent and stands before the ambassador like a statuesque figure. He seems disinclined to comment further.

Yet, he then boldly states, "I understand the want for my family and me to return to our homeland, but the urgency to do so should be tempered with the reality that neither the Professor nor I have any idea if we'll be required by the alien to make more appearances."

As the elevator door opens, Nikolai nods at the ambassador and he and Harold enter the lift. Harold immediately uses his cell phone to call home, but once again the airwaves are so overloaded that his call does not go through.

* * *

Meanwhile, watching the televised Security Council meeting with interest from his secret bunker, the billionaire executive planning the escape trip to Mars begins to text his contingent of extremely wealthy colleagues:

"The results of this important U.N. meeting are encouraging and may eliminate the urgency of pursuing the scheduled Mars colonization launch. I shall closely monitor all developments and progress toward the agreed-upon disbanding of the weaponry mentioned. However, I urge you to continue your training until the alien contacts world leaders and the Moon returns to its past position in space, plus those two physicists confirm that the threat to our world is over."

* * *

On the brief helicopter ride back to JFK airport, Harold makes another attempt to call home but has the same response and no connection. The President again thanks and offers his appreciation to Harold and Nikolai. Although grateful for the recognition, Harold once again feels the madness and dark gloom of doubt creeping into his mind.

Nikolai quickly picks up on that and sends him a telepathic message. "Comrade, why so glum? I sense the clouds of indefiniteness gathering on your horizon and spreading like a winged dragon across your mind."

Overhead through the large windows of the plush aircraft, rays of bright sunshine glisten and burst inside as if they are sparkling jewels within the clear blue sky. Seeing the bright sunshine seems to pull Harold out of his momentary doldrums.

He mentally replies to Nikolai, "I'm just homesick and worn-out from all this. I'm tired of manic-depressive Technicolor dreams with an alien disk and voice in my head. I'm wary of being thought of as a designated misfortune-teller trying to predict if an apocalypse has or hasn't been averted. I feel like I've been going around and around in a revolving door, and in a pressure cooker that has a stuck safety valve."

Nikolai, in his usual composed demeanor silently declares, "Come on, cheer up! Round and round, huh? Then You should be relieved, for one should never become dizzy from doing a good turn."

Harold manages a weak grin and cerebrally cites, "You're like a bulldog that's always in control. Me, I have an indisposition that malingers. I envy that you'll be met with a kiss and hug from your loving companion. I have my kids, of course, but at the moment I feel lonely and deeply miss the affection and love I got from my beloved, Elisa."

Nikolai shoots him a huge sardonic smile and returns comments about all the morose things that encompass Harold and what they've both been through.

"Hmmm, I see. Well, while I sympathize with your situation and understand the tension from the events we've both encountered of late, that small growth above your neck is your head. It is a smart enough brain to know that life is forward living ... in the now... so, I suggest you quit lingering in the past and make an effort to reestablish a relationship with a woman to whom you're attracted. Surely, even someone as homely as you ... must know some nice lady that would make a loving companion."

Harold knows he means well, but raises a hand to stop Nikolai's silent banter. However, before he can do that, at about that same time the helicopter begins to land at JFK airport.

Harold scoffs, "Stop it! You sound like my daughter."

Nikolai grins and mentally states, "I wasn't making any sound. It was just a mind whisper."

There's a slow curl of his lips as Harold launches his mental reply.

"I recall when I had private thoughts ... and long for the day when this disk in gone from my skull and I can have them once again."

"Where's the fun in that?" goads Nikolai. "This way, we cannot tell a lie and must unconditionally trust one another."

"Yes, I know that," relays Harold, "but there are some things that are not meant to be shared with others ... like suggesting that I'm homely or should find another woman to care for me."

"Okay, Comrade, suit yourself ... but when you do, try matching the color of your socks and shoelaces."

Harold glances down at his feet and finally realizes what Nikolai's referring to. They then have to break off their mental connection and watch as the President prepares to exit and turns to his two riders. He first hands Harold a business card.

"After I leave, the helicopter will proceed to fly you both to Trenton. When you arrive, a safe ride home for you has been arranged. We're told that some revelers have gathered outside your residence, Professor. I've alerted the authorities to make certain they prevent any vandalism or harm from coming to either you or your family."

He then adds, "The card I gave you has a phone number on it. Dial it, and then type in the code I wrote on the back. That will get you into my staff, who can then contact me. If you hear from that Resstore, or whatever his name is, please let me know what he tells you. Good luck in dealing with your military superiors, General. Thanks again for what you've both done."

With that, they each shake the President's hand. He deplanes and walks toward Air Force One waiting for his arrival and the trip back to D.C. When he's on board his jet, the pilots of the helicopter rev up the engines as the aircraft lifts off and swiftly departs for Trenton.

On the short flight back, Nikolai again makes a mental connection with Harold.

Nikolai remarks mentally, "Comrade, are you as curious as me about where our friendly alien is and why he hasn't contacted us about the decisions made at the U.N. today?"

"Curiosity is the one thing holding me together," replies Harold. "I'm hoping the positive vote to disband will pay off like a Vegas slot machine, but like you, I wonder what Rehtorb's reaction is and if the decision is enough to stave off the Creator's wrath."

"Yes," moans Nikolai. "Let's hope this action takes the project of nuclear disarmament to fruition, for I look forward to having things and life back the way it was before all this."

Chapter 24

During their flight, Harold's cell phone signal finally gets through and he calls home to let Ted and Steve know that a ride home has been arranged and that they didn't need to come to the airport. Harold's relieved to learn that the crowds of protesters in the streets near his home have lessened and those present now are not causing any violent threats.

When arriving at the Trenton airport, Harold and Nikolai depart the Marine One helicopter. They are once again met by an armored, military Humvee. As Nikolai walks across the tarmac towards it, the driver's door opens, and out steps the same Marine Sergeant, Long, that picked them up at JFK airport in New York. Nikolai's face forms a broad grin and he shakes hands with the Sergeant.

Harold does as well and remarks, "This is quite a surprise to see you again, Sergeant Long."

The Sergeant explains, "After letting you out at JFK, I was given orders to drive here and when you arrive to get you and the General home safely. It's not out of the way, since I'm stationed at the Marine Barracks near D.C."

Harold and Nikolai again enter the armored vehicle and the Sergeant drives them off the airport and onto the highway towards Harold's suburban home.

Harold's apprehension about what they'll find at home seems to have diminished since Ted informed him that the aggressive protestors near their home have dispersed and departed. Nikolai's eyes focus on people they pass that seem fatigued with conflicted emotions. Although the U.N. vote was as manna from heaven, they still seem tense ... with some still acting profoundly sad.

He comments, "From the expressions on their faces and the demeanor of those we've passed, I'd conclude that they are without question not yet convinced of the solidarity of those nations that voted to disband their nukes and other weapons."

Harold's also been attempting to read and interpret the attitudes of those that they pass. He abruptly turns toward Nikolai whose expression reflects one of doubt and angst.

He asks Nikolai, "Is that what you believe is their reaction ... or is it your own opinion and impression?"

Nikolai replies in a cynical voice, "A smart person will not climb a mountain. He will go around it. My dread is that those who faced that nuclear mountain at the U.N. agreed to climb it and disband when in truth they have no real intent to scale the mountain ... and only stalled till they can go around it."

The Sergeant grunts and his eyes divert from the road momentarily to meet theirs in an intense stare.

He asks, "Are you saying that this thing might not be over and that there's still a lunar threat to the world?"

Trying to be tactful, Harold attempts to answer, "Sergeant, we have to assume that the U.N meeting solved the issues of disarmament and that all nations who made their pledge and vote to disband will follow through with that commitment. Any other consideration at this time by either the General or me is mere speculation and is not a response based on anything other than our being anxious."

Nikolai shakes his head and with a wave of his hand adds, "What he said!"

The Sergeant's reply tinges with sarcasm, "Thanks, I guess! Point well taken ... and just how far is it around that mountain?"

* * *

As the Humvee turns onto Harold's block, those in the vehicle observe that although the street itself is devoid of people, Harold's front lawn is not. There must be almost a hundred packed on his large front lawn, holding signs and waving banners welcoming the General and him home.

Harold soon recognizes that many of those that are present are his Princeton students. Many hold signs proclaiming: WAY TO GO – DR. KNOW!–NO NUKES ARE GOOD NUKES. Harold grins and begins to wave out the window, as the vehicle approaches the front curb and walkway.

Seeing all this, Nikolai inquires of Harold, "You know all these young folks? And who is Dr. Know?"

When the Sergeant pulls up and stops, Harold reaches for the door handle and pauses to answer Nikolai.

"Many of them are in my classes at Princeton. Dr. Know is me. It's the nickname my physics students gave me a few years ago and that's what they all call me now."

Nikolai and the Sergeant both smile. They too roll down their windows and wave at the friendly crowd. Harold shakes hands and thanks the Sergeant and then opens the vehicle door. He steps out on the walkway and is quickly met by the throng of students, parents, and well-wishers, as they applaud and gather around him. He maneuvers his way through the crowd and up the walkway toward the house. He notices Morgan, Ted, and the others standing on the front porch waving. Nikolai also thanks the Sergeant and he too exits the vehicle to cheers and congratulations.

Once both men are safely on the porch, Sergeant Long salutes, waves, and then drives away. They each wave goodbye to him, and then exchange hugs and kisses with their loved ones. Harold acknowledges the crowd and some of his students begin questioning him.

One near the porch asks, "Dr. Know, what was it like inside that huge spacecraft? Any idea how their propulsion works?"

Realizing that some in this throng of people must be reporters, he wishes only to go inside and relax with his family.

Harold patiently replies, "Imagine if you will a craft as big as Rhode Island. Then, consider how many species of plants and animals you'd be able to store and raise inside such a craft. That is mostly what we saw, thousands of aquatic and land animals inside huge soil terrariums and interior seas and lakes. As for their propulsion, I can only reveal that although we have no idea of the method, whatever it is capable of traversing vast distances of space in days, not years or eons as would be the case by any presently known Earth vehicle."

Another asks Nikolai, "We understand from news reports, General, that you too are a nuclear physicist. Do you think your nation will comply with the decision made at the U.N. today?"

"I am not a politician," remarks Nikolai, "I certainly hope they abide by the decision, for it would not be wise to do anything else."

A young female student asks, "Dr. Know, will the Moon be placed back in its original orbit and the present high tides and volcanic activity cease?"

"I cannot say for certain what will occur with the Moon's orbit, other than Rehtorb, the alien, stating that the Creator will not send it to destroy us if we comply with his demand. I suppose that's where faith comes in, and although I've been lacking in it most of my life ... I have developed a new appreciation for it."

After answering a few less complicated questions, Harold waves to the crowd and bids them thanks. He suggests that they go home and be with their families. After he and Nikolai go inside, twenty minutes later, all of them have left the yard and are indeed returning home.

* * *

Inside their home, Morgan, Rita, and Katya escort the men into the den. Harold and Nikolai seem exhausted and each finds a spot on the sofa to recline. Harold sprawls out on the sofa and upon the other end of it, Nikolai leans back and props his feet onto a leather ottoman. Ted and Steve each pick a comfortable recliner and all of them relax and begin to chat amongst themselves.

In the kitchen, Rita and Anya rinse off dirty dishes from breakfast and Morgan takes a loaf of bread and begins to cut the crusts off slices.

She then walks to the doorway into the den and asks her dad, "Did you all eat any lunch? I fixed tuna fish sandwiches for ours ... and there's potato salad and green beans if you'd like."

Harold raises his head and pats his stomach. He glances over at Nikolai that raises an eyebrow and also places a hand on his belly.

"Come to think of it, we've been so focused on that meeting that we haven't had anything to eat or drink."

He swings his legs off the couch and sits up. "I could eat, how about you, Comrade?" he asks.

Nikolai nods his head and the two men saunter off into the kitchen, where Morgan and the other two women set the table with plates and glasses, plus the sandwiches and two veggies. They and the other two men join them sitting at the table, as Harold and Nikolai snack on the light lunch.

Morgan goes to the fridge and asks, "We have soda and grape juice to drink. I can also make you some hot tea or ice tea. If you prefer, I'll pour you a glass of cold water."

Nikolai casts a sheepish grin and says, "No water, I've had my limit of that for the day. The grape juice sounds good, thank you ... and thank you all for your being so considerate to me and my family."

Morgan removes the juice, and then fills Nikolai's glass, "You're more than welcome, General."

Harold remarks, "If the situation was reversed and I was in your home, I've no doubt you'd do the same for us."

"Dad, what would you like to drink, and would anyone else like something?" she asks.

He replies, "Water's fine with me, hon. Thank you!"

As Harold partakes in the lunch, he brings up an idea.

"You know, I think it's time we all got on with our lives and go celebrate tonight. I'll make reservations in town at one of my favorite restaurants and we can all go out for a nice, family dinner."

Morgan grins and happily comments, "That sounds wonderful, Dad."

Nikolai chimes in, "Yes, but, Comrade, having been whisked away from Russia in such a way, I have but a few rubles on me and cannot afford such a thing."

"Nonsense!" declares Harold. "It's my treat and I am happy to do it. We all deserve a relaxing evening, after what we've been through."

Katya leans over and kisses Harold on the cheek, "You are so kind, Professor. How can we ever thank you for your generosity?"

Nikolai seems squeamish and states, "I will pay you back, Comrade. I promise you that. I feel as if I'm a bankrupt man that's fallen overboard and forgotten how to swim."

Sensing Nikolai's melancholy, Harold sends him a telepathic reply.

"And good moaning to you too, Comrade! Look, it's not your fault that any of this has happened, so quit beating yourself up about it. When you get home, just send me a few million of your rubles and that'll square us."

"Would that I had such wealth, I'd gladly share it with you as you are with us. You are a good man with a wonderful family, Comrade. God has greatly blessed you." reflectively states Nikolai.

"Yes, He has," remarks Harold.

Harold pauses, and then speaks, "I am only beginning to understand how much God has blessed me. At best, I was an erstwhile Catholic. My opinion of God was that if He was real, to me it seemed like this world was nothing but an ant farm where on occasion He used a magnifying glass and the rays of the sun to scorch and burn the life out of good, loving people ... like my parents and my beloved, Elisa. It took a devout alien from another world to open my eyes and warm my cold heart. I shall forever be thankful for that."

Morgan's eyes fill with tears and Ted's fighting to not let his emotions cause him to weep. He stands and places a soothing hand on his father's shoulder.

His voice cracks as he says with deep conviction. "Dad, I've never been prouder of you or happier than I am at this moment."

Morgan wipes away tears, nods, and rises to her feet to go hug her dad.

* * *

After assessment from the others over what type of food they'd prefer, it was decided by Harold to call ahead and makes reservations at a fine dining restaurant offering steaks, seafood, and Italian food. He was happy to learn they were still open and serving. He had to call three services before finding one that was still operating and then arranged for a stretch limo so that all eight of them can ride together.

Before they're ready for the night out, Katya and Anya inform Morgan that all they have to wear is what the alien packed in the luggage and that none of it is suitable or formal enough to wear to a nice restaurant. Being almost the same size as Morgan, she solves that problem by offering the two Russian women some of the more formal wear she keeps in her closet upstairs.

"I have several dresses and gowns that I left there for when I come to visit, Dad."

Katya and Anya agree and each tries on and discovers they fit into the dresses Morgan offers them.

Nikolai does not change out of his uniform and Harold and the other men wear collared shirts, ties, and slacks. Morgan again helps her father coordinate his outfit.

When the limo arrives that evening, the men are ready and await downstairs in the den for the ladies. The first to come down are Morgan and Rita. They have curled their hair and put on make-up, plus they each wear colorful springtime attire and heels. Morgan is wearing a low-cut, strapless gown accentuating her ample bosom. Each looks lovely. Harold sniffs the air, noting Morgan's wearing the same scented perfume that she did in the graveyard that day.

Nikolai stands and his attention is drawn toward the stairs as Katya and Anya gracefully descend the steps. He first greets Katya, whose hand he takes, kisses it, and grins.

"You look amazing, my love."

He then turns to Anya, whose long blond hair is pinned atop her head revealing her long, graceful neck. Like Morgan, she is wearing a low-cut, black gown with spaghetti straps that accentuate every curve of her bosom and body. Nikolai looks at her and she giddily twirls before him in her borrowed heels and with her arms elegantly extended. He almost speaks but holds his tongue as his lips curl into a sneer. Noticing that, she places both fists on her hips and shoots a firm glare at her father.

"Well, Father, how about me?"

Nikolai clears his throat, glances over at Harold who tries to suppress a laugh, and then Nicolai remarks, "That's a very nice dress you almost have on. As I've heard before, if a moth ever got hold of that gown, he'd die of starvation."

Anya snarls and protests, "I suppose the only time I look good to you is on Halloween."

Nikolai laughs and goes to hug his pouting daughter.

"I'm just kidding you, my sweet angel. You look divine ... it's just that I'm not used to you looking so ... adult."

He leans over and kisses his lovely daughter on the head. She forces a smile and they then adjourn to the awaiting limo.

Once they are all inside, Anya pointedly adds, "I feel like Cinderella riding in her carriage going to the royal palace."

Their time together is full of mirth and sharing of a great meal. Nikolai, due to the expense is reluctant to order his usual four glasses of vodka, but Harold insists he orders whatever he wants. Overall, the evening proves to be relaxing and enjoyable for all. Anya is noticed quite often by some single men sitting at a nearby table. A few stern and squinted iron stares from Nikolai cool their libidos a bit, but Anya seems amused by the attention.

Back home afterward, the ladies all excuse themselves and go upstairs to change into more modest clothing. The men again go into the den to chat. Nikolai breaks out one of his last remaining cigars and lights up. Harold hands him an ashtray off a nearby end table.

Not having taken his cell phone, Harold sees it lying on the coffee table where he'd left it. He picks it up and begins to scroll through the logs to see if he's had any calls. He's surprised to see that Albert called him from Texas. He is about to play the voice mail message that was left when Morgan and the girls come back down and into the room.

He puts the phone down on the table and asks, "I'm going to get some water, anyone care for something else to drink before bedtime?"

Not getting any requests, Harold glances at the cell phone, not noticing that it's set on silent vibration mode instead of ringer mode. He strolls off into the kitchen to get a glass of water. Morgan joins him.

"Thank you, Dad. We all had a wonderful time tonight. That's the first time in five years that you, me, and Ted have all been together ... the last time being—"

He cuts her off, "At your mother's funeral. Yes, I know. This was a special night and duly needed by all of us."

Snuffing out his cigar with half of it still useable at a later time, Nikolai strolls off into the living room he passed when coming into Harold's spacious home. He's followed by Morgan and Rita, who watch curiously as he opens up the fallboard, which is the part of the case that folds down to protect the keys when the piano is not in use.

Morgan asks him, "Do you play, General?"

Nikolai moves the piano bench out enough so that he can sit on it. He cracks his knuckles and stretches his arms.

"Yes, my father taught me when I was but a young boy, and then I studied composition and collaborative piano at a Russian conservatory before my twentieth birthday. Do you, play, Morgan?"

"I can plink out a few simple tunes, but my mother was a virtuoso. She was the last to sit where you are now."

"I see," declares Nikolai.

He points to the framed photo portrait lying on the top of the piano.

He queries Morgan, "Is that a photo of your mother?"

"Yes, Dad likes to display it here in a place where she always seemed happiest in this house."

"I can understand why," Nikolai says. "She was a beautiful lady indeed. It's so tragic that her life was cut short by that accident."

"Yes, my dad has not been the same since it happened."

"Do you suppose your father would object if I were to play this grand Steinway ... in her honor?"

"No, I'm sure it's okay. He loved it when Mom played, and to have someone as proficient as you do so again will no doubt be a thrill for him."

Nicolai nods and glances back into the den where Harold and the others are still gathered. He turns to face the keyboard. With a surprising dexterity for such a big man, he begins to play a classical arrangement. The music sifts through the air into the den, affecting Harold with a resonance that he hasn't heard in over five years. The harmonious sounds coming from Nikolai's talented fingers mellow and draw him like the tempting calls of sirens to sailors in a lost sea. He rises, as do the others, and joins Morgan and Rita in the living room. Harold finds an armchair, sits down, closes his eyes, and lets his mind drift as he listens to the sweet, spirited, melodious music coming forth from the piano via Nikolai's gifted and nimble fingers. A broad smile crosses his lips and he feels more relaxed than he's been in several days.

When Nikolai's playing ends in a dramatic conclusion, Morgan and all clap and applauds Nikolai's performance. He swivels on the piano bench and faces Harold.

Obviously moved, Harold, coughs into his fist, and then clears his throat.

"That ... was amazing, Nikolai. I know you told me you were a pianist, but listening to you play ... well, it was incredible. What is that piece called?" asks Harold.

Nikolai exhales and also seems somewhat emotional.

"It is Tchaikovsky's Piano Concerto No. 1, that your American, Van Cliburn, played in 1958, and won the Tchaikovsky Competition in Moscow," he explains. "He was only twenty-three years old, and my father, already a member of a Russian symphonic orchestra was but twenty-seven years old and present during the contest.

"Afterward, he met Van Cliburn, had a photo taken with him, and Van Cliburn later autographed it for him. It sits on my piano at home and besides my family, it is my most prized possession."

* * *

Before going to bed in the upstairs guest bedroom, Katya removes the two framed photo portraits of young Nikolai and his father. She places them on a dresser near the foot of their bed.

Seeing them as he sits on the edge of the bed, he asks, "Those were on our bedroom wall at home. What are they doing here?"

"All I know is that when I unpacked this suitcase, they were lying inside. Why the alien placed them there ... I have no idea."

Nikolai seems stunned and by his expression, he is upset and confused.

"That's truly bizarre! They're the only such photos I have of him. We must be very careful to see that they get safely back home to Russia."

With that, they turn out the lights and slip under the light blanket and sheets. Still curious about why the photos were sent, it takes Nikolai over an hour before he falls asleep.

Chapter 25

After showering in his bedroom, Harold stares at the glowing digits on the alarm clock on the table next to his bed. He too is still wound up from all the enjoyment he's had that night. Although he tries to sort out the thoughts he starts to indulge in now, he cannot seem to shake the uncertainty that begins to consume him.

His hands fumble to open a drawer in the bedside night table, whereby he withdraws a prescription bottle of pills. Having brought a glass of cold water up with him, he opens the bottle, taps out a couple of the pills, and using the water he opens up and swallows down the meds prescribed to help him sleep.

He turns off the lamp next to him, lies back, and then attempts to clear his mind of any negative thoughts. He raises the glass and places it and the cold water within it on his temples. Fidgeting, he begins to experience the assumption of a headache that haunts the fringes of his consciousness. There develops a driving pain, which forces his mind into a pit of deep and dark despair. As if in slow motion, a syncopation of voices in his mind begins calling to him in muted tones and scrambled words he can't seem to understand.

Not realizing that he's now asleep and dreaming, his bewildered mind attempts to make sense of the sorrow he's experiencing. His thoughts struggle to interpret the voices and the sobering impression that they're delivering him the bad news. He tosses and turns in his bed, lamenting that his mind cannot rid itself of the confusion.

Moaning, he kicks away the covers from his feet. In a startling vision, there are rapid flashes and images of headlights on a highway and tires squealing on the pavement. He hears a shrill female scream from the car, glass shatters and the car flips over two times in the darkness. Even asleep, his body begins to perspire as horrid memories buried for five years form a ghastly vision in his subconscious, guiding him through a dismal doorway to the past that he never again wanted to revisit.

Even though he realizes that this is a nightmare, the imagined last moments of Elisa's life and her screams echo through his troubled mind. He's avoided facing this demon for all these years, but he cannot vanquish it now. Nor can he even in fitful slumber bring himself to look upon her torn and twisted body again. However, once more he hears the screeching sounds of metal, and glass, hissing steam emitting from the crumpled radiator, and the pungent smell of gasoline.

On the pavement, as he arrives after the crash, he witnesses the sticky ooze and smell of her blood amongst the twisted metal in which she was entombed. He recalls the terror that consumed him that night and though in deep slumber he attempts to resist the terrible memories and traumatic event that he seems incapable of scrubbing from his mind. The next thing he's aware of is the sound of his own voice waking him after he takes notice of himself screaming. Sweat pours from his brow and he's trembling.

The dim light of dawn comes pouring in through his bedroom window and he bolts up in bed ... where a concerned Nikolai gathers him by the shoulders to calm him.

"Easy, Comrade, you've been having a nightmare. It's okay; you're awake now and home in your bed."

Harold's wild eyes roam across the room and he swings his feet off the bed and onto the carpet. He tries to focus on Nikolai and slowly his head begins to clear. Nikolai is fully dressed and composed. Harold now understands that what he experienced was all a very bad dream.

Nikolai assists him up on his feet. He shakes his head and a concerned Nikolai helps him into a nearby soft chair. Still flustered by his grim nightmare, he reaches for the glass of water on his nightstand. The water is wet, but no longer cool, which is okay for it moistens his lips and seems to calm him a bit. Wearing only an undershirt and a pair of boxer shorts, he stands and his expression forms a congenial smile towards Nikolai.

"Thanks! I think I'm alright now," he tells Nikolai.

"Good, for I know nightmares can be awful things. I too had a most unusual dream. It's daylight now, so go get cleaned up and dressed, and then come down to breakfast. Katya is making us kasha porridge and butterbrots."

Harold smacks his mouth, noting that he needs to brush his teeth. After sweating so much in bed, he also needs another shower.

"I've heard of kasha, but what the heck is butterbrots?" he asks.

"It's a kind of sandwich made of a single slice of bread and one topping such as butter or ham ... with boiled or fried eggs."

"Sounds good. You go ahead and I'll be down after I shower, shave, and get dressed."

* * *

Fifteen minutes later, when Harold jaunts down the stairs and into his den, the first thing he does is check the voice mail that Albert sent him last night. He'd forgotten about it till just now and he's puzzled why it is on the carpet when he recalls having left it on the coffee table. When he turns it on and checks the call list, he notices that Albert called him four more times. Since the phone was in silent mode, it must have vibrated off the table. Somewhat concerned now, he puts his finger over the voicemail icon to retrieve Albert's first message.

He listens as it states, "Harold, John called me from New Mexico and told me that they'd taken another laser measurement from the Moon. To be certain of his findings, I took my reading about ten minutes ago—"

Before he can finish listening to the message, the front doorbell rings. Irritated by the insistency of whoever is doing it, Harold lays the phone down and goes to see who it is that is on his doorstep at 6:15 a.m. With Morgan and the others also curious and looking on from the kitchen doorway, Harold opens the front door to find two Army officers standing before him.

They remove their hats and with somber looks on their faces inform him, "Sorry to be here so early, Professor, but your colleague, Dr. Goodfellow in Texas has been attempting to get hold of you. When he couldn't reach you, he got hold of the military to come to check on you. Is everything alright?"

Harold sighs and answers, "Yes, we went out to dinner last evening and my cell phone has been on silent mode. I was just checking his voice mail when you came to the door."

One of the officers smiles and seems relieved. "Good, then we'll leave you to your breakfast. I'm glad everything's okay. Dr. Goodfellow said it's urgent and asked that you please call him ASAP."

"Thank you, officers. I shall do so as soon as I've heard the rest of his voice mail."

After they've left, Morgan inquires from the kitchen, "What was all that about, Dad?"

He replies, "They'd gotten a call to come to check on us to see if everything's okay. I assured them it is. Let me finish checking this voice mail and I'll be right in there."

With that, Harold picks up his phone and continues with Albert's message.

It states, "Harold, I'm afraid my readings agree with John's. The Moon has once more begun its steady descent toward Earth. Given the rate, we estimate that we have less than three days before it reaches the critical point where our world begins to suffer severe consequences leading to mass casualties and eventual utter destruction soon after that. Please call me back ASAP. Perhaps there's something you and the General can do to help stop this madness."

Harold's legs wilt under him and his face goes flush. This is not the news he'd hoped for and his fears are coming true. Either the news from the U.N. meeting was inadequate, or else those that agreed on disbanding ... are instead going ... around the mountain.

Chapter 26

In the kitchen, Nikolai senses the angst in Harold's mind. He immediately mentally questions Harold about what is wrong.

"What is it that is bothering you, Comrade? Did you receive bad news from your colleague?"

Harold's hands shake nervously as he tries to push the icon on his contact list to phone Albert. After he manages to do so, he then replies to Nikolai.

"Yes, the worst kind of news. He tells me the Moon has once more continued its trajectory toward Earth."

Before he can say more, Albert answers, "Harold, thank goodness you've finally called. Did you listen to my voice mail?"

"Yess, I'm afraid I did. It's not the news that I wanted to hear."

Albert sighs and remarks, "No, it's not. Have you heard any more from that alien about what's going on and why the U.N. vote hasn't been enough to forego the continuance of the Moon's perturbation?"

"No, I have not, but I certainly hope to have him contact Nikolai and me about this matter and how it can be rectified before it's too late," states a worried Harold.

"I understand. Please keep me informed of any progress in that matter. Is there anything we can do to help?"

"Nothing but pray ... and trust we still have hope."

* * *

Having joined Harold in the den, Nikolai overhears the conversation. Like Harold, he no doubt wants to know why this is happening and why Rehtorb has not been in contact with Harold

While the others in their families gather in the kitchen and anxiously begin to discuss the news Harold received, Harold has Nikolai join him privately in the home office. Once inside, Nikolai begins taking note of the many wall-hung diplomas and certificates of achievement that Harold has on display. Harold goes behind his large oak desk and sits in his padded swivel desk chair. He scribbles on a pad, noting how many days are left before the deadline.

Nicolai's eyes roam around the richly oak-paneled walls. One wall is complete with a matching oak bookcase and a cabinet filled with books on physics, astronomy, and scientific magazines. Lying on the corner of Harold's desk is a recent copy of the journal, "Aerospace Science and Technology." Nikolai picks up the magazine and begins flipping through the pages.

He comes to an article and begins reading the headline: "Reducing The Drag Coefficient On Hypersonic Missile Systems."

Nikolai comments, "This was an interesting article you wrote. I was one of the peers that reviewed it and found it to be quite informative. Of course, in Russia, we already practically applied this system and achieved working hypersonic missiles."

Harold looks at Nikolai with a stern expression, "Yes, and our government is aware of that fact. I will not affirm or deny that we have that capability as well, but all of these methods and advances in rocketry do not lessen the threat of war, but only serves to make it more likely."

"Agreed," Nikolai states in a pessimistic manner. "So are the threats from space in the form of Russian anti-satellite orbiting weaponry. Such technology dwells on the edges of 'Star Wars.' Plus, my nation is also aware of your experiments with a high-intensity laser satellite that can home-in on fired missiles to knock them out of the air before their warheads are engaged."

"I know of no such functional weapon, but if our scientists achieve that capability, then no doubt your nation and China will soon have it as well. If our world survives ... space war might indeed leave the realm of science fiction and become a reality."

"The capability of disengaging communication satellites would impede and result in any nation's ability to wage war. It would be dangerous reversibility making warning systems go dark," replies Nikolai.

Harold agrees, "Right! GPS-guided drones, missiles, and intelligence gathering would be lost with no way to rapidly assess a foreign attack."

"Of course, none of that matters at the moment ... if we can't fix and comply with the demands of the Creator and his natural satellite ... our Moon."

Both men seem frustrated and somewhat leery of discussing the real issues on their minds. Nikolai closes the magazine and sighs.

He pauses and then says, "Any idea how we can communicate with Rehtorb to ask him what's going on and where we stand in this conundrum?"

Harold responds, "I'm hoping he will be contacting us soon. Perhaps if we both use our telepathic abilities we can contact him, maybe such efforts will get through to him."

The two men do all they can to concentrate and call upon Rehtorb to come forth and inform them of what has to be done next.

The two mentally confirm, and then send a strong, emotional message: "Rehtorb, wherever you are, we plead with you to appear before us so that we can determine what we are to do to avoid the impending disaster. Since we've learned that the Moon has continued its diversion toward Earth, we must assume that the decisions made at the U.N. are not sufficient to satisfy the Creator. Please ... show yourself and let's discuss other options."

After using the disk in their brains to transmit the message, they sit silently, hoping that somewhere in the cosmos, wherever Rehtorb might be that he will receive their plea and come forward.

Minutes go by and yet Rehtorb does not appear as they've hoped. Both men seem disparaged by this fact and each looks at the other wondering if perhaps they've heard from their alien mentor for the last time.

"I do not understand his reluctance to follow up and tell us what needs to be done," declares Harold in a desperate voice.

A frustrated Nikolai states in a sarcastic tone, "Perhaps he's gone to a crematorium on another human-inhabited world to gather ashes to sell to some cannibalistic planet as "Instant People."

Neither man laughs at the absurdity of that remark, but each silently blasphemes their alien abductor and heretofore guide for refusing to show up.

From his billfold, Harold removes the card the President gave him.

"I need to contact the President and let him know what Albert told me about the Moon. "What else can we do now?" asks Harold in a surrendering manner.

Nikolai shakes his head and shrugs. "As you told your colleague ... we pray and hope."

* * *

Several hours pass without any contact from Rehtorb. Harold and Nikolai return to the den where the others of their family gather. When they learn that no word has come about how to avoid the ultimate fate of the world, Morgan suggests that they gather together and pray. Harold joins the others as they kneel in a circle, hold hands, and began to recite their prayers. Being Russian Orthodox Christians, Nikolai, Katya, and Anya, all manage to produce short, heart-felt words to their Lord and Savior, Jesus Christ, and Mary, the Holy Mother. Harold's kids all do the same. When it comes to Harold's time, the words simply do not come to him and he's overcome with emotion.

Sitting next to him, Morgan squeezes his hand and whispers, "That's alright, Dad. Let's recite the Lord's prayer."

With that, they each begin to vocalize the prayer that Jesus taught His disciples.

* * *

After speaking with the President and giving him the bad news, Harold and all the others eat a light dinner, and then reluctantly accept that another day comes to an end without a resolution to solving the problem and avoiding disaster. Nikolai and Harold retire to their bedrooms, noting that tomorrow's sunrise will mean that it is one day closer to the deadline set by the Creator.

For Harold, sleep does not come easily and he repeatedly sends Rehtorb cerebral messages, beseeching him to please come and let him know what needs to be done. He receives no response. Around 2:30 a.m., an exhausted Harold finally drifts off to sleep.

In his troubled slumber, he finds himself alone atop the crest of a hill. He sees a valley below and a bustling city where the people are boarded up in their homes avoiding yet another deadly biologic virus. All the stores are closed and the streets are void of any pedestrian or vehicle traffic. He walks silently down the deserted streets, only witnessing one individual stirring a half-block away. Near an alleyway, he observes a suspicious-looking man attempting to deploy and set off a briefcase-sized atomic bomb.

Harold's mouth opens, but in his nightmarish stupor, he has no voice and cannot scream.

He hears his somnambulant mind screech, "Come on, you Milk-fed, All-American boy genius. Get it together and stop this insanity."

He finds himself sprinting toward the man with the atomic bomb. The man sees him, rises, turns, and races away. Harold hears cynical laughter and the strumming sounds coming from the briefcase as a timer clicks off seconds until a detonation occurs.

Once he reaches the briefcase, Harold stops and glances around looking and hoping that someone will come to help him defuse this threatening device. His eyes catch a glimpse of Morgan ... peeking out of a window from a nearby home. He then sees Ted, Nikolai, and Katya opening a front door and peering out into the stillness of the silent streets.

His head feels like a hard stone and despite his desire to wake up, he cannot. His eyes focus on the timer as it counts down from thirty seconds ... twenty-nine ... twenty-eight. He bends and fiddles with the wires and tries to make sense of the mechanisms to stop the bomb's pending detonation only seconds away. All of a sudden, he feels corrupted and betrayed by the alien he's met and whom he trusted. He hadn't wanted or asked for the stressful undertaking that has become his and Nikolai's cross to bear. He deplores the dependency of such responsibility being placed upon them both. Now, he is facing this bomb about to explode ... taking both his life and that of his friends and family.

He urgently attempts to maneuver the proper sequence to cease the countdown and avoid certain death, but when the timer reaches six ... five ... four ... he stands and looks over his shoulder at Morgan, who now reminds him of his beloved Elisa. His mind hears the triggered mechanism whine ... and then ... a flash as bright as the sun. As if in slow motion, his eyes lift and he gazes once more at Morgan at the window and Nikolai, Ted, and Katya in the doorway.

His mind again screams for he looks down to see that his flesh is on fire and the skin from his arms drips away as if it is a liquid wax. Terrorized, he watches as Morgan's lovely face melts in the extreme heat from the bomb, and Nikolai, Ted, and Katya's skin crumbles in microseconds. Now only skeletons, their bones collapse, and when the calcium frames that were a moment before living beings, are now but a bunch of crumpled ash remains.

His eyes search for Morgan, but all he momentarily saw of her was a barren skull with hollow eye sockets devoid of life or flesh. Glancing at his hands, they too are devoid of flesh. In a storefront window somehow amazingly still intact, he catches glimpse of his reflection. The screaming skull and bones reflected therein bear testament to him being dead ... and not realizing it. On a bony heel, he turns and all he can think of to say to Morgan and the others is: "I'm so sorry I couldn't stop this from happening. Please forgive me."

He bolts up as he'd done the morning before after having a nightmare. He yells and panics. This time, however, it is not Nikolai standing over him. Instead, he opens his bloodshot eyes and beholds himself lying in a large meadow with green trees near a slow gurgling, clear stream. He's wearing casual clothing. The early morning sky is clear and azure blue, and a gentle breeze stirs the waving green grass that he lies upon. Butterflies flitter about and his senses catch wind of the sweet scent of Jasmine and Gardenias. He stands and turns, now uncertain if he's really awake, dead, or still dreaming.

As he stands, he hears a low, guttural growl coming from the woods around him. Terrified, he beholds a large male lion with a thick mane lazily stepping out into the opening, bearing its long frightening fangs at Harold. His instincts demand he takes flight and flees from this carnivorous creature, but his legs will not move. He panics and feels as if his heart is about to burst out of his chest. Sensing that he's about to be attacked, he imagines his life flowing away as if it is a river.

He wonders, why is everything moving so slowly... like blind horses in a mill. Closing his eyes, he awaits the certain mauling to come. Instead, from the woods marches behind the lion ... a white as snow lamb. It prances up to the lion, which then lies down on the soft grass with the lamb sprawled out right next to the lion's massive jaws. The lion bends over and licks the lamb, whose baa, baa sends chills up Harold's spine. The impression of it all stuns and surprises Harold.

It is then that he hears a voice calling to him from unknown regions of his brain. As cobwebs weave around his very soul, the welcome, familiar voice is as pollen to a bee.

"Harold, wake up. Your nightmares are over. Go now to your friends and family downstairs. Something is coming on the news that concerns both you and the General. I have not abandoned you ... and will soon come for both of you once more."

Harold recognizes the majestic mental voice of Rehtorb and his body stretches as he sits and yawns. He now realizes that before he was still asleep and dreaming. He sits up in bed and his eyes search the bedroom for Rehtorb, but it is only the alien's temporal voice that he hears.

Immediately, Harold mentally reacts, "Rehtorb, thank God! We were afraid you'd left and weren't going to come back and inform us if something went wrong. You do know the Moon's again coming toward Earth."

"Yes, of course," responds Rehtorb. "All should know that they cannot hide things from the Creator. He knows the hearts of every life He's formed from cosmic dust. You, humans, are like notes the General played on your piano. Those notes die away after they're born on the keyboard, but still, the sounds of the music live on as echoes in the mind. You, humans, are to the Creator as a melodious song, with a resonance that lingers and makes Him sing. Yet, it also causes His own heart to break because ... you do not obey Him when He offers you mariners of the flesh a lifeboat. Instead, your species defy Him and refuse to get into it.

"No, that which was promised at the meeting will not lessen the waves to come from the tempest. As frightened children in the dark, humanity has chosen instead to stir up clouds of deception. That's exactly what the evil entity I spoke about wants. With his interference and your humanistic misleading manner, the brutal swords of war have not been beaten into plowshares as was promised. So, rise and know that I will soon come again for the two of you."

Silence prevails, as Harold stands, his knees knocking and his hands trembling. With Rehtorb finished speaking his mind, he is both stunned and relieved. His relief comes in the promise that Rehtorb will come to him and Nikolai. That he will, Harold interprets is likely to be another chance to bring hope to the world. He quickly heads off to his bathroom to brush his teeth, shave, and dress casually before going downstairs.

* * *

Downstairs, Morgan and the other women are in the kitchen preparing breakfast. While the other men sit drinking coffee and watching the morning news on the television, Nikolai seems edgy and begins to explore a long hallway leading from the den. At the end of the hallway on the right wall, he comes to a wooden door. From his expression, it appears that he is curious as to what lies behind that door. With one hand, he attempts to open the door but finds it is locked.

About the same time, as Nikolai stands there in front of the locked door, Morgan comes into the den to announce that breakfast will be ready in five minutes. She asks that someone go upstairs and let her Dad know. As she turns to go back into the kitchen, she notices Nikolai standing by the hall door. She instinctively walks down the hall toward him.

Seeing him snooping, Nikolai sighs and remarks, "Sorry! I don't mean to be nosey, but I had a peculiar dream last night about a door ... this door. Now, in reality, I am seeing it for the first time. May I inquire ... where does it lead?"

Morgan politely replies, "That's the doorway to the basement. It was a special fun place that my mom and dad shared. When she was killed in the car accident, Dad locked the door and as far as I know, he has not been down there since."

"I know this sounds crazy," comments a puzzled Nikolai, "But in the dream, I saw a table tennis game, a pool table, a long table with hockey pucks on it—"

"That's called a shuffleboard table," Morgan interrupts to inform him.

"Yes," he remarks. "And the walls were clad with the same rich oak paneling as your dad's office. There was a large fireplace, plus in the corner of the room was a table with two facing chairs. On the table, was a chess set with an incomplete game in progress. Now, why do you suppose I dreamt such a thing about a room I didn't even know exists?"

Morgan's expression reveals her surprise and she informs him, "That is surreal, General, for you just described that basement room in its entirety. My Mom was a female ping pong champion in high school and college. Dad could never beat her at that game. He did, however best her when it came to shooting pool, which he attributed to his knowledge of physics and basic inertia. There is a fireplace and the real uncanny thing you mentioned is the unfinished game of chess. The night before Mom's accident, they started the game, but did not finish it, vowing to return and do so the next night ... which obviously—"

Morgan cannot finish, for tears begin to form and she bursts out crying. Nikolai quickly takes her in his arms and hugs her to him.

"I know of your sorrow, dear one. When I was six years old, my father was killed in a plane crash. One never gets over such a tragedy, but know that your mom and my father are in a better place now in the arms of our Lord."

He then shakes his head and is truly amazed by his dream.

He states, "That I had such a dream proves to be based upon stark reality makes me wonder if perhaps what I experienced wasn't presented to my slumbering, unconscious mind by some divine power. I am most curious by what that means."

Chapter 27

After breakfast, Harold calls Nikolai into the office to discuss a matter. There, he informs Nikolai of Rehtorb's message and that they'll both soon be hearing from him again.

Nikolai asks, "So, did he indicate why the Moon has again continued its descent toward Earth?"

"No, but he did inform me of a deception and that the Creator sent a "lifeboat" ... that I'm assuming was the opportunity to save ourselves by doing what was promised at the meeting. Evidently, those commitments made there were false and the Creator knows that."

Before Nikolai can ask more, Ted races into the room in a panic. His expression appears as if reflecting an approaching, pent-up storm, yet his words of warning seem unutterable and don't come out as he planned.

"Dad ... the T.V. You must see ... come please, it's awful!"

Harold and Nikolai cease their conversation and quickly follow Ted into the den where all the others sit and behold the startling news alert on the television screen:

"This is not a drill and is a warning from the Federal Emergency Management Agency, FEMA, which issues this disaster response from the U.S. Military. Nuclear missiles have been fired from Russia, China, and North Korea toward the U.S. Shelter in place and if possible, immediately go below ground level. If you are within twenty miles of the detonation of a bomb, do not attempt to flee or go outside, as the risks of radiation will be extremely dangerous.

"The following U.S cities are in jeopardy as the missiles have been characterized as being launched via submarines and land-based ICBM's from Korea toward Washington D.C., Los Angeles, New York City, Houston, Dallas, Omaha, and Huntsville, Alabama. Retaliatory missiles are also en route to those opposing nations and the U.S. Anti-Missile Defense System has been activated to hopefully prevent the warheads from reaching their targets."

Morgan and the other women panic and begin heading toward the locked basement door. As they do, before Harold can reach for the key in a drawer next to an end table, Rehtorb suddenly materializes in the den.

"Fear not!" exclaims Rehtorb to their minds. "What is warned shall not come to be. This act was not a deliberate attempt by any of the nations involved to commit the first strike or start an all-out thermonuclear war. It was achieved by another wicked entity that sought to create chaos and bring about a war amongst those powerful nations, essentially dooming all life on the planet.

"We have seen to it that all the missiles fired are intercepted, dissolved, and neutralized. At this time, I bid that you, Harold, and you, General, come with me where I will explain what has occurred and prepare you for another amazing oncoming display of the Creator's power. What happens after that shall determine whether or not His actions will lead to Him becoming a dove or remaining a hawk when deciding your planet's fate."

Rehtorb's appearance and his words are as mirth incarnate, for the breath returns to all in the room at the news that millions of innocent Americans, Russians, Chinese, and North Koreans will be spared and that the missiles have been destroyed.

Before anyone can comment, Harold, Nicolai, and Rehtorb quickly vanish from the room, leaving the others stunned, but hopeful that the world will take note of what comes next from the Creator. They all bend to their knees and say a prayer for both men, for the world, and then thank God for this alien intercessor, Rehtorb, for preventing a global catastrophe.

* * *

After fifteen minutes of special alerts, the networks break in to announce a special update.

The News Anchor of Fox News declares, "I know most of you must be very frightened and confused as to how something like this could happen ... and be wondering why D.C., New York, L.A., Houston, Dallas, and other cities haven't been destroyed. We're now being told by the news services and the military at the Pentagon that all the missiles were fired by mistake and that somehow after they traveled into space where the warheads separate and deploy toward their programmed targets ... have all mysteriously vanished into thin air. That sounds suspiciously like the previously inexplicable vanishings of world leaders. It is presumed at this time that the alien whose voice was heard at the U.N. and his species' advanced technology is likely responsible for that miracle. If so, then thank God for his intercession.

"Word out of Washington is that Russia, China, and North Korea have been in contact to acknowledge that there was no intent of a first strike. What is troubling, however, is that what we're attempting to get made clear is how nuclear subs with all the failsafe devices and nuclear protocols they are required to follow can have something like this occur within the ranks of three of the most powerful navies of the world. North Korea also proclaims it did not fire its rockets either, blaming it on some outside force jamming its computers and reprogramming them to fire the rockets. It will no doubt take several days or maybe months ... if we have that long ... to learn what happened and why. Still, we can all breathe a bit easier for now, and instead of facing the apocalypse via nuclear annihilation, all we have to deal with now is the lunar threat that according to astronomers has once more begun its convergence toward Earth."

* * *

Outside of Harold's home and across the street is parked a black van with the lettering "City of Trenton Water Department." Inside the back of the van are numerous surveillance monitors and computerized equipment to record thermal imaging and powerful electronic listening devices that tap into mobile phones and boom-type audio microphones that can be pointed toward the residence to record what is said inside the house. Two men from the FBI observe the monitors and listen in to what's being said inside Harold's home.

One of the men says to the other, "You'd better call this in and report what we have. Then see if they want us to continue with the surveillance."

The other man in the van uses his cell phone to call Washington.

A female party he's calling answers.

In code, he says, "This is Roy Kline. Please leave word for the boss that we need to speak with him about the sewer problem he wanted us to check out."

The female voice complies, "Okay, he's pretty busy with a project the mayor gave him, but I'll give him the message and have him return your call as soon as possible."

"Thanks, Gladys. He knows my phone number."

After hanging up, the two men get back to their monitors and adjust the volumes on some of the listening devices. Fifteen minutes later, the agent's cell phone rings and he answers it.

"This is Roy." He pauses, and then again replies in code, "Yes, boss. We just wanted to let you know that we checked out those two manholes ... and there might be a sewage issue down there, but we aren't sure. So far as we can tell, the heavy sludge has moved on out of there. We didn't see any rats and what's left there seems to be a bit clogged up."

The male voice on the other end remarks, "Okay, let me know if the sludge gets any worse. I'll let the commissioner know what you've found out."

"Sure thing, boss. We've still got a camera down there and will monitor it in case the sludge returns."

When the man in the van hangs up, the man he called in Washington D.C., the FBI Director, uses another secured line to make a call. When the party he's dialing answers, he taps in a numerical code and the line goes directly to the desk of the U.S. President in his Oval Office.

President Battle picks up the phone.

"Hello Director, what's the word from Trenton? Please tell me that after avoiding a certain nuclear catastrophe our two contacts with the aliens are okay."

The Director tells him, "Via code, I received word from the agents monitoring them. They tell me that the two men are no longer at the house and that the agents have no indication if the alien contacted them, nor how or where the two men might have gone. They just disappeared."

Frustrated, the President sighs and remarks, "More vanishings I suppose. That's a contagion we must stop. Okay, then all we can do is hope they've made contact with the alien and will learn what next needs to be done." He pauses, and then sternly expresses, "Furthermore, I want answers from our admirals exactly how their billion-dollar submarines launched nuclear missiles without mine, the Pentagon, or the captain's consent."

"Yes, Sir! The Russians, Chinese, and Koreans are trying to find out the same thing. If there's a terrorist threat capable of doing such things, then the security of ours and every nation is in jeopardy."

* * *

Meanwhile, Harold and Nikolai find themselves transported not to Rehtorb's huge spacecraft, but rather to some smaller triangle-shaped craft. The space they materialize into is an apparent airlock of some sort, with shiny metallic walls and a circular ceiling about twelve feet tall. They are also surprised to learn that they are wearing the same two helmets as before that Harold stored in the guest room closet after they were sent back from their first encounter on Rehtorb's enormous craft. They realize the air they breathe comes from the life pack attached to their backs. Soon, a round metal portion of the wall with what appears to be slotted louvers begins to fan open to reveal a passageway into the vessel. Just inside the next room stands Rehtorb. His helmet is removed and for the first time, the two men view his head and shoulders. Harold's first impression is that Rehtorb's expressionless white and red pupil eyes that they first saw when he was wearing the helmet must have been coverings from some sort of goggles, for the eyes they see now have lids that blink and eyes shaped somewhat like their own, except their coloring is entirely ice-blue.

Rehtorb cerebrally welcomes them, "We located your helmets and life packs at your home and placed them on you before waking you and opening the airlock."

He points around the room, where several others of his kind sit at consoles and what must be the guidance controls of this craft. They all turn and Harold silently swears that they smile at him with their large, thin lips. Nikolai notices it too and he returns their odd smile with one of his own.

"As you can see, we do not need our helmets here, and since we are in our environment and a manufactured gravity, we don't need the suppressor units like I wore to avoid Earth's extreme gravitational force," explains Rehtorb.

Harold mentally asks, "I'm assuming you got our mental message and that we're here because you have something to tell us about why the U.N. decisions failed to satisfy the Creator."

Rehtorb motions for them to follow him. They do so and he guides them into another section of the craft where they behold a rounded, convex wall with what appears to be some sort of viewing screen, similar to a huge high-def television. Rehtorb has them sit in the two chair-like devices he's prepared for them. He waves his hand at some control lights on a wall panel and the lights begin to dim inside the room.

Seeing this, Nikolai leans back and crosses his arms. He facetiously quips, "Oh, I do hope that I haven't seen this movie and that they have a cartoon before the main feature."

Harold hears a startling wheeze, followed by a couple of loud snorts like that of a donkey's braying. He glances toward Rehtorb and in the dim light reasons that ... for the first time they may have just heard the alien's strange laugh.

Rehtorb quickly gathers his composure and emotionally states, "What I am about to show is a real-life moment from what we obtained by visual monitoring of a meeting at your U.S. Pentagon. It was held in what is known as a SCIF room. Are you both familiar with what that is?"

Harold silently answers "Yes, that stands for 'Sensitive Compartmented Information Facility,' and is an enclosed area within the Pentagon that is used to discuss and process classified information."

Nikolai agrees, "Yes, it is also comparable to what my government has in the Kremlin. It's where the highest-ranking officers of the military discuss top-secret issues."

"Yes, it is exactly that and what you're going to see is the reaction of those high-ranking officers about what occurred at the U.N. meeting. This was before the unintended firing of missiles from the submarines and land-based rockets from North Korea," declares Rehtorb.

They all watch the wall. Soon, what appears in three-dimensional images are the Joint Chief of Staff, plus four of his military counterparts: an Army General, a Navy Admiral, a Marine General, and an Air Force General appear on the screen. They are in the SCIF room sitting around a table. The Chief of Staff begins the discussion.

"Gentlemen, I've called you here because I have concerns about what transpired today at the U.N. As noble as the cause and outcome that was voted upon there and approved, I have grave reservations about whether or not our nation's enemies will truly comply with the idea of complete disarmament of their nuclear, biologic, and chemical weaponry. To me, such a notion is sheer folly, and for the U.S. to adopt that policy and remove all our means of defending other nations and terrorists by removing our vast arsenal of atomic weapons is suicidal and irresponsible."

Stoked and anxious, he pauses and takes a drink from the glass of water before him.

The Navy Admiral responds, "I agree that the principle of the idea is tempting and hopeful, but like you, General, I fear it is not reasonable to assume that other nuclear powers will follow the resolution and truly destroy that which they also know is the chief countermeasure to prevent us or any other nation from attacking them."

The Marine General adds, "Unless there is complete compliance to this idea, and if we agree to it and it happens, we become sitting ducks with a missile defense system that isn't ready to fend off and destroy a vast amount of hypersonic nuclear warhead rockets fired toward our cities and populace. We do have in place the 'Star Wars' orbiting laser system that in real-life exercises has shown that it can destroy incoming missiles, yet it too is untested against an all-out atomic barrage or the new hypersonic missiles that Russia and China have produced."

There is a moment of silence, and then the Chief of Staff wishes to hear from the Air Force General.

He turns toward the General and asks, "What's your opinion on all this, General Norton?"

General Norton clears his throat and states, "Although I understand every point made here, must I remind you all that the alien and the two men that have become its spokesmen have repeatedly told us that God will accept nothing less than full compliance with His demand. The oncoming lunar threat, those three days of darkness, plus all the other inexplicable occurrences, and the show of advanced technology by the aliens convinces me that the world will indeed only survive and be better off without nukes and the other chemical and biological weapons designed to kill.

We all have families, and gentlemen, my own is scared stiff and greatly worried. I have four grown kids and eight grandchildren that I'd like to see live out their lives without the threat of nuclear war. Their first sign of hope came from that meeting this morning, and to remove that hope from them and all of humanity seems to me to be ... barbaric."

The Chief of Staff delivers an assertive response, "General, we all have a family to consider in this matter and none of us wants for them to be threatened with nuclear war. Still, it has been our nation's policy for the past seventy-five years to deter our enemies from using their stockpile of atomic weapons against us by procuring and having enough of our own to ensure that those enemies know they too will be annihilated if they attack us. That remains the sole deterrent against Russian, Korean, Iranian, and Chinese aggression. We could only be certain of no retaliatory response from those four and other nations that oppose our government if they too remove and destroy all their nuclear weapons ... and honestly, do we think they truly shall? I sure as hell do not."

With that last argument, the images on the screen begin to fade away. Rehtorb raises the level of light again and he turns toward Harold and Nikolai.

"What eventually was agreed upon in that meeting was that no matter what the political decision and outcome might be, the military would resist destroying 'all' the nukes and would covertly retain as many as possible as one General called it, as their 'Ace in the Hole.' I've shown you but the one meeting, but we intercepted six others from opposing nations that were almost verbatim to the one you just saw. In each case, the powers in each nation seek to pretend to go along with the removal of all nukes, while in reality, they plan to conceal as many as possible to keep an advantage over their enemies.

What they should know, but don't is that nothing can be hidden from the Creator. So, now you understand why the decision at the U.N. has not solved the problem. It isn't enough to agree only for a moratorium on nuclear weapons, for only a complete and universal disarmament of each type of weapon is acceptable."

Nikolai stands and somberly transmits, "That there is resistance to the idea of complete nuclear disarmament disappoints me but does not surprise me. As I've noted before, such efforts to do so have gone unresolved for many decades and the problem has been a point of contention that many governmental administrations have tried to solve but failed."

Harold adds, "Basic mistrust among those opposing nations has been the cause of that failure. Yet, how much more proof must military leaders see of the power of God before they realize their only choice is disarmament? It's madness not to accept and comply with the U.N. decision."

Rehtorb agrees, and then telepathically states, "That is the only choice. We will soon be taking you to the place where the two final displays from the Creator will begin to play out. If after those two, if there is no mutual confirmation of compliance, then I'm afraid life here and your planet will be terminated."

Harold asks bluntly, "Where are we going ... for that matter, where are we now? I hope we aren't 7500 light-years from Earth again."

Rehtorb clarifies, "We are in our vessel that is similar to what your 'Star Trek' series referred to as a 'Shuttle Craft.' We are in a secret base underneath a Southeastern Pacific Island. We shall remain here until tomorrow morning when the last of the Creator's displays will begin. Thereafter, there are but three days left until the deadline and your Moon reaches a critical point in its descent."

Harold's voice cracks as he replies, "Then I think I speak for the General when I tell you that we'd prefer to be with our families ... should that ultimate catastrophe occur."

"I understand that desire," says Rehtorb. "However, your presence is required by the Creator at this site where your world will be witnessing what is to come. If after they've seen, believe, and demand that all must comply, then all this will be over and the Moon will return to its original orbit in space. If they do not, then we will return you to your families, for the Earth will after that soon no longer exist."

* * *

On several news networks, people are being interviewed about the incident where the missiles were supposedly fired by each nation without the consent of their leaders. On CNN one man that was a retired, former captain in the military begins to describe the protocols required before nukes can be used against a foreign adversary.

The News Anchor introduces the captain, "We're speaking now to retired Captain, Rex Lane, whose former job it was to direct and supervise an elite team that is assigned and responsible for carrying out the use and deployment of nuclear missiles housed within numerous nuclear submarine silos under his jurisdiction. Please, Captain Lane, can you describe to us without giving away any classified information the process of what happens should an opposing nation fire nuclear missiles at the U.S."

The captain explains, "Okay, let's say our satellites with infrared sensors and radar systems, plus ships at sea confirm missile launches. When an ICBM missile leaves the atmosphere, it breaks up into the warhead, debris, and decoys intended to confuse our sensors.

"People in control centers in Alaska and Colorado are quickly challenged to identify and locate the warheads, and then determine where to intercept them. Once that's done, they give the order to fire interceptor missiles from a west coast base or one in Alaska. Thirty-six interceptors are hidden in silos at these two sites, each carrying a 'kill vehicle.' This method is said to be akin to having a bullet hitting a bullet. There's rumored to be a laser system in orbit and one on the F-35 fighter jets that can destroy missiles, but I've had no confirmation of that being true."

He continues, "Once all this begins, the Pacific command has about five minutes to characterize the incoming launches, determine their trajectory and targets, and then alert the public through FEMA 's public alert system, as was done this afternoon when the missiles were deployed from the sea and land."

His voice cracks and he pauses to take a drink of water from a glass, "Of course, there isn't enough time to evacuate the masses from cities, so what it equates to is the old "duck and cover" scenario being in effect. People beyond the blast area should go underground if possible, and not go outside afterward to try to flee the effects of the fallout. They most likely would be in a more dangerous situation doing that than staying put."

The News Anchor then asks, "So who is it that makes the final decision to fire our missiles in a retaliatory response?"

"That final decision lies with the President alone and is not negotiable nor can it be countered. At all times, there is a military officer near the President that carries with him in a briefcase and the codes necessary to launch nuclear weapons. Once a threat occurs, the President must respond rapidly and decisively to a nuclear attack by an enemy. Land-based missiles would reach the U.S in about thirty minutes ... much less time if they are hypersonic. Missiles launched from enemy submarines might reach their targets in only fifteen minutes," explains the captain.

The News Anchor continues to inquire, "Is the President then the sole authority in deciding whether or not to push the button ordering the annihilation of millions of humans?"

"Yes, I'm afraid so," replies the captain. "If you're asking me if I think being able to override that singularity decision is a good idea, then I'd have to say, yes I do. I understand taking the ultimate decision out of the hands of the military, but to have only the chief executive making that choice seems dangerous to me. I've heard legislation has been proposed to include the Secretary of Defense, the Secretary of State, or maybe the National Security Advisor as other choices to input their compliance or denial with the decision for using nuclear weapons."

"It hardly seems logical that given the short response time required that each of those officials would have enough time to decide to respond or not respond. So, after the decision is made to deploy the missiles, what happens then?" asks the News Anchor.

The captain tells him, "It depends on the circumstance, but if there's time, the President will call an emergency meeting of his top advisors. In very few words, they would inform him: Here are your options, and here are the consequences. He will have about six minutes to make his decision. After that happens, and he chooses the launch option, his order is conveyed instantly to the war room at the Pentagon, where then there is a launch order issued to all those with military nuclear weaponry; the 'gold code' is authenticated and the sequences for launching the nukes via subs, from land-based silos, and jet bombers proceeds ... whereby the apocalypse begins."

The News Anchor shivers and remarks, "It's insane! There is no wonder God deplores such a thing." he pauses, and then asks, "So, can you tell us the procedure after you receive a launch command?"

"Well, other than the inexplicable unintended launches made today, the first thing I'd say about the protocol and process is that no missile is launched by a single person. There is what we referred to as a buffer area as "the no lone zone". In silos, there is infantry present to guard the weapons, with instructions to shoot anyone approaching a nuclear weapon alone.

"Launching a nuclear weapon requires two people working in concert, following the same orders. They must then input the same target package sequence and type of weapon to be fired presented to them by the National Command Authority.

"If missiles are somehow accidentally launched, as may have been the case today, they wouldn't have the input of arming codes, nor the target package programmed into them. So, they'd not get very far because the guidance systems wouldn't contain any instructions. With no arming codes, they won't explode.

"There is a system used called, PAL, which is a failsafe system that without its permissive codes will neutralize and not arm the warheads. So far as I know, Russia and other nuclear nations have similar protocols in effect to eliminate unintended firing of nukes."

"That is informative, thank you, Captain," comments the News Anchor. "Hopefully any future launching of missiles will comply with that protocol. Better yet, I hope they do not need to launch, for nukes hopefully won't exist after this ... or else we may not exist.

"Since most of the missiles launched today and all of them from the U.S. were launched from nuclear subs, can you tell us more about those in our fleet?" inquires the News Anchor.

The captain describes the fleet, "The exact number is classified, but I believe the U.S. has enough Ohio-class subs capable of carrying twenty-four SLBMs, known as SSBNs. That means Sub Launched Ballistic Missiles. Our most technically advanced submarine is the Virginia-Class. Russia has thirty-three subs, some being the huge typhoon sub also capable of launching ballistic missiles. The People's Liberation Army of China has a new Type 096 model sub with similar capabilities.

"The thing to remember about such subs is our Trident versions each carry eight times the total blast power exploded by all sides in World War II. Each sub has the equivalent of four-thousand Hiroshima bombs in but twenty-four missiles that contain eight to seventeen warheads. Any one of them can destroy an entire continent."

The News Anchor reacts, "God in heaven, that is incredibly scary, for it came too close to that scenario becoming real today."

He declares in a hushed, somber tone, "Thank you for coming, Captain, and explaining all that to us. I for one hope all those that pledged this morning at the U.N. follow up and do what was voted upon."

Chapter 28

Harold transmits an inquiry to Rehtorb, "May we at least call home to inform our families of what's going on and that we are alright?"

Rehtorb mentally replies, "They've been told that we needed you again and that no harm will come to you."

Nicolai then questions, "You say we are at a secret base underneath a Southeastern Pacific Island? Where is that exactly?"

Rehtorb enlightens them, "I won't reveal the exact location, but only tell you that it's under one of your remote islands inside a hollowed-out cave. It's been here for several thousands of years, as have our bases in Antarctica, and was created by volcanic activity and expanded by my race ever since we've been monitoring your planet."

Harold then wants to know, "You said the evil entity caused the nuclear missile launches, who or what is this entity, and where is it now?"

"An evil, elusive one," declares Rehtorb. "He's known as an archangel who opposes the will of the Creator. His kind has caused chaos, plus millions of deaths and destruction throughout the universe for eons."

"You're describing that which we refer to as Lucifer," states Nikolai.

Rehtorb responds, "I know, and your planet is but one of many where he contributes to death and destruction. He and his underlings thrive upon doing their best to harvest human souls throughout the cosmos and promote evil in this world and all worlds. With the Creator's help, we attempt to suppress his malevolence, as we did when we destroyed those nuclear missiles before they could explode. He has been driven off your planet for the time being into another dimension, but eventually, he shall return to reclaim more souls of those that do not obey the Creator."

"What happens next that requires our presence?" asks Harold.

Rehtorb explains, "Though you don't realize it, the time has passed and it is now mid-morning of the following day. Before the sun sets, the Earth will be drawn to the place where the final exhibit of the Creator's power will be displayed. It is here, that your voices shall join with mine to have the nations of Earth act to comply with the Creator's wishes."

* * *

Before noon on this day, people on Earth are reacting to the threat of the lunar deviation and the narrow escape of avoiding nuclear war. Various groups are reacting in various ways. Religious zealots clamor at the doors of churches to get in. In many churches, newly repenting people are getting baptized. Cults brandish signs like "Come Take Us!" appealing to the aliens to please remove them from this dangerous planet. Rowdy, violent gangs and terrorists defy the law by setting fires to buildings, stealing, assaulting innocents, getting drunk, and into fights throughout large cities in the U.S. and around the world.

Immigrants that made their way into the U.S. from foreign nations frantically attempt to make their way back across the U.S. border, heading north or south to remove themselves from the cities that might become targets for nuclear bombs.

Militaries around the globe remain on high alert status to respond to any aggression at a moment's notice. People with telescopes in their backyard study the sky, attempting to see for themselves what's happening with the Moon.

The Russians and Chinese display tanks and military transports carrying huge missile rockets rolling down main streets in Moscow and Beijing. Korea follows that same example.

Meanwhile, some homeless drifter sitting under a tree in San Francisco knows nothing about a world threat or what's been happening.

* * *

At Apra Harbor naval base in Guam, the U.S. Trident submarine that fired the nuclear missiles is docked. Inside a military compound, a tribunal of high-ranking naval officers is conducting an inquiry with the Captain of that submarine.

The Base Commander in charge begins the questioning.

"Commander, as you know, our Trident submarines are a pivotal part of the U.S. nuclear Triad. Although this base is not your home port, all of us here, plus our political leaders want to know exactly what occurred yesterday when your submarine fired six nuclear missiles without the consent of the President or the Pentagon. Please start at the beginning and explain how that happened."

The stern Sub Commander begins to inform them of the details of that dire incident.

"At the time, we had orders to patrol the waters within a hundred kilometers of Guam. We were topside and doing routine reconnaissance to identify any topside or underwater threats. Without any direction from myself or the executive officer, the diving alarm sounded and we began to submerge. I gave orders to override that, but the helm was unresponsive and we had to clear the deck."

"Once on board, you immediately tried to counter the order and attempt to resurface?" asks the JAG Commander.

"Yes, Sir!" replies the Commander in a firm voice. "I first asked who gave to order to 'pull the plug,' and then sought to have the helmsman cease the submergence, make the corrections, and return topside at once."

"And did he obey that command?" asks the Sixth Fleet Commander.

"He tried to comply with the order but the helm was unresponsive. The Diving Officer confirmed that and we continued to submerge to a depth of around forty-eight meters, and then leveled off."

"What was your response then?" questions the Base Commander.

"I immediately ordered an Emergency Blow, but the control room confirmed that too was unresponsive, so we remained submerged."

"Then what control of your boat did you have?" inquires the Fleet Commander.

"Not much, if any. A few moments after that the Weapons Officer excitedly informed me that the readouts from the control panels were indicating missiles were being prepared to fire and that the warheads were being armed. My exec and I immediately ordered a shutdown of all weaponry systems, but once again, the crewman was unable to perform that function. Essentially, someone or something had taken over the controls of the boat."

"Which crew was on duty at the time, the Blue or the Gold crew?" inquires the Base Commander.

"The Blue. As you know, when at sea, we do drill after drill to ensure everyone is prepared. All of those men are well-trained and there are many safeguards in place to prevent the inadvertent or unauthorized launch of any missile or nuclear torpedo. However, before we could shut the system off, the Weapons officer confirmed that the six missiles were showing programmed targets and were ready to fire, which moments later did launch without anyone's authority."

In a stern voice, the JAG Commander asks, "Are you saying that despite all the failsafe devices and the required PAL protocols that those missiles simply armed, aimed, prepared, and launched themselves?"

"Without any doubt, yes, Sir! That is what happened," responds the assertive Sub Commander.

The Fleet Commander sighs and crosses his arms, "How long has your submarine been deployed on your current mission?"

"Before this, we were scheduled to be at sea for another two weeks before returning to base for a routine refit and maintenance check."

"Has every man in your crew been certified by Squadron personnel? Has anyone on your nuclear weapon launch order decryption teams, plus the Strategic and Control Team not been adequately trained?" asks the Base Commander.

"Sir, as I mentioned, everyone onboard has been certified and efficiently trained and qualified to perform their assigned tactical missions and duties. I am confident that none of what occurred was due to some personnel deficiency or subterfuge."

The tribunal pauses a moment to quietly speak among themselves.

Once they've done that, the Base Commander makes a statement, "Commander, we know that the pumps, motors, generators, turbines, valves, and other parts of a submarine are operating in the harsh environments of corrosive seawater and high pressures from the ocean depths, thus often requiring maintenance to operate properly."

He looks at the records before him. "It appears that your boat was in port forty-six days ago for Upkeep and Refit that took almost four weeks to complete. Afterward, you went out for two weeks on a Sea Trial to be certain that all repaired systems and every other control system were operating properly. Is that correct?"

"Yes, Sir!"

"Then you are sticking by your answer that despite your sub being tested and ready for any emergency, this one is still attributable not to any human error, but rather one of equipment failure?"

"Yes, Sir! That is what I'm telling you, and if you ask the Russians, Chinese, and Koreans, I'm told they had the same type of malfunctions and firing of missiles that we did."

"Very well, Commander. Is there anything else you can tell us that we might need to know?"

"Yes, Sir! I've neglected to tell you of one other very relative and critical issue that no doubt has not been mentioned to the media."

The Base Commander and the other two men lean forward and listen carefully.

"By all means," replies the Base Commander. "Say what you have to say."

The Commander sneers and reveals, "The other eighteen nuclear birds ... did not launch, however, they somehow instead vanished instantly from inside the boat."

"What?" screams the Fleet Commander. "Are you saying that we have eighteen Broken Arrows that just disappeared?"

The steely-eyed Commander replies, "No, Sir! I'm saying that technically ... we have twenty-four Broken Arrows.

He pauses a moment, and then makes a final statement, "As difficult as this all must seem, how much more unbelievable is it that those launched warheads somehow vanished and didn't explode once they were deployed above the atmosphere?

"All the men on my boat have been assigned to me for several years. Each one of them proudly wears the silver or gold dolphins on their chest. Each of them loves our country. Each man trains and works tirelessly to do their job and defend our country should enemy aggression from nations with opposing ideologies begin a nuclear first strike. What occurred yesterday was an uncontrollable abomination that I pray will never again occur."

The Commander's voice trails off. He sighs, shakes his head, and then drops his arms into his lap in frustration.

The JAG Commander looks at the other officers and responds, "Very well, Commander. As you know, a formal review of this matter will be forthcoming. So too will a detailed inspection of the boat's equipment. Although I believe what you've told us, though inexplicable ... it is true. Perhaps, if we all survive, we can come to an understanding of how this egregious act was committed. Thank you for your testimony. Engineers and electronic specialists are flying in to try and make some sense of this matter. Your boat will be sequestered at the harbor until it is cleared of any malfunctions. You and your crew will be detained and undergo standard psyche and polygraph tests. Thank you, you're dismissed."

Chapter 29

After Rehtorb shows them the covert Pentagon meeting, he asks Harold and Nikolai to accompany him to another section of the craft.

Harold asks him, "I have no sense of direction inside here. Are we stationary and parked, so to speak, or are we moving? I can't tell one way or the other."

"At the moment we are stationary," states Rehtorb. "Come, I will take you out onto the base and show you some of our technologies. Since you are each a physicist, I wager you'll understand and want to develop some of what I'll show you for your species. You must retain your helmets and life packs, for the atmosphere has been altered and is conducive to our species, not yours."

When an elevator-type conveyance descends and it stops, the passage opens upward to reveal the massive underground, undersea cavern. Both Harold and Nikolai sigh and become wide-eyed at what they behold. It appears to be a city hollowed out of this massive cavern complete with fantasmagorical futuristic buildings. There are various shapes and sizes of flying vehicles encircling and racing about.

Harold imagines this to be as if they are all part of the animated George Jetson Family. He notes that Rehtorb is not wearing his gravity suppression belt, nor are all the other aliens he sees. He reasons that a lower gravity herein has been somehow produced. He notices that he feels lighter and his steps are also. The atmosphere is somewhat hazy and there is no evident source providing the illumination.

Nikolai notices what appear to be small alien youths scurrying about on their eight-appendage, octopus-type legs. Apparently, between the three of them, they are playing some sort of a game of tag using stalagmite-looking humps to leap upon and scurry over with their nimble eight legs. He's amazed at their dexterity and how rapidly they can move.

Rehtorb escorts them around and through the amazing underground city, pointing out several distinctive yet unusual landmarks and how the base is lit using luminescence from unique flowers brought from their home planet. There are some families seemingly enjoying the calmness within this secretive facility. When they pass by what appears to be some sort of construction site, Harold and Nikolai get a clear understanding of the strength each mature alien has in those elephant trunk-like arms of theirs. Even in the lesser gravity, they lift huge square boulders that would strain a ten-ton forklift. Several of the males easily grab and maneuver the boulders into place on the structure they are building.

As the odd excursion continues, they pass one edifice whereby several adult aliens are standing next to something Harold thinks resembles a tavern. When Nikolai steps toward the open doorway, Rehtorb stops him and shakes his head.

"I wouldn't go in there just now. Those are some of the star pilots and they tend to get a bit rowdy and imbibe intoxicates after their missions. Two of them were the ones operating and disintegrating the missiles launched from land and those submarines."

Hearing that, Nikolai's ears perk up. He remarks, "Hold on! Are you saying this place ... is a saloon? He licks his lips. "I know it's early, but do they happen to serve any vodka in there?"

Rehtorb stands in the doorway and points at the bar. One inebriated alien sways back and forth as he dips his trunk arm and long phalanges into what appears to be a vase or jar. When he removes his arm, his fingers are covered in a thick, creamy, brown substance. Instead of placing it up to his thin lips, instead, a long, thin, blue tongue-like appendage emerges from the center end of his arm trunk and laps up the gooey substance. Harold then hears what he interprets as a belch from the alien.

Seeing this, Nikolai snarls his lip and asks, "Good Lord, what is that mushy mess? And is that proboscis from his trunk-like arms ... a tongue?"

Timidly, Rehtorb replies, "I suppose you might refer to it in human terms as being a tongue. We refer to it more as a flavor scoop. That deplorable brown substance you saw him partake in is my species' worst addiction and vice. I believe it's known as Jiff, although some favor a substance called Peter Pan or Skippy."

Harold tries to suppress a snicker, but then can't help but burst into laughter. Nikolai joins him.

Sarcasm drips from Nikolai's words, "Are you saying that your kind gets drunk ... on peanut butter? Which do they prefer, the creamy or chunky style?"

As both men share in a belly laugh, Rehtorb's brow furrows, though neither man knew he even had brows.

Rehtorb's voice becomes stern and he proclaims, "I assure you that this is no laughing matter. Jiff overdose has ruined and broken up many relationships. Some that become addicts have even smuggled the raw leguminous peanut seeds to our planet and have been raising the illegal, banned plants in Earth soil and oxygen-sealed terrariums.

"They then deal them to others that sell them to our youthful urban dwellers for astonishingly high prices. Only on your planet are our kind permitted to partake of the horrid butter made from that product. If I were permitted by the Creator, I would smother every peanut pod and plant. I'd prohibit its consumption and destroy every jar of this intoxicating, tepid vintage."

Noting that Rehtorb is serious causes the two men to cease their banter and teasing. Instead, he continues the tour and points out some of the astonishing technology and futuristic inventions they have. He shows them a microwave appliance that in addition to heating items, can also instantly cool or freeze them, depending on what it is one wants to do. Another amazing item is what appears to be a three-dimensional computer monitor.

Rehtorb shows them machines that use a new form of energy, whose power source he claims he cannot reveal. Harold notices that because of their lack of a flexible waist, the furniture they've seen in alien homes is levitated by what Rehtorb claims to be a magnetic gravitational force of some sort that allows them to recline and shift positions as required.

They soon pass a very interesting-looking building that Rehtorb proclaims is a secured, covert facility. Nevertheless, he escorts them inside where they see a device about the size of a walk-in shower. It has brass-looking tubes encircled about the top quarter of it, and below around the bottom quarter of it is an amazing, complex-looking, shiny metallic apparatus. Just above that is what seems to be some sort of transparent tube twisted into a pretzel-like shape. It alternately glows in the colors blue, green, and red.

Curious, Harold asks about the device, "What is this thing and what does it do?"

Without hesitating Rehtorb declares, "We call it a window to the past."

Nikolai studies the queer-looking machine before him.

"Hold it! Are you telling us that this machine allows you to time travel?" he asks.

"No," declares Rehtorb. "It only allows us a holographic view of moments in this world or any other that happened in the past. Only the divine can travel backward or forward through time."

Harold states, "That's truly incredible!"

He and Nikolai both seem to have quickly developed a new appreciation of this remarkable alien being. He has many good qualities that appeal to them and they know that he wants what they want ... to be able to save this world and all the treasures and pleasures it brings to all.

As Rehtorb winds down his tour, Harold hears his stomach growl. He realizes that neither he nor Nikolai has had anything to eat or drink in a while, and both men are hungry and thirsty. Rehtorb notices Harold's lean look and apparent loss of energy.

He tells them, "Let's go back to the transport vessel. I had some consumable human food and drink brought in for you. After you consume them and rest awhile, I'll inform you of what to expect when the Creator's assortment of astonishing power begins."

Chapter 30

Later that afternoon, Harold and Nikolai are led by Rehtorb back into the room with the wall and large three-dimensional screen. They once again take their seats on the odd chairs and Rehtorb again dims the lights.

He spreads and waves his long, thick arms at the screen, reminding Harold of what Elisa once read to him in the Bible about how Moses raised a staff over the Red Sea, whereby the powers of God parted the waters and allowed the Israelites to pass over dry land to escape the wrath of the Pharaoh's army and chariots.

As Harold and Nikolai behold the life-like images beginning to appear before them, each seems to realize that what's about to occur will be spectacular, and even more amazing ... it will be real."

The first image they see is that of the serene fields in England on which the mysterious formation of massive vertical and horizontal boulders makes up the circular landmark known as, Stonehenge.

As several tourists stroll around viewing the array of large stacked stones, there is a sudden bright flash of light. Instantly, the entire grouping of stones disappears ... to be quickly replaced by several Moai, like those monolithic ones of the Easter Island statues. Everyone who witnesses this amazing, curious, and inexplicable exchange stands silent and stunned for a moment. Then, they begin to panic and back away from what some seem to believe is a paranormal event that perhaps might be from some witch's spell. As if voyeurs, Harold and Nikolai realize what celestial power is responsible for this amazing feat.

The image switches from England to Xi'an, China, and inside the mausoleum of, Qin Shi Huang, the first emperor of China. Once again, as visitors to the huge exhibit of the eight thousand Terracotta Army, marvel ... as in a flash, each one of these iconic figures vanishes and is substituted by more Moai statues, each the size of the soldiers they replace. The same type of reaction occurs among the people there, and although neither Harold nor Nikolai speak Mandarin, they can each tell by the outcries and panicky attitudes of the people that this too is a seemingly traumatic impossibility.

The next image comes from the Giza Plateau, on the outskirts of Cairo, Egypt, the home of the Great Pyramids, and the mysterious, ancient image of, The Sphinx. As three Egyptian archeologists pass by on the backs of camels and a few yards from The Sphinx, again in a bright flash, a breathtaking and indescribable event takes place. The mighty human-headed lion carved from natural rock instantly vanishes and it too is replaced by a huge Moai carved from Lava rock found on Easter Island.

Seeing this, Harold nods at Nikolai and sends him a quick comment, "This indeed is incredible and quite a brilliant display of God's superiority. I think we now know under which island this base is located."

Nikolai nods and agrees with that assessment.

Next, the screen displays an aerial view of Mount Corcovado, otherwise called, Sugarloaf Mountain, in Rio de Janeiro. Atop this mountain and overlooking, Rio, is an iconic, imposing, and inspiring ninety-eight-foot-tall monument of, Christ the Redeemer, whose presence represents peace and harmony as it spreads out its arms that represent the cross and a loving embrace while watching over the city.

Following in the same pattern as the other incidents, after the flash, in an instant, this monument dissolves and is replaced by a Moai of the same height. In the city, cars can be heard screeching their brakes and even crashes occur as those driving are distracted by what they see atop the mountain. Flustered bystanders along the city streets, houses, and shops exit their abodes to walk outside, stop, and with great concern and tribulation observe this startling occurrence. Many kneel and begin to cross themselves and say prayers.

The scene fades and Nikolai moans, as the image of patriotism in Russia known as, The Motherland Calls Statue comes into view. This two-hundred-seventy-nine-foot-tall statue of a winged female holding a sword aloft and weighing slightly eight-thousand-eight-hundred tons rapidly fades away. It too is replaced by an equally tall Moai statue.

Harold then experiences the same type of reaction, when the iconic, Statue of Liberty, on Liberty Island in New York Harbor, also quickly vanishes and in its place is yet another exact-sized Moai.

In a somber cerebral manner, Harold comments, "I pray that we become independent of a need for the weapons God wants to be destroyed. All our poor, huddled masses are indeed yearning to be set free from that terrible menace. Maybe this fascinating demonstration is what will at long last bring about that change."

Next, the image displays the five-hundred-sixty-foot-tall, Juche Tower, on the east side of the Teadong River, in Pyongyang, North Korea. Fortunately, all visitors have exited and no one is riding the elevator to the top. Nor is anyone in the observation area at the summit. Like all the other mysterious vanishing landmarks this one also disappears and is replaced by a Moai of equal height. All who witness this disappearance are spellbound and at a loss to explain how it is possible.

As Rehtorb, Harold, and Nikolai look on, the image of the Taj Mahal, in India appears. Almost at the speed of light, after the bright flash, the two forward white-marble towers leading into the magnificent edifice disappear and are each replaced by Moai statues. As at other locations, those who witness this are mortified by what they see.

A similar occurrence happens in Punjab, Pakistan in the city of Lahore, where the two tall front brick prayer towers of the famous Badshai Mosque, vanish. In their place are two equally tall Moai statues. Similar stunned reactions are evident on the faces of those Muslims who have come to worship inside the elaborate Mosque built in the year 1671.

In northern California at the Sequoia National Park, several tourists amble and stroll through the serenity of the huge trees, winding their way down a trail to view the two-hundred-seventy-five-foot tall, General Sherman Giant Sequoia tree. This thirty-six-foot diameter tree is the world's largest tree by volume and has proudly stood through time. It is estimated to be around two thousand years old. Unlike the other targets of these incredible vanishings, this is the one living monument that is firmly implanted into the soil in which it has flourished all these years. However, it is not spared the indignity of being uprooted and chosen to display the Creator's superiority over all living things; for it too vanishes and is swapped with an equally tall and broad Moai.

As this lengthy process continues many other landmarks suffer the same fate. In the U.S. the, Hollywood Sign, vanishes and is replaced by an assemblage of Moai statues. In London, the iconic towering, Big Ben, the clock is replaced.

Among the many other notable disappearing landmarks are: In China, the giant two-hundred-thirty-three foot tall statue, the Leshan Giant Buddha; In Turkey, the monument to the Trojan Horse at Troy is replaced by a Moai; in Paris, the iconic, Eiffel Tower is not spared; in Washington D.C., the Washington Monument is replaced by a Moai of the same height; in Japan, the target is the famous, Tokyo Tower; in Israel at the Jerusalem Citadel the, Tower of David built in the fourteenth-century vanishes and is supplanted by a Moai; and finally, the entire ancient pyramid of, Chichen Itza, once the center of the Mayan empire disappears and a series of huge Moai replace it.

* * *

Once these amazing incidents conclude, Rehtorb has Harold and Nikolai follow him out of the room and into another portion of the transport vessel. There, both men are given an update on what the Creator's plan is for that evening. Both men are surprised and they each ponder their upcoming roles in what is to happen next in this shroud of mystery.

* * *

Back in Trenton, the members of Harold's and Nikolai's families have their attention captured by the news coming forth from the networks, the televised videos, and the scheduled programs being continuously preempted by breaking news alerts.

Morgan gathers herself close to Steve on the sofa and remarks, "I sure hope Dad and the General are up to speed on all these tragic events and that with that alien's help can save us."

The News Anchors for every network have reporters stationed all across the U.S. and the globe. What they're recording and showing seems too astounding to be real, for the videos they're sending back to their networks are incredible.

On ABC, the young female News Anchor switches to a field reporter in downtown New York City. The televised view shown on Broadway in Times Square is the rising sea waters that have encroached upon the land and flooded that entire area of downtown Manhattan with six inches of saltwater.

On NBC, a male field reporter situated in the lower ninth ward of New Orleans shows a video where the streets are equally as flooded as they were after the levees broke during Hurricane Katrina. In switching the news to the west coast, the video displays San Francisco Bay wharfs being flooded over. In fact, on the whole of the west, east, and southern coastlines, low-lying cities like Miami, Houston, and others are experiencing similar flooding from rising sea waters. Those floods are causing widespread panic and destruction.

Fox News is reporting that oceanographers have learned that the temperatures of the world's largest two oceans, the Atlantic and Pacific, have increased by almost ten degrees within the past ten hours. In long-dormant calderas across the globe, numerous volcanic eruptions are occurring.

Perhaps the most frightening report in the U.S. comes from the geologists assigned to measure the ground pressures caused by the immense underground cauldron of super-heated magma under Yellowstone National Park. The geologists report that the ground swells have risen over fourteen inches in the past two hours, which indicates an almost certain eruption of that super volcano that's been dormant for over one-hundred-sixty-thousand years.

On top of all the other dire reports and videos pouring into the networks, a few of the more prominent vanishings and replacements by Moai are trickling into news desks.

The young ABC female News Anchor states, "I'm now being told that our Washington D.C. and New York City reporters have some astounding videos to show us. Mack, we'll start with you. What is it that's occurred in our nation's capital?"

The field reporter describes the video now playing as it shows the tall Moai statue that has replaced the vanished Washington Monument.

The stunned reporter says, "The puzzlement here in D.C. is as you can see the disappearance of the iconic Washington Monument, and in its place is what I'm told is a carved, one-piece monolithic statue known as Moai, like those found on the mysterious remote Easter Island in the Pacific Ocean ...

only several times larger than any known to exist there. In questioning some of the scientific minds at the Smithsonian and Georgetown University, they mostly responded by saying it's pointless to try and explain this, for there is no known technology that is capable of such a thing. We're also learning that this isn't the only such incident, as other reports of famous landmarks vanishing and being replaced by these behemoth statues all across the globe."

* * *

Governments around the world use Earth observation satellites to obtain high-quality photographic data of Easter Island. The European Space Agency's Sentinel 2 satellite is the first to be in a position to focus its panchromatic, high-resolution cameras on the island. The image it records proves to be amazing, for all those missing landmarks come into view and are in place and scattered about the remote island. As always, the information produced in the framework of the Copernicus program of the ESA is made available free-of-charge to all its users and the public, thus allowing the downstream to media services that quickly print out the island's photographs and send them around the globe to every network and media outlet. The U.S. networks immediately break in with updates and post the incredible Easter Island photos online for all to see. The talking heads on each network attempt to make sense of the imponderable and immediately begin making plans to send their field reporters to the island for more coverage.

* * *

By dusk of that same day, as Morgan, Ted, and the others partake of their evening dinner, they hear a siren-like alarm being sounded on Morgan's, Ted's, and Steve's cell phones. Each pauses their meal to see what is happening that would cause an alarm to be broadcast to their phones.

They each have a message from the "Emergency Broadcast Network" to tune into an upcoming worldwide broadcast televised announcement. All of them quickly abandon the last remnants of their dinner and go into the den, where Morgan turns up the volume on the T.V.

At first, there is nothing but a blue screen with the words, "Stand By" displayed. A few moments later, however, the women all gasp, and what they see provokes them to lean forward on the edges of their seats ... for on the screen seemingly composed and coming over the ridge of what appears to be a deep crater is Harold. Close behind him comes Nikolai. The two men appear side by side as the sun begins to set over the ocean behind them.

Harold speaks first, "Fellow humans, I am Harold Simpson. My comrade here, Russian General, Nikolai Belinski and I appeared before you at the U.N. Security Council meetings and now come to you via an alien-produced broadcast from Easter Island here in the southern Pacific. By now, most of you know this island is littered with famous landmarks from various nations around the world. It is important to know that none of the exchanges made with Moai statues was accomplished by aliens or any unknown human technology. No, it was done as part of God's plan to convince world leaders to follow through on their promise to rid the world of biological, chemical, and nuclear weapons."

Nikolai steps forward and explains, "Although that promise was made, the aliens have shown us covert meetings made in private among several of the nuclear nations that defy that agreement and have thus nullified the promise by the Creator to spare our world from the oblivion that it will encounter should that agreement not be honored."

Harold then adds, "For most of this day, the General and I have been the guests of the aliens and I assure you; they want as much as we do to have this outcome spare our world and eliminate the threats posed to humanity by these terrible weapons. They too want to avoid a lunar catastrophe.

"However, someone once told me that to all governments and their militaries ... you cannot change what you refuse to confront. I find it inexplicable that after three days of experiencing unfathomable darkness some paranoia would prevent any and every nation on this planet from complying with what was decided and directed by their U.N. ambassadors. I include my nation in that context of deceit as well as a few others."

Nikolai then surprises everyone by announcing, "So, if you won't believe us and if this present remarkable demonstration of God's power still isn't enough to convince you, then it is our privilege to introduce you to the alien whose telepathic voice has been heard at the U.N. and among several of the world's leaders. Many of you have inquired about him and a few even doubted his existence, but I assure you he's real. He's been very cordial to the professor and me, and he loves and obeys the Creator. At this time, we'd like to introduce our alien comrade, Rehtorb."

All across the globe, people are glued to their television screens as the very tall, odd-looking alien again wearing his helmet and life-pack, plus the gravity belt comes into view. With his eight octopi legs, he scurries up the crater and stands next to the two humans.

With his temporal means of communication, he introduces himself, "Attention humans! What I'm about to tell you comes directly from the Creator. After tomorrow, there is but the completion of one more day before your Earth can avoid being destroyed by the approaching proximity of your Moon. To avoid that, obey the following: By 11:00 a.m. tomorrow, ten of the international press must be flown from Santiago Chile to Easter Island. When they arrive there, they will then be flown here to Easter Island to be temporarily boarded in one of the island's vacant hotels. All residents of the island were evacuated a few weeks ago after geologists predicted that the island's five dormant volcanoes were likely to produce a massive volcanic eruption. That was a manufactured gambit used to persuade the island's inhabitants to evacuate. However, I would caution those evacuees to avoid returning until our effort on this island is complete.

"As a final demonstration of his majestic power, the Creator shall after noon Chilean Standard Time cause an unbelievable event unlike any the world has ever known. The press shall then report at 4:00 p.m. to the rim of this caldera on which we stand. At that time, all of you on Earth shall again be presented with another announcement and revelation. My species and I pray that this matter is resolved peaceably and that we can move on and leave your beautiful planet to be enjoyed by you and your ancestors until such a time as the Creator returns His Son to invoke judgment upon you all."

With that, Rehtorb, Harold, and Nikolai turn and look back down the sloping crater toward the massive lagoon at the bottom of the Rano Kau caldera below. The televised view shifts toward that lagoon. All the world watches in awe as the caldera's thirty-two-foot-deep waters begin to be siphoned away into the ground, leaving only the vast array of Totora reeds. As astounding as that seems, what happens next seems impossible. The ground itself begins to crack and part ... to reveal the rising of the triangle-shaped craft that Rehtorb refers to as their transport vessel. Otherwise, it is known to all those humans watching as a large UFO. It slowly ascends from inside the large caldera with the Totora reeds and other plants draping across it and falling away as it rises.

Those watching this Easter Island video feed from home, from the Pentagon, the White House, the Kremlin, Beijing, and other national headquarters are mesmerized by what they're seeing. Within three minutes the craft rises and silently floats over the landscape to pause and settle down within two feet of the ground, apparently defying gravity to hover just above it as the ISS had done at Thule Airbase.

Rehtorb again projects, "Our transport vessel shall remain here until tomorrow evening, at which time the finality of this matter will be decided. As you've been told, no one can hide what's in their heart from the Creator. Any nation or terrorist group attempting to withhold <u>any of the weapons</u> mentioned will only lead to your destruction. Should there be no universal compliance, by midnight tomorrow, tidal dissipation and the angular momentum of the tidal forces under the Moon's approach will begin to severely affect your world. It will take the lives of billions of your species. By noon of the following day, complete annihilation will occur."

At home, the television broadcast quickly ends and the feed returns to show a local News Anchor. She has a profound look symptomatic of stunned fascination and fear reflected on her face. She nervously places a hand on her right ear. From the earphone she's wearing, comes instructions from her producer inside the control room. She winces and then focuses on the camera.

"That certainly was a mind-blowing experience. We've all wondered what the alien looked like, now we know. He's certainly not physically like us. Although he did not seem exceedingly terrifying, the words he spoke to our minds certainly were. I'm told there is no indication of how that apparent worldwide transmission was accomplished, but for certain it was effective and quite candid.

"What we don't know is what the Almighty's demonstration will be tomorrow, nor why the reporters are being summoned to Easter Island. Let's hope that whatever happens ... is convincing enough to result in a firm decision to comply with the demands for nuclear disarmament.

"Of the two gentlemen that were there on Easter Island, and whom we've seen and heard at the U.N. meetings, Professor Harold Simpson is a resident and was evidently selected as the alien once told us ... by God Himself to represent humankind and bring word from God about how we may avoid an apocalypse. They each gave impassioned speeches at the U.N. when the vote was made to remove nuclear, biological, and chemical weapons, but as we've learned, that directive was not carried out. After tomorrow, that leaves our world but one day to avoid the consequential destruction from the Moon's approach ... which is already causing havoc and a loss of life among many of the world's coastline cities. Indeed, for the sake of all of us, let's pray our nation and all nations will come to their senses and quit attempting to deceive God. We urge you, leaders, not to betray all of the rest of humanity."

Chapter 31

Back in Trenton, Katya comments to the others, "That certainly was a tremendously impressive and frightening presentation, but I was surprised that the whole of it was transmitted in the Russian language."

Steve tilts his head and then states, "That's not what I heard. I understood it all and they were speaking to my mind in English."

Rehtorb's mental transmission, plus Harold's and Nikolai's vocal transmissions, were sent out to all humans and each heard and understood what they were transmitting in their native language.

* * *

After the transmission is over, Rehtorb escorts the two men up a ramping device back into the transport vessel. There, they have quickly transported a few miles away into the main Easter Island town of Hanga Roa.

Rehtorb projects, "You must be tired, so we've prepared a place for you to rest and sleep here in town by opening up one of the hotels. We connected the power to it, so you'll have lights and water in case you wish to bathe and void your bowels. Tomorrow morning, we shall come for you an hour after sunrise. A morning meal is being prepared for you. If you thirst, there is a machine in the lobby of this hotel in which there are various liquids. I'm told there are also human consumable sweet carbohydrates therein of which you may partake. I leave you now and prepare for the coming day. I will contact your families and let them know you're safe."

"Thank you, Rehtorb," replies a grateful Harold. "We'll see you tomorrow and hope it isn't the last one we humans all have left."

* * *

After the two men exit the craft, Rehtorb, and the shuttle leaves, Harold and Nikolai walk out of the Hotel and begin peering around outside. The incredible view they witness of this barren island is stunning. Not only is there the daunting row of imposing Moai statues on pedestals, but they are still amazed, as scattered all across the daunting landscape are dozens of familiar-looking landmarks ... all now stationed randomly across the island's hillsides. Harold is particularly amazed and concerned when he sees the Statue of Liberty and Hollywood sign in front of the Washington Monument. The Sphinx is in front of the Chichen Itza Pyramid, and the Eiffel Tower is side by side with the marble towers from the Taj Mahal. A massive Buddha sits next to Big Ben. The huge General Sherman Sequoia Tree stands tall and planted firmly into the Easter Island soil.

Both he and Nikolai are still astonished by this site and seem speechless as they re-enter the hotel to the rooms they've chosen for the night.

Two hours later, after raiding the vending machine and finding only sodas and fruit juice to drink, Nikolai begins to explore the premises of the vacant hotel. When he locates the hotel's bar area, he begins to snoop and finds a locked cabinet where the adult beverages are kept. Not able to locate a key for it, Nikolai instead locates a heavy brass vase containing fake flowers. He empties the flowers and uses the vase as a hammer to pound the locked door of the cabinet. After several powerful blows, the lock surrenders and the door creaks open ... revealing its paragon, the array of alcoholic beverages. It takes Nikolai but a few moments to locate two bottles of vodka. His face lights up as bright as if he'd found a buried treasure. He smacks his lips, secures the bottles, and heads off back to the room he took next to Harold's.

Harold is exhausted and ready for bed. He lies back with his head propped up by pillows and sipping on a cold bottle of Coke. His mind wanders as he thinks of Morgan, Ted, and the others back home. Even after Rehtorb does contact them, they must still be worried beyond imagination. Annoyed that he cannot be with them, he groans under his breath, finishes his drink, switches off the light, and slides down in the bed to get to sleep. Before doing so, he once more recites a second prayer, asking God's help to avoid any impending doom.

Twenty minutes later, from the adjoining room separated by a locked door, he's aroused when hearing a rowdy Nikolai croaking out arias from a Russian opera. Harold finds this most interesting, yet disturbing, as he is fatigued from all that's gone on that day.

When the singing gets louder and more rambunctious, he rises from his bed and goes to open the door to Nikolai's room. The door is locked, and despite his knocking on it and calling his neighboring crooner, Nikolai does not answer or cease his wailing.

Harold begins to pound on the door and yells, "For crying out loud, you crazy Russian. Stop that infernal racket. I need to get some sleep."

The door lock slowly disengages and Nikolai opens the door. Soused, Harold sees the two empty bottles of vodka lying on the floor next to Nikolai's bed.

"What's the matter, Comrade?" asks a highly intoxicated Nikolai. "Don't you appreciate classy ... classic Russian Opera?"

Harold shakes his head in disgust and comments, "Not this night, I don't ... and where did you get hold of that liquor?"

Nikolai stumbles backward and points with a shaky hand at the two empty bottles.

"There's a self-service bar in the hotel. You'd be surprised at how useful a brass vase can be to partake in imbibing elements from that bar," replies Nicolai in a stammering voice.

Harold shrugs and scolds his Russian friend, "Okay, I get it. I suppose you needed it. So, enjoy tomorrow's hangover, but please ... end the arias for the night and allow me the opportunity to get some sleep. You should too, as tomorrow we'll either reach the pinnacle of what we've been trying to achieve ... or else it'll be humanity's last hurrah. Please, get some rest."

"Okay, my crabby, mentally connected, Comrade."

He staggers backward and almost falls. Swaying and with eyes that look like boiled onions he looks up at Harold in a somber manner.

He remarks in a poignant slur, "Honestly, I wish I was home in Russia with my beautiful wife and daughter. I've about had all of this intrigue and intrepid suspense I can take. Are we to be ... or not to be?"

With that, he belches and falls back into a chair.

* * *

By the dawn of the next day, the chosen grouping of international reporters is in flight on their way to Chile, and then onto the plane waiting to transport them thousands of miles away to Easter Island.

Rehtorb does as he promised and wakes Harold and Nikolai around 8:00 a.m. island time. Harold raises, showers, and dresses in the same clothes he had on the day before. He then prepares for the upcoming day and the breakfast promised them by Rehtorb. Nikolai is less enthusiastic or responsive and it takes him a while to shrug off the effects of ingesting enough vodka in one night to send a normal person into a coma. Still, after a hot shower and doing his normal number of sit-ups and push-ups, his blood is flowing again and he's ready to take on the day ... albeit with a jack-hammering headache.

The two men join Rehtorb back in his transport vessel and they all return to the underground cavern and secret base. There, they are served a breakfast fit for any human. Rehtorb even has coffee served, of which they partake. Nikolai uses it to calm his nerves and hopes his headache will subside.

He mentally asks Rehtorb, "I don't know how or where you got this food, but thank you! What're the plans for the day, and why did you want those pesky news reporters to come to the island?"

Harold raises his head and listens, for he too wants to hear Rehtorb's reply.

"Today, the Creator will bring your species to its knees and all humanity will know that God is God," declares Rehtorb.

Harold and Nikolai both seem surprised that this alien finally refers to the Creator as God.

Rehtorb picks up on their thoughts and responds, "Yes, I know I called Him God, and he is that. My species prefer to call Him the Creator, and yes, we also believe in the Holy Trinity, as your Christians do. At any rate, what He's about to do will be dramatic and so amazing that surely not even the most cynical and suspicious of national leaders and militaries can resist complying with the Creator's will."

Harold winces a bit and asks, "Just what is it He plans on doing? I hope it doesn't result in deadly consequences to human lives."

Rehtorb answers, "What will happen poses no immediate threat to humans, yet it will be of such a magnitude that all humanity will shiver at its implication."

* * *

At about 11:00 a.m. island time near the Arabian Sea in the Strait of Hormuz, two huge oil tankers each loaded down with almost eight million gallons of crude oil steam their way through the Persian Gulf on the way to foreign ports in Europe and America. As they move slowly through the calm seas, there is a sudden lurch, and then the vessels immediately pop upward as if like a cork ... raising their ships far above their Plimsoll-line that notes the maximum, safe depth they can be immersed when loaded with their heavy cargos. The captains of each vessel instantly panic and direct sailors to go check the cargo holds to make certain they haven't hit something that would cause immediate flushing of oil into the sea. What the sailors see when they and other concerned crew mates check the cargo holds puzzles and astounds them.

Instead of thick crude oil, the entire hold is empty with not a drop of oil. Even more puzzling is there is no sign of any leak or encroachment to the ship's hull. It remains watertight and solid.

One sailor gasps and remarks, "Holy mother of God. Where did it all go?"

Another older and salty sailor comments, "I've no idea, but I do know the skipper is going to be very pissed off."

On the other tanker, there's a similar reaction as the same thing happens to them as well.

* * *

Meanwhile, among the largest oil-producing nations, in Iran, Iraq, Kuwait, Saudi Arabia, Canada, China, Russia, Venezuela, and the United States another incredible event is about to take place. Being the world's largest exporter of oil, the oil and petroleum transits from Kazakhstan transferred to other European countries via rail cars, trucks, oil tankers, and pipelines all suddenly become bone dry.

In refineries across America and other nations, that equipment that was busily converting crude into usable petroleum suddenly discovers that the gas and oil have been replaced by ordinary water. The same is true for every oil and natural gas well, pumping station, or explorative rig, whether on land or in the large platform derricks at sea. Pure water replaces oil at every level of the industry.

Gas in every fueling station on the globe, all diesel, gasoline, ethanol, kerosene, LPG propane, and natural gas are turned into water. Solid fuels like coal become useless white powder. All manufacturers that use petroleum as a base of their final product rage when they find that their petroleum-based material has become water.

The oddity of this dramatic transformation is the selective and exacting changes that do not affect certain fuel-consumption vehicles and generators. All in-flight airliners loaded with kerosene or naphtha jet fuel are not affected. Railroad engines in transit are exempted from this phenomenon, hospitals and medical offices requiring electricity, plus all buses, taxis, ships, automobiles, emergency generators, and basically, any necessary facility or vehicle with combustion engines requiring petroleum is exempt from this inexplicable occurrence. Thus, all fossil fuel transportation itself is not shut down; yet re-fueling of those transports will now be impossible.

At the same time, even in bright sunlight, solar farms all around the world begin to lose power coming from their solar cells. That loss of power causes the grid to reduce to near zero in amp output in mere minutes.

Wind farms throughout Texas, California, and the breezy southwest falter and come to a halt as the winds drop and completely subside.

Hydroelectric plants around the globe still have water passing through their generators, but like the previous unexplained blackout in Vegas and California a few weeks ago, the generators at these large dams fail to produce even one volt of electricity. Thus, blackouts on the dark side of the Earth cause total darkness to become prevalent, while on the daylight side of the world, all things requiring electric power cease, even those produced by nuclear-powered plants.

Basically, except for those exempt things like people carrying transports and hospitals requiring electricity, every source of power known to humankind has stopped working ... and all fossil fuels have either dried up or become water.

* * *

Without the power to transmit over their towers, cell phones quit working along with the loss of radio, television, and Internet connections around the globe. It doesn't take leaders and the public long before panic and paranoia occur. Not knowing if their nation is the only one with a loss of power, the militaries, foreign and domesticate once again are at their highest levels of alert status, yet have no connection or other means of establishing data needed to make security decisions.

Inside the silos and among the mobile-launch systems of all nations, it becomes quickly evident that even EMP-resistant weaponry and missile-launch systems no longer operate and perform their readiness commands. Satellites go dark and no nation can contact any other from space or by other means on Earth. Any efforts to send the satellites command signals are nullified.

On the seas, destroyers, aircraft carriers, nuclear submarines, and all other ships still function, but their weapon systems are all neutralized by some unknown source. All the world's ability to wage an all-out nuclear war or defend itself from its enemies, provide powered electrical energy to its masses, or refuel vehicles has come to a screeching halt.

Even military armory and every caliber of machine gun, cannon, rifle, or handgun somehow becomes inoperable.

* * *

Back home in Trenton, their families deal with the loss of electrical power as well as the inexplicable inability of their cell phones to work, plus the gas burners on the range top and oven have no gas flowing to them. In checking throughout the neighborhood, they find that others deal with the same outages, and yet some automobiles still start and run properly, so the vehicle batteries must work, but why do they? Why also does the water pumped through city pipes still work?

Miraculously, Ted's car is one that still starts and has fuel. In a drive around town, Ted and Steve learn that there is no generated electrical power, and even more curious, that despite the pumps at gas stations not working, the managers are finding out that their station's underground tanks have no gasoline or diesel, but are instead filled ... with water.

Morgan tries to turn on a small battery-operated black and white television she brought with her when she and Steve were out camping, but its batteries are dead and it won't turn on either.

Ted and Steve drive slowly against crowds of humans that begin to flood the streets after all the businesses shut down and folks attempt to get home to their families. They see a police car on the side of the road and an officer at the intersection directing traffic. They stop to ask the officer if he's aware of what's happening.

The officer shakes his head and says, "Sir, I have no idea. I've tried to reach dispatch on my car radio, but neither it nor my cell phone is working. All traffic signals are out and stores are closing. I tried to switch on my wig wag lights and forge a way home to my kids and wife, but even those don't work. So, I'm here trying to keep people from rioting or stealing. You'd best get that car out of here before things turn violent."

Ted and Steve thank the officer and turn to drive back home.

* * *

When the plane carrying the group of reporters lands at the airport in Hanga Roa, on Easter Island they are met by Rehtorb, who both frightens and excites them with his presence. Their cameras and video recording devices still work and are unpacked and loaded onto a bus driven by Harold. He drives them to the same hotel where he and Nikolai were boarded the night before. Naturally, Harold is bombarded by questions, and none of them know of oil and power outages.

He ignores them saying. "You'll have to direct your questions to your alien host, Rehtorb. Your being here is his idea, and for what reason, we've not been told."

When the group reaches the hotel, they are greeted by Rehtorb, who is somehow transported there. Some wonder if this is the same alien or merely another that looks just like him.

Rehtorb cerebrally communicates to them, "I am, Rehtorb. You may each locate and choose a hotel room. When you've unpacked, the Professor will drive you around the island where you will be able to take photos and videos of the landmarks brought here by the Creator. Your battery-operated devices work and there's electrical power on the island. A meal has been prepared for you in the hotel dining room. Later, before dark, you will be taken to the caldera, where there shall be one final demonstration and a reveal that will surely convince your governments to unanimously agree to disarmament."

Chapter 32

By the time nightfall arrives in Trenton, it is dusk on Easter Island. The reporters are all gathered there at the edge of the Rano Kau caldera as Rehtorb directed.

In Harold's home in Trenton, Nikolai's daughter, Anya, stands near the television talking to her mother and Morgan about the danger they are in and how they hope Harold and Nikolai will soon return home.

When the unplugged television suddenly comes on behind her, Anya almost jumps out of her skin with fright and surprise. The others gasp as well and the first image displayed on the Hi-Def screen is that as before on Easter Island where the waters of the caldera part and the astounded viewers in Harold's den, the reporters present, and also everyone around the world whose television sets miraculously displays this event watch as the alien transport vessel once again rises and floats silently over to a spot on the land. As before, it hovers above the ground, and then Rehtorb, Harold, and Nikolai walk down a ramp that opens onto the ground there at Easter Island.

Rehtorb's image becomes the focus and he begins to transmit to the world, as reporters video the incident.

"Oh, you children, in whose image the Creator made. Listen to my words. Despite the wonders of his supremacy displayed, you have repeatedly denied His will. You flatter Him with promises from your tongues but have been deceitful and unfaithful in the performance of that covenant.

"Time after time over the centuries, He has restrained His anger and did not stir up His full wrath. He knows that you are all made of flesh, like a passing breeze that does not return. How often you have rebelled against Him, though he has gifted you with your very lives and provided you with an eternal soul and all the pleasures this Earth and Heaven can afford.

"Now, He grieves, and yet you continue to put Him to the test time after time. He has stood by watching with much sorrow, as opposing tribes of nations have beaten back what you proclaim as enemies and given over millions of your brave ones to the swords of war. Now, with these powerful nuclear, biological, and chemical weapons, you have made it impossible for any human to have a safe sanctuary anywhere on your planet. Total

270

annihilation is possible from weapons whose sole purpose is to deliver total mutually assured destruction of your species and all living things.

"As you've noticed, He has loosed His power to deplete your energy sources. Only the images you're witnessing and created by our technology are the transmittable communication available to you at this time. Your Bible says that Christ changed the water in wine. Now, the Creator changed oil into water and depleted electric energy.

"Before the Moon goes dark and destroys you, and those looking through the windows to eternity give up their souls to Him; before all created symphonies of this world cease; before the blossoms of springtime fade and the cord of life is severed, and before your dust returns you to the ground from which you came ... you humans have this one final chance ... not to resist His will, but to obey Him, and bow humbly before your maker."

Rehtorb then dramatically waves his long, strong arms at the reporters.

"You were all brought here to record and note the following:"

He outstretches his arms and from the skies above him, a shadowy darkness begins to envelop the island. Methodically, Rehtorb's enormous alien spacecraft slowly descends from above, blanketing the skies for fifty miles in each direction.

The reporters cry out, most likely because they fear it might come down and crush them. However, it comes to within about a hundred feet of the ground and stops, hovering as if like an ominous dark cloud.

Harold too is a bit worried seeing the huge craft dominating the skies and blocking out the evening stars and setting sun. Rotating green, gold and red lights start to rotate underneath the bottom of the craft. Silently, upon the ground directly beneath the center of the huge craft, a ghostly mist of green fog begins to appear.

Harold, Nikolai, the reporters, and all those watching from around the globe are curious as to what will come forth from the emerald-colored haze.

The green mist soon lessens, and then materializing is what seems to be a circular blackness the size of a six-foot round storm drain. Inside this dark shadowy circle, there suddenly emerges the noticeable silhouette of human beings. As if a portal to another dimension, the humans commence to exit the darkness in groupings of three. Seeming somewhat startled, they step forward out of the swirling mist and into the open.

Whatever is directing the transmission of images from this island settles in and focuses upon the men and two women coming forth from the black-hole circle of darkness.

To the surprise of everyone except Rehtorb, the trios of humans cautiously and silently file out onto land. At first, Harold and Nikolai do not recognize who these confused-looking people are. Most of the males have dirty clothing, some with rips and tears in their pants and shirts. The men display gaunt faces donned with several weeks' growth of beard stubble. The women too wear unclean clothing and seem on edge and frightened.

Although appearing in soiled clothes and emaciated, soon the reporters, plus Harold and Nikolai identifies many of the previously disappearing Presidents and leaders. They and all watching on television are surprised to see these that so mysteriously vanished have safely returned.

In all, there are thirty-six national leaders, in twelve trios that come forth. Each appears somewhat astonished by this method of reemergence onto Earth. Most of them are alarmed when they look upward and see the sky blocked off by the huge spacecraft.

The reporters, selected from nine different nations begin to search out the leaders to interview and question them.

The first question most leaders want to know is: "What is that above us and where are we?"

Next, they ask: "Is that tall thing with the octopus legs standing over there, Rehtorb?"

The U.S. President is met by two that immediately welcome him back, but then begin peppering him with questions.

"Welcome back, Sir! It's wonderful to see you again, Mr. President. After you vanished and didn't re-appear, everyone thought you were dead."

President Nash Garrett nods his head and remarks, "Dead? Yeah, at first I thought I was too, and wondered if instead I'd been deposited in hell. All of us were transported to some other world with diverse races of human-like beings on a planet that I presume is somewhere in our galaxy. How we got there and were returned, I've no idea."

Seeming weak and before going on he asks for a drink of water. A reporter hands him an unopened bottle of water, which he eagerly opens and gulps down.

He sighs and continues, "However, for the past few weeks, we've been with those other beings in their apocalyptic world. Their civilization and most of their population were destroyed by nuclear war and a viral pandemic unleashed upon their planet by a warring nation. That nation's violent actions also consumed it as well as many others."

He pauses and glances up at the amazing, huge craft above him.

"We were in the outlands areas of the planet not yet irradiated and were still somewhat habitable. There was very little to eat and drink, plus we had to hold up in caves to avoid the cold and predatory animals in search of prey. Some of those who were generous enough to shelter us died from the attacks made upon our grouping when out in the open. I soon came to the assumption that we would all die there with those others of our reluctant hosts."

"Well, you're back now, Mr. President. We are here on Easter Island in the Pacific," the reporter states. "The object above is an enormous alien spacecraft."

"I see, and is that Rehtorb over there?"

Listening to the conversation, Harold approaches the President.

"Yes!" states Harold, "How is it you know of him and his name?"

The President remarks, "Hello, Professor Simpson. One of the most amazing things to occur was that when we were in the caves, a vision appeared to us as a hologram, displaying the events taking place on Earth. We were all startled by the vision of the U.N. Security Council meeting and the alien voice that commanded all nations to disband their nukes, biological, and chemical weapons. That vision of the atomic blast inside the Security Council meeting room was incredibly frightening. We also had a vision of you too, Professor Simpson, plus General Belinski speaking at both meetings."

He pauses to take a drink, "I must contact my good friend, Vice President Battle, who was no doubt sworn in and is the acting President. I shall be pleased to reassume my duties in that office ASAP, but please, delay any more questions for later. Right now, we gentlemen and ladies are exhausted and have more important things to discuss ... mainly about this matter of nuclear disarmament and disbanding other weapons of mass destruction."

He gathers the others around him and they begin to chatter in some language that each seems to understand, but neither Harold nor Nikolai comprehend anything they're saying. The grouping of leaders nods and shakes their heads at whatever the Russian, Chinese, and U.S. presidents are explaining. Once their gibberish is complete, President Garrett approaches Rehtorb.

The two begin to converse verbally, "We are ready to present our decisions to the world, Rehtorb," says President Garrett. "You have our word that what has been decided is definite and when we reassume our duties as the leading officials of our nations our orders will be carried out."

"Excellent, President Garrett," transmits Rehtorb mentally. "I'll introduce you and the others, and then you can each reveal your decisions to the world. Speak in your own language and our technology will interpret it for other nations in their language."

He also explains to them where they have been and that it was God that transported them to the failing planet to experience the after-effects of what nuclear and biological war can do to a planet.

Somehow, at the same time as Rehtorb is explaining to President Garrett, he is also mentally transmitting the same info to all the leaders.

President Garrett nods and the three leaders who a moment before walked from the mist hand in hand, are introduced to those watching. The first to speak is President Garrett.

"By the technology available to us via Rehtorb and his species' system of broadcasting, though on a planet we're told that is about two-hundred light-years away from Earth, we were still able to view all that has transpired at the U.N. meetings and of the agreements voted on and made there, but not fully acted upon and carried through by our colleagues.

"Although deposed of our political positions temporarily, as re-united leaders of our nations before we vanished, we each now reclaim those positions to bring to you the following unanimous decisions made between us. To explain more, here's the President of Russia."

The Russian President is heard by those from other nations in their native tongue.

He explains, "Thank you, Mr. President. In weighing the consequences of what will happen should the orders of the Creator not be followed, we ...

meaning every nation and supreme leader present, do declare an immediate removal and disarmament of all stockpiled nuclear weaponry within our nation's territories, islands, and those in outer space. This order is to be implemented immediately and has been approved by all thirty-six of the leaders." He pauses and then pronounces; The Chinese President will explain more."

In Mandarin and interpreted by Rehtorb's technology to all nations, he tells those watching, "Thank you, Mr. President. Fellow humans, the answers and solutions to this problem are quite simple. Despite what we leaders imagine will be suspicion from our militaries and generals, all of us that must deal with the well-being of our nations have concluded that for us and our planet to survive, we have no choice but to comply and disband all nuclear weapons, plus biological and chemical ones. As the commanders and chiefs of our nations, that order is as stated to be carried out by all functions of each of our governments and militaries ... immediately ... and without question."

After they speak, each of the fatigued leaders shakes the hands of the men and women with whom they shared their amazing survival venture and this momentous decision.

Rehtorb steps forward and Harold and Nikolai recognize his thin lips forming in a sly smile.

He steps forward and begins to transmit, "The leaders of your world were sequestered on that planet, not by us, but rather by the wise Creator. As you have heard, they have returned and shall be transported back to the nations from which they vanished. As you also heard, they reached a unanimous decision to obey the Creator's order to disband all nuclear weapons and the other two deplorable ones. As messengers for the Creator, I can report to you Earthlings that this is the decision the Creator wanted and is one... He accepts ... therefore ..."

All around the globe, people watching this dramatic moment sigh. One can almost hear the echo of their collected breathing as an entire populous gasp... holds its breath ... and then enthusiastically exhales while waiting for the mental transmission and final confirmation of what they've been longing to hear.

Rehtorb continues dramatically, "The outstretched wings of the angel of death shall pass by your world. The clouds of uncertainty and trepidation above and within the homes, tabernacles, mosques, temples, and sanctuaries of the world shall be lifted. The populace of your world will no longer be as serpents struggling in a vulture's grip ... for the venomous spite of nation toward nation shall be like a blown-out flame no longer able to spew fire down upon you. No nation, like a looming spider, shall be capable of casting its web and stinging bite across continents to randomly cause the supplementary offerings of innocent souls.

"Your Moon shall realign in its proper orbit at a safe distance from the Earth. Your previous sources of energy shall return as before. So too shall your landmarks be returned unharmed to their original places. Your communication satellites and devices will again work.

"There will be no more days of darkness summoned for humanity, for the threats of thermonuclear war, or those involving biological, and chemical weapons will be gone forever.

"Tomorrow's hope will come, for my crew and I shall see to it that this covenant is carried out. We shall at once perform that which we were directed to do. We've made many friends here and will part from your world wishing you all well. Do not forget who created both you and all of us. He loves you, lives in the unobtainable light, and shares His creations with everyone. He'll guide you through this life ... and if you love and believe in Him ... He will safely bring you into His kingdom once your time on this Earth is done."

With that, Rehtorb signals to his large transport with a device he grips with his long fingers. Inside the vessel, three crewmen begin what appears to be some sort of a computer program. Lights sparkle and gleam as whatever it is that's controlling the devices begin to whir.

From the top of the huge spacecraft, a metallic rod ten inches in diameter lifts and raises about fifteen feet into the clouds above. A moment later, a metallic screen around the rod slowly releases as if it is an umbrella opening. The ends of the eight rods holding the metallic mesh are cone-shaped with center holes resembling the barrel of a gun.

The clouds above the craft begin to trickle and spark as if they are on fire. Then, there are loud swooshes of air as some sort of crimson ray shoots forth from the ends of the eight rods, lighting up the skies like the fourth of July. The rays travel upward toward space and others travel down into the ocean, while the remaining rays span and encircle the globe with a web resembling a maze covering the skies like a swarm of red fireflies.

The striking effects of these mysterious rays cleave into their intended targets, which moments before were horrible mechanisms of war and death ... to now be left as ineffective, blunt non-operating instruments of conflict turned to ash.

* * *

Soon after this momentous decision is made, the group of national leaders mingles with the reporters attempting to answer their questions as well as possible. Harold and Nikolai are surprised when President, Nash Garrett, and Russian President, Leonid Rosknova, seek them out. Both men shake hands with the Presidents and seem humbled by their attention.

Harold speaks first, "President Rosknova, I am Harold Simpson, and of course, you know, General Nikolai Belinski."

Again, Presidents Garrett and Rosknova communicate in this odd language.

President Garrett, then replies to Harold, "Yes, Professor. We know who both of you are, for we were, as I stated, able to watch and listen to the speeches you each gave at the U.N. One reporter informed me that you've both been very cooperative with President Battle in working to solve this matter."

Harold tells him, "Thank you, Sir. We've no idea why we were chosen to be spokespersons, but we are delighted that you and the others have banned together to solve the dilemma. If I may ask, Sir, what language was that you all were speaking and understanding?"

"My apologies, Professor. Let me explain: When we first came to realize we were on an alien planet far from home, we also discovered that only a few spoke a second language not native to their nation. So, without our interpreters, we could not converse intelligently with each other. However, on the third day, we suddenly spoke and began to realize that this mysterious language we somehow learned overnight was a central one that everyone understood. It was miraculous and changed our perspectives of each other.

We've retained that ability, for as you can hear, we still have that universal language skill even back here on Earth."

President Rosknova pats Nikolai on the back and smiles at him.

Speaking to him in Russian, which Harold understands.

He says, "Comrade Belinski, my congratulations on your efforts in this matter. Although my colleague and the temporary substitute were probably not enamored by your close association with the Professor, I believe that relationship has shown great promise in displaying détente between our two nations and the ability to build lasting friendships between us. I know that is true between President Garrett and me. The Chinese president is also coming around I think."

Nikolai thanks him and asks President Garrett, "Did Rehtorb arrange for you all to speak to your nation's military leaders and Cabinet members? I admit that I am pleasantly surprised that you all accomplished this universal disarmament so easily after all other U.N. efforts proved to be unsuccessful."

President Garrett grins and whispers to Nikolai and Harold, "Well, we each made it an irrevocable executive order, but I think it helped that Rehtorb went to them previous to our return and said to them that the Creator was reserving the worst pits in hell for those that delayed or disobeyed our orders. Yes, we saw those meetings as well on the cave walls."

Harold and Nikolai glance over at Rehtorb, who is surrounded by reporters firing off questions at him. He answers a few, but after five minutes of pandering to their ploys of getting some sound bites for the stories they'll report, he dismisses them and waves to us ... as if pleading for our help in relieving him of their incessant curiosity.

Seeing Rehtorb's plight, the President motions to Harold and says, "It appears our gregarious alien is getting a full-on dose of human-frenzied media interrogation. We leaders have to go sign the agreement we made and get Rehtorb to zap us all back home like he says he can."

"I assure you, he can do that," replies Harold pointing to himself and Nikolai as examples.

"Okay then," asserts President Garrett. "So, you two go scatter those pesky reporters away from him and we'll get this ball rolling."

As Rehtorb begins to rumple his octopi legs to move back from the reporters, Harold and Nikolai face them and politely steer them toward others to interview.

"Come on, fellows, he's given you enough info for tomorrow's headlines. Go question someone else and use your satellite phones to call your bosses ... which probably work now ... and wire your photos and videos in so that the world can rejoice in this victory," declares Harold.

One insistent reporter angrily demands, "Wait! Where are the six crewmen that disappeared from the ISS. What happened to them?"

As all the reporters look to Rehtorb for an answer to that, he, Harold, and Nikolai disappear.

*　*　*

After Rehtorb, Harold, and Nikolai teleports back inside the huge transport vessel, each reporter and national leader is also teleported to their home nation. The leaders are ecstatic to be reunited with their families. Inside the huge spacecraft, Harold and Nikolai prepare to be teleported back home, but Rehtorb takes a few moments to converse with them telepathically.

"By now, each of those nations and several covert terrorist groups has learned that every nuclear weapon and warhead on Earth has been neutralized and will no longer detonate. That's true for submarines, land-based missiles, ones on jet planes and drones, plus those in orbit on satellites. We have done that with our technology and via instructions from the Creator. Nuclear fission is still possible for use in powering ships and submarines, plus nuclear power plants that produce electricity. Hospitals can still use their nuclear diagnostic equipment. However, never again shall nuclear energy be capable of producing thermonuclear weapons."

Harold projects to Rehtorb, "You have our deepest gratitude for helping make this amazing concession happen. I have no idea how you've accomplished neutralizing so many nukes, but I do not doubt your technology and its incredible abilities. Nikolai, me, and all of humanity thank you from the bottom of our hearts."

Nikolai happily follows with, "The future bows before us now as a vision of hope and promise. As Harold put it, we all thank you."

A joyful Harold replies, "Yes, it's true. Instead of doomed souls on a doomed planet, the snarling beast that was ... has been caged and tamed. For almost two weeks, life has been dreary and uncertain, with humanity itself feeling like a hunted stag. Once again it holds promise, for instead of vaporizing flesh in a blinding flash hotter than our Sun, you have worked your magic and turned the dragon itself into vapor. And hopefully, no longer will viruses, nerve gas, or some other deadly agents be used in war for military purposes."

"For certain, comments Nikolai, "People around the world must be celebrating as if they are a bunch of giddy fawns frolicking like they are children. I can just imagine happy faces blooming bright again akin to spring flowers."

Harold mentally states, "Yes, the future is once more become a thing at rest, something to be experienced onward by a vision that will sometimes bring pleasure and at other times perplexing moments ... yet always lingering with a promise of opportunity and triumph of achievement."

Rehtorb inserts a somber remark into their blossoming wave of celebration, "Although biologic and chemical agents shall also never again exist as weapons, pandemics such as the one your planet endured with the Covid-19 outbreak will remain a possibility. The threats of a nuclear apocalypse are no longer a threat, but I doubt the engines of war shall ever truly cease grinding for you humans. As I noted before, the ideologies of your politics and tribal nations seem irrevocably in disrepair, so I suspect after the honeymoon between the superpowers of the world is over, the argued differences of opinion in how to best promote human rights, how to govern, defend, plus operate those nations will once again lead to a frigid climate of disharmony, lingering suspicion, and eventual more crossed swords."

Nikolai refuses to let his mood swing to one of doubt or worry.

He projects his reply, "Most likely, you are correct, Rehtorb, for distrust and disharmony seem to be the template and temperament of our species. However, due to this phantasmagoria event allowing us more tomorrows, I cannot permit myself concern over what might be and rejoice in what is. I praise God for His mercy, and praise you and your species for helping save us."

Harold agrees with that statement. He then asks the question last posed by the reporters.

"What did happen to those six crewmen on the ISS? Why didn't they emerge from your spacecraft with the others?"

Rehtorb responds, "Do not concern yourselves. You shall see, but not yet."

Chapter 33

What Nikolai described to Rehtorb is how the rest of the world reacts after learning of the executive orders that saved the Earth from being destroyed by nuclear war, chemical, and biological weapons, or by the approaching Moon. As the Israelites were led out of bondage from Egypt and away from the oppressive Pharaoh, those born from 1945 till now are finally freed from living under the bondage of weapons that were capable of destroying not only their lives but those of their children, grandkids, great-grandkids, and every individual being born on Earth.

Eliminating that enormous menace, despondency, and the shadow of death seemed before as unlikely as rocketing to an unapproachable star. The extreme tension was always there in the back of everyone's mind, with most refusing to even think about an enemy firing an avalanche of nuclear missiles with warheads exploding over their homeland, yet knowing it could become a definite possibility.

Each person appreciates and is thankful for the elemental forces that God displayed to convince the national leaders to make the decisions He required. Most agree that His using the aliens as messengers was a brilliant strategy, and all are thankful that the aliens used their superior technology for good rather than wielding it as a threat.

Throughout each nation on Earth, people express their joy. Faith in God blossoms among many that before were either agnostics or apathetic. Churches become packed, financially supporting missions, and most praise God and send Him their prayers of thanksgiving. Emotions of mirth lead to various celebrations and parades where people join in the bliss by wielding signs of hope. There is fanciful entertainment by famous musicians and orchestras play uplifting songs of optimism and joy.

The generators at Niagara Falls again begin to store and produce electricity. So too does it happen all around the world where there had been complete power blackouts. Solar power again works, and winds once more blow to churn the electric-generating wind farms around the globe.

The reporters take hundreds of photos depicting the displaced famous landmarks on Easter Island and are astonished as anyone when they all vanish and return to their normal places among the nations from which they came. Needless to say, all those that had missing icons were overjoyed by getting them back to where they belonged.

In oil fields around the world, pumps once again shell out the oil that was turned into water. In the cargo holds of all the tankers, and on oil platforms, the water reverts to oil. Refineries operate as before churning out petroleum. Gas station owners and customers rejoice that their tanks are once again filling automobiles across the world. Airliners, truckers, and railroads again have jet fuel and diesel to resupply their transports.

In New York, Hollywood, and Washington D.C. all tourists celebrate the return of national symbols. In the skies above, the full moon shines down from its normal heavenly perch ... again at a safe distance away. All the high tides and increased volcanic activity immediately cease and calmness prevails over the world as floodwaters recede and clean-up begins.

In space, NASA, Russia, Japan, and the Europeans agreed it was time to send another crew up to the ISS to resume experiments and collect data. They begin making plans to do so, while the families of those six crewmen that vanished grieve and are bitter that their loved ones did not return with the others on Easter Island.

Now that all of humanity became aware that it is not alone in the universe, astronaut applications pour in for those eager to join in space exploration. Meanwhile, the affluent One Percent that paid hundreds of millions for the rocket ride to Mars to escape and colonize that planet are not disappointed when the billionaire that designed and built the rockets cancels the launch. They are a bit miffed when he refuses to fully refund their payments for the ticket. Instead, he claims the residual funds shall be used to build more rockets and colonization equipment, plus possibly using the new EM Drive type non-propellant technology as the means to get there.

* * *

It is a happy homestead that both Harold and Nikolai re-enter, where their families are rejoicing with the masses as they watch and listen to the festivities on television, once again powered by the reoccurrence of electricity.

When the two men materialize in the guest bedroom again and stroll cheerfully into the den, Morgan and Anya race into their father's arms to hug and kiss them. Ted, Steve, Rita, and Katya soon all join in the welcoming. Pure ecstasy prevails, as Harold and Nikolai are offered cake, cookies, punch, and several finger foods that were prepared.

Nikolai eats a few chocolate chip cookies, but then asks, "I don't suppose there's any vodka in the house ... is there?"

With that, Katya reaches into the seat of a sofa and slowly pulls out from between a cushion and end rail a bottle of Stolichnaya. Nikolai's lips curl and his eyes light up like a neon sign.

"We figured you might be a bit thirsty when you returned, my love," proclaims Katya. "So, Harold's wonderful kids pitched in and bought you this."

Harold grins as Nikolai's handed the beverage of his choice. As before, Nikolai licks his lips, opens the bottle, and then chugs down a big slug of his favorite brew. When he's done, he wipes his mouth with the back of his hand. He expresses a flash of gratefulness with a huge grin from ear to ear on his face. Soft waves of satisfaction seem to calm him.

"That's smooth and supple as a rose!" he declares, as he rolls the strong drink around in his mouth, and then eagerly swallows it. "This is most appreciated and as welcome as an old friend. My sincerest thanks to you all."

Harold's eyes flicker and he facetiously suggests, "Enjoy yourself, but save enough of that so it doesn't again loosen your lips to warble out more of those midnight arias. I'd like to get a full eight hours without being disturbed by your cackling."

For the tiniest bit of a second, Harold sees reflected in Nikolai's emerald eyes a look of disdain as the big Russian downs another slug of vodka.

The mocking brittleness in his voice confirms Nikolai's teasing counter.

"Not to worry Comrade. I assure you I shall be content tonight to only humming soft lullabies and falling asleep in the arms of my beloved."

A half-hour later, Nikolai, sets the bottle down on an end table. Although a bit tipsy, he's not drunk. He follows Harold as the two adjourn in private to Harold's office. There, the two friends sit and discuss Rehtorb.

"After all we've seen and been through together, I am a bit disturbed that he zapped us back here and didn't even tell us goodbye," states a disappointed Harold.

"Yes, me too," responds Nikolai. "I suppose he was anxious to wrap things up on this planet and return to his own to be with his family. Still, it would've been nice to have had one more opportunity to let him know how grateful we are."

"What do you suppose we do now with these disks planted in our heads? I doubt they can be removed by any human surgeon. Shall we always be able to converse mentally between us?" asks a concerned Harold.

"I'm not sure, but although we didn't ask for it, we have retained that mental ability," declares Nikolai mentally.

Harold projects his non-vocal reply, "Yeah, I suppose it's alright, even though at times I'd prefer you didn't know everything I'm thinking."

When they're through, Nikolai follows Harold back into the den and stops near the entrance to the hallway. His expression changes to one of confused curiosity. Harold picks up on Nikolai's sudden apprehension.

"What's wrong? You're puzzled by something," Harold states in a concerned voice.

Nikolai pauses and glances down the hallway at the basement door he'd dreamt of that night. As if in emotional turmoil, he walks down the hall and stops in front of the door.

He glances at Harold, who seems awkwardly uncomfortable with Nikolai's gazing at the door.

He projects, "I had a strange uncomfortable dream about this door," he transmits silently to Harold. "Morgan informed me it goes to your basement, which holds some prized reminiscences you spent down there with your wife, Elisa."

Harold winces and a gathering of old memories begins to flood his mind. He recalls the days of intense competition he and Elisa enjoyed when playing ping pong, shooting pool, competing at shuffleboard, cards, and the last game of chess they played but never got to complete.

Nikolai cerebrally informs him, "Morgan told me that after Elisa's death, you locked the door and haven't been down there since."

Harold feels tightness in his chest as he joins Nikolai in the hallway next to the door.

"Yes, that's true. That room was the happiest place in our home, and when I went down there without her, too many precious memories flooded over me. Not being able to share them with her caused me too much pain, so I've avoided going down and locked the door."

Nikolai's uneasy as he describes his dream, "I understand that Comrade, but for some reason, I had that strange dream ... and in it, I saw the table tennis game, the pool table, the shuffleboard, card table, plus the chess pieces and the unfinished game. There's also warm oak paneling on the walls like that you have in your office ... and a stone fireplace with a large screen television set mounted over that fireplace."

Harold's face forms a queer look of wonder, "Yes, all those things you describe are accurate, but how is it you could know that?"

Nikolai verbally speaks, "I've no idea, but suppose we go down there and finish that game of chess. Maybe then, your heartache will soften a bit and the uneasiness you have will be lessened."

Harold considers Nikolai's suggestion and at first rejects it, for a surge of more memories flood over him. After a few moments pass, he reconsiders the proposal and fumbles through his pockets for the set of house and car keys he carries. With nervous hands, he removes the keys and glances at Nikolai who stands there in anticipation. Finding the proper key to unlock the door, he places it into the keyhole and dislodges the lock.

His legs wobble and he sighs deeply. Nikolai places an arm on Harold's shoulders and stops him from heading down the stairs.

Noting the gloomy look on Harold's face, Nikolai remarks, "Hold on. If it's going to be so upsetting for you, close the door, lock it and let's go back to the den. Besides, I suppose I need to get ready to go catch the plane back to Russia tomorrow morning."

Harold gently removes Nikolai's arm and glances down the dark stairway. He then flips on the air conditioner and light switch to the basement and then begins stepping down the stairs.

At the foot of the stairs he glances around and affirms, "Thanks, I'm okay. Besides, you may be right."

Harold pauses a minute to savor the memories shared with Elisa in this place. The images flood his mind and seem as clear as though they'd happened only a day ago. He realizes that down here to him ... Elisa's essence hasn't faded with time. He notices all the precious mementos they collected together, all of her college trophies for being a champion ping pong player; the baby shoes of Ted and Morgan that she had bronzed and placed on pedestals; the framed copy of both kid's birth certificates; plus, the framed photo collage on the wall of his and her wedding. All these things now bring him happiness and alleviate the dread he had before of coming back down here into this sanctum they so loved.

Harold nods and tells Nikolai, "I have no ill memories of anything bad happening down here. I suppose it's time to make more happy ones, starting with you my good friend. Let's work on finishing that game of chess. After I beat you at that, how's your pool game?"

Nikolai grins and follows Harold down the stairs into the happy playpen. Once in the basement, Harold points across the room at the chessboard and the unfinished game. Nikolai nods and breathes in the somewhat still stale air not yet completely overcome by the air conditioner that's been turned off for five years.

He starts toward the chess table with Harold, but as he does his eyes roam about the room, noticing the dusty pool table, the shuffleboard, and the ping pong table. He sees the large screen T.V. hanging on a wall, plus the photo collage of their wedding. He then focuses upon something that catches his eye atop the wood-carved mantel over the fireplace. He ceases walking, turns, and then approaches the three 8" x 10" photo portraits on the mantel.

Harold notes the sudden odd look of confusion on Nikolai's face as he stares at the three portraits. Nikolai takes one in his hand to examine it closely. Harold mentally senses an icy chill seeming to overcome Nikolai. He watches as his friend's face twists and sneers. He then holds out the photo toward Harold with a stunning look of sheer bewilderment.

Nikolai's voice becomes weak and almost pleading as he asks Harold, "How is it that you have a photo of my father standing next to this woman? And is that you as a child standing by them?"

Harold then registers his surprise at Nikolai's absurd proclamation and assumption.

"Your father? That photo is of my dad and mom with me as a kid. Those other two are of me with Elisa and them a few months before my parents were killed in the crash."

Nikolai grabs the other two photos and his face reddens with confused anxiety.

He repeats the certainty of his claim, "The man in these photos is most definitely my father. See that simple line fish tattoo on his right arm ... he got that after he took me to be baptized in church when I was five. It's a Christian symbol and he had one tattooed on my right arm as well. I'm surprised you've never noticed it."

He rolls up his sleeve to show Harold, who stares at the tattoo on Nikolai's arm and the one on his dad's arm in the photo. They both seem to match.

"Hold on! Are you trying to tell me that—"

Before Harold can finish his stunned remark, Rehtorb suddenly materializes inside the room. He raises an arm to stop Harold's reply. In one arm he carries the suitcase he sent with Katya when she and Anya first arrived here. He lays it down onto a nearby small table.

With his normal placid manner, he begins to telepathically enlighten them why he's come.

"Yes, hold on, both of you, for I have something important to show and tell you. Please sit down, as I am about to show you a grouping of hologram images supplied via the time machine that you saw at our underwater base. As I told you then, it allows one to view incidents from the past. You will witness the same type of three-dimensional images produced and seen at your first U.N. Security Council meeting."

As a bewildered Harold and Nikolai take seats in two armchairs facing the fireplace, Rehtorb opens the suitcase and removes the two framed photos of young Nikolai with his mom and dad. He hands them both to Harold, whose jaw drops as he beholds the exact doppelganger of his father. He then turns toward Nikolai, who in turn stares back at him. Both seem vexed with no idea of how to calm the anxiety building within them. Harold mentally confirms to Nikolai that he too is confused.

Rehtorb then dims the lights and closes the basement door at the top of the stairs. In the quiet darkness the sudden image of Nikolai's thirty-two-year-old father, Oliver Belinski, appears as if he's there inside the room. He bends down and hugs his six-year-old son, Nikolai, whose face reflects the love he has for this good man.

Nikolai squirms in the seat and watches as his deceased Mom, herself also a young woman hugs her husband. He bids them each goodbye, enters his car, and drives off toward the airport where he's leased a single-engine plane to fly to his concert in Poland.

The image then fades to a moment during the flight, when the father's plane experiences engine trouble. He attempts to correct the loss of fuel, but the plane's engine sputters and catches on fire.

Rehtorb explains, "Nikolai, your father reports a Mayday over the plane's radio, but flying through mountains on a snowy, winter day, he doesn't know or have time to report his exact location before the plane dives headlong into the icy waters of a remote and very deep lake in Lithuania. Unknown to him, the plane's transponder isn't working properly, so no one knows where his plane goes down."

Nikolai watches as the plane strikes the water. His breath catches in his throat as he sees in stark color and clarity the terror on his father's face just before his head crashes into the front cockpit window and the icy waters begin to swallow up the plane.

Harold too is mesmerized by what he sees happening.

Nikolai shivers with trepidation leaps out of his chair an "Enough! I do not wish to view the moments before my father dies."

Rehtorb quickly corrects him, "No, he does not. Watch what happens."

Puzzled and apprehensive, Nikolai sits back down and watches the life-like action of the hologram before them. His father is still conscious, and fights to remove the pair of pants he's wearing that are caught under the cockpit's dash on something. Blood trickles down his forehead. He unzips and loosens the pants around his waist, struggles out of them, and then kicks out the door to the plane that is now half-submerged in lake water.

As he scrambles to exit the sinking plane, he notices the shoreline about fifty yards away. He quickly reacts to the lake's chilling thirty-eight-degree temperatures and desperately kicks off his shoes to start swimming toward the shore. It takes all his effort, but he soon reaches the shoreline and crawls up onto the bank. His body shivers as he lays there. His rapid breath exhales fog while the heat from his wet body also produces steam to rise off it around him.

Exhausted, he glances around at the landscape and tries to stand. He falls back twice, before getting to his knees and forcing his chilled limbs to react. Knowing that his body's temperature has fallen to a near-critical point and that he'll freeze if he doesn't move to find a warm place, he manages to stand in a squatted position.

About thirty yards away, he sees a paved roadway, so he strains and shuffles towards it. His feet must be close to being frostbitten and his head seems to swirl. His eyes roll back in his head just as he reaches the edge of the road. He falls backward and collapses unconscious onto the ground.

In the meantime, Harold and Nikolai notice a car coming over the top of a hill on the road. Inside the car, Harold recognizes the woman driving. It's a younger version of his mother, but he doesn't mention that to Nikolai, and hopes that he doesn't pick up on that. As her car approaches the roadside where Oliver lies unconscious, she sees him there and squeals to a stop.

With snow coming down and a slight breeze, the wind chill must feel like it is in the '20s. She stops, opens her door, and races out to see if she can help this poor man. Showing amazing dexterity, the lovely twenty-eight year old, Malina Kowalski somehow manages to drag him over to her car and get him inside onto the passenger seat. She then closes the door and goes to her trunk where she removes two blankets, a towel, and a leather cap with woolen ear flaps. She takes them and gets back into the car's driver seat.

Nikolai and Harold stare in awe as she unbuttons Oliver's wet shirt, removes it, and then wraps him in the two blankets. She uses the towel to dry his wet hair as best she's able. She places the cap over his head, careful not to further harm his injured forehead, and pulls its woolen ear muffs down. She starts the car and places its inside heater on high. She then heads off down the highway.

The scene switches to a hospital in Vilnius, Lithuania. Oliver lies in a hospital bed; his head is bandaged and he has an oxygen tube up his nose. He's awake but seems rather weak and timid from not knowing where he is.

Malina is talking to a doctor. Harold and Nikolai hear the doctor speak in English, but he did so in Polish.

"He's very fortunate to be alive. He wouldn't be if you hadn't found him and brought him here," states the doctor.

"He seems to have been in an accident," says Malina. "He had no shoes or pants and I saw no other cars around where I found him. What is wrong with him, doctor, and who is he?"

"He had no identification on him, and when we asked his name, he could not recall it. He doesn't know where he lives, how old he is, if he was in an accident, or if he's single or married. He did, however, wear what appeared to be a wedding band. The authorities weren't able to locate any evidence of an accident, and there were no witnesses they could find to identify him or how he might have been injured."

Hearing that, Nikolai bristles, and his lips tighten in anguish. He waves at Rehtorb to stop the images and he once again stands.

"Are you implying that my father, who didn't die in the plane crash, lost his memory and couldn't recall being married to my mother, or that he had a six-year-old son back home in Russia?" asks a frustrated Nikolai.

Rehtorb ceases the hologram and attempts to explain what happened after the crash.

"Your father suffered two lingering, permanent disabilities. The concussion he got from the crash, plus the fact that his body went into extreme hypothermia caused him to have severe retrograde amnesia. That condition lasted the remainder of his life. With no identification, no witnesses to the crash, the plane sinking into forty feet of water, and him not remembering his name ... and despite the wedding band, there was no way he could recall that you and your mom were back home grieving and thinking he was dead."

Nikolai reaches into his vest pocket and removes the remnants of his last Cuban cigar. He nervously bites off one end of the cigar and spits out the remnant. His hands tremble and he nervously uses a lighter to ignite the tobacco. He exhales and faces Harold.

He then tells Rehtorb, "Please, go on then ... explain what happens next."

"Your father's true identity is never revealed, nor does he have the ability to remember anything that occurred before the crash. Such memory loss is rare among your species, but it does occur in some cases. In this incident, it did with him."

More images appear in the darkness. This time, it is of Malina and Nikolai's father sitting together in a porch swing at her home in Poland.

Rehtorb explains, "Nikolai, your father physically recovered from his ordeal. However, he also suffered nerve damage to the ligaments in his hands. Even if he'd remembered that he was a virtuoso pianist, he'd never have been able to again play that instrument.

"The Polish woman that saved him returned several times from her home in Poland to visit him during his recovery. In time, they grew quite fond of one another and after six months they became engaged. Even though he was affluent in Russian, he told her he had nothing to offer her ... not even a name."

Nikolai puffs on his cigar, stands, and then walks into the hologram and up to the image of Harold's mother on the swing. His shaky finger points at her and he sighs.

"No need to go any further with this. I can see where it's leading. She's a lot younger there than in the photo Harold has on his mantel, but it's his mother, isn't it? My father's infirmity and loss of memory, along with this woman's affections ... the two fell in love and got married, didn't they?"

Harold now stands and tries to speak, but words escape him and he plops back into the chair.

Rehtorb continues, "Yes, Malina referred to him as a John Doe, so he takes John as a first name, and then adds the last name of Simpson, that she makes up from one of her cousins.

"So, they marry in Poland eight months after he's released from the hospital. She becomes pregnant a few months later, and for some reason John cannot fathom, he's drawn to them moving to Alabama in the United States. After getting a passport, they use the money she got from her parents' dowry and leave on a cruise ship from Paris to the U.S."

Harold again stands and declares, "At first they live in a dingy apartment, but then each finds work and they lease a decent house in the suburbs. My father, John / Oliver, goes to work as an intern on the railroad. Three years after I'm born, he becomes a full-time railroad engineer driving freight trains all across the nation. Malinda, my mother becomes employed in a pre-school, daycare facility and later is a kindergarten teacher."

He stops and both he and Nikolai stand face to face staring at one another as if ... it's the first time they've truly seen each other.

"Finally, Nikolai breaks the ice between them as he speaks vocally, "Yes, I noticed when we first met, you have his same expressive gray eyes. Now it makes sense why that is."

Harold grins and replies, "And you have his long fingers, his physique, and strong arms."

They remain silent for a few moments and Nikolai tamps out his cigar. For several moments not a word is spoken, and then Rehtorb takes them both by the shoulders and pulls the two together.

He grunts and snorts as he instructs, "Go on! Each of you ... <u>hug your brother!</u>"

Harold can barely contain himself and his eyes water. Nikolai remains stoic, but it's obvious that he too is touched with emotion. The two men that were good friends before embrace each other for the first time as brothers. The smiles on their faces say it all, for each is overwhelmed.

"I have a brother! You ... are my brother, Nikolai." states a joyful Harold.

"Yes, it is remarkable, for sure," declares Nikolai. "I was a wayward child of six without a father that did not die as my mother and I thought. Instead, fate decreed he begin a new life with the woman that saved him. Even one of your American Hollywood screenwriters couldn't make that up. At any rate, none of that anomaly is of your doing, my brother. You too had to mourn for him and your mother when they died in that awful car accident."

Harold holds Nikolai at arm's length and is exceedingly pleased to have a brother. His second hug is accompanied by a broad smile.

He teases with a comment, "Great, my brother's a dark and handsome communist ... I mean when it's dark, he's handsome."

Not to be out clichéd, Nikolai remarks facetiously, "And my brother's a capitalistic college professor whose genius is squeezing a minimum of thought into a maximum of verbiage."

Each glare seriously at one another ... and then bursts into laughter. About this time, Morgan opens the basement door and sees the ten-foot alien, Rehtorb, stooping a bit inside the room's nine-and-a-half-foot ceiling.

"What's all that racket going on down there? Oh, hi Rehtorb! They were wondering if they'd see you again."

Harold smiles and waves a hand to her, indicating that all is well and for her to close the door. She smiles back and does exactly that.

Rehtorb then wittingly asks in his mental way, "Do either of you semi-intelligent humans know what an Emordnilap or Semordnilap is?

Nikolai snarls his nose and sarcastically remarks, "Yeah, I caught a couple of those little critters in a bear trap when I vacationed in Siberia. They were a bit too stringy to eat though."

Harold corrects him, "Yes, well, to accurately answer your question, I recall that from my freshman English class in college. It's similar to a palindrome, except the letters aren't exactly from the front and backward, so it's called a Semordnilap."

"That's correct," states Rehtorb. "Your species often seems to do things backward, so one of you geniuses try it using my name."

Harold mentally begins to spell Rehtorb backward. After he does, both he and Nikolai realize what Rehtorb is telling them. They each throw up their hands, sigh, and laugh.

Nikolai exclaims out loud, "It spells, 'Brother!' Well, you sneaky, sly, old alien. Is that your name, or have you been going by that because you were trying to tell us something?"

"Yes, that was an Earthly moniker I assumed. It's likely that neither of you could pronounce my true name. You're also correct that I did that so that if you didn't get it then ... you might after I revealed your father's situation ... but you were both as dense as ever."

With that, he snorts and gurgles a few times as his lips form that goofy looking smile they've come to recognize.

Harold sneers and fakes annoyance, "Okay, Not-Rehtorb, we get it now."

Harold swears he sees Not-Rehtorb place his long tentacled fingerlings over his lips to suppress a laugh. Then, as things calm down between them, the alien embraces the two humans with his trunk-like arms and then backs away from them.

Nikolai then asks Not-Rehtorb about something that has been puzzling him, "One more thing ... back before my brother and I went to that first U.N. meeting we each had a dream about you. Then, a few nights ago, I had a strange prophetic dream about the games and things down in this room. Did you implant that dream in my head and the ones before the U.N. meeting?

Not-Rehtorb pauses, and then remarks, "The human mind is very receptive in a somnambular subconscious state. Therefore, it is easily prone to envisioning mental suggestions directed to it."

"So, what you're telling us is ... that yes you did implant those dreams in our heads," chides Nikolai.

Not-Rehtorb transmits, "The disks that were transplanted inside your brains will no longer function once I'm gone. Don't worry, for they will pose no physical threat to you. It was through the disks that you experienced those dreams.

"I must go now. I shall miss this world and the two of you, my human friends. The Creator chose well in selecting you, which was in part due to the close relationship of which He wanted you each to learn. He too likes a happy ending. I'm glad to say this one has that. Together with His wisdom and power, the three of us helped Him bring about a tremendous change that makes your world and the universe much safer."

He starts to fade away, as both men reach out and beckon him not to leave.

The last words they hear in their thoughts are, "Farewell, and may the Creator continue to bless you!"

Realizing that is their final farewell, Harold turns to his newly discovered brother, glances around the room, and then strolls over to the game table with the chessboard.

He motions for Nikolai to join him, where the two of them sit, size up the positions of chess pieces, and then they each begin to make their strategic chess moves. What they instantly realize is that neither can sense nor read the thoughts of the other as they had been able to for the past weeks.

Harold states as Nikolai makes a move that threatens his queen, "Terrific! When I need to know what you're thinking, it all disappears and I have to rely on instincts. It may turn out that I hate the brother I love."

Nikolai winks at him and then like a striking serpent makes the move that then places Harold into "Checkmate."

He then states, "I already miss that marvelous alien. Yoda didn't leave us with, 'may the force be with you.' It wouldn't have surprised me if he had."

"Yeah," replies Harold. "I'm just glad Darth Vader nor Obi Wan Kenobi told him they were our father."

* * *

A day later at NASA control in Houston, they receive an unexpected video transmission from inside the International Space Station. To everyone at NASA's surprise, what they see astounds them, yet also causes them to celebrate for the live images of all six missing, bearded, and ragged-looking crewmen float happily inside the crew compartment and they transmit this message to Control.

"Come in, Houston. Are you receiving our video feed? Brace yourselves, for you aren't going to believe what happened to us and where we've been for the past few weeks."

* * *

Three days later near sunset, Ted, Morgan, and their spouses bid so long and head back to their homes. That same day, Harold bids goodbye to his brother, Nikolai, his sister-in-law, Katya, and his niece, Anya as they return home to Russia.

Nikolai leaves him a letter stating: "My dear brother ... I like the sound of that. Brother, although humankind has dodged a bullet this time, the Bible tells us that there will one day be an Armageddon and that an anti-Christ will appear upon the Earth. Christ will return to defeat that evil and to judge the living and the dead. We witnessed many of the signs of such an apocalypse during our current crisis, and I am confident that among humanity's nations there will once again in our future be wars and rumors of wars that will occur.

Our violent history and differing points of view in governing will cause more clashes of ideology ... and more human blood will be spilled and soldiers sacrificed. As Not-Rehtorb told us, we are a warring, tribal species. However, for now, our world is at a stage where we can no longer annihilate each other with atomic weapons. That and the demise of chemical and biological weapons is a win-win-win for humanity. Henceforth, no matter how temporary this peace is, we should relish it and seek to live righteous lives. Up till now, my father and son were the only two men I ever told that I love them. I leave you now, expressing to you my friendship, my admiration, and my undying love for you and your beautiful family. Until next time, your brother, Nikolai."

* * *

Days later and once again home alone and in his bathing suit, Harold goes out back and hops into the lukewarm waters of his swimming pool. Now May, it's still a bit chilly in the 78 degrees outside temperature, but to him it's exhilarating.

He swims up to the side of the pool, glances up into the sky just above the treetops, and gazes at the full moon rising on the horizon in the twilight of the oncoming dusk. He grins and shakes his head. Only a few stars are visible at this time, but the ones he takes special note of are the three sisters of Orion. In his mind, he envisions, Rehtorb, the tall alien that befriended him and Nikolai and who helped give all the world a future.

He treads water and holds onto the coping at the edge of the pool. He sighs and then wonders what his brother Nikolai and Not-Rehtorb are doing at that moment ... so very far away in Russia. Is Nikolai downing vodka and puffing on one of his new stashes of Cuban cigars?

He ponders, is Not-Rehtorb resting on a floating lounge, racing around with his kids on those octopi legs of his, or has he been given a new assignment to go save another planet in the vast galaxy of our universe full of humans that defy God's will?

Harold's truly calm and happier than he's been in a long time. He asked for and received permission to skip teaching this summer's physics class at Princeton. Instead, he and his brother Nick, as he's started calling Nikolai ... arguing that a three-syllable name is too long for a guy that might start hanging out more in New Jersey. Of course, Nicolai responded to that by renaming Harold as well ... calling him ... "Hare." Naturally, Harold vetoed that, so each went back to calling themselves by their full names.

They agreed to meet in the Maldives for a long vacation together. Nicolai received a Presidential citation from Russian President Rosknova and a furlough from the Army for three months this summer.

As Harold's arms hang onto the poolside, his eyes catch the glimpse of something flittering rapidly across and in front of his face. He focuses on four metallic green hummingbirds with red-colored throats visiting the feeder he keeps in the large oak tree a the end of the pool. The tiny bird eagerly feeds on the sweet nectar, to then flit away and zip around the yard at warp speed. Harold then notices the rapidly beating wings of the birds swooping forward and stopping just a few feet from him on the poolside. As he'd once done with a butterfly, for the heck of it ... he holds up a hand and sticks out his index finger. It produces a "déjà vu" experience.

To his complete astonishment, one hummingbird zips and lights with its tiny feet on top of his finger. The other three rapidly flap their wings, hover across from him, and tilt their heads, as if to be sizing up this human before them. The one on Harold's finger warbles and hums, unafraid and waving its head at him as if to say hello.

Harold holds his breath, and then softly whispers, "Hello little friend. And what wonders from God must await us both with tomorrow's dawn?"

ABOUT THE AUTHORS: C.S. RAMAHON

Shannon Cindy

Above is Shannon. She has five grandchildren and lives in Fort Worth, Texas with her two best friends Cindy and Andy. Cindy is technically a collaborator to Shannon on all the novels and screenplays they've completed. Because Cindy is dyslexic, Shannon is the author and writer of the team. Rather than just use her name, Cindy and Shannon created the amalgam **C.S.** with **C.** for **Cindy** and the **S.** for **Shannon**. The last name, **Ramahon,** is also an amalgam of their true last names. Therefore, **C.S. Ramahon** is the pseudonym for their books and screenplays. Having a BBA degree in business management and marketing from Baylor University, Shannon also did post-graduate studies in psychology and the human condition. Now retired, professionally she has been a building contractor, a real estate developer, building material distributor, a manufacturer's representative, an office manager, and an industrial sales rep. Retired, she now seeks to promote their novels, screenplays, poetry, and also her songs.

A devout Christian, she is a member of the Methodist faith, loves sports, attending Baylor games, and Texas Rangers baseball games.

Also retired, Cindy was in the Navy stationed off the coast of Viet Nam on the aircraft carrier, U.S.S. Ranger. She is a former aircraft inspector for the U.S. Department of Defense having served in that position for over forty years. She was last stationed at Lockheed in Fort Worth where she was the government inspector on the F-16 fighter jet and the highly technical F-35 joint strike fighter jet.

She and Shannon have lived together for over 22 years and attempt to develop entertaining characters and stories for their readers.

* * *

We value the opinions of our readers. We are thankful to (you) the reader that leaves a one or two-sentence review at **Booksellers or on our email address below** about what you thought of the book.

Email us at: shannindoe@yahoo.com

Other Titles Available by **C.S. Ramahon:**

Tree Weavers: A Paranormal Fantasy Thriller in the Amazon Jungle

The Last Angry Word: Dark Tale of Retribution

Poultry-Geist: G-Rated Comedic Romp About "Fowl Play"

:

Five New Novels Upcoming:

Down Da Road: Comedic Adventure Tale With a Sasquatch

Bleakwood: Paranormal Murder Mystery and Mayhem

Hooten Holleran: An Avid Baseball Fan's Afterlife Adventures

Hostage of The Moon: An Original Werewolf Saga

Forged By The Blood: Historic Fiction About an Alamo Survivor

Context of Eternity: A Time Travel Tale About Christ